The Rake's
Unconventional Mistress

In The Regency Ballroom Collection

Scandal in the Regency Ballroom – Louise Allen
April 2013

Innocent in the Regency Ballroom – Christine Merrill
May 2013

Wicked in the Regency Ballroom – Margaret McPhee
June 2013

Cinderella in the Regency Ballroom – Deb Marlowe
July 2013

Rogue in the Regency Ballroom – Helen Dickson
August 2013

Debutante in the Regency Ballroom – Anne Herries
September 2013

Rumours in the Regency Ballroom – Diane Gaston
October 2013

Rake in the Regency Ballroom – Bronwyn Scott
November 2013

Mistress in the Regency Ballroom – Juliet Landon
December 2013

Courtship in the Regency Ballroom – Annie Burrows
January 2014

Scoundrel in the Regency Ballroom – Marguerite Kaye
February 2014

Secrets in the Regency Ballroom – Joanna Fulford
March 2014

Juliet Landon's keen interest in art and history, both of which she used to teach, combined with a fertile imagination, make writing historical novels a favourite occupation. She is particularly interested in researching the early medieval and Regency periods and the problems encountered by women in a man's world. Her heart's home is in her native North Yorkshire, but now she lives happily in a Hampshire village close to her family. Her first books, which were on embroidery and design, were published under her own name of Jan Messent.

Chapter One

Richmond, Surrey. 1814

'Well?' said Letitia, closing the door of the parlour behind her, shutting off the gentle hum of voices. 'What do you think? Shall you beg Mama to come and rescue me, or shall you tell her how capable I am?'

Garnet placed an arm through hers and pressed it to her side. 'Mama *knows* how capable you are, dearest. She simply didn't want you to do this all on your own, that's all. It doesn't fit in with her plans for any of us, least of all her eldest daughter.'

'Well—' Letitia smiled, acknowledging the truth '—she always knew I'd go down a different path. She must have expected it. A pity she couldn't find time to come and see for herself, though. She knows how to make her displeasure felt, doesn't she?'

Persephone, Garnet's twin, was like her sister in everything except in the degree of assertiveness. 'Oh, Mama's displeasure is no rare thing these days, Lettie,' she said. 'You know how easy it's been to set up her bristles since we lost Papa. You're well out of it, but not too far for us to visit whenever we like.'

'You approve, then?'

'Of *course* we do,' the twins chorused. '*Very* select. Seven lovely young ladies. Hanging on your every word. So respectful. Yes, Miss Boyce, no, Miss Boyce.'

'Stop!' Letitia begged them, laughing. 'It's only their first term. They'll soon be pitching the gammon like the rest of us.'

The white hallway was bright with spring sunshine that bounced off the jug of creamy lilac blooms and shone in patches upon the pink-toned Axminster rug. Through two open doors could be seen a polished post-chaise with the Boyce crest upon the panel, a liveried postilion sitting erect upon one of the horses while another waited on the pavement beside the folding steps.

A large bay gelding was brought to a standstill behind the coach, its rider showing no sign of impatience as the three, with arms linked, came to stand beneath the elegant white portico, still finding last-minute messages to send, approvals to be repeated, thanks and farewells mixed like potpourri.

'Lord Rayne is to escort us back to London,' Persephone whispered, unable to prevent a deeper shade of pink creeping into her cheeks. 'He's *so* gentlemanly, Lettie.'

'He's taking us to Almack's this evening,' Garnet added, her eyes shining with excitement. 'It will be the most *horrendous* bore, but Mama insists on it.'

This, Letitia knew, was intended to convince her that they would not enjoy it much and that *she* would enjoy it less, even if she too had been invited by the handsomest beau of their acquaintance. She glanced up at him, then wished she had not, for he caught her eye in a look that seemed to reflect, with added amusement, a certain perception that was by no means enthusiastic. Without prejudice, her glance might have agreed with her sisters' description of him as the most perfect tulip, the best-dressed, the most eligible *parti,* a Corinthian out of the very topmost drawer.

But Letitia *was* prejudiced by the other epithets she had heard, not so glowing, that although he was wealthy and titled—and who in their right minds could ignore that?—he was also a rake. And what was her mother doing to allow her younger sisters to be seen exclusively in his company, she would like to have known. Granted, her lovely sisters had reached their twenty-second birthday some months ago, quite a serious matter for any ambitious mother. But Lord Seton Rayne, younger son of the Marquess of Sheen, must by now have had every heiress in London hurled at him, despite his reputation, and still he had not made a permanent choice.

The look Letitia caught, the one that made her turn hastily away, seemed to have read her like a book. His slow blink returned to her, telling her in words as clear as the town crier that she might disapprove all she liked, but *she* had nothing to fear, that unmarried females who ran seminaries were of no interest to him except as objects of amusement, however well connected they might be.

But if Letitia hoped to avoid an introduction, it was not to be. 'Come,' said Garnet, gently urging her forward. 'Will you not allow me to present Lord Rayne to you before we leave? My lord, you said how you longed to meet our elder sister. Well, here she is.'

He bowed from the saddle, touching the brim of his grey beaver with the silver knob of his whip, his dark eyes taking in her tall figure as if—she thought—he was about to make a bid at Tattersalls for a good general-purpose sort of hack. 'Miss Boyce,' he said, 'I am pleased to meet you at last. I had begun to suspect that you were a figment of your sisters' imaginations.'

'I can well believe it, my lord,' she replied, unsmiling. 'I suppose you must meet so few women of independence, these days.' Making it clear that this briefest of exchanges was at an end, she turned away to place a kiss upon her sisters' cheeks, to shoo them into the carriage and to watch them move off, waving merrily.

Responding to a signal from his rider, the bay gelding took his place on the far side of the carriage and pranced away, swishing his tail as if to cock a snook at the lone figure on the pavement who could not quite understand why she felt so buffle-headed and gauche. Had she been unnecessarily defensive? Had she taken his greeting the wrong way? Would he have noticed? Did it matter if he had?

She walked back into the shadowy hall, studied the nearest brass doorknob, then turned it and entered the room, relieved to be back in her natural element. Seven heads lifted, sure that Miss Boyce would find something complimentary to say about their drawings of daffodils.

It was not that she begrudged her sisters a single moment of fun with the pick of London's available bachelors, never having enjoyed being caught up in the social whirl of balls, routs and drawing-rooms, house-parties and assemblies. Her twin sisters did, and popular they were, too. Well mannered, well dressed and gregarious, they graced every event with their petite charm and blonde curling hair, not least because there were two of them. Good value by any hostess's standards. By their demanding mother's standards they were worth their weight in gold *and* a liability, for she could not conceive how one could be married without the other, and where did one find two equally wealthy titled bachelors, these days? The twins were just as sceptical.

The problem of mates for her eldest daughter had rarely occupied Lady Boyce's sleepless nights as it did with the twins, for Letitia might as well have been a boy for all the interest she showed in finding a husband. For her, the school-room had never been a place to escape from, her father's vast library had been a favourite haunt, and a visit to a museum, a lecture on the structure of the ode, or a discussion on Greek vases and their classification was more in her line than an obligation to dine with her mother's gossipy guests in their gracious Mayfair home. She did, of course, do her duty in this respect, but most of her friends were artists, poets, politicians and writers.

Her late father had understood his daughter perfectly—her socialite mother did not. After her father's sudden death in the hunting field, Letitia had made her bid for complete freedom away from her mother's dominance. Her father would have approved, though it was her mother's elder brother, Uncle Aspinall, who had helped her to purchase Number 24 Paradise Road in Richmond, in the county of Surrey. He had also been the only one of her relatives, apart from her sisters, to approve of her plan to open a seminary there.

'A *seminary*?' Lady Boyce had said, as if her daughter had blasphemed. 'How do you ever expect to attract a *husband*, Letitia, if you're stuck in a seminary with young *gels* all day? Really, how *can* you be so vexatious?'

'I shall not be stuck in it all day, Mama,' she had said. 'It's not going to be *that* kind of seminary. And they won't be much younger than seventeen, just on the eve of their coming-out. There's so much they ought to know at that age,' she added, remembering the deficiencies of Mrs Wood's Seminary for the Daughters of Gentlemen. 'If Papa had not talked to me about interesting things, I would have been as tongue-tied as most of the other girls at Mrs Wood's.'

'And tongue-tied is one thing no one could ever accuse *you* of being,' her mother retorted, not intending the compliment. 'But I wish you would consider *my* feelings for once, Letitia. How I'm going to explain this to my friends I really don't know. They may look on eccentricity in the older generation as something to be expected, but no one expects it from a twenty-four-year-old who ought to be turning her mind to raising a family. It's *most* embarrassing.'

'It was never my wish to be an embarrassment, Mama, and I have nothing against men, or marriage, or families, either. But I have never been able to understand why educating one's mind is acceptable in a man, but frowned on in a woman. Papa never thought women's brains were inferior to men's, did he? It was he who taught me to read.'

'Your Papa, God rest his soul, had radical views about most things, Letitia, but when he left you a sizeable legacy to do with as you pleased, I doubt if he ever thought it would please you to run completely wild, buy your own house and make an utter cake of yourself.'

'Uncle Aspinall doesn't think so, Mama. And thank heaven for it. Without his help I don't think I could have managed half so well.'

This comparison did nothing to mollify Lady Boyce. 'Aspinall,' she snapped, 'has no children of his own, which is why he knows so little about what parents want. I hardly expected he would side with me on this matter, and I was right as usual, but if he likes the idea of having a *blue-stocking* for a niece, there's little I can do about it. Indeed I suspected you were inclined that way when you tried to conceal a *Latin dictionary* in your reticule when we went to Lady Aldyth's rout party. Was there *ever* such a trial to a devoted mother?' Lady Boyce's imposing figure described a convincing swoon that would have done justice to Mrs Siddons, landing gracefully on a striped brocade settee with lion's paws feet.

It was from both parents that Letitia had inherited the height that had not afflicted her sisters to the same extent. For a woman, she was taller than average, which had never done much to help when she was obliged to look down upon so many of her dancing partners. Sitting down with men to talk was more comfortable for both parties, Letitia being blessed with a serene loveliness that, combined with an ability to talk interestingly and without affectation on any number of current affairs, captivated the more liberal-minded men of her acquaintance. Whether it helped for her to have fine ash-blonde hair that strayed in wisps over her face and neck resisting all efforts to contain it, or to have large eyes the colour of thunderclouds rimmed by unusually dark lashes, or to have a figure that Juno herself would have been proud to own, were not things that occupied Letitia's mind, for in the wide unchartered territory of men's preferences she was lamentably ignorant.

The priority in most men's minds, her mother had told all three of her daughters, were that they should remain innocent, be adept at all the social graces and, above all, show no inclination to be bookish. If there was anything a man deplored above all else, it was a woman who knew more than he did on any subject except domestic matters. The twins had no wish to argue with that, but Letitia understood that it was far too generalised to be true, for there were men she knew personally who had accepted her exactly as she was, bookish or not. Unfortunately for Lady Boyce, these same men were not interested in marrying her eldest daughter, either, because they were already married or too engrossed in their own special subjects to be leg-shackled to a wife and family.

If Letitia was affected by this lopsided state of affairs, she never let it show except, occasionally, by an inclination to pity both the men and women who lived by such shallow conventions. Nevertheless, the stark truth was that book-learning and marriage rarely mixed and that, as she had now earned a reputation as being 'Lady Boyce's unconventional eldest daughter', she was highly unlikely to find a mate of *haut ton* as her mother would have preferred.

'What will people say?' whined Lady Boyce for the fiftieth time. 'That I threw you out to make shift for yourself? You have no need to earn your own living, Letitia. It's simply not *done* by women of your standing, you know.'

But it *had* been done, and so far Lady Boyce had been too busy to visit Number 24 Paradise Road, relying on the twins' information to fuel the smouldering fires of her disapproval. Naturally, she urged them to tell Letitia about the ball she was planning, the guests she would be entertaining, the visits, the soirees, the titled men they were meeting. They had brought her a copy of the newly published novel by the author of *The Infidel*, which all society had talked about last year. They were sure it would not be available in Richmond for some time, though their mother had deemed it a wasted gesture. 'Lettie will not read *that* kind of thing,' she had told them.

'What kind of thing, Mama?' they had asked, innocently.

'*That* kind of thing. Novels. Racy novels.'

'Is it racy, Mama?'

'Oh, I don't know, dears. It looks racy to me. What's it called? *Waynethorpe Manor*? *Sure* to be.'

'So you haven't read it, Mama?'

'Me? Read such rubbish? Why, no, of course not.'

'Then how can you judge it, Mama?'

'Oh, I flicked through it when I was in Hatchards, and I could tell. I don't see Letitia reading it unless it explains how to tell a Turner from a Reynolds, which I'm sure I don't care about unless there's a difference in the price.'

Meant to tease, the conversation veered predictably into areas about which Lady Boyce had strong views, but no knowledge. The twins smiled and took the book to Richmond, just the same.

Letitia picked up the brown paper package and opened it, finding the three volumes of brown leather tooled with gold lettering. She peeped at the title page of the first one.

Waynethorpe Manor
A Novel in Three Volumes by the Author of *The Infidel*
London
Printed for the Mercury Press, Leadenhall Street
1814

She closed it again, smiling. But seven faces could not conceal their curiosity. 'May we read it, Miss Boyce? Please may I be the first? Is it the new one? *The Infidel* was *so* romantic. My mama told me I should not be reading it, but *she* read it. I *know* she did.'

Letitia chuckled. 'Perhaps I shall look through it first, and, if I think it's suitable, I'll lend you my copy. I would not wish to offend your mamas. Now,' she said, glancing at the clock on the mantelpiece, 'it's almost time for our accounting lesson. Mr Waverley will be arriving at any moment, and we must not keeping him waiting. Leave your paintings as they are, and we'll come back to them after tea. Come, girls, into the parlour.'

Rewrapping the volumes, she carried them away to safety.

The Honourable Bartholomew Waverley was indeed arriving on foot as she spoke, to take the Friday lesson that would, in theory at least, initiate Miss Boyce's pupils into the mysteries of household accounting that every good wife, wealthy or not, needed to know. It was the kind of thing Letitia included in her curriculum, which other seminaries did not, and so far there had been plenty of parents who agreed with her that it was essential learning. Mr Waverley had been a friend of Letitia's since they had met at a lecture to which her father had taken her many years ago in London. By good fortune, he lived in a beautiful house that faced north-west across Richmond Green, and his willingness to become involved as escort, guide and tutor was one of the reasons why Letitia was sure she could take on such a responsibility. Their relationship was warm, but never more than that—more like that of brother and sister. They were both quite content to have it so.

Mr Waverley was not only a reliable friend, but also an excellent companion who saw nothing remarkable in Letitia's exceptional interest in subjects deemed to be a man's territory. They attended meetings and discussion groups together where his keen mind and knowledge of things scientific and mathematical balanced nicely against her preference for the arts subjects. He was, in fact, the perfect friend. He stood with his feet upon the fanlight's semi-circular shadow that fell upon the Axminster. 'I'm standing on your cheese segments.' He grinned.

'So that's what I can smell. And, yes, you *are* invited to dinner. Come inside, Bart. The girls are in the parlour already.'

'With Gaddy?'

'Yes, Gaddy's in there, too.'

Miss Gaddestone was Letitia's cousin who lived with her by dint of a reciprocal arrangement whereby she received board and lodging for her services as chaperon whenever she was required. And since several of the tutors employed by Letitia were gentlemen, Miss Gaddestone was always there in a corner of the room for the sake of propriety and to keep an eye on good manners. She was kindly and well liked, a stickler for correctness who took her duties very seriously, sitting there with her basket of sewing, saying little, but hearing all.

The exchanged smile needed no explanation, for both of them were aware that one or two of the pupils harboured fantasies about Mr Waverley that had very little to do with accounting. He was tall and pleasant-faced, brown-haired and courteous with well-manicured hands, and eyes that smiled easily. He was also the son of a viscount, wealthy and unmarried, quite a catch for any woman, if he had shown the slightest interest. Naturally, the pupils were sure that he and Letitia were more than just good friends.

'I'll go in, then,' he said.

'Yes. The twins have been.'

'Oh? Not Lady Boyce?'

'No. They brought me something, Bart.'

He studied her laughing eyes, almost level with his. 'Not the book? But you've already got your copies. Did you tell them?'

'Heavens, no. Mama's sure it's not suitable reading.'

'She's probably right, dear heart.' He smiled. 'So do I get to read it now? Come on, that's part of the bargain, remember.'

'All right. You can take it home after dinner. Go on in.'

'Promise?'

'I promise.'

It was getting late by the time Mr Waverley left, though Letitia had not minded having the three boarders stay up for an extra hour or two of good conversation, since the morrow would be Saturday and free from lessons. Miss Gaddestone had contributed with hilarious tales of her childhood in rural Wales, and their next-door neighbour at Number 22, Mrs Quayle, with whom the three young ladies had their rooms, had connections with society women that made her a fount of fascinating information, mostly of a cautionary nature.

By the light of a single oil lamp, Letitia unlocked the drawer of her writing-desk and carefully lifted out a scuffed leather-bound book where the pages of the first half had grey well-thumbed edges, the second half still pristine. It seemed to open by itself at the last page of handwriting.

Unscrewing the silver top of her inkwell, she peered in to check the shine of liquid against the light, picked up her quill and studied its sharpened end. 'Stop prevaricating,' she whispered to it. 'Go on, write it. It's what you want to say. Write it, before you forget.' Obediently, the quill dipped and began to describe.

He sat the huge bay gelding like a god, scowling at the sun until he was obliged to acknowledge her, though she did not wish it. His eyes she could not see, though she knew how they looked at her, how they refused to light, but scanned in one glance from head to toe, touching a nerve of her anger, making her fists clench, halting her breath. She said something ungracious that did not, as she had intended, make him smart, but dismiss her as too clever by half and not worth his time.

She felt her heart thudding, her eyes wanting, but not wanting, to take in more of him, his gloved hands on the reins, now reaching to pat the glossy neck before him, settling his mount as she wished he would settle her. She had never felt so unsettled. So overlooked. There are more interesting things, she told herself, to occupy your thoughts. Yet for the life of her she could not will them to return.

The quill was laid to rest as a shuddering sigh wafted across the page, and for several moments she stared at the words as if someone else had written them. But that was what writers must do to record every scrap of information that came their way, especially writers to whom such things came with exceptional rarity, as one had today. Was it worth recording? she asked herself, closing the book and returning it to the drawer. Yes, it was. Comfortable or not, she could hardly afford to let it pass, her experience of men being what it was.

The ride to Hampton Court Palace on the following day, ostensibly to visit Mr Waverley's elderly mother, was augmented by five of Letitia's pupils, two of whom were local day girls who, if they had wished, could have stayed with their parents. So while Miss Gaddestone and Mrs Quayle rode in the barouche, the others rode their own horses, some of which were stabled with Letitia's. As a good horsewoman, she had been keen to introduce riding lessons into her list of subjects, there being too few young ladies of seventeen, she said, who knew how to look easy in the saddle. She had no say, however, regarding the quality of the mounts their fathers had provided for them, which was something she would have to work on, once things became more established.

The cavalcade of one carriage and seven riders ambled along the river path to the village of Hampton with not quite the striking image Letitia had had in mind at the outset, though she did not believe they would be much on show at a place like Hampton Court. The last time she had visited, the gardens had been overgrown and the elderly inhabitants too intent on their feet to notice any passing horseflesh.

While Mr Waverley rode round to the south side of the palace where his mother had a grace-and-favour residence, Letitia led the way round to The Green, and from there in through the West Gate, which, she had been informed, would lead them directly to the place where they could leave the horses and go on foot into the courtyards.

What Mr Waverley had failed to mention was that the large area from gate to palace, known as the Outer Green Court, was the province of the cavalry academy where recruits underwent intensive training before joining Marquess Wellington's army in Spain. Along the left-hand side ranged the red-brick barrack block, the yard in front of which was packed with mounted men in blue tunics with silver frogging across their chests, white pantaloons tucked into shining boots, tall fur helmets, with braids, tassels, belts and buckles, sashes and saddle-cloths, curved scabbards and yards of silver cord. As the barouche and six riders began to cross the parade ground, large glossy horses with stamping hooves and jingling harness moved off in synchronised groups, with civilians around the perimeter to watch the exercise.

But Letitia's elderly coachman, slightly deaf and revelling

in his audience, could not hear her call to him to stop, the blast of a trumpet coinciding with her warning and, at the same time, spooking several of the horses. Almost unseating two of the pupils, the mounts half-reared and pranced out of control while others scattered and wheeled, preventing Letitia from reaching the coachman who, still oblivious to the danger, thought it unlikely that a group of cavalry would take precedence over his carriage and pair. In this, however, he was mistaken, for the cavalry recruits threatening to mow him down were the 10th Light Dragoons, who believed by divine right that they took precedence over everything at all times.

Torn between stopping the carriage and rounding up her struggling pupils, Letitia yelled at Miss Gaddestone who was half-standing, waving her arms like a windmill at the advancing line of dark blue tunics in the hope that they would wait. Using a more immediate approach, Mrs Quayle took up her parasol like a golf club and swiped wildly at the coachman, sending his top hat bouncing like a football under the feet of the cavalry horses. She said afterwards, by way of apology, that she had been aiming for his shoulder. Nevertheless, it brought him at last to an abrupt halt.

The six attractive female riders having trouble with their mounts and the coachman having trouble with his dignity were immediately surrounded by the elite cavalry corps, aged from eighteen to twenty-two, who were not so disciplined that they could conceal their grins in view of the farce before them. Nor could they totally ignore the plunging, whirling, side-stepping and reversing mêlée that blocked their way. Unable to resist the temptation, a few of the young men caught the reins of the worst-behaved horses just as their commanding officer, on a very large bay gelding, rode through the ranks as if the Red Sea was parting for him, and came to a halt beside the coachman's box.

Beneath the black fur of his helmet, the officer's expression was thunderous as he barked at the furious coachman. 'I take it you were never a part of His Majesty's Services, man?'

'No, sir. I was not!'

'Then you may not be aware that a blast on a trumpet is some sort of *signal*, and that not even a dimwit with half a brain would take a carriage forward across a line of cavalry unless he had a *death wish*. Who is in charge of this *nursery*?'

'I am responsible for the safety of these young ladies,' Letitia called out to him. 'And if the commanding officer had *his* wits about him, he would have seen that all was not clear *before* he issued his command. I hope this will be the worst that can happen to your men when they go into battle, for they will be—'

Although the two antagonists had recognised each other instantly, Captain Lord Rayne had decided not to listen, turning his mount away before her insults were finished, snapping and barking at his men and Letitia's coachman, bringing order to the chaos so quickly and efficiently that even the horses obeyed him. Letitia was the last one to pass him, but neither of them cared to acknowledge the other by so much as a glance, and she was left to bring up the rear, seething with anger and humiliation under the barely controlled grins of the men and the wide-eyed stares of the spectators. There was a scattering of applause as she left.

The drumming of hoofbeats on the gravel behind her made her turn to see a young cavalryman with a boyish face drawing alongside, holding out a battered top hat that had once been black. 'Captain's compliments, ma'am,' he said.

The discomfiting episode of the parade ground was bound to have repercussions that would follow Letitia's party, quite altering the purpose for which she had brought them, which was to see the palace architecture and for the riding experience. Now, the excited pupils were far more interested in the young men who had dashed to their aid—which was how they preferred to see it—than in the beauty of the patterned brick chimneys, and they begged to be allowed to watch, if only for a few minutes, the men performing their battle drill. Letitia could hardly refuse. So, leaving the girls with their two chaperons, she went off in search of the grace-and-favour apartments where Mr Waverley's mother lived.

The maze of stone-flagged passages in the Tudor part of the palace soon gave way to the more recent but equally convoluted muddle of courtyards and poky chambers of the William and Mary additions, which had once been the royal apartments, but were now shabbily redundant. After wandering without success from one long passageway to another, she sat down upon a dusty windowseat in a small bare room that might in earlier days have been a butler's pantry. Looking out on to yet another cobbled courtyard, she tried to remember by which side she had entered it, and which might conceivably be the south side.

Before she could draw back, a tall uniformed figure strode through the colonnade opposite her and stopped to look about him. Almost identical in dress to dozens of others, there was no mistaking the set of the powerful shoulders, the length of muscular leg, the officer's arrogant bearing that singled him out from all the rest. She did not watch to see where he went, but held herself flat against the cold wall, hoping that the sage-green velvet habit would not be seen against the mossy brick-work. He was the last, the *very* last person she wished to bump into here, of all places.

Listening for the smallest sound, she held her breath while

trying to distinguish the rattle of roosting pigeons and the thudding of her heart from the hard echo of a footfall upon stone floors. It grew louder, then stopped at the doorway and took a step inside.

Lord Rayne ducked his head beneath the lintel. 'What's this?' he said, softly. 'Abandoning your chickens, Mother Hen?'

Letitia glared at him, then looked away, fixing her eyes on the flaking distemper of the opposite wall, disdaining to answer such a nonsensical question. She felt very vulnerable, for though he had not bothered to close the door, the passageway behind him was completely deserted.

'Mute?' he said, coming forward to rest a hand high on the wall near her head. 'Interesting. You had plenty to say a few moments ago out there, Miss Boyce. Would you not like to continue, now I have your undivided attention?'

One lightning-quick glance told her that his eyes were as brown as chestnuts, hard and mocking, and that it would not be the first time he had ever had a woman so completely at a disadvantage. Still, she refused to give him any more ammunition, it being clear that her ungracious retort yesterday was remembered and that he was angered by today's unladylike response in front of his men. It *had* been unladylike. There was no getting away from that.

'An apology, then? Would that be too much to ask?'

'Yes, my lord. It *would*. Please leave me alone,' she said with as much dignity as she could summon, though he must have heard her voice waver. He was uncomfortably close on purpose, she thought, to intimidate her.

'Leave you alone…here? Ah, no, that would be ungentlemanly, Miss Boyce. You are either hiding, or you are lost. Which is it?'

Taking refuge in silence, she turned her head to one side, her cheeks burning under his intense scrutiny, her mind working furiously towards a way to resolve this dreadful hindrance. Not for the world would she give him the satisfaction of an apology, nor even an explanation. But he was between her and the door and, although hoydenish behaviour was not her style, whatever he chose to believe, a quick dash for freedom seemed to be the only way to extricate herself.

Riding habits, however, were not designed for the quick dash. No sooner had she gathered up her skirts with one hand than his long leg moved to prevent her, his body pressing her back against the wall with a determination she could not break. She felt the shameful pressure of his thigh against hers, and the warmth of his face, so closely restricting. 'Let me go!' she whispered. 'You insult me, Lord Rayne. This surely cannot be the gentlemanly conduct you offer my sisters.' She pushed against his shoulder with her riding crop, but even her well-built frame was no match for him, and there was little she could do to prevent his mouth slanting across hers, taking the apology she had refused to offer.

It was no mere peck, and when she tried to end it by breaking away, he caught her chin to bring her back to him, stopping her protests with another angry kiss more searching than the first. Even through the thickness of uniform, braids and buttons, she could feel the surge of authority that he felt obliged to impose, left over from the earlier incident and now aggravated by her refusal to yield. His arms were controlling her, determined to humble, demanding submission. It had nothing to do with desire, she was sure, but with obedience, the same obedience she had refused him earlier before crowds of onlookers.

'No,' he growled, 'this is not what I offer your sisters, Miss Boyce. I am not offering anything, but *taking* your apology. No one is allowed to walk off my parade ground yelling insults at me, not even a woman. Besides, I've never taken a kiss from a schoolma'am before. It's a novelty. Worth repeating, I think.'

'No...*no*!' Letitia snarled. 'Don't *dare* to handle me so. Get off me! I owe you nothing, and that was *not* an apology. I never apologise to *hooligans*.' Her voice, hoarse with rage, spat out the last word as she found a space to bring up her riding crop with a backhander that would have left a mark had he not caught it in time.

Her fury was not only for his contemptuous embrace, but for herself, too, for she ought to have seen it coming, or at least made it more difficult than she had. There was also the painful truth that her first kiss from a man had been taken from her with such ill will rather than for reasons of tenderness and affection that she had always believed were the prerequisites for lovemaking. His intention had quite obviously been to chasten her, making it doubly humiliating.

He held her wrist and riding crop in mid-air, clearly taken aback by the vehement eruption of her fury, his other hand ready to catch her next move. He watched her brilliant flintstone eyes spark and glisten with rage, her beautiful mouth tremble with shock, and the flippant words he was about to deliver, the laughing retort, did not emerge as he had intended. His eyes grew serious, suddenly contrite. 'A woman of independence *and* courage,' he said, relaxing his grip. 'Steady now.... I've had my say, and I would not wish you to believe your sisters have a hooligan as an escort. Can we not call a truce now?' He held out a hand. 'Friends?'

But Letitia whisked away out of his reach as if he'd offered her a viper. 'After that *disgraceful* behaviour towards a lady, my lord? If you can believe I need *that* kind of friendship, you must indeed be more queer in your attic than the rest of your kind,' she snarled. Lifting her arms, she replaced her hat over her brow, wishing she had worn a veil. 'Stand aside and allow me to find my way out of this *damned* place.'

He might have smiled at the strong language, but his mouth formed a soft whistle instead while his eyes took in the neat waist and voluptuous curves, the arch of her back and the proud tilt of her head on the long neck, which yesterday she had kept hidden. He cleared his throat. 'I know this place like the back of my hand. I will be glad to—'

'I'm sure you *do*, my lord. Every little nook and cranny. I can find my own way, I thank you.'

'What were you trying to find?' he said, ignoring the innuendo.

She had to give in, or run into yet more problems. 'The Gold Staff Gallery. Lady Waverley's apartments.'

'Number 17. So you know Lady Waverley, do you?'

'No,' she said, enigmatically. She swept past him through the door, but a distant shout put further bickering at an end.

'Lettie! Lettie, where are you?'

Relief swept over her, flooding into her voice. 'Here!' she yelled. 'I'm here…*Bart*!' The voice cracked on the last note, giving her away.

Mr Waverley strode round the corner, quickening his stride at the sight of her, reaching out. 'Lettie, where've you been? You here, Rayne?'

'How d'ye do, Bart. Miss Boyce was lost,' said Rayne. 'We were on our way to find your lady mother. Number 17, isn't it?'

Smiles, indulgent and comforting, warmed Mr Waverley's face. 'Little goose,' he said, tucking her arm through his. 'You'd get lost in your own backyard, wouldn't you? Thank'ee, my lord. That was kindly done.'

'You…you *know* each other?' Letitia whispered.

'As lads,' said Mr Waverley. 'Both at Winchester together. Live in the same town, too. I never went in for all *this* stuff, though.' He grinned, flipping a hand towards the silver frogging across Rayne's broad chest.

But despite the sage-green velvet that covered her own breast, Letitia could still feel the imprint of that bulky silver braid, the ache in her arms, and the assault of Lord Rayne's mouth upon her lips. That was bad enough, but worse still was the pain of his contempt, which she believed was less for her indiscretion on the parade ground than for the fact that she was, as he put it, a 'schoolma'am' and therefore less entitled to his respect than her sisters.

Chapter Two

Far from being disturbed by the parade-ground incident, Letitia's five pupils rode back to Richmond brimming over with excited chatter about the way they had been saved from bolting horses or, at least, being thrown and trampled to death. Their exaggeration served two purposes—first, in masking Letitia's quietness and, second, in providing Mr Waverley with all the details that she did not particularly want to repeat.

He had not attached any importance to finding Lord Rayne there at the palace, or to the fact that he had been helping Letitia to find her way about. It was, he agreed, a devilish place in which to lose one's bearings. And it was not Letitia who asked him about Lord Rayne's exact function as a captain of the 10th Light Dragoons, but Mrs Quayle and Miss Gaddestone, who were still chuckling like girls about the poor coachman's top hat.

'He trains cavalry for Marquess Wellington,' Mr Waverley told them. 'Not just the 10th Light Dragoons, the Regent's Own, but other regiments, too. He's done his share of fighting, but he sold out once and was re-commissioned. There's no one better than Rayne for preparing young lads for battle. He lives with his brother and sister-in-law up at Sheen Court for some of the time.'

Mrs Quayle of Number 22 knew his brother. 'That's Lord Elyot,' she said to Miss Gaddestone, holding her broken parasol across her knees. 'Lady Elyot's a lovely lady. She's on the Richmond Vestry Committee, in charge of the strays that wander into the town.'

'Stray dogs?'

'*Women*, dear,' said Mrs Quayle, pursing her lips, implying a certain condition. 'Lord Elyot is Assistant Master of Horse, you know. The Royal Stud is there at Hampton Court, so he and his brother work hand in glove with the King's horses. Breeding,' she whispered, raising an eyebrow and leaning towards her friend. 'Horse mad, that family.' She might as well have said 'breeding mad'.

Letitia made no contribution to the conversation, nagged by the thought that it was her own untypical defensiveness that had brought about that outrageous scene in the little room, not in defence of her charges, which would have been under-standable, but in defence of her own position as their guardian. Had it been anyone else but Lord Rayne who had appeared, she would probably have said very little except to admit their mistake. But at first sight of him, it was as if all the hostility in her being had rushed to the fore, to pay him back for the perceived slight she herself had provoked yesterday. It was all so farcical, when she cared not a whit what the dreadful man thought of her.

Yet she cared very much that she had been shown such shocking disrespect, kissed by one of the most notorious rake-hells in town, not because she was what he wanted, but because he suspected that was what would upset her most, a blue-stocking, worth in his eyes only the novelty value. So much for leaving the protection of her family. So much for independence.

After dinner she pleaded tiredness, leaving her two companions, Mrs Quayle and Miss Gaddestone, to their own company. This was the time she usually reserved for writing her thoughts while she was unlikely to be disturbed.

Tonight, the pen refused to speak for her.

For the best part of an hour she struggled for a way to translate her confusion into words, to describe the physical sensations and to explain her emotions, but this time not even anger would untangle itself sufficiently to make the slightest sense, and eventually she closed the book in weary surrender. Perhaps tomorrow she would be able to see it better from a distance.

That, she told herself, was half the problem, for while she could see perfectly to read and write, to sew and draw, she needed her spectacles to be able to see *anything* clearly at a distance, and only amongst friends would she have been seen wearing them. If only she'd had the courage to wear them that afternoon, she might have been able to anticipate the trouble before it happened. Locking away her notebook, she reached for her reticule and took out the leather- and silver-banded case that held her plain steel-rimmed eyeglasses.

Coldly, they clamped each side of her face, but instantly each dark recess of the room came to life with detail, the faint rose pattern on the bed-curtains, the reflections on glass and metal, the sharp moulding around the ceiling. The lamp flame was a little miracle.

Her maid, Orla, entered with a tray, smiling at the bespectacled figure that stared about her in wonderment. 'The day will come, ma'am,' she said, 'when every other lady will be wearing those.'

'In public? Never.'

'In public, ma'am. You mark my words.'

Letitia was silent. Her father had refused to wear his except in private. Letitia had been with him when he approached the fence and ditch all wrong, and she had never hunted since, knowing that it could have been her. He had died in her arms.

Her inability to put down in words what she had gained by the experience of that disturbing day kept sleep at a distance. Her success as a writer of novels depended to a large extent on her sincere and often vivid accounts of passionate relationships, which, for the most part, were the result of an active imagination combined with brief and surreptitious observations. It was not a satisfactory method for any writer of integrity, even though her first novel to be published, *The Infidel,* had been a runaway success. The second, recently published, seemed just as likely to please, if her pupils' eagerness was anything to go by.

Her notebook was her lifeline, a personal record, added to daily, where not only her own thoughts and experiences were logged, but other people's, too, including those of her pupils, relatives and friends: their mannerisms, figures of speech, and the tales they recounted. Descriptions of places were important, too, which had been one of her reasons for wanting to visit Hampton Court Palace that day. She needed the details, the colours and scale, the sounds and patterns. She had returned with an indigestible muddle of emotions, too contradictory to string together in words.

But therein lay another problem—that of writing about relationships when she had only her own to draw on. If she wished to continue giving her readers the kind of detail they craved, it surely made some sense for her to gain a deeper understanding, a more informed perception of the human heart in all its seasons. Some had dubbed her novel 'racy', even 'scandalous', because she had followed her characters into places where other writers had not, but as long as she remained anonymous, she was perfectly safe from the disapprobation of those who felt shamed by such personal matters. How could any young woman enter matrimony, she wondered, without knowing the first thing about the state of mind, and body, of the man she would be tied to for the rest of her life? If her own pupils read her books, then so much the better for them. No one would ever suspect her, Lady Boyce's eccentric daughter, of writing about people in love.

Later that night, however, long after Orla had plaited her tresses into a silver pigtail as thick as a wrist, the notebook was brought out for a second airing to receive a scattering of adjectives, which, while they added colour to a new kind of scene, had little to do with the emotion that simmered behind it. Nevertheless, as she climbed back into bed, she could not resist taking a look at two faint bluish marks on her upper arm. 'Lout!' she whispered. 'Ill-mannered *boor*!' He would have laughed about her with his comrades, for certain, marking up a score for the superior male sex.

At that moment, the thirty-three-year-old lout in question lay sprawled across his bed staring up at the dim pool of light made by a single oil lamp on the canopy. He had scarcely moved for the last hour, but now he rolled off to the edge and sat there with his dressing gown gaping, his hands dangling in repose between lean thighs.

Feeling unsociable and critical of his behaviour that afternoon, he had left the company of his brother and sister-in-law, unable to convince himself that Miss Lettie Boyce deserved all she got. Nonplussed by his uncharacteristic discourtesy, he wondered what devilry had made him follow her, insisting on playing out an incident that would have been better put behind them. A bevy of silly females and a deaf coachman were not, after all, the worst thing that could have happened to disrupt his exercise. To make matters worse, the woman he had shamed was the elder sister of the twins he was currently escorting, the sister they had fondly told him about.

He had formed a picture of a dowd, a frumpish bookworm securely on the shelf. He had caught a glimpse of her yesterday when she had clearly formed *her* own picture of *him* and decided he was not worth her civility. So he had not suffered any guilt at dismissing her as a sharp-tongued hen-of-the-game, even without a closer look. But today he'd seen her on horseback, superb, stylish and proud, the only one of the women to keep control of her mount. Later, he had come across her in that grubby little room where her dignity had been no less impressive, defying him, refusing to be intimidated, spitting fire from her remarkable eyes and rousing in him the kind of aggression he kept only for male opponents with whom he fenced and boxed. Never before had he vented it on a woman.

She was a beauty, too, once he'd got close enough to see: tall and athletic, and undeserving of the 'schoolma'am' he'd taunted her with. Now he would have to find a way to put things right, if only for the sisters' sakes, his first try having been justifiably rejected. He sighed and stood up, dropping his gown to the floor. The thought of seeing the bubbly twins again did not, for once, give him any particular pleasure.

His chance came quite unexpectedly at church next morning when the two Misses Binney asked him if he could find the time, just once, to attend their supper party in the company of his brother and sister-in-law. 'It's several months since you've been,' Miss Phoebe Binney complained, touching his arm with the tip of one gloved finger. 'You brought Mr Brummell with you last time, remember. Such an interesting man, and such good company.'

'Dear Miss Phoebe,' said Rayne, taking her hand between his own, 'I remember it well, and so does he. But I usually return to barracks on Sunday evening ready for work in the morning.' From the corner of his eye he could see the tall plume of dark blue feathers on a velvet hat moving towards the west door, and he knew that, if he stayed talking to Miss Phoebe, his chance would be lost.

'Oh, dear. Then you won't be able to get to know our latest addition to Richmond's talent, will you?' Miss Phoebe's eyes searched, pausing at the vicar's latest captive. 'Miss Boyce, you know. Bart Waverley has promised to bring her with him again. Such a bright star. Her father was Sir Leo Boyce, the architect of those magnificent... Well, of *course*. Your parents are neighbours, are they not?'

But Rayne's refusal had already begun to veer like a weathervane towards acceptance. 'I can return to barracks early tomorrow, Miss Phoebe. Thank you, I look forward to this evening.' Surrounded by several other females, the plume was fast disappearing down the path towards the lychgate, leaving Rayne in little doubt about the reason for the haste.

The terraced three-storey building on Maids of Honour Row facing the Green was well known to the Richmond set as one of the most popular literary salons outside London, not only for its attraction to 'blues and wits', but as a place of political neutrality where complete freedom of speech was actively encouraged. The home of the two elderly Misses Binney, both of them highly intelligent and well educated, its guest lists were noted for assembling people of all ages and experiences, the only requirement being that their manners must be impeccable and that they must contribute to the evening with at least a modicum of cleverness. Needless to say, an invitation to one of their 'supper parties' was an honour few ever declined and, as the best society hostesses were celebrated for their brilliant repartee, the contribution of women to the discussions, whatever the subject, was treated with due seriousness.

When Rayne arrived with Lord and Lady Elyot, the drawing room already buzzed with conversation, and the first notes of a song on the piano, followed by a voice, then laughter, made them smile even before the door closed behind them. Heads turned with greetings, absorbing them into the pool of black and grey, ivory and amber, the blue-white flash of diamonds and the wink of a quizzing-glass.

'Ah, Rayne, old chap. Come over here and tell us about...'

Courteously, he nodded, but preferred to wait a while. This was not the kind of place to which he would normally have come to pursue a woman, nor was he quite sure why he'd accepted the invitation so optimistically when Miss Boyce was unlikely to give him the time of day, let alone engage him in conversation. She was not his type anyway; he preferred his women friends to be affable and accessible, not needing too much effort on his part and certainly not as enraged as she had been by his kiss, even if the reason behind it was controversial. Unsurprisingly, she was a complete innocent and more than likely to stay that way if she was as determined as she appeared to be to redirect her social life. A *seminary*, of all things. Why, with the blunt Sir Leo had left her in his will, she must be one of the best catches of the decade, but for her non-conformity.

'Eccentricity is all the rage these days,' murmured a sweet voice in his ear. 'There are plenty of them about, if you think on it.'

Rayne smiled. 'Amelie, my dear, what are you talking about?'

Slipping an arm through his, Lady Elyot squeezed gently. 'You know well enough what I'm talking about, brother-in-law dearest. I'm talking about the one your eyes could not keep away from in church this morning. The one who sits over there in the corner talking to Miss Austen. It's not like you to be so hesitant. Nor, come to think of it, was it like her to dash off without coming to speak to us. I don't suppose she was the reason you changed your mind about delaying your return to Hampton Court, was she?'

He looked down at her, catching the teasing in the lustrous dark eyes, remembering the time, nine years ago, when he and his brother had first seen her in Rundell and Bridges choosing silverware, both of them wanting her, as most men did. Even after bearing three children, she was still a stunningly lovely woman, gentle and compassionate, whose love had tamed his brother's wild heart as no other woman could have done. Rayne trusted her opinion as much as his brother's.

'Nonsense,' he said with a sideways grin. 'Whatever gave you *that* idea? You've met her then, have you?'

'Well, of course I have, love. I was one of the first people she contacted about opening a seminary in Richmond when there are already six others, not to mention all the boys' academies. As a member of the Vestry, I was probably in the best position to discuss the idea with her, and had she not proposed to make hers different from the others in many ways, I'd not have been so encouraging. Besides, I know her mother, as you do.'

'What ways?'

'Subjects about which young women of a marriageable age seem to know so little these days. The art of conversation, for one. That's sadly neglected by so many mamas. She takes them on visits to places of interest, to art galleries and studios of the leading painters, visits to the House of Commons to hear debates, to the theatre and the royal palaces. She wants them to learn better riding and driving skills, too. You'd be surprised how many young women are unable to ride really well,' she added, waving to a friend across the room.

'No, I wouldn't,' he said.

'I believe she has a lot to offer that others don't. We have Kew just across the park and I'll lay any odds that half her pupils' parents have never been to see the gardens, let alone the succession houses. She intends to teach them how to keep household accounts, and to plant a herb garden, and to cook with them.'

'To cook? What on earth for?'

'Seton dear, you're so old-fashioned. What do you expect a wife to do these days? Stand around like a gateau and simper?'

'Gateaux don't simper, dear Amelie. And I think it sounds like an expensive exercise, since you ask.'

'Ah, but Miss Boyce is no fool. She knows one cannot start such a venture on a shoestring, but don't be supposing her fees are anything like the usual. Nothing but the best for Miss Boyce's pupils. She had the house extended and refurbished before she moved in, and her pupils are from Richmond's best families. Colonel and Mrs Lindell's daughter is one, the vicar's eldest daughter is another, and Sir Mortimer Derwent's girl, too. Oh, and Sapphire Melborough from up on the Hill.'

'Mm...' said Rayne. 'Interesting. Quite a handful.'

Whether he meant the entire package or Sapphire Melborough alone, Lady Elyot did not ask, though she might have been able to guess. 'With her connections,' she said, 'she's had no problem attracting the right kind of client. How do *you* find Lady Boyce these days? Has she tried to interfere with your friendship with the her twin daughters yet?'

'Not yet.'

'She will.'

'She'll only try it once, Amelie.'

'Oh, so you're not *so* keen, then?'

'There are plenty of other fish in the sea. Lady B. is a shark.'

'Yes,' she whispered, 'but some will be harder to catch, I believe. Like the elder Miss Boyce.'

'Hah!' said Rayne, laughing off the suggestion. 'I wouldn't even know which bait to use to catch *that* one. I leave her to the *literati*, m'dear.'

Lady Elyot withdrew her arm, responding to her friend's repeated beckoning. 'Well, you *do* surprise me, Seton dear. I would not have thought you were too old for a challenge as lovely as that. Stay with the safe twins, then. You can hardly miss there, can you?' She drifted away before he'd realised he'd forgotten to ask her who the Miss Austen was, talking so earnestly to Miss Lettie Boyce. But her taunt rang in his ears rather like a warning bell, overlapping the cheery male greeting behind his shoulder.

'Seton, good to see you here. Having an evening off?'

He was aroused from his reverie just in time to catch the remains of a smile on Bart Waverley's attractive face that had been directed, not at him, but at Miss Boyce, who had clearly been heading in his direction until she saw who he was about to address. Then she had smoothly stopped by the side of Baron Brougham, the Member of Parliament who was talking to Sir Joseph and Lady Banks, greeting all three with a kiss to both cheeks, turning her back upon the two who watched.

'Oh, that looks rather like a cut to me,' said Mr Waverley with a laugh. 'I wonder what we've done to deserve that.'

'I cannot imagine,' said Rayne. 'Who is the lady in the corner, Bart? Did I hear the name Austen correctly?'

'Miss Jane Austen. She's staying here with the two Misses Binney. Lives over at Chawton. Shall I introduce you?'

'Yes, if you will. She looks like a homely sort, and I feel a bout of charity coming on.'

'Then a word in your ear, old friend. A little less of the con-descending manner. Miss Austen and most of the ladies here could give you an intellectual run for your money any day of the week, so if you start off in patronising mode, you'll find yourself tied up like a bull in a pen. Just be warned.'

'Thank you, Bart. What is Miss Austen's forte?'

'Writing,' said Mr Waverley. 'Even Prinny is one of her admirers.'

'Good grief. Then I'd better tread carefully.'

'The trouble with you, Seton, is that you've never fished in deep waters, have you? Come on, I'll introduce you.'

With the metaphors becoming increasingly visual, Rayne and Mr Waverley waded through the company to reach Miss Austen, only to find that they had been beaten to it by both Lady Elyot and Mr Lawrence the court painter, both of whom had been waiting in line for the chance to speak with her.

Nor was it quite as easy as he had thought to capture a few moments of Miss Boyce's time when she was surrounded by artists and poets, publishers and politicians, writers, actors and musicians and, in one case, a painted scent-drenched playwright who seemed desperate to hold centre stage until Miss Phoebe and Miss Esme, her sister, drew him kindly towards the supper table, still declaiming *King Lear.* Rayne eventually discovered her standing with her back to him, listening intently to Mr William Turner talking about his latest tour of the northern counties, a small untidy man whose strong Cockney accent was at odds with those who asked questions of him.

Among others, Miss Boyce wanted to know what his plans were for the Royal Academy Exhibition. 'You only presented one painting last year, Mr Turner. Will there be more than one this year?'

He obviously knew her, fixing her with an impish glare down his beaked nose, rather like an outraged gnome. 'Virgil,' he said. 'Begins with a D.'

'Dido?' said Miss Boyce, promptly. 'Dido and Aeneas?'

The amusement and applause was as much for the master's pretend-anger as for Miss Boyce's sharpness, but he scowled and shook her hand, telling her she had no business to be guessing in one. Then, because there was some turning and teasing, she saw who stood behind her and allowed the ravishing smile to drain away, edging past her friends with a quick look of annoyance over her shoulder, which, Rayne suspected, may have been partly to do with the fact that a pair of steel-rimmed spectacles rested halfway down her nose.

Striding away towards the supper room, she attempted to outpace him, but was prevented by a group of chattering guests who hesitated, then parted to let her through, allowing Rayne to meet her on the other side of them. 'Miss Boyce,' he said, 'may I help you to some supper?'

Rather than move her spectacles up, she tilted back her head to look down her nose, just as Mr Turner had done a moment earlier. 'Help, Lord Rayne?' she said, scanning his figure like the proverbial schoolma'am with a tardy child. 'Help? Why, no, I thank you. Your assistance, I seem to remember, comes at the kind of price I'm not prepared to pay. Go back to your gaming tables and whatever Sunday-evening company you usually keep. You seem to be out of your depth here.'

'You look even better with spectacles than you do without them,' he replied, refusing to flinch under the lash of her tongue.

'And you, my lord,' she said, removing them with a haughty flourish, 'look much better *without* them.'

'You flatter me, ma'am.'

'No, do I? I beg your pardon. I didn't mean to.'

'Still way up in the boughs, I see. Isn't it time you came down?'

'To your level? Heaven forbid. I fear I should be trampled on.' Tucking her folded glasses into her reticule, she turned away, heading once again for the supper room.

Rayne's own brand of cynicism would, at times, have been hard to beat, but this woman's meteoric put-downs would have silenced most hardened cynics. He followed on, more slowly, watching the swing of her hips under the charcoal-grey beaded half-dress over pale grey satin, the low-cut back and peach-skin shoulders, the long wisps of moonlight-blonde hair escaping from her chignon to curve into her graceful neck. Needled, curious, perplexed, he followed her to the array of food, not sumptuous, but plentiful. But it was not easy to identify the tiny pieces of something, the squares of something else, rolls and balls garnished with greenery, jellies and glasses, and a confusion of cakes.

Without a word, he took the plate from her hand, placed a selection of bite-sized delicacies upon it and gave it back to her, poured two glasses of lemonade and bade her follow him. 'This way,' he said, as if he could sense her relief. He found a vacant sofa beside a table and waited for her to be seated before he asked, 'May I?'

She glanced at the space beside her as if to estimate how much of it he would need, then she nodded, refusing to meet his eyes, taking the lemonade from him with a mechanical 'thank you', and placing it on the table. 'Is this all for me?' she said, looking at the plate. 'Where's yours?'

'I wondered if we might share it,' he said, watching for her reaction.

She made a small involuntary move backwards as if trying to steel herself for something very unpleasant. 'I have suddenly lost my appetite,' she said. 'And anyway, such a gesture would be taken to mean that I have accepted you as a close friend, which is very far from the truth, my lord. If it were not for the fact that you are known to be on good terms with my sisters, I would not be sitting here with you like this. Certainly not sharing a supper plate. Mr Waverley usually does this for me.'

'I accept what you say entirely, Miss Boyce. So may I suggest that, for the time being, you pretend that I am Mr Waverley?'

Dipping her head with a genteel snort of laughter, she turned her dark grey eyes to him at last. 'Lord Rayne, my imagination is in perfect working order, I assure you, but there are some things it would find quite impossible to tackle. That is one of them.' As she spoke, her eyes found the black frockcoat and white breeches of her friend, resting there affectionately. 'Mr Waverley's manners are faultless,' she said. Picking up one of the tiny squares of pastry, she placed it absently in her mouth, still watching until, catching her companion's amused expression, she realised what she had done. Instantly, she stopped chewing and blinked.

'There, now. That wasn't difficult, was it? Having vented some of your spleen, you've found your appetite.'

Swinging her head away, she finished the mouthful. 'Fudge!' she snapped. 'I have not *vented my spleen*, as you put it, in years. In fact, I'm not sure where it is, so long has it been unvented. Here, have one of those. They're quite good. But don't take it as a peace offering. You may be the bees' knees with my sisters, my lord, but if they knew what I know, they'd not be so convinced that you're as gentlemanly as all that.'

'Yet you have agreed to sit and share supper with me,' he said, taking two of the tasty pieces.

'Don't be bamboozled by *that*,' she said.

'Why not? Is it not true?'

'Because,' she said, taking another piece and studying it, 'there is a limit to the length of time I can stay blue-devilled, that's why. I have rarely had reason to hold a grudge against anyone, so I lack the practice. I suppose it's a form of laziness, but I find the effort not worth the reward. I might have been able to keep up a high dudgeon for a few more weeks if there were not so many people known to both of us who would wonder why I insisted on being so uncivil to you. Which I *could.*' The piece disappeared into her mouth at last.

'Oh, I have absolutely no doubt of that, Miss Boyce.'

'But,' she munched, 'I should find it so *tedious* to explain. Naturally, I can accept that men of your…*experience*…may become confused from time to time about who to bestow good manners on, and who not to. That's not the problem. The problem is that when one is on the receiving end of shabby behaviour, one tends to take it personally. If I'd known you had such an aversion to women like me, my lord, I would never have ventured near the parade ground yesterday. Not in a million years. And had I known that your tolerance extends only to women of my sisters' sort, pretty, gregarious women, you may be sure I would have taken my pupils round to the back entrance. So, you see, it's not so much that I've decided to forgive and forget how insulting you can be towards *some* women and mannerly towards others, depending on who is watching, but that I really cannot be bothered with people of your sort. The world is so full of really *interesting* people to spend time with, don't you agree?'

Taking the glass of lemonade, she downed half the contents in one go, replaced the glass on the table and, withdrawing her spectacles from her reticule, replaced them on her nose. Then, treating him to an innocent wide-eyed stare, she rose. 'Thank you for sharing your supper with me,' she said sweetly, and walked away to join a group, linking her arm through one of them like a favourite niece.

Leaning back, Rayne let out a silent whistle like a head of steam being released. 'Whew!' he murmured. 'The lady is certainly not stuck for words, is she? I think there may be more work to be done here, old chap, before this episode can be closed.'

Chapter Three

Creamy white pages danced with shadows. Hovering like a merlin, the loaded quill point swooped, squeaking on the line, eager to tell what it knew.

Even George Brummell himself would have approved of the cravat, spotless white, perfectly creased against the bronzed outdoor skin around the jaw, touching the dark curl of hair before the ears. One could not tell whether the hair had been combed or not, but the way it rumpled on to the forehead might have taken others some time to achieve. A broad forehead, straight brows, deep watchful eyes, still mocking, a nose neither hooked nor bulbous, a wide mouth without fullness, but showing perfect teeth. Taller than me, for a change, and, I suspect, no padding upon the shoulders. My sisters say he boxes, shoots, fences and hunts, and this I can believe for he has the athlete's grace and assuredness, thighs like a wrestler's under skintight white breeches, well-shaped calves. The tables were turned, this time. I was amongst people I knew and liked, at ease and not inclined to sham a confusion I did not feel. I see no need to like him for their sakes, but I will say that, as far as looks go, he must be called a Nonpareil. Would that his manners matched his appearance. My sisters must see quite another side to him, which makes one wonder which side is the right side and which the reverse. Outwardly, some semblance of politeness must be maintained, I suppose. In Miss Austen, for example, I detected no other side than that which I saw her present to everyone, whether they knew of her books or not. Such a delightful lady, well into her thirties, she has asked me to call on her tomorrow before her return to Chawton. To be granted a private meeting—what could be more excessively civil?

As usual, the cathartic labour of love released her pent-up thoughts and tumbled them on to the page, ready for use in another form in the story she had only recently begun. It was work that had to take second place nowadays to the needs of the seminary, still occupying several hours of each day. Apart from the emotional satisfaction of daily creating her own characters and scenes, the financial reward was a bonus she had never anticipated. *The Infidel* she had sold for £80 to the publisher who had seen in her writing an extraordinary talent, and the first edition had sold out in less than a year, bringing in a reward of £200. That had been more than enough to spur her into the next one, *Waynethorpe Manor*, just published with a subscription list that took up the first three mottled pages and glowing reviews from *The Lady's Magazine*, and even *The Lady's Monthly Museum*, usually cautious about what it recommended.

For a woman possessed of such an independent spirit, the delight of being well paid to do what she most enjoyed was a welcome boost to her confidence that had given her the courage to set out along her own path. Her father's legacy and her uncle's active encouragement had made it possible. Now she was truly a woman of means, and if that brought with it a certain non-conformity that made her family uncomfortable, then it would have to be so. She could devise her own romances and walk away from them without the slightest loss of sleep.

Her enthusiastic publisher, Mr William Lake, had never met his most popular novelist face to face, however. Not even Letitia could bring herself to talk to him about her work, so Mr Waverley was the one who took her manuscripts to Leadenhall Street, to convey Mr Lake's comments and to negotiate on her behalf. This had been, so far, a very satisfactory arrangement which meant that, for his services, Bart was usually given his own copies to read before anyone else, and a vicarious share in her wild success. Knowing the author only as Miss Lydia Barlowe, the publisher had agreed that the creator of *The Infidel* should be known only as 'A Lady of Quality', since it was abundantly clear to him that, with a friend of such superior breeding as the Honourable Bartholomew Waverley, that was what she was sure to be. It was not his business, he assured the go-between, to probe any further.

Leaving her young charges to the Monday-morning care of the two elocution, play-reading and singing tutors, Letitia set out alone to the Misses Binney's house, wearing a favourite but rather worn velvet pelisse of faded lilac, keeping the nippy April breeze out with a swansdown tippet inside the neckline. She had noticed last night that Miss Austen had worn a long-sleeved brown gown trimmed with black lace, an acknowledgement of the death of the Queen's brother last month.

This morning, the mood had lightened to a white gauze gown under a sleeveless spencer of pale green quilted silk complemented by a soft Paisley shawl and satin slippers made to match. Partly covered by a pretty lace cap, her dark curls framed her sweet face, though, in the daylight, Letitia could see shadows beneath her brilliant eyes and the delicate, almost transparent skin that she understood had once been flawless. Life, she saw, had not passed Miss Austen by without leaving its mark upon her, though she moved with the grace of a much younger woman, her welcoming smile as open as ever.

Their meeting last evening had been too brief for either of them, with so many others awaiting their moment of glory, and now Letitia could not hold back a pang of guilt for the strain that more talking might impose.

'My dear Miss Boyce,' said Miss Austen, 'it's no strain to talk to those who share a love of good literature. Especially—' she twinkled '—without the background noise. That's what I find most difficult. The politicians do tend to *boom*, don't you find?'

Letitia loved her puckish sense of humour. They sat opposite each other by the long window that looked out across The Green where people strolled like coloured beads caught in the sun. 'I think the playwright did his share, too...' she smiled '...but I must not be too harsh. He is to escort us all to Mr Garrick's Temple after lunch. He knows Mrs Garrick well, so we shall be introduced.'

'Then we shall not say another critical word about loud voices. I take it you have tutors to come in daily. Are they there now?'

'Indeed. Elocution and music on Monday mornings. The "voice day" we call it.'

'Music...ah! It *is* important,' she agreed, 'for every woman, young or not, to be able to entertain her guests and to sing for her supper, too, when asked. Not to contribute in some way would be exceedingly poor form. But I have always thought it to be a little…well…insincere, even dishonest, to pretend to an enthusiasm one does not possess, as if other people's likes and dislikes carried more weight than one's own. Without sounding pompous, Miss Boyce, this is why I think you and I could become good friends, for you do not appear to me to be afraid of showing what you do. For a young woman of your background, the pressures to conform must have been very great indeed. But here you are in a fashionable place like Richmond, running an exclusive seminary, which I own I would rather have attended than The Abbey at Reading. It's nothing short of courageous. I suspect there is very little you would hesitate to try, despite what society thinks of it.'

Beneath such a misplaced tribute, Letitia was faced with an instant dilemma of whether to accept it with thanks and to say nothing about Miss Austen's suspicion, or whether to confide in her about the writing, which no one but Mr Waverley knew of. It was a decision that could not be delayed, for upon her response would depend the true nature of any future friendship. On the one hand, Miss Austen would see nothing especially difficult in admitting to a profession at which she herself was a success but, on the other, the kind of writing for which 'A Lady of Quality' was known would most certainly not come within Miss Austen's approval. The friendship would end before it had begun. Letitia could not bring herself to shock so excellent a writer whose books she truly admired, for it had been made quite clear during their previous discourse that Miss Austen's opinion of writers who 'stepped over the bounds of propriety with too colourful imaginations', as she had delicately phrased it, were definitely not to be recommended.

Nor was there any chance that Letitia might admit to being a writer *without* saying what she had written, or how very successful she was, the very idea of pretending to be unpublished being too full of pitfalls to contemplate. So, in the time it took her to smile, she decided upon an even greater deception as the price of Miss Austen's much-needed regard and the approval of a like-minded spirit.

'You honour me with your friendship, Miss Austen,' she said. 'I don't know that I would call it courage, exactly, but I believe my bid for independence of mind may have begun as soon as I gave my first yelp. Or so my mama always maintains. May I ask about your next book? Is it soon to be published?'

'About May, I think. It seems so long since I began writing it I can sometimes scarce remember what it's about. It isn't quite the seamless progress it appears to those not in the business,' she explained. '*Mansfield Park* was begun in the year 1811, almost three years ago, but there are usually some overlaps when parts have to be revised or even rewritten, and then I may find I have two books in hand, the one I *thought* was finished and the one I'm in the middle of.'

'I see. So when one is published, you re-read it after quite an interval? That must be quite refreshing.'

'In a way. But I'm always struck by what *could* have been written, rather than what I actually wrote. Several years later, one's experience of life is slightly changed. Small changes, but enough to make a difference.' Her tone became wistful, reflective. This was exactly what Letitia needed to know.

'Experience is vital, then? Does not the imagination and observation make up for what one can never hope to experience in life?'

Miss Austen sighed, speaking with less assurance.

'Marriage is what you mean, I suppose. Yes, on that subject you may be right, for I shall never enter that estate now and you yourself have taken a brave risk in placing yourself outside your family's protection. And although I can observe some of the tenderness of married love from my relatives, that's probably as far as I need to go in my stories.'

'But before that? In the wooing? The relationship of lovers?'

There was a pause, and the hands that lay in Miss Austen's lap began to move and caress. 'That, too,' she said. 'There were two occasions: one of them I had hopes of, the other could never have progressed. I withdrew my consent immediately. It was a mistake. Without love, you see.' She smiled sadly as the moment of pain lifted. 'One needs to *feel* the love. It's the same with writing. One *can* write about the anguish and uncertainty; one can write about the wonderful sensitivities of the mind, men's minds, too. But as I get older, I realise that it's the true experiences that have informed my writing as no mere imagination could possibly do, even though it was quite some time ago now. There's no substitute for sincerity, is there? I think my readers would demand it from me now, Miss Boyce.'

'I'm sure they won't be disappointed in *Mansfield Park*. I look forward to reading it. Have you another one planned?'

'I have another,' she smiled. 'I shall call it *Emma*. And this heroine will have faults, for a change. They cannot all be so perfect, can they?'

They continued to talk for another half-hour, which was much longer than Letitia had intended. By the time of her departure, they were on first-name terms, had exchanged addresses and had given promises to write and to visit. They embraced at their farewell, Letitia both elated and cast down by her most significant artifice. Deception on such a scale weighed heavily upon her.

There was one thing, however, that afforded her some relief, for in denying her writing, she had been spared the obligation that would inevitably follow of having to talk about her stories. Miss Austen had seemed happy enough to explain her published heroines' attributes and foibles, but Letitia could never have done the same with anything like her skilled understanding. Perhaps, she thought, that was because she did not understand them as well as Miss Austen understood hers.

Another aspect of her meeting with the famed Miss Austen was the conviction that, whatever the authoress had meant to say, there was no substitute for experience. This was something that no page in her notebook was ever likely to supply. She was going to have to take the bull by the horns, one day very soon. The question to be answered was—how?

Her return to Number 24 Paradise Road, taken at a very brisk walk, coincided perfectly with the mid-morning break when the pupils gathered in the garden room to take a cup of chocolate and a biscuit while conversing, as a good hostess should, with the tutors and chaperons. Their lessons that morning had been more in the nature of rehearsals for, in five days' time, all seven pupils were to entertain an invited audience of local guests, including tutors and parents, at the Richmond home of Sir Francis and Lady Melborough whose daughter Sapphire was a pupil at Letitia's seminary.

Understandably, they were nervous, but nerves, they were told, were no excuse for trying to opt out of it, or for unnecessary displays of modesty. The second half of the morning was a run-through of the singing, leaving the piano solos and duets, the harp-playing and poetry recitals, for the days ahead.

The afternoon sun and sharp breeze were perfect for their outing to Hampton House, the home of the late Mr David Garrick. That same morning, Letitia's pupils had been studying one of the actor's most acclaimed roles as Shylock in Shakespeare's *The Merchant of Venice*, and the invitation to visit Garrick's Temple to the Bard had come at a most opportune moment, even if the exuberant playwright Mr Titus Chatterton was hardly the one she would have chosen to escort them. But Mr Chatterton and the old Mrs Garrick were personally acquainted, and this was the kind of connection one needed if six adults and seven young ladies were to descend upon a frail ninety-year-old widow all on the same afternoon.

To buffer her against Mr Chatterton's incessant theatricals, Letitia had requested the company of their elocution tutor, Mr Thomas, whose popularity was almost on a par with Mr Waverley's. The latter was also one of the party, riding horseback like everyone except Mrs Quayle and Miss Gaddestone, who sat behind the coachman, his dignity having been restored by the presentation of a replacement hat from the late Mr Quayle's wardrobe. This time, Letitia warned the girls, they were unlikely to interfere with any cavalry drills.

It was when they rode through Bushy Park's avenue of chestnut trees towards the Diana Fountain that Letitia realised how close they were to Hampton Court Green where the cavalry offices and stables were situated and that, as they turned right on to the avenue of limes, they had been recognised. A group of helmetless recruits sat on the white-painted fence waiting for orders, swinging round to ogle the riders who passed behind them.

Coming under the multiple stare of male eyes, the seven young ladies adjusted their posture and became alert as if, Letitia wrote in her notebook that night, someone had pulled their strings and brought them quietly to life. At the same time, several of the horses reacted, too, exchanging whinnys and pricking ears, rolling eyes and prancing under tight reins, responding to unintentional messages.

Letitia reined in her pretty grey Arab mare. 'Keep going!' she called, resolving to have their riding tuition increased now that the good weather was here to stay. Waiting until they had passed her, she brought up the rear alone since Mr Chatterton, with his captive audience of two ladies, rode beside the barouche. The other two men were some way ahead, oblivious to the cavalcade behind them. From the corner of her eye, she could see the uniformed young men donning helmets, mounting horses and heading for the gate that would release them on to the avenue. Soon, the drumming of hooves followed her, keeping a respectful distance but ready to overtake her pupils as soon as she relinquished her rearguard position.

One young man, more reckless than the rest, cantered on to the grass beside her, laughing at his comrades for their prudence. A sharp command brought the young man's mount wheeling round on its haunches and, before Letitia could turn to look, the captain's bay gelding was beside her, towering over her dainty mare, garnished with tassels and braids and padded with several inches of white sheepskin under the ornate saddle. Shining black boots and silver spurs caught her eye, but she would not look at him. In front of her, the swish of a tail away, Jane Doveley's horse had taken a fancy to walking crab-wise, highlighting yet again the sad fact that all was not as it should be with the young riders and their mounts.

'I see you could not stay away, Miss Boyce,' said Lord Rayne in a voice that held more than a hint of amusement.

'This is the way to Hampton House, Lord Rayne. We are obliged to avoid the public highways, but the last thing we need is a cavalry escort. We have our own chaperons, I thank you.'

'Not very effective, are they? They don't even know we're here.'

He spoke too soon. Responding to the calls, Mr Waverley and Mr Thomas had turned and were cantering back, astonished to find that their duties had been taken over by at least a dozen mounted men. The first help Mr Thomas offered was to take Miss Doveley's horse by the bridle.

Mr Waverley greeted his old school friend and asked—foolishly, Letitia thought—if he intended to go to the Garrick house with them.

'No, he certainly does not!' she replied with more emphasis than she had intended. 'Poor Mrs Garrick would suffer a fit of the vapours to see such a crowd on her property. Please return, my lord. We shall go on nicely as we are.'

'What you need, Miss Boyce, is a good riding instructor for some of your young ladies. Do you not agree, Bart?'

'Well, I, er…'

'The good riding instructor to be yourself, of course,' said Letitia. 'So, having got that detail out into the open, perhaps you should know, my lord, that it doesn't matter what Mr Waverley thinks about it, their lessons are in *my* hands, and I shall arrange any extra ones myself, I thank you.'

'No need to take a pet about it, Lettie,' said Mr Waverley,

reasonably. 'Rayne's only making a suggestion, and there's no one more experienced than he.'

'Yes,' said Letitia. 'That's exactly what I am afraid of.'

'And if he was offering me his help, I'd take it. He might even reduce his fee for seven of them.'

'You mean I'd be expected to *pay* him for an hour in the company of my pupils? I think not. And anyway, Lord Rayne is fully occupied with his own business all week, and our weekends at Paradise Road are not for lessons. It's quite out of the question.'

'I could make an exception,' said Rayne. 'I'm sure the parents would notice the difference.'

'I'm sure the parents would also notice the difference if some of the mounts they've provided were not the ones they've had since the girls were ten, or the ones they use to pull the family dog-cart. But that's not for me to tell them, unfortunately.'

'But *I* could,' Rayne persisted. 'Coming from me, and knowing that it was myself who'd given them some schooling, they'd allow me to find them something more suitable for their daughters. These nags hardly add much to *your* image, either, do they? Unless your intention is to entertain, of course.'

'My image is my own affair, my lord,' she snapped.

His low reply was meant for her ears alone. 'Yes, my beauty, and I could make it mine, too, if you could curb your sharp tongue. The nags are not the only creatures around here that need some schooling.'

She pretended not to have heard, but she had, and the words bit deep into her shell, angering and exciting her at the same time. Why did he think, she wondered, that it was not obvious why he wanted access to seven attractive young ladies on a regular basis, with her personal approval? Did he think she was a dimwit not to see what he was about?

'Your persistence must be an asset when you're teaching battle tactics, Lord Rayne, but I find it irritating. Thank you for your offer, but I prefer to do these things in my own way and in my own time.'

She had not, however, made any allowance for the timely interference of Miss Sapphire Melborough, whose parents were important members of the Richmond set and who, at almost eighteen years old, saw in Lord Rayne a close resemblance to Sir Galahad of Arthurian fame. What she knew of his reputation made him all the more dangerously attractive to her. By falling behind her companions and by making her dapple-grey dance about naughtily, she allowed herself to be caught by Lord Rayne's hand on her bridle and brought back to the wide path, blushing in confusion. It was doubtful whether the performance had fooled anyone, Miss Melborough being one of the better riders, her mount usually well mannered, but it served to reinforce Lord Rayne's argument tolerably well.

'Oh, thank you, my lord,' she said, slightly breathless. 'I cannot *think* why Mungo should choose to be so wilful when I was trying so *hard* to do everything Miss Boyce has told us about looking where we're going.'

'Perhaps,' said Rayne, with a glance at Letitia, 'Miss Boyce also finds it difficult to see where she's going.'

'But Miss Boyce is the most *elegant* of horsewomen, my lord. You must have seen that for yourself. And her beautiful grey mare is…'

At the merest signal from Letitia, the beautiful grey mare bounded forward on delicate hooves towards the barouche, which was approaching the village of Hampton, and although her instructions to the coachman were hardly needed, neither would she stay to hear the silly exchanges between those two, or to his impertinent observations about not being able to see. It was not hard for her to believe that this deficiency was partly behind his offer, knowing as she did that, in order to correct anyone's riding, one must be able to see perfectly. Yet she did not think his offer was entirely for her sake, either. The man was nothing if not an opportunist.

Entering the riverside grounds of Hampton House, she left Mr Waverley and Mr Thomas to dismiss the cavalry in whatever way they chose, going with the playwright Mr Chatterton to meet their hostess in the sadly neglected mansion that David Garrick had lovingly referred to as 'his pretty place by the Thames-side.' Bound to the upkeep of two grand houses under her husband's will, old Mrs Garrick was now reduced to doing almost everything for herself and understandably did not wish anyone to see the dilapidations of the house. She was happy for them to go down to Mr Garrick's 'Temple to Shakespeare' by the river, which is what they had most hoped to see.

It was a domed, octagonal, brick-built place with steps up to a portico of Ionic columns and a room beyond where, they were told, the actor used to entertain his friends or learn his lines in full view of the river. A statue of the bard was here, too, with objects said to have belonged to him, though the glass cases were dusty and a mouldy smell hung in the air. Between them, Mr Chatterton and Mr Thomas, a young Welshman with the most perfect diction, took it upon themselves to be the guides.

Miss Gaddestone, Mrs Quayle and Mr Waverley hovered on the edge of the group while Letitia, hoping for a few moments to herself, wandered down the sloping lawn to the water's edge. A weeping willow swept the grass with new fronds like pale green hair and, as she passed through its curtain, a figure moved away from the trunk and into her view. Against the mottled shadows, she had not noticed him.

The fur helmet was cradled under one arm, his dark hair caught by patches of light, thickly waved and long enough at the back to be tied into a pigtail, which she knew was a badge of this regiment. She wished he had stayed with them.

He followed as she turned away, though she felt rather than heard his presence. But there was nowhere for her to hide and her impulse to run was held in check, and she was gently steered away from the direction of the Temple, feeling rather like a hind evading a dominant stag.

'Out of the frying pan into the fire,' she snapped. 'I came here to avoid the commentary, but perhaps I should have braved it, after all. Don't captains have duties to perform on Monday afternoons?'

'Surely, Miss Boyce, you would not begrudge me a few moments of your time?'

'Oh, be assured that I would, my lord. I thought I'd made that plain last night at the Misses Binney's. However, if you are also hoping to claim a few moments of Miss Melborough's time on the way home, I would rather you respect my wishes and do your flirting when she is under her parents' protection, not mine. I cannot be held responsible for what *you* get up to. Is that too much to ask?'

'Not at all. I am happy to oblige. So, having dismissed the young lady from our thoughts once and for all, I wonder if you would care to reconsider your objections to allowing some help with the riding problem. You admit that you do have one?'

'I neither admit nor deny it, Lord Rayne. It is my concern and nothing to do with you. Thank you for your offer. The answer is still no.'

They had been walking quickly, and now Mr Chatterton's distantly garbled ranting came to them on the breeze combined with the honking of geese on the water. The winding path had taken them downhill out of sight of the Temple and into a dell where they came to a standstill, their antagonism almost tangible as they faced each other like a pair of duellists waiting for the next move.

'Do you answer no to everything, Miss Boyce, as a matter of course?' he said, softly.

She hesitated, suspecting that he had re-routed the subject towards something more personal. She could not be sure. 'No,' she said, 'but I find it a useful tool to use when an alternative won't do.'

His head bent towards her. 'Surely you don't think there is only one alternative, do you? There are many tones between black and white, you know. There is *maybe,* and *perhaps*, or *let's discuss it*, or *what exactly do you have in mind?* And dozens more.'

'I know exactly what you have in mind, Lord Rayne.'

'Tch! Miss Boyce!' he exclaimed in a dramatic whisper. 'That is the most unintelligent thing I've heard from you so far. Would you believe me if I said the same to you?'

'No, of course I would not.'

'I should hope not indeed. Still, if you're quite determined not to accept the best offer you'll have for some time, then so be it. We shall consider the matter closed because Miss Boyce has a bee in her bonnet about my precise intentions. Which, by the way, are not at all what she thinks.'

'Lord Rayne,' said Letitia, looking towards the silver ribbon of water and the blobs of white floating upon it, 'I think we ought to return. I have nothing to gain and much to lose by taking a walk alone with you. Perhaps you should allow me to walk back on my own.'

'I do not think you should be allowed to go anywhere on your own, Miss Boyce. Will you take my arm up this bank? We'll go up towards the house.'

'I'm not exactly *blind*, my lord.'

'So defensive,' he said, crooking his arm for her. 'Come on. Mind that branch.'

She hesitated, unaware of any obstruction on the path. It was shadowed and dappled with greenery, and it would be unnecessarily foolish to ignore his offer of help, and she *was* defensive, and insecure, and a whole lot of other devices acquired during years of having to battle against convention, her mother, her desires, her poor eyesight and its disadvantages. Her hesitation was interpreted as obstinacy.

'Can you not bring yourself to accept help of *any* kind?'

'I can't see any branch!' she yelped.

Unable to stifle a chuckle of exasperation, he went behind her, bending to unlatch the skirt of her sage-green habit from a mossy twig projecting from a branch. 'Now,' he said, offering his arm again, 'shall we go, or shall you fight the elements single-handed?'

Subdued, she took his arm and used his steely strength to negotiate the overgrown path up to the house, unsure how she had come to this point in a relationship that could not have begun in a worse manner. She understood that everyone had at least two sides to their characters, but so far she had allowed him to see only one of hers. It was her own bizarre two-sidedness that concerned her most, for she was not sure which of the two was the real Lettie Boyce, nor did she approve of the deception she was being forced to present, especially to those close to her. For some reason she could not explain, it mattered to her that this man's opinion should be placed on a firmer footing.

'Lord Rayne,' she ventured, not quite knowing what to say.

'Miss Boyce?'

'You may have…well, you see…I am not quite what you think.'

'And you are about to tell me what I think, are you? I thought we had agreed on the absurdity of that, just now.'

'I *meant* to say, if you will allow me, that I may have given you the impression that…well, you spoke earlier about my sharp tongue, and—'

'And the fact that you might personally benefit from a little schooling? Yes, I remember, Miss Boyce. Are you taking up my offer, then?'

'Lord Rayne, you are the most *odious* man of my acquaintance.'

'Abominable,' he agreed, smiling broadly.

Chapter Four

As a result of her meeting with Miss Austen Letitia came away with a feeling of relief that she had not revealed anything of her own writing. Yet with every sentence she wrote, she was reminded that, apart from one derisory kiss from the odious Lord Rayne, her heroine and her heroine's creator were both still innocents with fervent imaginations. Although the kiss was very clear in her memory, it had not been given in the right circumstances and was therefore untypical.

Mr Waverley had told her that afternoon how much he was enjoying *Waynethorpe Manor* as much as, if not more than, the first novel. His mother, he told her, had begged to be the next to read it.

'Is that wise?' Letitia asked him before he left that evening.

'She's one of your most avid readers. Of course it's wise.'

'I hope she doesn't suspect…'

He took her by the shoulders in brotherly fashion, laughing at her touchiness. 'She doesn't suspect anything, Lettie. She and Lake are well acquainted, and he's told her that the author is a certain Lydia Barlowe, but no more than that.'

'Perhaps I should have used different initials.'

'Nonsense. No one is ever going to make the connection.'

Her friend's approval of *Waynethorpe Manor*, however, satisfied her that the author's lack of emotional experience had not in any way affected his enjoyment, though whether she could convince her readers for a third time remained to be seen.

'What's the new one about?' he asked.

'About a young lady called Em...er...Perdita, rather like one of my pupils, in some ways.'

'Which pupil?'

'Any one of them. Inexperienced. Looking for excitement.'

'Looking for love, you mean.'

'Yes, that, too,' she said, giving herself away at each reply. Surely Bart would recognise the heroine?

'You have only to look at the material right under your roof.'

'What d'ye mean?' she asked, rather too sharply.

'I mean your seven young ladies, who else?' They had reached the pavement where Mr Waverley's horse was being held by the young groom. Taking the reins with a nod of thanks, he spoke to Letitia in a confidential whisper. 'As a matter of fact, there is a young lady who might fit your Perdita's description, up to a point. The lass from Scotland. One of the boarders.'

'Edina Strachan? In what way?'

'Nothing I can quite put my finger on, but you must have noticed how inattentive she's become this new term. Her mind certainly isn't on her household-management accounts, and I'd swear she'd been weeping before she came to the dinner table yesterday. She moons about like a lovesick calf.'

'You don't think she might be in love with you, do you, Bart?'

'Good grief, no, I do not. She's either still homesick or lovesick, I tell you. Perhaps something happened while she was at home at Easter. You might keep an eye on the situation.'

'Yes, thank you for the warning. I will. I'll ask Mrs Quayle what she knows about it.'

But Mrs Quayle, the widow in whose house next door the three boarders had rooms, had nothing to add to Mr Waverley's observations. 'Homesickness, my dear,' she said that evening. 'It's only her second term away from home. We may have to work harder on her Scottish lilt, for if she cannot be understood, she's not going to make much headway in the marriage mart, is she? Perhaps we could get Mr Thomas to give her an extra half-hour each week?'

'So you don't think she's in love?'

'Who knows? With all those young Hussars swarming about, it wouldn't surprise me if all seven of them were. Don't worry, I'll keep a look out.'

'Yes. Thank you.'

That same evening, Letitia sat with the attractive seventeen-year-old Edina, whose guardian grandparents lived at Guildford. After talking at length about her family, it seemed that Edina was relieved to be away from their strait-laced Presbyterian influence and more involved with the kind of social life she had previously been denied. The symptoms that Mr Waverley had identified could not be homesickness, Letitia decided, therefore it must be love.

That evening, Edina's early signs were written into the notebook with some elaboration to make up for what Letitia had not personally observed.

* * *

The remainder of the week passed uneventfully except for
the visit on Thursday of Miss Garnet and Miss Persephone
Boyce in the company of Uncle Aspinall and Aunt Minnie,
the latter requiring a tour of the house and redesigned gardens.
Sir Penfold Aspinall, a bluff, good-natured giant who had
done so much to help his sister's eldest daughter to set up
house, approved of everything he saw, partly because he
trusted her good taste and partly because he liked the idea of
being surrogate father to his remarkable niece. His wife,
shrewish and disapproving, had come chiefly to take note
and then to convey to Lady Boyce every detail to which they
could mutually object.

The twins' main purpose in visiting their sister seemed to
be to catch sight of Lord Rayne, whose absence had been the
cause of some concern. They asked if it was true that he was
visiting her.

'Visiting me? You must be bamming!'

'Has he?'

'Of course not. Why would he visit *me*?'

'We heard he was riding with you on Monday.'

'Me and about twenty others on the way to Garrick's Temple.'

'Oh, well, if that's all.'

'That *is* all. I suppose he'll be escorting you on Saturday?'

'No,' said Persephone, pouting.

'Too busy with preparations for the foreign visitors. Apparently they'll all need mounts,' said Garnet. 'We shall go to
Almack's, anyway.'

'It won't be the same. He's such a tease.'

'Is he?' said Letitia, relieved to hear that his commit-
ments would keep him away from Richmond that weekend.

'Come to the garden and see my new summer-house. I think you'll like it.'

Aunt Minnie had found it first. She was taking tea there, dunking an almond biscuit in her cup before she heard them coming. 'Ridiculous waste of money, Letitia,' she said, brushing away dribbles of tea from her lace tippets. 'What are your fees for this place?'

'With extras, usually twenty pounds a term. More for the boarders.'

'Hmm! I don't know what your mama will say to that.'

Uncle Aspinall chuckled. 'It has nothing to do with Euphemia,' he said. 'Cheap at the price, I'd say. What are your young ladies doing now, Letitia?'

'French, with Madame du Plessis, Uncle.'

'Tch! French indeed,' said Aunt Minnie, sourly. 'That monster Bonaparte has a lot to answer for.'

But Uncle Aspinall had nothing but compliments to offer about the way his niece had furnished the rooms, the feminine colour schemes, the new garden layout and the adjoining conservatory. The hanging baskets, potted palms, window-boxes and newly planted vines had brought the garden well into the white painted room. 'Like a jungle!' Aunt Minnie carped. 'Ridiculous!'

It was not until Saturday evening when Letitia gathered her pupils into the downstairs parlour for a last check that she discovered an unwanted addition to the guest list that she could do nothing about when the invitation had been issued by Miss Sapphire Melborough, the daughter of their hosts.

Letitia kept her annoyance to herself, though she would like to have boxed the pert young woman's ears. 'I don't mind you inviting Lord Rayne, Sapphire dear,' she said, fastening the pearl pendant behind her neck, 'but it might have been more polite if you'd asked me first. And your parents. We have to be very careful about the audience, you know.'

'But they *like* Lord Rayne,' said Sapphire, understating the case by a mile, 'so I know they won't mind him coming with Lord and Lady Elyot. And I didn't think you'd disapprove, now that you and he have made up your differences. I told him about our concert and he said he'd like to hear me sing.'

'Next time, dear,' said Letitia, turning Sapphire to face her, 'ask me first, will you? He may be one of Richmond's *haut ton*, but the 10th Light Dragoons, or Hussars, whichever you prefer, have quite a reputation.'

Sapphire's bright cornflower eyes lit up like those of a mischievous elf. 'The Elegant Extracts is what I prefer, Miss Boyce. It's so fitting, isn't it?'

'It's also one of the more repeatable tags. There now, let me look at you. Yes, I think your family will be proud of you. Nervous?'

A hand went up to tweak at a fair curl, and the eyes twinkled again. 'With Lord Rayne watching me, yes.' Provocatively, she lifted one almost bare shoulder in a way that some women do by instinct. It would only be a matter of time, Letitia thought, before this one and her parents managed to snare the Elegant Extract, unless one of her own sisters did first.

'Stay close to Edina, Sapphire. I think she feels the absence of her parents and guardians at a time like this.'

'Yes, Miss Boyce. Of course I will.'

There was more to Letitia's annoyance than having to show friendship to a man she would rather have avoided. He had told her sisters that he would be too busy on Saturday to escort them when he must already have accepted Sapphire's invitation to hear her sing. Persephone and Garnet would be sadly out of countenance to learn that he was not as committed to them as they thought. Their mother even more so. All that was needed now to set the cat among the pigeons was for them to believe that *she* had invited him to the Melboroughs'. She could only pray that they would not come to that conclusion as easily as they'd learned of his precise whereabouts on Monday.

As it transpired, this particular problem faded into insignificance beside the others of that evening. Though she had made every effort to present her pupils to perfection in appearance, manners and performance, the one who outshone them all without the slightest effort was herself. Gowned modestly in palest oyster silk and ivory lace, her aristocratic breeding and her refined silvery loveliness drew the eyes of the appreciative audience before, during and after each individual contribution. Making good use of her gold enamelled scissors-spectacles that hung from a ribbon looped about her wrist, she was able to see most of what was happening while combining an image of seriousness with a charming eccentricity, for the folding spectacle was not an easy accessory to use.

When she was not using it, it seemed hardly to matter that she could see only the indistinct shapes of the guests for, with Mr Waverley to help her through introductions and to murmur reminders in her ear, she felt the disadvantage less than she might otherwise have done. It also quite escaped her notice that the admiring eyes of so many men turned her way, or that the women's eyes busied themselves with every perfect detail of her ensemble.

Miss Gaddestone, petite in a flurry of frills, mauve muslin

and bugle beads, and Mrs Quayle, like a plump beady-eyed brown bird, were the other two who knew the seriousness of Letitia's handicap, but who were too interested in their own roles to play chaperon to her as well as the pupils. They knew Mr Waverley would do that.

Sir Francis and Lady Melborough had taken a fancy to Letitia from the start, looking upon her at times as one of the family, though it had always been one of her policies to maintain a respectful distance between herself and the pupils' parents to avoid any appearance of favouritism. Lady Melborough was a perfect forecast of how Sapphire would look in another twenty years, kindly and flighty and of a more blue-blooded ancestry than Sir Francis. She had prepared well for this event, her house being the most perfect setting, high-ceilinged and spacious, gold-and-white walled, moulded and mirrored.

As a newly knighted city banker, Sir Francis was self-important and ambitious, handsome and middle-aged with an eye for the feminine form, and for his own form, too. He stood facing a very large gilded mirror to speak to Letitia where, with lingering looks, he could see over her shoulder both his own front and her back, the curve of which he thought was enchanting. Letitia found his closeness uncomfortable, his affability fulsome, his attentions too personal for politeness. She edged away, trying to identify Mr Waverley's brown hair amongst so many others, and when she noticed the unmistakable frame and dark head of Lord Rayne approaching from across the room, the sudden relief she felt was quite impossible to hide.

'Why, Miss Boyce,' he said, 'am I dreaming, or did I see a fleeting welcome in your smile? Do tell me I'm not mistaken.'

'It would be impolite of me, to say the least, Lord Rayne,

to admit any feeling of relief. Sir Francis is our host and I'm
sure he's doing all he can to make the evening a success.'

'Then I take it you would not appreciate a word of warning?'

This was the first time she had seen Lord Rayne in evening
dress, and she found it difficult to reconcile the former soldier
in regimentals with the quietly dressed beau in charcoal-grey
tail-coat, left open to show a waistcoat of grey silk brocade.
Whatever else she disliked about him, she could not fault his
style. 'Warning?' she said. 'Are you the right person to be
warning me of *that*?'

'Of what, Miss Boyce?'

'Lord Rayne, you take a delight in putting me to the blush.
But I shall not rise to your bait. You of all people must know
what I refer to.'

'Will I never be forgiven for that, Miss Boyce? Am I not
to be allowed to warn you of similar dangers from old married
men who ought to know better?' Despite the teasing words,
his eyes were seriously intent.

'It is not necessary. I am not a green girl, my lord, and I
have Mr Waverley to protect me.'

'Ah, Mr Waverley. So you do.'

Their eyes roamed together, identifying the elegant figure
in dark blue and white only a few paces away. Side by side,
he was talking and smiling with Mr Jeffery Melborough,
Sapphire's older brother, shoulders almost touching, their
backs reflected in the long mirror above a semi-lune table.
Before Letitia could withdraw her glance, a slight
movement in the mirror caused her to squint, trying to
understand why young Mr Melborough's hand was slipping
between the long tails of Mr Waverley's coat, its white cuff
almost disappearing.

'What's he doing?' she frowned. 'I think he's picking Bart's pocket. I must go and warn him.'

'No, come away…over here.' Lord Rayne's voice was suddenly commanding, his arm across her waist urging her forward. 'Look, here are Mrs Quayle and your cousin. It must almost be time for the second half. Ladies,' he bowed. 'May I procure—'

'But what if he *was* trying to reach Mr Waverley's pocket? Is there not one in the lining of the tails?'

'—a glass of punch for you?'

Face to face with the two chaperons, Letitia had little option but to abandon Mr Waverley to his predicament, whatever it was, in favour of the excited chatter covering every aspect of the evening, including Lord Rayne himself, as soon as his back was turned.

'Did you *know*,' said Mrs Quayle, 'that he actually *offered* for your house when it first came on the market? I had no idea, but that's what Lady Adorna Elwick has just told me. She's his sister, you know. Lives at Mortlake. Over there, with the tall gentleman. Her *beau*,' she whispered. 'Isn't she a *vision*?'

'Yes, I met her earlier,' said Letitia, recalling the stunning beauty in gossamer gold-threaded muslin that seemed to reveal more than it covered. The Merry Widow, they called her, with good reason. 'Strange that no one mentioned it before. Lord Rayne has said not a word.'

'Well, perhaps he doesn't want you to know,' said Mrs Gaddestone.

'That he wished to purchase my house? Why not?'

Miss Gaddestone opened her mouth to answer, but was checked by her friend's elbow connecting firmly with hers. 'Oh! Am I not meant to say?'

'Say what? Gaddy, what *are* you talking about?' said Letitia.

Helplessly, Miss Gaddestone blinked at Mrs Quayle, who rose to the occasion as if this was what she'd intended. 'Lord Rayne,' she breathed from half behind her fan, 'is still recovering from a thwarted love affair, his sister says. Number 18, you see, belongs to the Bostons, and Lady Boston is Lady Elyot's niece, and when the two of them lived there before they were married, Lady Boston and Lord Rayne formed an *attachment* to each other.'

'Before she was Lady Boston, you mean?'

'Yes, she was plain Caterina Chester then, but she—'

'Mrs Quayle,' said Letitia, 'what are you implying? That Lord Rayne wanted Number 24 so he could live near the lady he once had a *tendre* for? If that were typical, he'd have to offer for dozens of properties a year, wouldn't he? Anyway, Number 18 is empty for most of the year. I was told that the Bostons live up in Northumberland. Or is it Cumberland?'

Fluffing up her feather boa and settling it again upon her shoulders, Mrs Quayle tried again. 'It is,' she said. 'The Bostons keep a skeleton staff there. They come down from the north about twice a year. Still, it sounds to me as if he's not quite got over the lady, doesn't it? I wonder if she feels the same way.'

'I think you're probably jumping to conclusions,' said Letitia. 'Perhaps he had his sights on Number 24 because Richmond houses don't come on the market too often. Well, not the kind he'd want to buy.'

But the information, so carelessly given, found a corner of her mind into which it did not fit as snugly as it ought. The notion of Lord Rayne being capable of a lasting affection for a woman seemed uncharacteristic of such a man. More than that she would not allow herself to dwell on, though it became quite a struggle to prevent certain images from developing in her mind that had no business there in the first place. Especially when she did not even like the man.

As if she could not resist the chance to needle him for something as indefinable as that, she joined him towards the end of the interval as he and Mr Waverley were chatting together. Instead of greeting her with his usual smile, Mr Waverley was studying his shoes as if they had been the subject of some discussion while Lord Rayne's expression held traces of sympathy.

'Ye...es,' Mr Waverley was saying. 'Right. Ah, Lettie. It's all going rather well, don't you think?'

'It is indeed,' she replied. 'And just think, if Lord Rayne had been with my sisters as they expected him to be, he would have missed such high-class entertainment. But one must choose, I suppose, between hearing Miss Melborough sing and thereby pleasing two prospective parents-in-law on the one hand, or escorting two Miss Boyces and pleasing only *one* parent. It must have been a very difficult decision to make, my lord. I hope the concert is worth the sacrifice. Shall I let my sisters know who took their place, or shall you be the one to explain the problem?'

Rayne's eyes, heavy-lidded and patently bored with the subject, looked beyond her. 'There was no problem, Miss Boyce, although if you wish to make a drama of it, please don't let a detail like that prevent you. I realise how dull life must be for you without some kind of diversion, however small.'

'Yes, my lord. You can have no idea how tedious it is to put on concerts of this kind and to be making visits almost every day. Compared to the excitement of routine cavalry drill and the polishing of tack, we live very sedate lives. What is it to be on Monday? Ah, yes, our theatre evening. Oh, what a bore.'

'Lettie, I think Lord Rayne means that—'

'Bart dear, I know what he means.'

'If I may interrupt,' said Rayne, tonelessly, 'I believe we may have covered this ground only recently. We're getting to the "I know what you're thinking" part, if I'm not mistaken. Bart, would you be a good fellow and…?' He touched Mr Waverley's lace cuff with the tip of his fingers.

'Yes, of course. Will you excuse me, Lettie? I'll catch up later.'

Letitia stared at the prompt departure. 'What was that about?' she snapped. 'Why did you—?'

'Because, my sharp-tongued beauty, I have some advice for you.'

'Then I don't think I want to hear it, thank you.'

'Yes, you do. It's about what you saw earlier. With Mr Jeffery.'

'Oh. Were you giving him a set-down?'

'Not at all. It was a fudge between them, and Bart was embarrassed. Nothing was taken from his pocket. It was just a bit of nonsense. It would please Bart if you were not to mention it.'

'Oh, boy's pranks, you mean.'

'Exactly. There are certain things a woman is innocent of when she has no brothers.'

Letitia blinked, not knowing how to reply to that. Without knowing it, he had pinpointed a basic truth that lay behind her writing problem, not simply by being brotherless, but being without the kind of understanding that comes from years of observing what young males do, how they behave together, what they look like under the formal attire and what they say to each other. It was a private jest between friends. She ought to have guessed.

Caught unawares, she foolishly pursued the other matter instead of granting him the last word. 'So what am I to tell my sisters, my lord? I would not want them to think it was I who invited you here this evening.'

'Miss Boyce,' he said, visibly stifling a sigh, 'you appear to be rather obsessed by what other people think, despite your efforts to make it seem otherwise. If I were you, I'd leave me to deal with my own affairs as I think best and try minding my own business.'

'It will be very much my business, Lord Rayne, if my sisters were to suspect *me* of keeping you here at Richmond. In fact, they have already asked me if you have visited me. How foolish is that, I ask you?'

'Extremely foolish, Miss Boyce. I cannot think of a single reason why I should want to call on you at Paradise Road. Can you?'

'Not unless it was to take a look at the alterations I've made since *you* looked it over. Enjoy the music, my lord.'

The tiff gave her nothing like the satisfaction she had hoped for and, if it had not been for her pupils' efforts to please, and her own part in that, she would have felt even more irritated than she did. As it was, the parents were well satisfied that they had made the right choice of school for their daughters and that their money was being well spent on all the right accomplishments. In that respect, the exercise had been well worth the effort.

Sir Francis and Lady Melborough went even further by letting it be known that Lord Rayne had agreed to give their daughter some riding tuition and to find her a better mount than the one that had been Mr Jeffery Melborough's hack. Then, it was only a matter of minutes before first one father and then another approached Lord Rayne with similar requests, effectively appointing him as personal tutor to their daughters and charging him with the purchase of suitable horses to replace the present ones, to Letitia's quietly seething anger. The only saving grace in her eyes was that the extra lessons would be outside school hours and it would be the parents rather than she who paid him. The only one to miss out on this new arrangement was Miss Edina Strachan, whose relatives had not attended.

'You did that on purpose, didn't you?' Letitia said to him.

'I didn't actually have to *do* anything, Miss Boyce. It was Miss Melborough herself who broached the subject to her father and he who asked me what I thought. What I thought is what I'd already said to you. Simple as that.'

'You have a knack of getting your own way, that's all I can say.'

'I wish it was all you could say, ma'am. Unfortunately, I do not hold out any hopes on that score until you're taken in hand and held on a tight rein.'

'Which will not be *your* business, my lord.'

'Not yet. You'll have to be caught first. Goodnight, Miss Boyce.'

This was not, however, the last she heard from him that night, for as she stood listening to the quietly spoken vicar's wife, mother of Verity Nolan, the deeper voices of Lord Rayne and Lord Elyot came to her ears from the other side of a wide marble column, weaving around Mrs Nolan's opinions of the piano duets.

'Attracted?' said one, in answer to some question. 'Intrigued, certainly. I can't say I've ever come across such a combination of looks, intelligence and prickliness.'

'So well balanced,' Mrs Nolan was saying, eagerly. 'Of course…'

'You've had it too much your own way, Sete. That's the problem.'

'…there were times when the bass line was a little strong, but…'

'Yes, I know I have. She seems to think so, too.'

'What about the sisters? Not so much fun?'

'….but that's only to be expected. A little more practice, and…'

'Getting tedious, Nick. Too predictable. The elder one is a cracker, and I fancy the challenge. You can see why she and the mother don't see eye to eye.'

'So, you fancy taking on a *blue-stocking*.' There was low laughter and some words about no stockings at all that made Letitia blush. 'Well, give it a try and see how it goes. She may prove to be worth the trouble, if looks are anything to go by. D'ye think she's interested?'

'She's very green, for all her ways. And I think she may be interested, but she'd not admit it. I may need some help, Nick. Are you willing?'

'Of course. You helped me with Amelie. Just let me know.'

'Thanks, I will.'

'Miss Boyce?' said Mrs Nolan. 'Are you all right? You're very flushed, my dear. I was saying—'

'Yes, quite right, Mrs Nolan. More practice, I'm sure. Now, I must go and say farewell to Lady Melborough and gather my brood together.' Slipping away into the crowd, Letitia made her way in a daze between the chattering bodies, her mind reeling from the kind of talk she should not have listened to. As her first taste of the way brothers spoke to each other in private, it would have been more enjoyable if the subject of their speculation had not been herself.

It now became imperative for Letitia and her pupils to take their leave of their hosts, pack themselves into carriages and escape to the safety of Paradise Road away from the controversies surrounding Lord Rayne's unwanted presence. If he had not been invited, Letitia was sure she would not be feeling so annoyed, even if she ought to have anticipated some trouble, in view of her previous experiences.

Her farewell to her host and hostess, however, could not be rushed through in a few brief words, and when Sir Francis took her to one side, impolitely monopolising her attention, it was more than she could do to snub him by refusing point-blank to cross the threshold of his large library where he promised to show her a rare volume of John Donne's poetry before she left. Just to one side of the columned hall, the white double doors were wide open and, since anyone could see inside, Letitia saw no danger in following him.

John Donne was one of her favourite poets, but the library was not well lit and, when Sir Francis opened the book upon his desk and moved it across to show her the handwritten script, she found it impossible to see much except the first decorated letter. Deciding there and then that this was to be the extent of her obligation to him, she bent to look more closely as his hand smoothed over the pattern of words on the page. His body moved too close as only a father would have done, innocent but invasive, nevertheless. His breath smelled of brandy. She was tired, emotional and, she thought later, too keyed up to think sensibly, and what happened next was as much the result of her over-reaction as Sir Francis's uncomfortable closeness.

She moved away and took a hasty step backwards, hitting her heel against some unseen object, and crashing down over the top of it on to the carpeted floor, forcing a yelp from her lips.

Lights tipped and jerked crazily.

Hands reached out.

Shapes bent over her.

A man's face loomed through a haze of shock.

'No...no, don't *touch* me!' she whispered. 'I can manage alone.'

'Miss Boyce, take my hand. It's me, Rayne. Let me help you to get this footstool out of the way. You fell over it, I believe. Are you much hurt?'

Somewhere behind her, she heard the deeply cutting voice of his brother asking Melborough what in hell's name he thought he was doing to invite a young lady to be alone with him, telling him with unarguable finality that it didn't matter whether the doors were open or not, he should have known better. The thud of Sir Francis's footsteps on the carpet was swallowed into the soft hum from the hall.

Letitia struggled to sit upright against the desk. 'My eyeglasses,' she said. 'I heard a crack just now. They're hanging from my wrist. Please, if you would move your foot, my lord.'

There was a tinkle of glass as he obliged. '*Damn!*' he said. 'Oh...oh, *no*!'

Crouching down beside her, he removed the ribbon from her gloved wrist from which dangled the golden scissors-spectacles, one half now empty of glass, its pieces on the floor. 'I'm so sorry,' he whispered. 'I didn't see them there.

Why in pity's name doesn't he get some lights in here?' Carefully, he picked up the pieces. 'Truly, I'm sorry. I'll have them mended immediately. Leave it with me. Come, Miss Boyce, you should go straight home. Can you stand now?' Tucking the broken parts into his pocket, he held out his arms to her as Lord Elyot watched.

Although she had heard, only a few moments ago, how indelicate their talk about women could be, she made no protest as his arms enclosed her shoulders and gently pulled her upright, nor did she object when his cheek almost touched hers. She clung to his arm. 'Yes, I can stand, thank you. Ouch…oh, *ouch*! I'm all right, really. It was nothing.'

'No, you're not!' said Lord Elyot, sternly. 'You've had a nasty fall.'

'Not as bad as I've had on the hunting field, my lord.'

'That was years ago. Rayne and I will support you. See,' he said, offering her his arm, 'this is entirely proper. It will cause not the slightest comment for you to take both our arms, Miss Boyce. Will it?'

Obediently linking her arms through theirs, she winced visibly as the dull pain came pulsing into her knee and elbow. 'Thank you, my lord. You are very kind.' From the corner of her eye, she caught a look from Lord Elyot sent across her head to his brother.

'A little kindness goes a long way, eh, brother?' he said, softly.

Bustling towards them, Miss Gaddestone was all concern. Mr Waverley was not far behind, then came the others, flocking to her with smiles of sympathy and tender enquiries. Her arms were relinquished to others on a wave of affection that bore her out towards a waiting carriage, lifting her into it, settling her with rugs and cushions.

'Bart, will you…?' she began.

'Leave it all to me,' he said. 'Came a cropper, did you, Lettie?'

'In a manner of speaking,' she replied, catching Lord Rayne's eye.

Chapter Five

With so much to be said about the success of the evening, it was very late when the three boarders and Mrs Quayle left Number 24 for their beds next door. Everyone they had spoken to agreed that Miss Boyce's very select seminary excelled in the quality of the teaching and in the astonishing progress of the pupils. The only sad note was the absence of Edina's parents and grandparents, though Letitia did her best to sweeten the disappointment by drawing attention to the absence of her own family, too. It could not be helped, she said, if one's family could not always be where one wanted them to be.

Later, sitting up against a bank of pillows in her own bed, Letitia felt the sadness as keenly as her Scottish pupil, knowing that her sisters would gladly have come if their mother had chaperoned them. What would it take to get her here? she wondered. What would it take to win her approval?

Other incidents had left a sour taste in Letitia's mouth, the last one being by far the most serious and the one her friends had kindly glossed over as being no more than an accident, though they must have realised there was something more to it than that. She had been warned, and had assured Lord Rayne that she was capable of looking after herself, and now he would think she had brought it upon her own head.

It had also served her right for trying to manage without wearing her spectacles on such an important occasion, and now they were broken. Amongst her literary friends it mattered less, for most of them wore them openly. But tonight she had wanted to look her best, to be a credit to her pupils and to set an example of womanly perfection, as far as she was able.

But her efforts to hold herself above the reach of rakes had been less than successful, for the one whose attentions set up her hackles more than any other had discussed her with his brother as if she were a filly ready to be taken in hand. It was what he had rudely told her more than once. Perhaps that was the way they discussed her sisters also—her 'tedious, predictable sisters'. Unlike them, she had always been too threateningly bookish for any man to think of in romantic terms, and even Rayne found her—apparently—intriguing rather than attractive, a challenge, a diversion, nothing too serious. Nor had Bart ever shown her any romantic intentions.

Between bouts of reflection, her pencil on the page described the atmosphere, mannerisms, expressions and ensembles, the music and voices, the colours, the blurred flutter of fans and feathers, the perfumes and the faint, warm, male scent of the man who had lifted her from the floor, effortlessly. The pencil stopped, her head fell back upon the pillow, eyes closed, remembering. Was that how it would feel to be lifted, carried, laid upon a bed?

Busily, the pencil continued its word pictures. Her elbow and knee throbbed. She took another sip of warm chocolate

while constructing an image of Lady Boston who would, naturally, be ravishingly beautiful, not at all sharp-tongued or intellectual, and probably pining up in Northumberland for the
brother of her uncle-in-law. Was he within the permitted degree
of consanguinity? Did it matter these days? She fell asleep,
wondering about it, convinced that Lord Rayne did not intend
anything more than a light flirtation, being still half in love with
Lady Elyot's beautiful talented niece. Yes, she was sure to be
talented and experienced. A society high-flyer she would be.

Several times she woke when her knee and elbow pressed
upon something, sending her thoughts rushing back into the
angry pocket of her mind where Sir Francis's unfortunate lack
of manners hovered like a giant question mark over the messages
she was unconsciously sending out about her accessibility. Was
her learning attracting the wrong kind of man? Was it perhaps
to do with her care of younger women? For Lord Rayne to
overstep the mark was one thing, but for the father of one of her
own pupils to forget the respect due to her was nothing short of
shameful. By dawn, she felt as if she had hardly slept at all.

Monday morning, usually kept for music, was taken at a
leisurely pace over jugs of barley water and coffee, cook's best
biscuits and a continuous flow of laughter and discussion
about future events. Sitting outside in the garden, Letitia used
the opportunity to show them the new shoots of herbs, dill,
parsley, rosemary and thyme, and to make a game of recognising them by smell alone. Then there were formal thank-you
letters to be written to their hosts, leaving Letitia to put her
feet up in the roomy summerhouse where the footman came
to find her with the news that she had two morning callers.

'Lady Elwick and Lady Elyot,' he called to her.

She swung her legs down, but her guests would not allow her to stand for longer than it took to exchange kisses to both cheeks.

'We came to see how you are this morning…'

'…taking a ride through the park…'

'…and to thank you and the girls…'

'…for the concert. We must do it next at Sheen Court.'

Letitia was used to the twins' interwoven sentences, but she had not encountered these two sisters-in-law together until now. Lady Elyot was a dark classic beauty; Lady Adorna Elwick was fair and quite unlike her two brothers. However, she shared with them their noble parentage, so was entitled to be known as Lady Adorna from birth, whereas the title of Lady Elwick came via her late husband. To confuse matters more, she had been known from childhood as Dorna, and the name still held.

Lady Dorna laughed readily, caring nothing for the crinkles around her merry blue eyes, the same shade exactly as the flimsy morning gown and low-cut velvet spencer. Ribbons flowed from her ruched poke-bonnet, and a lacy parasol was furled into a spear as she took the chair next to Letitia. 'Isn't this *cosy*?' she laughed, looking about her at the cushioned benches, basket chairs and rattan tables. 'One could have a secret *rendezvous* in a place like this, Amelie. Couldn't one? Oh, what fun! I think mine is too small for anything as romantic as that. Perhaps I ought to enlarge it.'

Lady Elyot shook her head, smiling at her sister-in-law's artlessness. 'Dorna, you are shocking Miss Boyce, dear. This darling place is used only for taking tea and writing one's journal, isn't it, Miss Boyce? Tell Dorna I'm correct. Mind you, if I had it, I'd use it to do my painting in.'

'That is what I use it for, my lady. Writing *and* painting.'

'Of course you do. As soon as we met I could see you were artistic. Writing and art: two sides of the same voice. You keep a journal, do you? Most women seem to, nowadays.'

'It's one of the subjects we teach. That, and the art of letter-writing. Speech-writing, too. There are sure to be occasions when they'll be expected to say something intelligent in public.'

'You are *so* progressive in your thinking, Miss Boyce.' Sliding gracefully into the other basket chair, Lady Elyot lifted a ladybird off the arm and placed it gently on to the vase of tulips. 'There will also be times when they'll be expected to attend a local Vestry meeting. Our new Vestry Hall is only a few doors away from here. Why not bring them along one day, just to listen?'

'Thank you. That would certainly open their eyes. We shall all be going to the theatre this evening. The girls are studying *The Merchant of Venice* and, by chance, that's the play being performed.'

'A coincidence indeed!' said Lady Dorna, delightedly. 'We have arranged to go, too. We're to have dinner first at the Castle, then straight to the Theatre Royale. Now why don't you join us for dinner, Miss Boyce? You and your boarders. And your two chaperons?'

'Lady Dorna, it is more than kind of you to invite us, but we couldn't possibly all come. That would be far too many because our party includes Mr Waverley and Mr Thomas, the elocution teacher. He wants to come, too. Why do you not come to us instead? It would be much more convenient, I think. We shall be dining early at six o'clock in time for the performance at eight. Just a simple repast. We'd be honoured if you would share it with us.'

Lady Elyot was concerned about the short notice to Letitia's cook, but Lady Dorna had no hesitation in accepting. 'Why not?' she said. 'Seton hopes to be with us, too. What a party we shall be.'

'Is not Lord Rayne at Hampton Court today?' said Letitia.

'Yes, but he's returning in time for our theatre dinner.'

'That's not like him,' said Lady Elyot. 'Seton has never been too keen on Shakespeare.'

'Well, dear, that's what I put to him, but he tells me he's reforming.'

And perhaps, Letitia thought, Lord Rayne has received another invitation from Miss Sapphire Melborough who, like the other day pupils, would be attending with their parents. With this certainty in her mind, she found it hard to accept that she was being used by the scheming young woman as a way of including Lord Rayne in her social life, whether she approved or not. If that were the case, there was little she could do about it, but she would have preferred the Melboroughs rather than herself to have the pleasure of feeding him.

To her relief, Mrs Mappleton, the cook, seemed quite unperturbed by an extra five guests to cater for. Mrs Brewster, the housekeeper, after indulging in the obligatory astonishment, soon began to warm to the idea of entertaining an extra two lords, two ladies and a captain. It was still before noon, enough time to send for more meat and fish, to prepare more side-dishes and desserts, and enough time for Letitia's pupils to decorate an enlarged dinner table. It was good experience, she told them, opening the double doors between dining and drawing rooms, thinking how right she had been to buy the extending table and matching chairs from Gillow of Lancaster. Lady Boyce had insisted it would be too large for

Letitia's purposes. Rather than set thirteen places, however, she sent an invitation to Mr Titus Chatterton, who lived near Mr Waverley on The Green, asking him to dine with them. He was an entertaining guest, for all his face paint and flamboyance, and one could not help but like him.

For the remainder of the day, she showed her pupils how a good hostess must prepare for last-minute diners without the slightest sign of improvisation or muddling through, and without upsetting one's cook or housekeeper.

By the time the first carriages rolled up at the door, the day pupils had returned home and the duty of receiving the guests was shared by the boarders as part of their education.

Acting as assistant host, Mr Waverley took the head of the table with Lady Dorna to his right while Letitia and Lord Elyot took the opposite end, and although there were more ladies than gentlemen, the arrangement could not have been more comfortable for the three youngest ladies for whom this was a kind of lesson. The guests appeared to understand it well, this being the first visit for four of them, and even though good manners forbade any show of amazement at Letitia's exquisitely tasteful surroundings, it was impossible for them not to appreciate the ivory-handled cutlery and fine engraved glassware, the blue-and-white Wedgwood dinner service matching the posies of bluebells and white lilac filling every space between silver dishes.

It was too early in the year for fresh green vegetables, but root varieties had been made into a pie, with a fricassee of turnips, and roasted potatoes, still a talking point. Nor was there any shortage of lamb, gammon or game, salmon and sole, pies and rissoles, sauces and garnishes and, as the guests were so appreciative and unpretentious, the meal flowed easily along with good wines and home-made orange wine for the younger ones. Tarts and cheesecakes, blancmanges, fruit jellies and creams were toyed with as the talk, inevitably, veered towards the contrast between the pupils' study of Shakespeare and their greater penchant for the novels such as *The Infidel* and, more recently, *Waynethorpe Manor.* The general opinion seemed to be that they could not have been written by a woman, in spite of what the title page told them.

Letitia had no opinion to offer on that, but laughed as she offered her poor excuse. 'Variety? My pupils are encouraged to discuss whatever they read, whether it's classical or popular fiction. If it's well written, it's readable.'

Captain Ben Rankin, Lady Dorna's good-looking friend, was intrigued by this view. 'So you've read them, too?' he said.

'Indeed I have, Captain. I would not otherwise allow my young ladies to.'

'And you approve, I see. Does Mr Thomas approve, too?'

The articulate young Welshman came readily to her rescue. 'If Miss Boyce approves, then so do I, sir. We don't necessarily read these stories *out loud*, as we do with Shakespeare, but—'

But the company had already dissolved into laughter at the idea of anyone reading *The Infidel* out loud, and Letitia's pink cheeks went unnoticed except by Mr Waverley and Lord Rayne who, sitting five places away from her, was finding it difficult to give his undivided attention to Mrs Quayle on one side and Miss Strachan on the other.

As they left the table, he caught up with Letitia. 'Allow me to thank you, Miss Boyce, for including me in your party. That was a memorable meal.'

She had had little choice in the matter of his inclusion, but saw no advantage in saying so. 'Thank you, Lord Rayne. It's given you the opportunity to see how I've changed things since you last saw the inside of the house.'

'I never saw the interior until now.'

'Oh? You would have bought it unseen?'

'My agent saw it. He recommended it to me, that's all.'

'I see. I had heard...' She must not tell him what she'd heard.

'Otherwise?' Deliberately, he looked across the room to the group where Lady Dorna stood talking. 'My sister means well,' he said, in a low voice, 'but she inhabits a delightful world where realities and fancies mix rather freely. None of us would have her any different, but it sometimes leaves us with some explaining to do. Would you like me to explain anything to you, Miss Boyce?'

'No, I thank you. There is room for all of us. But whatever I heard about you wanting my house has completely escaped me. It's of no consequence.'

'None at all. I could never have made it look as handsome as it does now.' His eyes did not follow his compliment, but took a route over her piled-up silvery braids, her graceful neck adorned with a single rope of pearls, her beautiful shoulders and bosom framed by pale grey silk piped and latticed with silver satin.

'No, a house generally does better with one mistress, my lord, rather than a succession of them. Take my *tedious, predictable* twin sisters, for instance. Even they might be at odds about some details. By the way,' she whispered, as if about to disclose a confidence, 'the blue-stocking *elder* sister is *not* interested, despite what you believe. I cannot *think* how you came by that notion, my lord, unless you share the same kind of problem with reality as Lady Dorna. Could it be that, I wonder?'

Lazily scanning, his eyes came to rest on hers, slowly re-vealing an understanding of where her phrases originated. They widened, then smiled, then grew serious again as she reached the end of her disclosure. 'So,' he said, quietly, 'the ears make up for the eyes, do they? No use for me to apolo-gise, I suppose?'

'No use at all, my lord. It merely confirms what I knew already.'

'That's the pity of it, Miss Boyce. It only confirms what you *thought* you knew already. But we've had this conversa-tion before, haven't we? Both of us have preconceived ideas about the other. You believe I am shallow. You *think* I believe you to be—'

'A *challenge* is what you said. You fancy a challenge. Forget it, my lord. You could never hold my interest. My sisters, however…'

'Whom we shall leave out of it, if you please.'

'They'd not be pleased to hear you say that.'

'Then they'd better not hear it, had they? As I was saying, you appear to believe I cannot be serious about a woman, and that what you overheard confirms it, and that I could only be interested in you for the novelty value.'

'I didn't *imagine* that, my lord. I *heard* it.'

'I was being uncivil, on purpose. It was not meant—'

'Oh, *spare* me!' she snapped. 'I'm so looking forward to hearing some *good* acting, aren't you? See,' she said, turning, 'the coats and capes are being brought in. Mr Waverley… Bart…where are you? If you will take three of the ladies in with you, and perhaps Lord and Lady Elyot will take…' She bustled away, managing and marshalling four people into each of the three coaches until, quite by accident, she was the only woman left with one male guest. 'Lord…er…*Rayne*?' she whispered. 'Oh!'

Leaning against the hall table with feet wide apart, he was quietly laughing. 'Managed yourself into a corner, Mother Hen?' he said. 'Come on, then. You and I are going to walk it. It's not far.'

'I know how far it is,' she growled. 'It's not that.'

He did not move. 'You want me to carry you there?'

'Tch!' She sighed, wondering how she could possibly have done something as foolish as this. She would rather have walked with Mr Chatterton in his high-heeled shoes than with Rayne, whose arrogance both excited and annoyed her.

The footman bowed and withdrew, leaving them alone in the hall with a mountain of misunderstandings to keep them apart.

He waited, then reached her in two strides, backing her into the hard edge of the opposite table. She gripped it, leaning away from him, seeing for the first time the crisp detail of his neckcloth, the white waistcoat and its silver buttons, undone at the top. Again, she breathed the faint aroma given off by his warm skin, but now there was to be no making of mental notes for her writing when he was so frighteningly close, no time to express how she was affected, or the sensation of her heart thudding into her throat.

He placed a large knuckle beneath her chin, lifting it. 'Yes, my beauty, I know. This is not what you planned, is it?'

'Don't call me that! I'm not your beauty, nor am I—'

'And you can glare at me all you want, but this evening you will do as I say without argument and without biting my hand off. Do you hear me?'

'I shall—'

'Do you *hear* me? Without argument. Just for once, if you please.'

She nodded, looking at his mouth, then at the faint bluish shadow around his jaw, then back to his eyes that had noted every detour. His thighs pressed against hers, and she understood that, suddenly, he was struggling to suppress an urge to do what he had done once before. She must prevent it. 'Let me go,' she whispered.

He did not move. 'Where are your spectacles? Have you another pair? Do you have them with you?'

'In my reticule. Let me go, please.'

'You will take my arm,' he commanded, 'and you will be civil.'

'Yes, I will be civil.'

'I have your word on it?'

'Yes…now *please*…let me go.' She took hold of his wrist, expecting it to move but, when she looked again at his eyes to find the cause of his delay, she saw how his gaze rested upon the staircase as if to measure its length. Panic stole upwards, fluttering inside her bodice. Her fingers tightened over the soft fabric of his coat-cuff. 'No,' she whispered. 'Don't…please don't.' She saw the reflection of the two wall-lamps in his eyes, heavy-lidded with desire.

'I could,' he said, 'but I suppose they will not delay the performance of Shakespeare for us, so we'd better go. Come, my beauty, adjust your shawl. There, now take my arm, and try to remember what you have agreed.'

Speechless and shaken, she did as she was told. Arm in arm they went out into the cool evening, pulling the heavy door closed behind them.

* * *

Earlier that afternoon she had formed a clear plan of where everyone would sit, herself being nowhere near Lord Rayne. However, arriving at the theatre only a few minutes later, Letitia found her plans already displaced by the earlier arrival of the day girls, their parents and friends. Although Miss Sapphire Melborough clearly hoped that Lord Rayne would join her parents in their box, he merely bowed politely, held a few words of conversation with her mother, then rejoined Letitia, taking the two seats left over after the others had taken theirs. It was not at all what Letitia had intended, and Rayne knew it as he quelled her budding protest with a stern glance, positioning her chair next to his at the back of the box and almost herding her into it with one uncompromising word. 'There,' he said.

She delayed for as long as she dared but, in the end, there was nothing for it but to accept the situation when the musicians in the pit ceased playing and the curtain glided upwards. The scene of merchants and their clients against a background of Venetian waterways would normally have riveted her attention. But this time she was sitting close to Lord Rayne against the high back of the box with a partition on one side of her, and her usually obedient concentration was distracted by the sensation that, for all her determination to deny him any sign of encouragement, he had won that round with ease.

He had another way of putting it, in a whisper, when she turned slightly to glance at him. Catching her angry expression, his unsmiling eyes made his advice all the more telling. 'Stop fighting me, my beauty. I intend to win.'

Turning her attention to her reticule, she drew out a pair of pocket spectacles that swung inside a mother-of-pearl cover, holding them to her eyes as if his words meant nothing. But the spectacles trembled, and she knew he had seen before she transferred them to her other hand.

That evening at Richmond's Theatre Royal was to be remembered for many reasons, the chief of which was the way in which Lord Rayne attended to her needs as they had not been since her father died, not even by Mr Waverley. Independent to a fault, she had intended to take charge of the event, putting herself last, as usual, in spite of there being enough adults to watch over the three boarders. But if she had thought they would prefer her to the others, she was wrong. They did not need her, and she had no other role to play except to stay by Rayne's side, where he wanted her.

'Miss Melborough is hoping you will visit her,' she said.

'Then she will be disappointed. This evening, Miss Boyce, I am with no one but you, and you will not get rid of me.'

'Hasn't this gone on long enough, my lord?' she said, demurely, opening and closing her spectacle-cover. 'You've made your point, I think. You've had your fun and enjoyed the stares. But these girls are my pupils, and you place me in a very awkward position by paying me this attention one evening and then, as you are sure to do, paying the same kind of attention to someone else next time they see you. They all know you and my sisters are seen in each other's company. They know that Sapphire's parents are keen on an alliance. I am not unused to being talked about in one way or another, but this evening will not be easy for me to live down, my lord. Perhaps you think you're doing me some kind of favour, but I assure you, you're not. Surely you can see that?'

Handing her a glass of negus, he took the spectacles from her and popped them into the opening of the reticule that hung on her arm. 'It's a great pity, in a way,' he said, 'that you overheard what you did, for now it will be harder than ever for me to convince you that I am not simply flirting with you.'

'You are mistaken in the matter, Lord Rayne. I was convinced you were doing exactly that at our first meeting. I'm afraid I cannot be unconvinced, nor would any woman be, in the same circumstances.'

'That would not have happened to *any* woman, Miss Boyce.'

'No, of course not. How often does one encounter a short-sighted, lost schoolmistress? Not one of your greatest challenges, I would have thought.'

He sighed. 'Miss Boyce, will you try to dredge from the depths of your *deep* intellect something we agreed on before we set out? Something you gave me your word on, if you need a clue?'

'Yes, my lord, but—'

'Good. Then keep it, will you?'

'But you haven't answered my question.'

'Oh? I thought I had. I wish you would listen as well as you talk.'

'Odious man!' she muttered.

Mr Waverley was amused by the new partnership. 'What's happened, Lettie? The fellow's sticking to you like glue. I think he's smitten.'

'Fudge!' she said. 'Bart, rescue me. Walk home with me. Don't leave me alone with him. He's only trying to show Miss Melborough that she has some competition, that's all. I know the kind of tactics such men use.'

'Maybe, but Sir Francis doesn't look too pleased about it, either, does he? He's been sending you the oddest looks. What's *that* all about?'

She did not explain. She had noticed the crowded Melborough box during the interval but, without peering through her lenses, had not been able to see who the visitors were. Nevertheless, she was receiving the distinct impression that Sir Francis, who would normally have been amongst the first to ingratiate himself with her, was keeping well out of her way.

Undeterred by her watchful escort, she managed to speak to many of her friends, her pupils' parents and their friends, too, and had thought that, as they began to seat themselves for the second half, she might be invited to join their ranks. But Lord Rayne was having none of it and, disregarding the interest and envy of her pupils, he steered her back to the same chair with the utmost propriety, giving them little to gossip about except that their guardian was once again being claimed by him.

And indeed there was nothing to which she could object except his closeness; no touching, no arm across the back of her chair, no flirtatious remarks, no compliments except in his eyes. It was, she thought, as if his aim was to familiarise her with his nearness as he would with an unbroken young horse. Which, after all, would have been the way of any suitor except this one, for whom conventional methods were usually too slow.

Years of watching her vivacious sisters take centre stage, however, had caused her to develop an unhealthy cynicism, enabling her to see through and partly to despise the ploys men used, the foolish games they played. And in view of her previous encounters with this particular buck, she was unlikely to let go of her conviction that she was being used as some kind of instrument in one of his games in full view of the pert and eager Miss Melborough, not to mention her ambitious parents. While she could not help but absorb the exciting vibrations from the man at her side as she had never done before with anyone, it was her steely common sense that pulled her emotions back from taking precedence over her writing, which needed information of this kind more than her starving sensitive heart did. If it was common sense, then it must be right, for what else did a woman like her have to rely on?

Agog with curiosity to see whether Lord Rayne would walk back to Paradise Road with Miss Boyce, her pupils were almost as excited to hear him call farewell to his relatives and to see him take one of the carriages with Letitia and Mr Waverley, which seemed to them a little odd when Mr Waverley lived almost next door to the theatre. Mr Chatterton and Mr Thomas had only yards to go. What the pupils did not discover is that, by tacit consent, Mr Waverley, Lord Rayne, Miss Gaddestone and Miss Boyce stayed up until past midnight in the drawing room, drinking red wine from sparkling cut glasses through which the candlelight danced and winked. Talking like old friends, not one waspish word was heard between them. Then the two men left, Lord Rayne having accepted a lift back to Sheen Court in Mr Waverley's phaeton.

It was usual, at the end of each day, however late, for Letitia to enter notes into her book before they suffered from distortion or, worse, amnesia. This night, the notebook stayed locked in her drawer while she lay against the pillows to watch the shadows move over the bed-curtains, not because she was too tired to write, but because her thoughts were torn by conflict, her heart entering a period of slow ache in anticipation of the pain that was sure to come unless she armoured herself against it. Of *course* he was teasing her. Her sisters said he was a tease. This was nothing but a game to him. Nothing but a game.

* * *

For the next two weeks it began to look as if Letitia's reading of events was accurate, the only communication from Lord Rayne being a formal note of thanks for an enjoyable evening, then a brief visit in person to return her mended spectacles. But since she was out with her pupils at the time, they did not meet. In a way, she was relieved to have missed him, for she had nothing to say except to offer him her thanks.

She was even more certain of her ground when, only two days later, she took her pupils to London to the Royal Academy Annual Exhibition at Somerset House where she found her sisters and mother in Lord Rayne's company. By chance, Miss Melborough was not one of the party, having twisted her ankle the day before and, in some discomfort, had been left to work on her watercolour until their return.

Letitia's sisters, as always, were glad to see her and to unload on her their latest experiences, shopping trips and parties, their mama's dinner party and the men who had caught their attention most. Lady Boyce greeted her eldest daughter more formally with a stand-off embrace and a showy kiss past each cheek that could hardly have been called motherly. After relating to Letitia what she had missed by not being at home, her remarks centred around the attention being shown to Garnet, especially by Lord Rayne. 'There'll be an announcement soon, Letitia,' she said, waving her fan to friends Letitia could not quite identify. 'Mark my words. I'm never wrong about these matters. I can always tell when a man is about to declare himself. Well, heaven knows, it happened to me often enough before your dear papa snared me. Lord Rayne is *very* keen, you know.'

'Yes, Mama.'

'So these are your *gels*, are they?' she said, glancing round. 'They look respectable enough. Isn't that Sir Mortimer Derwent's daughter?'

'Maura. Yes. They live in Farnham. She boards with us.'

'Your papa used to hunt with them. And there's your Mr Waverley. Still faithful, is he? Who are the other two?'

'That's Mr Dimmock, our watercolour teacher, and Mr Ainsley, our drawing master. Rosie has stayed at home with one of the girls, but the lady over there in brown is Mrs Quayle, our next-door neighbour. Would you allow me to introduce her to you? She'd be so thrilled.'

'Another time, dear. Nice to see you. Keeping well, are you?'

It was pointless for Letitia to reply when the orange turban had already turned towards other faces and, since that exchange appeared to be the sum total of her mother's interest, she adjusted her spectacles and moved away to the walls lined with pictures.

Softly, Lord Rayne's voice spoke into her ear. 'You're using them I see, Miss Boyce?'

She turned to face the dark serious eyes and immaculate form of the one man she had hoped not to see. 'Yes, my lord. Thank you for returning them to me. They're quite perfect. I cannot tell where the mend is.'

'Ayscough on Ludgate Street,' he said, gravely. 'My mother gets hers there. He recognised them.'

'He should. That is where they were bought. But please don't let me keep you from your obligation to my sisters. I had not expected to see them here, nor my mother. They don't usually show much interest in this kind of event.'

'I did not come with them, Miss Boyce. I came with Lord

Alvanley and George Brummell. Over there...see? They're helping me to find something suitable for my study.'

'Oh...I thought...'

'Yes, I can see you did. I believe that's what you were meant to think.' His quick glance in Lady Boyce's direction qualified his remark. 'If I may offer you a word of advice, it would be not to—'

'No, please don't offer me any advice, my lord,' she said, quickly cutting him off. 'It's no concern of mine what my sisters do or don't do. All I wish for is their happiness, not to interfere in it. Have you seen a painting you like?'

He paused, obviously not content to be diverted. 'I've seen one prime article in particular I like the look of, Miss Boyce,' he said. 'I wish it was as easy to purchase as a painting.'

'For your study wall?'

'For my study, certainly. For my wall, no.'

'Good day, my lord,' she whispered, trying to hide her flushed cheeks behind the panel of her bonnet. 'I shall leave you to make your choice.'

'And you don't wish to give me the benefit of *your* advice?'

'I don't wish to incur any more of my mother's disapproval than I have already, my lord.'

'By talking to *me*? Surely not.'

'She would misunderstand, and so would my sisters. Need I say more than that?'

'Usually you say too much, Miss Boyce, but on this occasion you have said too little. I thought you had become independent of Lady Boyce's management.'

'I have taken a very big step, my lord, but I have hopes that she will visit me, one day, not cut me out altogether. I am already well outside her plans.'

'But not her influence, apparently. Time you were, then. So, if I am not allowed to advise you, I shall tell you this. Lady Boyce may be allowed to keep a finger in your pie, for the time being, but, by God, she won't put a finger near mine unless she wants it snapped off. When I want a woman, I shall not be asking her permission.'

'Not even when the woman is her daughter, my lord?'

'Not the eldest one, no. Good day to you, Miss Boyce.'

Her cheeks were still very pink when Mr Dimmock joined her to discuss some of the paintings with her and found, to his dismay, that she had so far seen very few of them.

Chapter Six

Leaving William Lake's lending-library in Leadenhall Street, London, Lord Seton Rayne tossed a pile of books on to the seat of his curricle and climbed up beside them, having accomplished what he had promised to do for his mother, the Marchioness of Sheen, who had been unable to find extra copies for her friends anywhere. He was about to call to his tiger to loose the horses' heads when he noticed the tall hurrying figure of the Honourable Bart Waverley leap down the steps of the library and dash across to the other side of the street carrying a leather briefcase under his arm. This was singular, Rayne thought, because there had been no sign of Bart inside the library.

Watching the striding figure disappear round the corner, he then looked up at the windows above the library where the gold-printed words read, Mercury Press, Est. 1790. Publisher W. Lake, Esq. Did Bart know William Lake personally? Was there some business between them? Not being one to poke his nose into other people's affairs, Rayne let the matter rest beside a strange feeling that a connection was escaping him.

* * *

Later that afternoon, he made a detour through the winding corridors of Hampton Court Palace on his way from the barrack block and stables to his own apartments bordering the Outer Green Court, his home during weekdays. Pausing for a moment outside the dingy little room where he and Miss Letitia Boyce had exchanged kisses—oh, yes, she had *exchanged* kisses, he was convinced of that—he smiled and closed the door, continuing his walk round to the gardens on the sunny south side of the palace's grace-and-favour apartments.

Residents and their elderly guests strolled along the overgrown pathways and sat on benches in the shade, snoozing, reading, or watching the boats on the distant river. One erect resident, lace-draped, white-haired and bespectacled, held a book up high as if she were singing from it. She looked up as Rayne approached, lowering the book with a smile. 'Lord Rayne,' she said. 'Finished for the day?'

'I have indeed, Lady Waverley,' he said with a bow. 'And you?'

Her smile softened as she removed her eyeglasses. She was still a lovely woman, arched brows, cheekbones firmly covered. 'No, not me,' she said. 'I have some way to go yet.' She indicated the book and the pages yet to be read. 'It's the newest one Bart lent me. I've been so looking forward to it, you know. Of course, he must be allowed to read it first, dear boy. Come and sit with me a while.' She drew in a heap of soft shawl and lace, moving up to make room for him.

Rayne sat, removed his helmet, and ran a hand through his hair.

'Are you not supposed to powder your hair?' she said,

watching the gesture. 'I thought the Prince's Own had to wear powder and a pigtail.'

'We do on parade, my lady. Makes too much mess for everyday wear.' He looked at the book on her lap. 'Did you say Bart lent it to you? My lady mother is on Hatchett's subscription list, but she wants extra copies to give to her friends. They're very scarce. Where does Bart get his from?'

'From Lake the publisher. He's almost sold out of the first edition, apparently, but we've known him for years.'

'Ah! That explains it.'

'Explains what?'

'Why I saw Bart leaving the Mercury Press this morning.'

'Oh, did you? Well, he brought me this yesterday.' She tapped the book. 'It's his own copy, given him by the author. Perhaps he was there on some business for her.'

'He knows the *author*? So it *is* a woman, then?'

'Oh, yes, he knows her well. He meets Lake on her behalf. A young lady cannot go there on her own, can she? Bart's done all her business transactions with Lake from the very first book. He gets to read it, then he passes it on to me. Am I not fortunate? I doubt I could wait any longer.'

'Is that so?'

'Oh, I've pestered him for ages to hurry up and—'

'No, I meant about the author being a young lady. Does she live in Richmond, near Bart?'

'It may be that she does, but I'm not too familiar with who lives there, so I don't really know, and he refuses to tell me any more except that she's earning quite an income from these.' Again, she tapped Volume One, leather-bound and gold-tooled. 'Mind you,' she continued, 'I have no doubt that Lake is doing very nicely out of it. He's unlikely to be offering her the kind of deal he'd offer a man, even if she is more popular.'

'But isn't that why the author has Bart to act for her?'

She smiled her indulgent, motherly smile. 'Of course. But you know what dear Bart's like, don't you? He was never the forceful kind, was he?'

'No, my lady.'

The sounds of the late afternoon passed them by with a shower of dandelion clocks, as they thought about Mr Waverley's many fine qualities, of which forcefulness was not one. 'Will he ever marry, do you think?' said Rayne, gently.

The shake of Lady Waverley's head would easily have been missed, had Rayne not been watching for it. 'No,' she whispered. 'Shouldn't think so, Seton. Marriage is not for Bart's kind, is it?'

'It's not unknown, my lady.'

'But it rarely works. Best to stay single. He's happy enough.'

'He'd make a wonderful father.'

Lady Waverley took that as the compliment it was meant to be, and said no more on the delicate subject. Rayne, however, returned to the young lady author. 'A Lady of Quality, I believe she calls herself,' he said, smoothing a hand over his helmet's glossy fur. 'So I suppose I must not ask if you know the identity of this mysterious wealthy young woman.'

'Only Bart himself knows that, and he'd not *dream* of breaking a confidence, not even to his mother. Mr Lake knows her only as a certain Miss Lydia Barlowe, but that *must* be a nom de plume. No lady of quality ever had such a common name.'

Rayne bellowed with laughter. 'Lady Waverley, I do believe you're a snob,' he teased.

She agreed, smiling at the notion. 'Yes, dear, I believe I am.

It's one of the few allowances left to a woman of my age. That, and being able to sit and talk to a man like you, alone, without being suspected of flirting.'

'And if I were not so afraid of being called out by your son, I would indulge in some serious flirting with you, my lady.'

The smiling face tipped towards him. 'Does Bart go in for…for calling men out?'

'Duelling? Not by choice, I don't suppose. But if you're asking if he's well enough equipped to protect himself, then, yes, he certainly is. He could do some damage with pistol, rapier *and* gloves, too. And the young lady writer, whoever she is, has chosen an excellent business partner, with Bart's head for accounts.'

'It's pity he won't be offering for her. Even if she is a commoner.'

Rayne smiled, which Lady Waverley took for sympathy, but which was, in fact, nothing of the sort. Lydia Barlowe. *L.B.* How careless of her, he thought. How endearingly, wonderfully careless.

Letitia's proposal to visit Strawberry Hill House at Twickenham, just across the river from Richmond, had an ulterior motive that no one but Mr Waverley could be expected to guess, for it was where Mr Horace Walpole had written, in 1764, his famous Gothic novel, *The Castle of Otranto*. Others, including Letitia, were to follow this trend, literally, while readers made pilgrimages to the amazing house-cum-castle he had built to satisfy his every Gothic whim. No serious romantic novelist could afford to miss such a place with its towers and turrets, chapel, cloisters and chambers littered with historic curios.

The great man himself, son of a Prime Minister, had died seventeen years ago and now it was possible for visitors to look round by arrangement with the housekeeper, a favour that Letitia had gone to some trouble to secure for her party of pupils, tutors and chaperons. She was not inclined to hurry through the rooms, having made it so far with notebook and pencil, sketching and scribbling as they were shown into the long gallery, the library, past carved screens, mock-tombs and suits of medieval armour, gloomy portraits and up winding spooky staircases.

Miss Sapphire Melborough, however, having other things on her mind, had soon seen enough of Strawberry Hill and was incautious enough to enquire of Mrs Quayle, in an undertone bordering on despair, how much longer they might be stuck here. She had asked the wrong person, for Mrs Quayle was thoroughly enjoying herself despite the appropriate melancholic expression. She passed on the plaintive query to Letitia, which Sapphire had neither wanted nor expected her to do.

'Why? Who wants to know?' said Letitia.

'Miss Sapphire. She's had enough.'

'If it's her ankle, she can rest on the bench over there and wait.'

'I don't think it's her ankle, Letitia.'

Beckoning to her pupil, Letitia noted the pouting rosebud mouth. 'What is it, Sapphire? We're only halfway round. There's much more to see.'

'But I…well, you see…' Pulling in her bottom lip, she nibbled at it.

'See what? Are you unwell? Do you wish Mrs Quayle to…?'

'No, Miss Boyce, only that I expected to be home by now because Lord Rayne is to bring my new horse and give me my first lesson on it. I'm afraid I shall miss it if I stay here much longer.'

'Sapphire, I made it clear three days ago that on Friday we'd be having an extended visit. If you forgot to tell your parents, that is your responsibility. My claim on your time takes priority, I'm afraid, and when we've concluded our visit here, we shall be taking tea at the tea gardens in Twickenham. I told you that, too, if you recall. You'll have to have your riding lesson tomorrow instead, won't you?'

Sapphire could not stifle the sigh. 'Yes, Miss Boyce. But Lord Rayne will not be pleased to be kept waiting.'

'Lord Rayne's displeasure is not my concern, Sapphire. You'll be writing an account in your journal of this visit next week, so I suggest you pay attention to what you're seeing.' *Or not seeing. As if I care a fig about Lord Rayne's arrangements.*

The cream tea at Church Street's sunny tea garden could not be hurried any more than the tour of the house, so it was past time for dinner when the carriages arrived back at Paradise Road after taking the day girls home. Letitia did not go up to Richmond Hill House with Sapphire, having no wish to hear about the missed riding lesson.

There was much to be written about by candlelight that evening.

The following day, Saturday, was bright but blustery, a stiff breeze rattling the window frames and rolling the last of the blossom across the walled kitchen garden like drifts of snow. Wandering alone, Letitia peered into the glass frames while the covers were up, at the strawberry beds white with flowers, at the budding cucumbers, the tiny spears of chicory and lamb's lettuce. In the furthest corner, the gardener's son was shovelling gravel on to the path and raking it over. Like coarse oatmeal, Letitia thought, adjusting her spectacles more firmly on to her nose. Fine wisps of hair whirled around her face as gusts of wind moulded her cotton day dress into the contours of her body and, to find a place of shelter, she opened the door of the stone-built potting shed built against the high wall, and entered.

She was instantly enclosed by the earthy aroma of potted plants and trays of seedlings covered by layers of damp newsprint. Racks of tools hung along one side, with buckets and pots, hoses and string, raffia and bell jars. A long low bench was covered with sacking as if the old gardener had used it to indulge in an occasional nap, and a pile of sacks at one end suggested a pillow. Intrigued, she bent to look more closely, to confirm her theory.

A long curling hair lay upon the pillow, clearly not the gardener's. Lifting it carefully away, she held it up to the high dusty window where a beam of light caught its shining gold. A sound behind her made her turn sharply and to frown in annoyance at the hefty figure of the gardener's son filling the doorway. One hand was hooked over the top edge of the door. 'Can I 'elp you, ma'am?' he asked.

His question, and the quiet way he asked it, made her feel as if she'd naughtily strayed out of bounds. Nor did she like being trapped in so small a place. 'No, thank you…er…Tom, is it?'

'Ted,' he replied, not moving or looking politely away, as if he knew of her discomfort and was enjoying it. No more than twenty years old, he had already filled out with brawn, his shirt sleeves rolled up to show well-muscled sunburnt forearms, his front buttons opened too far down for any lady's eyes to dwell there for more than a second. 'Can I do anything for ye?' he asked.

Damsels being pursued and seduced by young males glowing with rude health was the stuff of her novels, and this the kind of situation not too far removed from some of the scenes in them, though so far no major part had been taken by the gardener or his son. Then, she had imagined a kind of helpless excitement rather than the raw anger she now felt at the threat of trespass by an uncouth lad. The girls and Mrs Quayle were in Richmond, shopping. Gaddy was still in her room. The gardener, Ted's old father, was nowhere to be seen. This present danger was very far removed from the harmless entertainment of fiction where one could turn a page and return to safety.

Still frowning, she asked, 'Have you finished the path?'

'Yes, ma'am. All done.' His glance at the sack-covered bench lingered and returned to her, but not to her face, and she knew how he must have seen the clinging cotton of her dress revealing her figure as she bent to the glass frames.

'Then I'll find you another task to do,' she said, suspecting that he would twist whatever she said to mean something different. 'Where's your father?'

'Oh, we don't need to bother about him, ma'am. He'll not be in for a while yet. Got a task for me, 'ave you? Is that what you want, eh?' He spoke slowly, insolently, his words taking on an intimacy far beyond their worth, his pleasant features as relaxed as his body, his blue eyes alight with anticipation.

'Ted, will you move away from the door, please? I want to go out.'

But he took his hand from the top edge, stepped further inside and began to close it, darkening the confined space. 'No, you don't,' he said. 'I know what you want. It's what all you young lasses want.'

Letitia's hand groped behind her, closing over the rim of a terracotta pot. In the very moment she brought it up to hurl at Ted's approaching head, the door re-opened with a crashing force, slamming it into the lad's rear end as he ducked to avoid the missile.

Like an angry bullock, he roared and turned to rush upon the intruder, but his progress was interrupted by a shining Hessian boot across his shins that sent him flying headlong into a stack of logs outside the door. The pot that Letitia had thrown shattered upon the door frame, and as she picked her way through the shards to find out who her rescuer was—supposing it to be Mr Waverley—she was in time to see the stocky Ted about to launch himself upon Lord Rayne.

Assuming that his lordship would certainly go down like a skittle, she let out an involuntary yelp of fright for, though she had once written of a brawl between two rivals, she had never seen a blow landed. She did now, but only just, delivered with such lightning speed that Ted did not see it coming at all. She heard a sickening crack as Rayne's fist connected with the cheek, and the grunt that followed, the thud as Ted fell back hard into the log pile where he slithered and stayed, swaying to one side.

'Get up!' Rayne snapped, standing over him.

Ted struggled and clawed his way up, holding an arm out against the possibility of a second punisher. 'Don't,' he mumbled.

'Get off home!'

'Yessir…I wasn't…I didn't….honest.'

'Out!'

Slouching, clutching at his face, Ted staggered away with a sullen glance at Letitia. 'She wanted it,' he muttered, 'as much as t'other one.'

This insult was not allowed to pass any more than his first had been and, before he had taken another step, he was yanked backwards by a strong hand beneath his arm, only to be knocked sideways by a fearsome blow beneath his jaw, laying him out into a patch of feathery fennel. This time, he did not move.

'Oh, you've killed him,' Letitia whispered behind her hand.

'If he opens his mouth once more, I will,' Rayne said, looking round for a water-butt. Taking up the full bucket of water from beneath the tap, he swung it back and discharged the contents over the prone body. Then, placing the empty bucket upon Ted's chest, he stepped back, removed Letitia's hand from her mouth and drew her like a parent with a child along the path to the door in the wall that led to the house garden.

Closing the door upon the last ugly scene, he released her. 'I'm sorry you had to see that,' he said, 'but unfortunately there was no choice. Are you all right?'

She nodded. 'Yes. Thank you for being there. I'm very much obliged to you. If I'd known he…oh, dear…it must begin to look as if I'm forever getting myself into…well, the truth is that…'

'The truth is, Miss Boyce, that you *do* seem to attract a rather immediate kind of response; while I can understand *why* it happens, I find it more difficult to understand why you *allow* it to happen. One could, I suppose, attribute it to not being able to see clearly, but surely that cannot always be the case.'

'Lord Rayne,' she snapped, coming to an abrupt standstill on the path, 'I do not *allow* any of these…these *incidents* to happen to me. Do you really believe that…oh…this is *too* much! Why should I care a fiddler's thumb what you believe? I have thanked you for dealing with this latest incident but, if you recall, you yourself behaved just as badly, if not worse, because Mr Waverley did not arrive in time to stop you.'

'Miss Boyce, Bart would not have arrived to find what I might have found just now if I'd been five minutes later. It's fortunate that I saw him following you as I entered the garden, but my point is that you need some protection before something truly serious happens to you. Bart is all very well, but he's not here when he's needed, is he? Nor does he have any obligation to be.'

'Why should a woman need protecting in her own garden, my lord?'

'Why? Because you appear to employ untrustworthy servants. That's why.'

'I don't employ him. He's the gardener's *son*, helping out.'

'Helping himself, more like. How many others has he helped out?'

Immediately, she remembered the long curling blonde hair that could have belonged to at least three of her seven pupils, or one of the maids. Surely that young lout had not forced himself upon one of them there, in the potting shed? There was a path that connected her garden with Mrs Quayle's next door along which the three boarders came to lessons each day. But could they also have used it at night to meet that dreadful man? It was unthinkable. They were all highly respectable young women. Like herself. Like the young heroines in her novels. Highly respectable, but eager for adventure, and very vulnerable. Were these young creatures simply more audacious than her, or more foolhardy?

'I don't know,' she said, 'but I intend to find out. If this incident has served no other purpose, my lord, it's certainly alerted me to the danger of—'

'Of not being protected sufficiently and of not being able to see what you're doing half the time. There's an easy remedy for both those problems, Miss Boyce.'

'That's *not* what I was about to say. You are determined to put me in the wrong. Very well, allow me to turn the tables, for once. In future, kindly refrain from organising my pupils' riding lessons while they're still in my care. I have first call on their time and I shall not be releasing any of them before the hour of five, unless there's a very exceptional reason.'

'So you think I'm free before the hour of five, do you?'

'You were yesterday, according to Miss Melborough.'

'Then she was mistaken. I told her father I would bring the new horse over after dinner, which is exactly what I did. I spent an hour or so with them in the paddock while it was still light. Are you jealous, Miss Boyce?'

'Of what, exactly?'

'Of me spending time with the Melborough wench?'

'Oh *do* rid yourself of that addle-pated notion, Lord Rayne. Spend whatever time you wish with whomever you wish, my sisters included, but don't expect me to tailor my time to fit yours.'

'Why not? You're prepared to accept all the advantages and compliments of having your pupils well mounted and taught by the best riding master while refusing to co-operate in any way. In fact, Miss Boyce, you appear to be hellbent on making it difficult for everyone concerned.'

Letitia was silent. He spoke no more than the truth, placing her yet again at a disadvantage. Fortunately, he did not pursue the matter while there were more side-saddle-trained horses to be acquired for the others. Enough time for her to revise her timetable, if she could swallow her pride.

They stopped just in front of the summerhouse as if by mutual consent, in view of what had happened earlier. So far, her anger had overcome other emotions, but now she felt again the sickly fear as the little shed had darkened and the man's swaggering presumption told her that she would not be able to hold him off. Was it mere coincidence that she had been made a target three times since placing herself beyond the protection of her family and friends? Had she been less than careful? In London, Uncle Aspinall had taken the place of her father, but now he, too, was miles away, and the only man to offer her his protection, as opposed to being recruited like Mr Waverley, was one of those who had treated her discourteously. And yet, just a moment ago, he had knocked a man down for less.

Rayne was waiting for a sign from her but, having no particular direction in mind, she took his left hand in hers and turned it to look at the knuckles that she was sure would hurt. A grey-blue bruise was already forming.

'I usually wear gloves,' he said. 'It's nothing.'

Removing her spectacles, she looked more closely. Tears prickled behind her eyelids as she was reminded of her narrow escape and, although she would not submit to pathetic weeping, she was unable to hide the delayed reaction that trembled her hands. Ted had not touched her except with his menace, which had been far worse than the thorough kisses Lord Rayne had given her.

Her shaky breathing was noticed as she struggled to control herself. His hand took possession of hers, with her spectacles, drawing her over the threshold into the shady summerhouse. 'Shh!' he said. 'It's all right. No harm done. You must tell your gardener that his son is not welcome. There's no shortage of labour. My brother's man will find someone for you, if you wish.'

'I'b dot crying, really I'b dot,' she sniffed.

'No, of course not.'

Even so, when he drew her very gently into his arms and held her like a bird against his chest, she stood quietly to absorb the safety and strength of his embrace. 'Why did you cub?' she whispered.

'To take you for a drive in my curricle.'

'But that would give the impression that we're good freds, by lord. And we're dot, are we?'

'By no stretch of the imagination are we good friends, Miss Boyce.'

'It would dot look good.'

'On the contrary, it would send out quite the wrong kind of message. Unless...'

'Unless what?'

'Unless I were to be seen taking you to my sister's house at Mortlake. A social call. That might just disguise any enjoyment we might be tempted to feel.'

She drew herself out of his arms. 'I should not be allowing this,' she said, wiping her nose in an unladylike gesture on the back of her hand.

'Because you may find that you're enjoying it?'

'Because I must set an example to my pupils. If they were to see...well, anyway...it won't do, will it? Young ladies of good birth—'

'Like yourself.'

'—like me, do not allow Corinthians to—'

'Thank you.'

'—to embrace them—'

'As they do in novels.'

'Lord Rayne, would you stop interrupting me for one moment while I try to finish what I'm saying? Please?'

'Certainly, Miss Boyce. What were you saying?'

'I don't know. I can't remember. You've put me off.'

'Then go and get changed, and we'll drive up to Mortlake.'

Predictably, she balked at his tone. 'Do all your female acquaintances promptly do your bidding, my lord?'

'Yes. All except one. Five minutes?'

'Multiplied by three. Shall you wait in the parlour?'

'I shall wait beside my curricle, if it's still there.'

'Well, then, try not to look like the cat that's swallowed the canary, if you please. We cannot have anyone getting ideas.'

'Put these back on,' he said, holding out her spectacles, 'and you'll see that I'm wearing my deepest scowl of discontent.'

'Thank you,' she snapped, putting them on as they entered the house. 'I don't quite understand why I'm agreeing to this. We have nothing pleasant to say to each other.'

Not in the least put out by her cynicism, he held the door open for her. 'Then we shall have to resort to our usual mode of bickering like terriers. See you outside in ten minutes.'

'Fifteen. Not a moment sooner.'

Ten minutes later she tripped down the front steps wearing a cream-muslin day dress under a spencer of apricot kerseymere and a floppy straw hat tied round the crown and under the chin with a long apricot scarf. Peeping from beneath the banded hem of her dress, a pair of apricot kid half-boots completed the captivating picture.

'Where are your spectacles, woman?' he said, curtly.

'In my reticule.'

'Well, you're not going to see much without them. Put them on.'

'I cannot. They ruin the effect.'

'Miss Boyce, you may take my word for it that the wearing of spectacles out of doors will become all the rage, once you are seen wearing them while being driven in my curricle. Now, put them on, if you please.'

Reluctantly, she fished them out of her cream silk reticule but, because she was wearing kid gloves, they swung upside-down before she could catch them. Taking them from her, he held them open at eye-level. 'Hold your head up...there... that's better. Now I can see you,' he said with a smile, adjusting a wisp of hair beside her cheek.

'You've obviously had some experience as a lady's maid,' she said, blushing at this very public intimacy.

'It would be useless to deny it. One must be versatile, these days.'

Climbing up into the confined space of the curricle, she bit back yet another rejoinder, realising that she would not always be allowed to have the last word with this man, as she did with her pupils, and that to allow him to have it, once in a while, was by no means as unpleasant as she had thought. Quite the opposite. Absorbed in Rayne's dexterity with whip and reins, with the classy paintwork and upholstery of the curricle and the prancing matched bays, she said very little, experiencing for the second time that morning the strange sensation that things were happening outside her carefully laid plans.

But the last thing she wanted was for her name to be romantically linked to his when it could cause nothing but problems and eventual heartache. Could she depend on his discretion when, only the other day, he had made his intentions plain? Would his daring sister jump to her own conclusions about their unsettled relationship? Would he encourage her to?

* * *

As it turned out, Lady Dorna's reaction to her brother's newest interest was to be the least of her concerns, for they were seen during that brief journey by at least five acquaintances of Letitia's sisters and mother, who would be eager to take the news back to London that same day. Known to be extremely fastidious in his choice of companions, Lord Rayne had never before been seen taking up a bespectacled female in his curricle.

Letitia was more disturbed by this unforeseen complication than Rayne, who brushed it off airily as being no one's concern but theirs. Forbearing to labour the point that she could ill afford to upset her mother more than she had done already, she said no more about it while imagining the indignation at Chesterfield House later that day.

Both the drive and the visit to River Court went well, Letitia making more effort than usual to respond to Rayne's charming company if only to show her appreciation of his earlier gallantry. It was unfortunate, she thought, that the problem of her mother's forthcoming exasperation could not be dealt with as promptly as Ted's.

As ever, Lady Dorna was delighted to see them together, and their return to Richmond began with some amusement at her assumption of a close friendship. 'Nonsense!' said Letitia as the curricle swung at full tilt out of the gates. 'One single drive doesn't mean anything at all.'

'Of course not. Quite meaningless.'

'I hope she doesn't think—'

'No fear of that, believe me, or she'd not have married Elwick, God rest his soul.'

'Was he a dear man?'

'Dear?' he said, easing the horses round onto the road with

a turn of his fist. 'Hardly. As dull as ditchwater. She didn't need his title. Didn't need his wealth, either. Can't think what she needed him for, come to think of it.'

'She has two beautiful children.'

He glanced at her, hearing a wistful note creep into her voice. 'So could you, Miss Boyce,' he said, quietly. 'Quite easily.'

So quietly did he say it that she could hardly believe her ears, though she blushed to the roots of her hair.

She would have preferred it if he had allowed her to go into the house alone, but he seemed intent on escorting her into the hall as if he'd known she might need some support. With a glance towards the hall table and its array of top hats, gloves and canes, the footman gave her the news she would rather not have heard. 'Sir Penfold and Lady Aspinall are waiting in the drawing room, ma'am. And Lieutenant Gaddestone and Miss Gaddestone are with them.'

'Then they'll be staying for lunch. Tell cook, will you?'

'I believe cook already knows, ma'am.'

'Good. Lord Rayne, will you stay, too?' She did not think he would.

His reply was unhesitating. 'Thank you, Miss Boyce. I will.'

'Are you sure?' she whispered, darting a look towards the door.

'Quite sure.'

'Then we shall be ten,' she told the footman, 'counting the three boarders and Mrs Quayle.' Removing her spectacles, she tucked them into her reticule, passed her hat and gloves to her maid, and went into the drawing room to meet her guests. With Lord Rayne close behind her, she found she could brave Aunt Minnie's hostile glare with more tranquillity than if she had been on her own.

Chapter Seven

～～～

Having met often at Tattersalls, White's Club and at Jackson's Boxing Saloon, as well as at Chesterfield House, Sir Penfold Aspinall and Lord Rayne greeted each other warmly. Letitia received the impression that Uncle Aspinall liked him, though Aunt Minnie could only favour him with a vinegary smile meant to show her disapproval of his appearance here at Paradise Road.

It is doubtful whether Rayne even noticed, being more interested in the appearance of another of Letitia's cousins, Miss Gaddestone's younger brother Lieutenant Fingal Gaddestone, who had been away at sea for almost three years. Rosie Gaddestone's girlish face shone with happiness, her arm linked through his as if to anchor him to her while his other hand held Letitia's. The two cousins had once been close, each of an independent spirit that recognised the need to break the family mould, which both of them had done successfully, but not without some anguish. Old Lady Gaddestone, Lady Boyce's sister, had died while he was away, some said of a broken heart, and Rosie had gone to live with her cousin Letitia rather than stay alone in London.

Disengaging her hand from his, Letitia could see the kind of changes that affected so many naval men: bronzed skin, lines around the eyes and mouth, a lean fitness and a newly assured manner that she assumed he had acquired as an officer. He was now a handsome young man with sun-bleached hair, a friendly smile and a teasing manner that made Letitia change the subject hurriedly and turn to her other guest. 'Lord Rayne, will you allow me to introduce my cousin Fin to you?'

'Certainly,' he said, stepping forward with a slight bow.

Both men drew themselves up smartly, pulling back their shoulders as if an extra half-inch could make all the difference.

'My lord,' said Lieutenant Gaddestone.

'Where are you lodging, sir?'

'Temporarily with my uncle and aunt in London until I can find a suitable place of my own. Then I shall settle down and live a normal life. Did you serve, too, my lord?'

'Briefly, in Spain. Cavalry. A few years of that was enough.'

'So now you're a man of leisure?'

'Not exactly. I train cavalry recruits at Hampton Court Palace. You must come and see, one day. My elder brother is responsible for the Royal Stud there. We shall need every available horse once the celebrations begin next month. It's going to be a busy time.'

Aunt Minnie could not resist asking, with a certain acid relish, 'And will you be escorting Miss Boyce, or her two younger sisters, my lord?'

Blandly, Lord Rayne studied her as if trying to make up his mind, then said, 'Lady Aspinall, as soon as I've made a final decision on that, you will be the first to be told of it. There, how will that do?'

Minnie Aspinall was not so stupid that she could not tell when she'd been snubbed for impertinence and, although Letitia thought she deserved it, she herself quaked at the damage it was doing.

The tension was broken by the arrival of Mrs Quayle and her three charges, and the meal progressed peacefully, the conversation to-ing and fro-ing with ease, neatly bypassing Aunt Minnie's simmering disapproval of her niece's friendship with Lord Rayne, her glowering silence being wasted on the company who had so much to say to each other. Letitia knew only too well that the news would be taken back, post-haste, to Lady Boyce and her twin daughters with predictable results.

However, Aunt Minnie refused to relinquish her role as critic and, as soon as she was able, reminded Rayne that Letitia's *dear* sisters had obtained vouchers for Almack's that same evening and were hoping to see him there. But to her great annoyance, he refused to pass on any message to her nieces except an enigmatic smile. She tried again on a different tack. 'Young Lieutenant Gaddestone and Letitia have *always* had a *tendre* for each other since they were children. He seems particularly interested in her now, doesn't he, my lord?'

'I suppose it's to be expected, Lady Aspinall. They must have plenty of news to exchange after an absence of three years,' he said.

She did not give up. 'Indeed, yes. He's done *terribly* well for himself, you know. Went out to the Americas with pockets to let and came back with a considerable share of prize money. Yes, he'll be a good catch for some fortunate young lady before too long. Of course, the army don't go in for prize money, do they?'

'No, my lady. They don't.' Cultivated through generations

of blue blood, the patronising smile in his voice and the quirk of one eyebrow was quite enough to remind her that her observation had backfired. Cavalry officers, drawn mostly from the wealthy aristocracy, could afford to fight for the sake of adventure and glory rather than for the pay, which was not good. Their colours, kit and horses usually cost a fortune, and few officers emerged wealthier than they were already. After that, Aunt Minnie confined herself to observing the two cousins and making plans for their future.

That evening, while her sisters were at Almack's, Letitia spent several hours writing her notes into her journal and continuing her story about the young Perdita who, by coincidence, was experiencing similar emotions and conflicts to herself.

She took her leave of him, allowing her hand to rest in his a moment longer than was appropriate for one who had only that day insisted they could never be good friends. To humour her, he had cheerily agreed, but the look in his eyes told a different story, and the pressure of his fingers was like a caress around her heart, adding to the slow thaw that had begun with his first disturbing kiss. He would never know what that had done to her. He would not understand how a maid could be melted, insidiously, by a gentle embrace offered that day out of compassion. What was an untutored girl to understand by this, except that he saw her as some trophy to be won? Was it too late for her to refuse him her heart? Had he already claimed it? 'Good day, my lord,' she said. 'Thank you for...'

'For what?'

'For the drive. For staying. For being here.'

He nodded, smiling with wicked brown eyes. 'Progress, Miss Perdita? Are we making some progress at last?'

She watched his two giant strides take him to his high curricle, revealing the length of his steely thighs and calves. Responding like quicksilver to his commanding hands, his team leapt away, leaving Perdita to watch him disappear into the blue autumn haze, already counting the hours before she would see him again.

Lord Rayne, on the other hand, had said nothing about progress to the author, nor had *his* wicked brown eyes smiled as he took his leave of her after luncheon. He had looked sternly at her instead. 'Well,' he said, 'don't be going on any drives with your cousin, will you? Naval officers don't have much practice with horses, and you two together would be a liability.'

'Thank you for your advice, Lord Rayne. Your concern is touching.'

'My concern is mainly for the horses. Good day, Miss Boyce.'

When shall I see you again?

Halfway across the pavement, he stopped and turned as if he had heard her. 'Tomorrow. At church. You'll be there?'

'Yes.' She nodded, startled by his reading of her mind.

His acknowledgement was curt to the point of incivility, his two strides to the curricle seat taken without another glance.

Her intention to be at church next morning, however, was upset by an incident that shocked the adults involved in the smooth running of Miss Boyce's select seminary.

Letitia and Miss Gaddestone were preparing to leave the house, waiting for Mrs Quayle and the three girls to join them, when the three arrived with serious faces, without their chaperon.

'Is she coming?' said Letitia, drawing on her gloves.

'Yes,' said Edina. 'She asks that you wait for her while we go on ahead. Shall we go?'

'Yes. We'll catch you up. Go with Miss Gaddestone.'

Once they were out of the way, Mrs Quayle entered the house through the back door, leading an unkempt Sapphire Melborough, who ought to have been at church in her parents' pew. Sapphire was sullen and indignant, her pouting mouth reddened as if she'd been eating strawberries. Her long fair hair, which should have been braided, hung down on to one muslin-covered shoulder, the fabric of which was loosened by the undone row of hooks and eyes down the back of her bodice. One hand held the front of her dress in place while the other carried her pink bonnet and reticule, and her prayer book.

If Letitia was lost for words, Mrs Quayle was not. 'I think,' she said in her severest tone, 'that this young lady has some explaining to do. First, she may like to tell us why she prefers to spend her Sunday morning in the potting shed rather than at church with her parents.'

Guessing the answer to that, Letitia started from a more obtuse angle. 'Where do your parents think you are, Sapphire?' she said.

'At church or at home, Miss Boyce,' the young woman whispered. 'They're away visiting for the day, but I pleaded to stay behind.'

'So you could come down to Paradise Road while we were at church?'

'Yes.' The blue eyes had lost their merry twinkle, taking on a heavy-lidded tiredness, guarded against probing personal questions.

'To meet the gardener's son?'

'How…how did you…?'

'*Tell* me! Never mind how I know.'

'Yes.'

Bristling with indignation, Mrs Quayle felt obliged to add details she knew Sapphire would not willingly have offered. 'The great hulking lout ran off, buckling his belt up, leaving this young madam—' she cast a jaundiced look at Sapphire's dishevelled state '—to pull herself together as best she may. Down on the bench they were, when I found them, rolling about like a couple of pups, and him with a black eye as big as a cabbage.'

'Yes, thank you, Mrs Quayle. Sapphire, come here and sit down. Did you walk down Richmond Hill on your own? Without a maid?'

'Charity came with me, ma'am, to keep watch.'

'To keep *watch*? For pity's sake, what has it come to? Where is she now? Still out there?'

'I don't know, ma'am.'

'Sapphire, how long has this been going on?' Before the girl could develop her fib, it was snapped off in a sudden burst of anger. 'Don't *lie* to me, young lady. The truth, if you please. How *long*?'

'Not long, Miss Boyce. Since I first hurt my ankle.'

Letitia closed her eyes, seeing the occasion in one quick blink. They had left Sapphire behind in Miss Gaddestone's care to finish off her watercolour in the summerhouse while the rest of them went to the Royal Academy. Gaddy would have dozed off. The gardener's son would have beckoned, offering Sapphire an irresistible alternative. She was not a girl to refuse that kind of adventure, as she herself had done. She would have pushed aside any reservations and taken whatever experience was waiting for her, and she would emerge at the tender age of seventeen knowing far more about a man than Letitia knew at twenty-four, a novelist who wrote about such relationships as if she knew what she was talking about. Sapphire's behaviour could not be excused or condoned, but neither could she be condemned out of hand for wanting to know exactly what would be expected of her in marriage, before committing herself to it.

'With the *gardener*'s son, Sapphire? Is that the best you could do? Could you not have waited for marriage?'

Sapphire hung her head as if in shame, but there was no trace of shame when she lifted it again to look Letitia full in the face. 'I could, Miss Boyce,' she said through swollen lips, 'but Ted's not like the men my parents approve of. He'll keep it to himself, not prattle and boast as others do, swapping details, comparing, laughing about it, giving one a reputation and a silly nickname to match. I wanted to find out what I need to know without everyone hearing about it. He's had lots of girls. He knows what he's doing. Not like some of them. And now I know what it's like. It was *not* what Mrs Quayle says, rolling about like pups. It was good, or I'd not have returned.'

'Have you no shame, Miss Melborough?' Mrs Quayle snapped.

Sapphire did not look her way. 'My body is my own to do with as I please. Yes, I know about bloodlines and all that, but experience with men has not stopped some women from making good marriages, and it won't stop me. The difference is that I shall be going into it with my eyes open. As men do.'

'And have you given any thought to the consequences, young lady?' said Mrs Quayle, unconvinced by the argument. 'Do you *want* to bear the gardener's brat? Will your own father recognise it, if you do?'

'There won't *be* any consequences of the kind you mean.'

'How can you be sure, Sapphire?' said Letitia. 'You run a very serious risk.'

'My father tells me one must be prepared to take risks in life.'

'I don't doubt he did, but I don't suppose he had this kind of thing in mind when he said it. Turn round and let me fasten you up.'

As Letitia might have expected, Sapphire's back was covered by tiny pink scratches that rough sacking would make upon delicate skin. But she was not prepared for the pale grey-blue rows of fingertip marks on the upper arms, shoulders and back as if some violence had been used. Finishing the fastenings, she turned Sapphire to face her. 'Tell me the truth, if you please. Did the gardener's son force himself on you?'

The blue eyes opened wider, astonished and innocent, and Letitia knew she did not lie. 'No, he didn't, Miss Boyce. Ted's not like that. I know it might be best for me to say that he did, but that wouldn't explain why I came down here on a Sunday morning when I told the housekeeper and Mama I'd be going to church, would it? I'd have gone straight there, not to your potting shed. I won't get Ted into any more trouble than he is already. Someone's already beaten him up.'

It would have been so easy for Letitia to tell her, but she held her tongue. This was not the time. 'Do you love him, then?' she said.

'No, Miss Boyce, of course I don't. It's not love we were after.'

'What *was* it, then?' said Mrs Quayle, sharply.

Letitia thought the question unnecessary, quelling Mrs Quayle's curiosity with a frown. 'My concern,' she said, 'is for your personal safety, which has been put at risk. And what on earth am I to tell your parents, when you choose to use *my* property to misbehave on while you were not supposed to *be* here? I shall have to insist that they find another seminary for you, Sapphire. Just when it was all going so well.'

'Do you have to tell them?'

Letitia recognised the plea for privacy, and there was a moment of hesitation before she replied, 'Yes, they must know. Certainly they must. They are responsible for you still, and I cannot pretend not to know what's been happening. That would make me as irresponsible as you. You must see that. I can only be thankful that it's been stopped before it gets any worse, though it will be bad enough if that young man has fathered a child on you. I pray it has not happened.'

'He must be got rid of *immediately*,' said Mrs Quayle.

'He will be. I should have done it sooner.'

'Why?'

'Well...er...because it's his father who's employed here, not Ted. He only helps out when he's needed.' She recalled Rayne's caustic and rather indelicate words about who else Ted had 'helped out'. 'Has he been associating with any of the other girls, Sapphire?'

'No, Miss Boyce.'

'Are you quite sure?'

'Yes, ma'am. Quite sure.'

Letitia sighed with relief. 'Stand up. I'll tidy your hair before I take you home. Turn round.'

'I'd rather stay here with you, ma'am, if I may. My parents won't be home until this evening.'

'Very well, but you must stay upstairs out of the way. I'll have your lunch sent up on a—' Her words were cut off by the insistent clang of the front doorbell, followed quickly by a loud commanding voice. 'Oh, no! That's Mama!' she whispered to Mrs Quayle. 'Quick! Take Sapphire upstairs.'

But it was too late to take Miss Melborough anywhere before the footman opened the door, his announcement obliterated by the loud greeting of Lady Boyce who had come on a mission of some urgency. *'Letitia!'* she bawled, then stopped abruptly to take in the unusual scene of her eldest daughter dressing the hair of a dishevelled young beauty, while her plump brown neighbour looked on with alarm written clearly on her face. With eyes sharpened by years of training, Lady Boyce saw that something was seriously amiss—a minor tragedy that demanded her personal investigation.

The hour that followed was one of the most difficult Letitia ever had to endure while defending Sapphire Melborough against Lady Boyce's embarrassing inquisition, far worse than Mrs Quayle's barbed enquiries. After ignoring repeated invitations to visit Paradise Road, she had chosen that Sunday morning to descend upon her daughter at last, not with smiles of appreciation, but solely to find out more about the relationship with the man she had earmarked for one of her younger daughters. Hoping to arrive before Letitia's return from church, she had intended to do at least half an hour of snooping. She did not enjoy having her plans dislodged, but she *did* enjoy demanding answers to searching questions, regardless of the fact that Miss Melborough's plight was no concern of hers. This kind of detail had never stopped her in the past, and nor did it now.

Usually able to hold her own in an argument, Letitia was this time no match for her mother, particularly on an issue that needed handling with great sensitivity. No amount of protectiveness towards Sapphire would do: that was seen as being on the side of the sinner. And as for Letitia's ideas of a seminary, it had already sunk to a level of vulgarity made worse by the noisy and untimely appearance of Charity, the young lady's maid who, more to save her skin than for any finer feeling, blurted out before anyone could stop her, her own innocent part in the role she had been told to play that morning. With additions.

Letitia's prayer for another unscheduled appearance in the form of Lord Rayne had no effect. If anyone could have dealt with Letitia's mother, he could. But he did not appear and, after Sapphire's eventual tearful departure to Letitia's bedroom, Lady Boyce needed no more convincing that she was right about the seminary being a grave mistake, already being regretted. Having made her opinions clear about the scandal of Melborough's daughter, she was not inclined to take luncheon with her niece, Rosie Gaddestone, or with Mrs Quayle and the boarding pupils. Instead, she launched once more into an attack upon Letitia, demanding to be told what she meant by driving out with her sisters' beau, making it look to the world as if she had stolen his affections. Did she realise what a disservice she was doing by this selfish behaviour? Did she realise the gossip it was causing? And the embarrassment? Did she *have* to wear those silly spectacles to draw attention to herself? Did she know how close Garnet was to being engaged to Rayne? Did she really believe a man like him could be seriously interested in *her*? Could she not see that she was not the kind of female such men married?

'Mama, you've not told me anything I don't already know. There is not the slightest possibility of marriage. Lord Rayne lives here in Richmond at the weekends and, because of my relationship to Garnet and Persephone, he and I are acquainted. Not good friends, Mama, just acquainted. He took me to Mortlake to see his sister, Lady Dorna Elwick, who is a friend of mine. There's no more to it than that. Garnet has nothing to fear.'

'And what about the theatre? I heard—'

'There were fourteen of us, Mama.'

'Well,' she said, looking round at the blue, white and gold décor, the walnut table and chairs, the embroidered seat covers and cushions as if they belonged in a dingy street tavern, 'it's bad enough for you to be doing *this* kind of thing, without trying to take your sister's future husband.'

'Are you not being premature, Mama? You know how Lord Rayne tends to…?'

'Yes, Letitia. I *do* know. That's the problem. And you're not helping matters, are you? And now this *shocking* scandal, too.'

'Which no one need know of, Mama, unless you tell them.'

'Then you must tell Rayne you no longer need his company,' she said, rising. 'That should redirect his interest. Don't ask him to lunch with you again, either. That young Waverley is more your type. Summon my carriage, if you please. It's time I was going.'

'But don't you wish to look round the house, Mama?'

'No time today. I have guests coming this evening.'

'I see. First things first, of course.'

Not being finely tuned to such nuances, Lady Boyce failed to pick up the cynicism. And had not Rosie Gaddestone entered the hall just as she was about to depart, she would have missed seeing her altogether after an interval of eight months. Her quick peck to each of Gaddy's cheeks was both hello and goodbye, delivered to Letitia with the same artificiality.

It was not like Letitia to weep over matters such as this, but the only thing preventing her on this occasion was not fortitude but the gentle clasp of Gaddy's arms around her shoulders and the scent of lavender in an embrace that lasted as the hall clock ticked and chimed over their heads.

'Has Mrs Quayle told you?' she whispered into Gaddy's lace cap.

'Yes, love. We're not having a good day today, are we?'

'No. Was Lord Rayne at church?'

'Yes. He asked about you. I said you'd been delayed.'

'We could have done with him here just now.'

'A change of heart, Lettie dear? That's not like you.'

'I'm not much like me at the moment.' She held her cousin away, her hands buried in the tiers of lace over her arms. 'Oh, Gaddy, what a business this is. Now we may be sure that Mama will tell anyone who'll listen what a mess I'm making of it.' *And unless Lord Rayne stays well out of the way, she will broadcast Sapphire's scandal far and wide. That's for sure.*

The next few days could not be counted amongst the happiest of Letitia's career when pupils, chaperons and tutors felt Sapphire's absence so keenly. Discreet excuses had to be given of how Sir Francis and Lady Melborough had accepted an invitation for their son and daughter to visit an aunt and uncle in Cheltenham during the summer months. Could anything have been more cruel?

The interview had been painful and humiliating, but not hysterically so, for Sapphire had appreciated Letitia's understanding and compassion and had accepted the blame for what had happened. She could no longer expect her parents to foster Lord Rayne's interest in her, such as it was, at least not until some months had passed. At all costs, said Lady Melborough, the disgrace must be kept quiet.

Letitia had agreed completely, but felt it only fair to warn the distraught mother that her daughter's maid Charity was not the soul of discretion, but that to dismiss her for her tactless outburst in front of Lady Boyce would have the opposite effect from the one they sought. If the story came out at all, Lady Boyce and Charity would be the prime suspects. This was not a thought to bring comfort to any of them, and Letitia's farewell to her ex-pupil had been tearful and affectionate. The outings that week were much less interesting without Sapphire's bubbly presence.

Letitia's first task on Monday was to summon Charlie, the elderly gardener, and tell him that his son was not welcome on her property, even though there was still much hard work to be done before Charlie could manage alone. His silent acceptance of the edict suggested that he already knew the reason, for he had seen Ted's injuries. It was time for him to get the come-uppance he deserved.

On Friday evening, Letitia sat before her book of household accounts and a pile of bills spread out under an oil lamp on the parlour table. The fading day was dull and blustery, the fire in the cast-iron grate throwing a soft pink glow over the skirt of Letitia's pale day dress, dancing between the deep frills of the hem. Her hair had begun to come loose from its pins due to the relentless twiddling of fingers while sums were added and columns scanned, and now a delicate veil of silver fell over her page as she wrote.

The light tap on the door produced only a murmur as the pen continued to scratch. 'Lord Rayne, ma'am,' said the footman.

'Oh!' The quill poised in mid-air. 'My lord?'

As always, Rayne's expression was hard to read, though his appearance at this late hour suggested that his visit was more business than social. 'Miss Boyce. I find you well, I hope?' His bow was formal, and he brought with him the fresh cold tang of the evening breeze and an energy that seemed to fill the room. His riding boots showed a film of dust.

She guessed what might lay behind the visit. 'Well enough, I thank you, my lord. Have you come directly from Sheen Court or from Hampton? Will you be seated? May I offer you a drink? I can send for some—' She pulled herself up short, remembering that she was not supposed to be offering him anything, not even the usual hospitality.

'No, I thank you,' he said, flipping up his coat-tails as he sat down. 'My visit will not take long. I've come from Sheen Court where I found a note awaiting me.' The hand that delved into his coat pocket pulled out a folded piece of paper, which he undid and passed to her. 'Perhaps you'd care to read it and tell me what it means.'

Feeling that she was being spoken to rather like an errant schoolgirl, she smiled, ignored the request, and sat down against the green-figured bolster on the sofa. 'I make it a rule never to read other people's letters,' she replied, sweetly. 'And if *you* don't know what it means, how can you imagine I shall do any better? Who is it from?'

He lowered it on to his knee. 'From Sir Francis Melborough. He sent it this morning by hand.'

'Then wouldn't it have been better to ask Sir Francis himself?'

'That is what I shall be doing when I've heard what you have to say about it. I prefer to be in full possession of the facts.'

'Would you care to summarise it? I cannot promise to have

anything at all to add, but I'll do what I can to help. I'm not at my best at this time of the day.'

'Very well. Sir Francis tells me that his daughter is no longer one of your pupils and that she's been packed off to Cheltenham with her brother. Do you have any comment to make on that?'

'No. Why should I? He's at liberty to do whatever he wishes...'

'With his daughter. Yes. So why has he withdrawn her from your seminary so soon after a very successful soirée at his home, and why did he go to the trouble of asking me to purchase a new horse and help her to get used to it only a week or so before sending her off to Cheltenham? Obviously there has been a sudden change of direction. Or is there a conflict of interests here that you could explain? Sir Francis tells me my services as riding master are no longer required.'

'Well, I'm sure you'll manage to find some other young ladies to occupy your spare time, my lord, as soon as you can find suitable mounts for them.'

'That is not the point, Miss Boyce, as you well know.'

'Oh, dear, then I've missed it. I told you I'm not at my best in the evenings.' A yawn behind her hand followed quite naturally.

'Don't try to bamboozle me with that flummery, ma'am. Your tongue and brain are as sharp in the evening as they are at any other time of day, or you'd not be doing your accounts, would you? Why have the Melboroughs withdrawn their daughter and sent her to Cheltenham?'

'I'm not at liberty to discuss the reasons with you, Lord Rayne. If Sir Francis gave you no reason, you can hardly expect that I will do so.'

'I see. Then I shall be obliged to draw the conclusion that you, ma'am, have devised some excuse to get rid of her because she's been occupying an occasional hour of my time lately, and that's your only way of making your displeasure felt. Or could it be some kind of retaliation for what happened in Sir Francis's library? You don't care for the Melboroughs much, do you, Miss Boyce? Are you gunning for the mother next, or have you done enough with this?'

'Lord Rayne, your imagination is working overtime. I will not stoop to answer your ridiculous allegations, but perhaps when you've had a good night's sleep you'll see that people *can* actually make decisions that have nothing whatever to do with you. Now, if you've said all you came to say, I suggest you go to the Melboroughs with your complaints and ask *them* for an explanation. And if that doesn't satisfy you, then you'll have to accept the situation, won't you?'

'Is this to do with your sisters? Have they told you to get her out of the way?'

Letitia came to her feet and waited for him to do the same. 'My lord, I have now heard every silly interpretation you can put upon the subject, including my apparent pique in expelling Miss Melborough from my seminary in order to punish her father for a tiny incident that didn't upset me in the least, except for a few bruises. After all, it was not the first time I'd been manhandled, was it? I happen to like Miss Melborough. She was an able pupil, and popular with all of us, and there is nothing my sisters could, or *would*, have said to make me do anything as irrational as what you suggest. Your insinuations do you no credit, my lord, and I urge you once again to abandon the puerile quest you and Lord Elyot discussed, if you have not already done so, and stay well away from

Paradise Road altogether. I shall no longer acknowledge you when we meet, and I shall instruct my staff not to admit you to my house.'

She ran out of breath on the last few words as she reached over to pull on the bell-cord, the clang of which could be heard above the howl of the wind in the chimney. In the silence that followed, the two antagonists stood without looking at each other, wondering who was being hurt most by this short, censorious exchange.

'There is surely no need—' he began.

'There is *every* need, my lord. I bid you good evening. Please don't come back. And rid yourself, if you will, of the notion that my sisters have any influence over me. You may like to suppose that there is some sisterly rivalry between us, but you'd be wrong. There is none, and there never has been. We have the greatest affection for each other. One of them will make you an excellent wife.'

'It won't do, Miss Boyce. You are not going to be free of me.'

The door opened. 'Yes, I am,' she said with a curtsy. 'Goodbye.'

Having been helped into his caped greatcoat and taken possession of hat, gloves and whip, Lord Rayne was about to pass through to the outer hall when the drawing room door opened and a voice whispered his name.

He turned. 'Miss Gaddestone. Good evening, ma'am.'

'Shh!' she said, sidling through the gap. 'Can you spare me a moment of your time, my lord? Please, just a wee moment?'

Without hesitation, Rayne followed her into the drawing room and closed the door quietly. A tall silver oil lamp spread a pool of light on to an open workstand bearing a pile of mending, with a needle-and-thread jabbed vertically into it. The armchair by the fire bore the hollow imprint of where Letitia's cousin had been sitting to do her sewing. Still with one finger to her lips, she indicated the opposite chair where he should sit. 'Keep your voice down,' she whispered, poking at the air in the direction of the wall adjoining the parlour. 'I dare say my cousin will not like it much my telling you this, my lord, but she could have done with you being here last Sunday morning. Oh, yes,' she said, seeing his eyebrows pull together in doubt, 'she told me so.' She smoothed the woollen stole over her knees.

'Why, ma'am? Has something happened?'

'She's not told you about Lady Boyce's visit?'

'Not a word. Is that not what she'd been hoping for?'

Rosie Gaddestone shook her head, bouncing the brown curls that spiralled around her face. 'Not *that* kind of visit. No indeed. Her ladyship can be very intimidating, you know. I've never known Lettie to be quite so upset by her. I took the three girls to church, as you know.'

'Yes, you told me Miss Boyce and Mrs Quayle would be delayed.'

'Then I came back here in case I could help, and when I got here Miss Melborough was with them. Then Lady Boyce rolled up, of all times to choose, when she must have known we'd all be at church.'

'You mean Lady Boyce arrived while Miss Melborough was here?'

'In this very room. That's why Lettie wished *you'd* been here, my lord. Such a to-do it was.'

Rayne sat back, his frown deepening. 'Can you tell me what happened, Miss Gaddestone?'

She looked doubtfully at the pile of mending. 'If Lettie has not told you of it herself, I suppose I ought not to be doing, either.'

'If it would ease your conscience, I've had a letter from Sir Francis telling me that Miss Melborough and her brother have gone to Cheltenham.'

Her face brightened. 'Yes, I suppose she'll have to be kept out of the way for a few months at least, won't she? Such a foolish featherbrained girl to throw away all her chances of a good marriage. Perhaps if she'd not been allowed to read all those romantic novels, she might not be so full of ideas. I cannot think it's good for—'

'And did you hear what Miss Boyce's reaction was?'

'I heard what her *mother*'s reaction was,' she said, stoutly. 'I should think everyone in the house heard Lady Boyce bellowing at the poor girl while Lettie was having a time of it trying to get a kind word in edgeways. Not that she was approving, you understand, but that was no way to set about the girl when she'd just been found... Well!' She took her fan out of the work-table drawer and fluttered it across her bosom. 'With the *gardener's lad*, as I heard later. Tch!' She took a deep breath, fanning frantically.

'Where, exactly?'

'In the potting shed. There's one in the kitchen garden, you know.'

'By Miss Boyce herself?'

'It was Mrs Quayle who found them, just before church. Lady Melborough turns her back for just a few hours and this is what she gets up to. Lettie was handling it all so well, as I heard, but once my Aunt Euphemia arrived and saw that there was some kind of problem that was *no* concern of hers... Well, it was that young maid...Charity...that spilled the beans, otherwise they'd no doubt have made something up. After that, poor Lettie didn't stand much of a chance, nor the girl, either. Then Aunt Euphemia gave Lettie a good set-down. They must have heard it in the *kitchen*, my lord,' she whispered, leaning towards him. 'Wouldn't even look round the house. Wouldn't stay to lunch. Didn't even exchange two words with me, her own niece. Tch!'

'So you heard what she said to Miss Boyce?'

'We all did. I told you, Lady Boyce doesn't do whispers.'

'She was still angry about Miss...?'

'About *you*, my lord. Seeing Lettie, to put it plain. She don't like it above half. She don't like it at all. I think that's what she came for.'

He nodded, pressing his fingertips together, beginning to understand. 'No, I gathered as much, but I didn't think she'd go that far.'

'Oh, she would, my lord. Aunt Euphemia doesn't like having her plans upset, you see.'

Without warning, the door suddenly opened very wide. 'Lord Rayne,' said Letitia, 'I have already asked you to leave. Would you mind respecting my wishes?' She stood to one side, leaving a gaping hole of escape beyond the room.

Rayne stood up, bowing to Miss Gaddestone. 'Ma'am, this is highly unconventional, but I wonder if you would mind allowing me a few moments alone with Miss Boyce?' He held out a hand to help her up.

Throwing a questioning glance towards her cousin, she accepted it. 'If you don't mind, Lettie dear? Or would you rather I stayed?'

'No, Gaddy,' Letitia said, wearily. 'It's all right, love. Just a moment or two, that's all. There's a nice fire in the parlour.'

Chapter Eight

Rayne closed the door and came to face Letitia across the hearth, this time with a kindlier expression. 'You should have told me,' he said, softly. 'Why didn't you tell me?'

'Because it concerns no one but those involved, my lord. And I wish my cousin had not discussed it with you.' Icily, she turned aside as he moved towards her. Passing the work-table, she jabbed the needle hard into the white linen. 'And if you have any more accusations to make, you had better make them in writing so that I can show them to my lawyer.'

'Lettie!'

'I am not Lettie to you,' she snapped, whirling to face him again. 'I am Miss Boyce, and I do not *ever* want to—' The words her mother had demanded stuck in her throat, refusing to emerge as the lies she knew them to be. She *did* want to see him again, but not at the price of her mother's revenge or her sisters' unhappiness. 'Lord Rayne,' she said, attempting to stay calm, to think rationally, 'I told you once before that this has gone far enough. Now I must ask you yet again to abandon this foolish game of…of chase…whatever you like to call it…and leave me alone. Your opinion of me cannot be so high if you can believe that I would expel one of my own pupils to spite you or her father. I am not in a position to break a confidence, but you had no right to draw such mischievous conclusions, and I want nothing to do with a man who finds it so convenient to put me in the wrong. I can do that for myself quite easily, but I don't deserve it from you, Lord Rayne, however much you wished to goad me.'

'And I deserve that set-down, Miss Boyce. That, and more. You are right to be angered and hurt, but may I say in my defence that, if I'd known Lady Boyce was here last weekend, I would have put quite a different construction on Sir Francis's letter. Miss Gaddestone did not divulge to me what the whole house must have heard, but I can guess well enough how your mother must have upset everyone, particularly you. Well, now you have said what she told you to say, using my unfair criticism as an excuse. It was quite unforgivable but, even so, I beg you to accept my unreserved apology. I admit that I have, in the past, taken some pleasure in trying to goad you, but never to earn your disgust.'

'You do not disgust me,' she whispered.

'I am relieved more than I can say. My conclusions do *not* reflect my high opinion of you, Miss Boyce, but rather the unusual tangents of my mind these days for which, like it or not, I hold you responsible. But if you think I intend to take the slightest notice of Lady Boyce's demands, then I must warn you again that no one dictates to me who I visit. I am well able to make my own decisions there.'

'I must interrupt you. I can understand your determination not to be dictated to, particularly by Lady Boyce, but have you stopped to ask yourself what this is all about, my lord? To insist on going against her wishes just to prove a point at my expense is hardly fair, is it, when I made it clear from the beginning that we have nothing whatever in common?'

Her heart lurched at his quick frown. Was it irritation, or pain?

'You think that's what this is all about?' he said. 'That I have no other purpose than to thwart a middle-aged matron, through you? Is that *really* what you believe? That I'm playing some kind of devious power game with you and your sisters in the middle?' Scowling, he dug his hands deep into the pockets of his greatcoat and hunched his shoulders. 'I don't know what Lady Boyce has told you about my friendship with Miss Garnet and Miss Persephone, but you may take it from me that I have *never* given them any reason to think that I have serious intentions towards them. Ask them yourself. They will tell you as much.'

'You may think that answers every question, my lord, but I'm afraid it doesn't. There's more to it than that.'

'What more?'

'Miss Melborough's indiscretion. Had Mama not arrived just then, it would have remained a secret. I would not have made it public at any price. She's made a foolish mistake but, at seventeen, she doesn't deserve to lose her reputation over it. My mother, naturally, doesn't see it like that. She will use what she knows about Miss Melborough to force me to do what she wants and, if I refuse, Sapphire's affairs and the good name of my seminary will be the latest gossip.'

'Blackmail? Heaven help us, she doesn't do things by halves, does she? Would she be so vindictive?'

'She's a very determined woman, my lord. I dare say she's been waiting to find a way to make me conform, and now she's found it.'

'She may lead a horse to the water, Miss Boyce, but she cannot force it to drink. I am not obliged to fall in with her plans.'

'Perhaps not, but I wish for my sake that you would. She is quite determined that, if anyone diverts your interest from my sisters, it will not be me. I am to keep you at a distance, though, after your earlier condemnation of my actions, that may not be too difficult.'

'For which I have asked your forgiveness.'

'I dare say Gaddy thought she was doing me a favour in telling you what happened. It would have been better if she had not, I think.'

'And I think that the sooner you are removed from Lady Boyce's influence, the better. Something will have to be done.'

'Oh, it will be. You can help by doing what I suggested earlier.'

'I heard what you suggested earlier, Miss Boyce. I have not the slightest intention of abandoning what you call my puerile quest.'

'Not even though I plead with you?'

'No,' he said, almost soundlessly. Taking his hands out of his pockets, he came towards her, moving her backwards, holding her at bay against the long velvet curtain. Tenderly, he moved aside a wisp of hair that hung untidily down her face, not knowing how the touch of his fingertips wiped her mind as clean as a slate. 'No, my beauty. Your pleading would have a hollow ring to it, wouldn't it, when I know as well as you that it's not what you want. You are not so hard to read, Lettie Boyce.'

'You are arrogant, my lord. Talking nonsense, too.'

'Sure of myself, you mean. Sure that your mama will not have the last word in my affairs. I've fought more devious foes than her, and won.'

Angrily brushing aside his hand as it came up to hold her chin, she dodged to one side, bumping into the overloaded workbox on her way to the door. 'Oh yes,' she cried, slightly breathless, 'this is all about men fighting the foe, isn't it? Winning at all costs. Don't spare a thought for those who are injured on the way, will you? For Sapphire. Or me. Or my pupils and tutors who depend on me. And for what? To prove a point? Is that all, when the relationship you seek to protect doesn't even exist?'

'You're wrong. It *does* exist.'

'No, Lord Rayne, it doesn't! It never has. You talk about knowing what I want, but what I want is to be left alone to get on with my life. I don't need any kind of relationship with a man of your experience, and I have no interest in boosting your notoriety by becoming your latest mode. A blue-stocking, no less. Rayne's latest excess, they'll say. His latest bright idea.'

His eyes narrowed, dangerously angry, and she knew she had overstepped the mark with her outspokenness. 'Enough!' he said. His many-caped greatcoat seemed not to hinder him as he reached her in long silent strides, and she was unable to evade the hands that took her by the shoulders in a firm grasp that bit through her fine sleeves. Turned roughly, she was propelled forward to stand before the gold-framed mirror above the white marble fireplace with no choice but to face herself and him, scowling and quarrelsome, lit by a halo from the lamp behind.

'Look!' he demanded. 'Look at yourself, woman, and for pity's sake stop this damned self-deprecating twaddle, will you? Once and for all, recognise what's there. Be honest with yourself, for a change.'

Before she could see what he was about to do, he had pulled the last two pins from her hair, loosing it over his hand and her shoulders like a shower of molten silver. She tried to turn away, but he made her stand, still gripped by his hands, her hair falling in a pale sheet across her face, obscuring what little detail she could just make out.

'Look there!' he demanded again. 'Tell me that's not beauty, if you can. Tell me that's not a sight to turn any man's head.' His voice was quiet but harsh with exasperation while he watched the reflections, his hand lifting her chin and holding it up, cupping it in his warm palm. 'Who gave you this absurd notion that you cannot be my woman?' he whispered through her hair. 'Mama, was it? Well, my beauty, if she thinks she knows more about what I want than me, she's mistaken, and blind, and jealous, and resentful that you're beyond her control. Unconventional and rare are the words for you, Miss Boyce, not blue-stocking. Intelligent and independent, stunningly beautiful, sharp-tongued, quick-witted, imaginative and talented, loyal, compassionate—'

'Stop!' she muttered, trying to remove her chin.

'And I don't care a damn how many pairs of spectacles she wears or where she chooses to wear them, this is the woman I have chosen, this snapping snarling vixen with the body and face of an angel who believes her mother's opinion to be more valid than her own. But this has little to do with silencing her, or about my personal dislike of being told what I can't have when I know otherwise. It's about what you and I both want. She lost you soon after your father, and now she's trying to control you from a distance because she needs to be needed. Well, that's too bad. I found you, Lettie Boyce, bawling me out in front of my own men like a vixen protecting her cubs, spitting and fighting when I cornered you, flaying me with your quick tongue. And that's when I wanted you. That's when I laid claim to you. And that's when you first responded to me.'

'I did no such *thing*,' she cried, wrenching herself out of his grasp at last. 'My response was to take a swipe at you, and it was no more than you deserved. I only wish it had connected.' Pacing away from him, she reached the other end of the room, fuming with indignation. Throwing the mane of hair over her head, she continued. 'And my mother is *not* controlling me, Lord Rayne. I am a free agent. I do as I please. I am not answerable to anyone, and I can find my own way out of my problems.'

'At my expense? No, Miss Boyce, that won't do. I shall not allow you to ditch me. You may prefer not to remember exactly how, but respond you did, in spite of your anger.'

'You are indelicate, my lord,' she whispered, holding a hand to her cheek. 'You have no right to remind me of that shameful episode. I shall not swoon because I am not a swooning kind of woman, but I must ask you to leave me. Your memory is severely at fault.'

'Then perhaps you could help me to restore it.'

'Perhaps you should go. I am very tired. I cannot...' She made a vague gesture with one hand as if to fend off an invisible enemy.

'Lettie,' he whispered.

'No...no, don't. Just go.'

From the kitchen below, there was a crash as if someone had dropped a tray. Then silence.

'Have you been into the garden today?' he asked, quietly.

She shook her head, wearily.

'Then I think we should go and take a look. Come on, my

beauty. The air will make you sleep better.' Slipping off his greatcoat once more, he held it for her to put on, adjusting its flopping capes. It was much too wide across the shoulders and the hem touched the floor. Warm with the faint aroma of horses and leather, it seemed to wrap her in its protection, as intimate as his embrace.

With an arm across her back, her ushered her through the dimly lit hall towards the back of the house and out through a door, past the new beds of gillyflowers and lilies of the valley, lavender and ferns. The light had almost gone, the wind swaying the trees above them, lifting the loose ends of Letitia's hair like a ruff of silver lace.

A few moments ago, she thought, she had been wrangling with him yet again, each of them wanting the upper hand, determined not to yield an inch, yet taking a certain pleasure from knowing that after the wrangling would come a period of calm to lift them to another level of friendship. He had been right, of course. She *had* responded, briefly, before she was able to stop herself, before her fury had returned. She could forgive herself for that, but it was most ungentlemanly of him to remind her of it.

Their feet crunched along the pathway, sending next door's cat leaping away to rustle the distant shrubbery. Ahead of them, enclosed on two sides by pink rhododendron blossoms, the summerhouse was closed for the night. Yet it was towards that sanctuary that their unhurried steps led them, as if to re-capture that precious moment when she had accepted the comfort of his arms. The memory of it was still fresh in her mind, contradicting all she had said to him earlier about not needing him. She did need him, even when they were at daggers drawn.

Responding to some unspoken signal, they came to a halt where they had stopped before, where the conflict in her mind was plain to see as she held her hair aside and looked across at the house, at the curtain-drawn windows, the conservatory shining with black and silver reflections, at the lights winking from the basement kitchen. Rayne took her by the hand, making the decision for them both. 'Come inside,' he said.

It was so much what she wanted him to say.

The summerhouse was still warm from the afternoon sun and, with the door closed behind them, the wind's roar softened to a whisper, muffling them in the quiet darkness of evening. Cares and quarrels faded into the shadows, heightening her anticipation. She thought he was about to take back his coat when his hands turned her to him, but they slid around her, easing her into an embrace as soft as thistledown, holding her against him as he had done before. This time, his fingers combed into her hair, grasping it lightly and tilting her face to receive his kiss that played over her lips and kept her spellbound with delight, fondling them with his sweet warmth. Unlike those first derisory kisses at Hampton Court, intended to humiliate and bring her to heel, these were offered with care and sincerity, received at first with a little hesitancy and then with a wonder that stirred something deep inside her like a suddenly discovered hunger.

There were things she needed to say to him, mostly negative, about how she must be left alone to sort out her problems, about how she had so far managed well enough without him. But they remained unsaid, banished like bad memories to the furthest reaches of her mind, overtaken by the physical needs of her body, disciplined for so long. The sheer luxury of surrendering herself to this man's arms, to his authority and care, seemed to her like the most dreamed-of boon she could imagine, and the hunger she had ignored for so long now raged within her, filling her with an ache to yield to him, allowing him to take over. After all she had striven for, stridently proclaiming her independence, setting up her own household, managing her own affairs, becoming a published author, all it took was such a man to show her how incomplete she was.

She might have wondered if, with his experience, he would take advantage of her extreme innocence as Ted had done with Sapphire. But she had nothing to fear, for Rayne knew better than anyone how not to force the pace with a woman so full of contradictions, and when he drew her towards the cushioned bench along the back wall, it was not to lay her upon it, but to sit her beside him in the close circle of his arms with his hand beneath the soft woollen greatcoat.

Even now she felt the confusion of her emotions acutely. 'What am I doing?' she whispered, breathless after his kiss. 'We can scarce find a civil word to say to each other, unless others are there. You came here on purpose to quarrel.'

'There are some things that have to be put straight,' he said, speaking into her hair. 'I cannot have you thinking that my first attempt to make love to you was the best I can do.'

Squirming, she tried to extricate herself, to no avail. 'Lord Rayne, if *that's* the only reason—'

'It isn't,' he said, laughing softly, holding her fast.

'You are indeed the most—'

'Odious man. Yes, I heard that before. Hush now, my beauty. You are not used to being teased, are you? So stop trying to find reasons for everything. Some things *are* unreasonable, and to you this looks like one of them. To me, it doesn't look that way at all.'

'Oh? Then how does it look, my lord?'

'Perfectly natural. You've had a disturbing few days, and when you needed me I was not here. Now I am, and I can give you the comfort you need. And more, if you want it. There's nothing to be ashamed of in wanting a man's comfort, sweetheart, especially when that's what he's wanted to do since he first saw you.'

'It may not do much for my good reputation, though.'

'There's a lot of nonsense talked about reputations, Lettie Boyce.'

'I know that women rise or fall by them.'

'Those who don't know the rules, yes. You believe that Miss Melborough's good name will be lost for ever if word gets round about her little peccadillo, but it won't be any such thing. She'll have a string of gouty old dukes dangling after her at Cheltenham, and she'll come back home as a duchess. You'll see. It'll take more than Lady Boyce to damage that one. After that, she'll probably take young Ted back into her service.'

'She wouldn't do that, would she?'

His laugh was low and husky. 'For a woman of your profession in charge of young ladies only a few years younger than yourself, Miss Boyce, you are remarkably ill informed about what they get up to. Did you have a governess, you and your sisters?'

They had, but Garnet and Persephone had socialised more than she had. The heroines of *The Infidel* and *Waynethorpe Manor* had not been typical of any young female she knew. She was trying to make Perdita more worldly, full-fleshed and rather extrovert, if anything, more ready to fall into adventure with a splash. Could her own preference for solitude be one of the reasons why Perdita was struggling with her image? Apart from her own ignorance of men, did she also need to investigate the real day-to-day behaviour of women, too? A seminary of seven privileged young ladies was hardly going to help much, with the exception of Sapphire.

'Yes,' she said. 'Then we were sent to Miss Wood's seminary.'

'That must surely account for it.'

'For what?'

'Lettie, I shall have to kiss you again,' he said, smiling. His hand had been roaming as they talked, challenging her mind to stay on course and to ignore what slow explorations were taking place under his greatcoat. Now, as he kissed her again and held her head upon his shoulder, the hand came to rest beneath the fullness of her breast, fitting it perfectly into the cupped palm. His timing was exact, for what would certainly have been a protest became instead a soft low moan of desire under his skilful lips.

Her hand covered his, pressing it even closer, directing all her senses towards the caress, to his kiss, and to his nearness. At once, the kiss deepened, luring her into a world of sensations about which she had yearned to know since she had started writing her first imaginative novel.

It had been an uncomfortable week, dragging its heels under the dark cloud of Lady Boyce's unreason. Letitia had felt particularly vulnerable, neither dependant nor free. Worse than that was what had happened to Sapphire, conveyed in one glance through those heavy-lidded eyes, not triumphant but fulfilled and knowing, confident and womanly. Mrs Quayle had been angered by the change, but Letitia had been moved by it, guiltily envious, sympathising with the girl's longing to discover what happened between a man and a woman in private without the fuss and publicity of marriage. It was exactly what she herself needed to know. Sapphire had taken matters into her own hands just as the heroine Perdita would do. Letitia would record it without a shred of evidence to go on except that look on Sapphire's face. Why could she not do as *she* had done and allow an expert to teach her here, in her own place, with no questions asked?

The answer was not far away: the risks were too great and too numerous. Courage was one thing, but experience of the sort she needed would cost too much, if a child should be the result of it.

Like a freezing mist the warning covered her, shrouding the enticing new world from view. Her hand closed over his and eased it away from her breast, clinging to it like a manacle. Her lips turned away from him with refusals littering his shoulder, whispering denials she could hardly expect him to believe. Shaking with the effort, her body stiffened and drew away, gathering strength to stand, distancing herself while drawing the greatcoat around her with a shudder. 'I'm so sorry...I led you on...it's my fault...I should not have...' she whispered.

He came behind her, placing his hands over her arms, smoothing her with his comfort. 'Hush, lass, it's all right, hush now. This is not about taking the blame for something we've discovered together. We have to talk about it, Lettie.'

'No, it's best to say no more.'

'That's foolishness. Come and sit with me for a while. Come. Side by side, over here.' Steering her, he lowered her into a basket chair and pulled up the other one near enough for him to lean over and take her free hand in his. 'It's no good walking away from this as if it wasn't happening,' he said, gently. 'We have to accept that there is something between us.

Yes,' he said, squeezing her hand as another protest began, 'there is, otherwise we'd not *be* here. And I can understand your reservations perfectly.'

'Can you?' she whispered. 'This cannot be what you're used to.'

There was a warmth in his voice as a smile entered it. 'Nothing about you is quite what I'm used to. Which is why it would be a great pity if you were to retire into your safe shell like a threatened oyster rather than face the situation with your usual courage. No, hear me out,' he said, stopping yet another protest at the unflattering analogy. 'You are known, Lettie Boyce, for being unconventional, independent, and too uncomfortably intelligent for most men. But I am not most men. I can accept all the reasons why you have chosen to remove yourself from Lady Boyce's contempt to a place where you can quietly get on with the business of being yourself and doing what you do best. But, sweet lass, I also believe that if you truly had the courage of your convictions, you would—'

'Are you suggesting that I lack courage? After what—?'

'I am suggesting that you are so concerned with what you may *not* do, that all those things you *could* be doing are passing you by. For a woman to defy convention is not such a crime these days, you know, and it can be made so much more enjoyable if she has someone to help her to do it.'

'In my mother's eyes, it *is* a crime.'

'And is your mother's opinion always regarded in such matters?'

'She would like it to be, but, no, it isn't. Not by a long way.'

'Then we are agreed that we need not take her into account. Which means that there are some things you would like to do which at present you are suppressing. Like taking a lover, for instance.'

Coming so soon after the last few wonderful moments in his arms, that struck a chord in her with more than usual force. 'It's not so much Mama's opinion on *that* which prevents me, my lord. You must know that the main reason for rejecting that option, if it should ever become one, is that the risks are too great. I stand to lose too much, as an independent woman.'

'In fact, they are not nearly as great as you suppose, but since you are not in the right frame of mind to hear about the alternatives to celibacy, you may like to hear about a different idea that would cause no loss of face. Indeed, it would be much more entertaining than dancing to your mother's tune whenever she calls it. Which is what you're doing at present.'

'I can't deny that. What are you suggesting? And what is it I'm not in the right frame of mind to hear about?'

'Since you ask, it's about the possibility of being my mistress.'

'You're right, my lord. I'm not ready to hear about that.'

'No, I didn't think you would be. Not yet. Nevertheless, Miss Boyce, I do not believe you're going far enough to present yourself as a woman of consequence, either here in Richmond *or* in London. Appearing occasionally with your brood at various public venues is all very well, but you could be singular in so many more ways, as I suspect you would quite like to be, if you were to have me beside you as your escort. Yes, I recall your earlier concern about being known as my latest eccentricity, but I believe it would be seen as the other way round, with some careful management. Besides, we are both secure enough in our habits to rise above silly remarks of that kind. What is more important, Lettie Boyce, is for you to take back the reins into your own hands, stop being controlled by your mother, and show the world that *you* have what other women lack. Uniqueness, style, wit and beauty. I was not entirely funning when I said that you could start a new rage by wearing your spectacles in my company.'

'You make it sound as if I secretly crave a wild social life, my lord. I don't, you know.'

'Not at all. Almack's is not the highlight of my week, either. But how many times have you been able to attend the evenings at the Misses Berry on North Audley Street since you left London? They still hold their evenings for intellectuals, and they still ask after you.'

'Not once since I left. But do you go there, Lord Rayne?'

'Whenever I'm invited. I could escort you and, if you prefer not to stay with your sisters at Chesterfield House, you'd be welcome to stay with my parents and me at Berkeley Square. My brother and sister-in-law would be glad to make up a party to the theatre or the opera. Or if you wished to attend a lecture, my brother and I would escort you, and Bart, too, if he's interested. You could take the town by storm, Miss Boyce, if you chose to.'

'Are you not forgetting that I have pupils to attend to?'

'No, I'm not forgetting. I'm seeing them as an addition to your image. They have their tutors and chaperons. They could all come, too. Just think, they'd make a perfect foil, and they'd provide a perfect reason for you all to be seen out and about, visiting, sightseeing.'

'I don't know what their parents would say.'

'The parents would love it. You'll have new ones begging to enrol with you. I can see you now with a bevy of well-mounted young ladies riding on Rotten Row. They'd all meet eligible men within days, and remember, they were not sent to you because you're like all the rest, but because you're different. You'll not lose any pupils by showing them more of the world than Richmond has to offer. But more to the point, *you* have nothing to lose by showing the world what kind of a woman you are, rather than trying to hide it.'

'And Mama? Can you imagine what she'll say to discredit me?'

Lifting her hand, he kissed her knuckles one by one. 'What do *you* imagine she'll say, sweet lass, when all her acquaintances are raving about the very exclusive and singular Lettie Boyce who rides a superb grey Arab mare, wearing the most divine Hussar habit made by Weston, and gold spectacles, with Rayne beside her, too, and a crowd of handsome *gels* and heaven only *knows...*' his voice took on the yelp of Lady Boyce's rhetoric '...how many chaperons and tutors, all of them Top o' the Trees, you know. You should just *see* them, my *de...ah*!'

'Stop...stop!' Letitia begged him, laughing.

'She'll not be tempted to disown you, believe me. If I know your mama, she'll be the one to claim it was all her doing.'

Still laughing, Letitia was bound to agree. 'I like the idea of taking all the tutors, too. We could take Mr Chatterton. He'd be in his element.'

'We could take Dorna, too. She loves a good show.'

'We could attend some of the celebrations next month.'

'All summer. My parents will be holding at least one ball and several dinners. I'd be honoured to partner you, Lettie.'

'You mean...as your...?'

'As my personal guest, my partner, my woman, whatever would make you feel safest and protected. That's something you've missed since you lost your father, isn't it?'

She nodded. 'Uncle Aspinall has been very good to me, but it's not quite the same. Aunt Minnie is…'

'Yes, but with me beside you, she poses no threat, does she?'

Memories of the lunch came to mind where Rayne had silenced the woman's sour-faced disapproval. 'No, none at all,' she said.

'Then allow me to be your escort, Lettie. I cannot take your father's place, but I could be as protective. I could also be something else to you, if you'd let me get closer.'

'As you did just now?' she whispered.

'As we did just now. Do you need some time to think about that?'

The last of the light had all but disappeared, leaving Rayne's head and shoulders in solid black silhouette against the window, with the smooth planes of cheek and brow just visible beneath a thatch of dark hair. Even in the darkness, she thought, his handsome features had the look of an aristocrat, regular and distinguished. How could she not want such a man by her side for all to see? How could she not feel protected and safe, even after their disastrous first meeting? The idea *did* appeal to her, for if her mother was unlikely to be silenced by simple disobedience, she would certainly be non-plussed by a stylish show of patronage from the Marquess and Marchioness of Sheen, no less. Whether the twins would forgive her remained to be seen.

'I *would* like to think about it,' she said. 'Yes. Thank you, my lord. I can see the advantages but, as a woman, I can also see the risks.'

'That particular risk,' he said, singling out the one in her mind, 'need not keep you awake at night, sweet lass. If it happened, you would marry me.'

'Oh.'

'That surprises you? Do you *still* think I'm playing games?'

'Well, as to that, my lord, I don't quite know what to think except that I'm more used to hearing about the women you've been seen with and then dropped, than those you've offered to marry. I cannot see in what way I shall differ from the rest in that respect. I'm not doubting your sincerity for one moment, only my own inability to hold your attention longer than any other woman. I have to say though,' she continued, warming to the theme, 'that the idea of being a little more…er…audacious…does appeal to me because I don't believe Mama will have a leg to stand on once she saw that I had your family's approval and that I chose to stay with them instead of with her. That would certainly give her something to think about. And I love the idea of taking the whole seminary up to London to mix their education with pleasure. Perhaps we could hire some riding horses from Mr Hall's Livery Stables, could we? I could even *rent* somewhere for us all to stay. Now, why did I not think of that before? That's a perfect idea. And I might even drive my phaeton again, if you were to sit with me. I usually ask Bart, but he's not—'

'Miss Boyce.'

'Yes?'

'Am I to deduce from that, that you have decided to allow me just a little further into your life? On trial, so to speak?'

'It does sound rather like that, doesn't it? I feel sure that if I were to take up your suggestion of being more adventurous and, dare I say it, a little more…er…*extravagant*, I could then…'

'Stylish and glamorous.'

'…begin to dazzle.'

'The audacious Miss Lettie Boyce and her dashing escort, her brilliant tutors, her strikingly lovely and talented pupils.'

She clapped her hands. 'That sounds rather like fun to me. What a pity Miss Melborough would not be with us. It's just the kind of thing she'd—' She stopped suddenly, responding to the capture of her hand, both of them struck by the same ingenious idea.

'She *could* be,' Rayne whispered.

Letitia agreed. 'She could. We'd only have to wait… well…a few weeks perhaps, and then if she's not…oh, dear…I *do* hope she's not.'

'If she's perfectly well, you could ask for her to return. Surely her parents would not insist on her staying all summer in Cheltenham?'

'Bringing her back to join us would let it be seen that all my pupils are of the highest *ton*. Mama would be utterly confounded, and she'd not be able to use Sapphire's disgrace against me if she wasn't *in* disgrace, would she?'

'Indeed she would not, Miss Boyce.' Reaching across through the darkness, he took hold of the greatcoat collar and pulled her towards him, meeting her mouth to take the kiss that awaited him.

'Oh, dear,' she said. 'Surely we cannot have solved all my problems at once, can we? Does this mean that things are beginning to sort themselves out?'

'Oh, I doubt it,' he said, caressing her cheek. 'No, this is just a hiccough. We'll soon find some more complications to make life more exciting, if we look hard enough. Are you ready to go in now?'

'My hair! What did you do with my pins?'

'Left-hand pocket.'

'Oh, so they are. Now, how am I going to see, I wonder?'

'What do you need to see? You know where your hair is. Here, give them to me. Turn round.'

Once again, but this time in almost complete darkness, Rayne acted as lady's maid, raking and twisting her long hair into a tight coil which he pinned up using the pins held between his lips. 'That will cost you another kiss, ma'am,' he said, turning her to face him. 'I'm expensive.'

Swooning in his arms, Perdita tried in vain to remember what she had been told about the impropriety of physical contact, apart from the assistance of a firm hand under her arm. But this was different, and both of them knew it, and these kisses were sweeter than anything she had imagined in the seclusion of her curtained bed. She did not believe any woman, unless she was heartless and cold, could have resisted his demands, but...

Wait a moment, Letitia thought. *Is* she going to resist his demands? Surely she's not going to leap into bed with him after a few kisses, is she? Is that what happens? Is that what I would do?

The quill pen was laid aside as she sat back to watch the lamp-flame's sinuous dance. Yes, it probably is what I would do, she told herself, but perhaps Perdita had better hold back until I know more about it. With a secretive smile, she re-read what she had written about those kisses. The idea of becoming Lord Rayne's newest mistress was by no means as far from her intentions as she had allowed him to believe, but for that to happen so soon would hardly provide her with the body of information she required about the lengthy art of wooing. No, he must be kept waiting until his patience wore thin;

meanwhile, she must not allow him to know how useful he was being in contributing to her literary talent.

It had been a stroke of genius, however, for him to offer help with her new image, a more daring Lettie Boyce whose lights need no longer be hidden under a bushel, whose pupils and staff would be seen and sought by society hostesses, as her sisters were. Now, she would have Lord Rayne's protection against anyone who felt threatened by her intellect, giving her the confidence she needed to wear her spectacles like an unusual fashion accessory and to see where she was going, at last. A small detail, but so very important.

Picking up the pen once more, she dipped it thoughtfully into the satin-black ink, thinking what a pity it was that her mother was more likely to be put out than delighted by the new development. It was a pity, too, that she would never be aware of her eldest daughter's literary achievements, though it was debateable whether that knowledge would embarrass her or make her proud.

The pen began to scratch. If she was going to wait, then so must Perdita. *'No…no,' said Perdita. 'This must not continue, sir.'*

Chapter Nine

At breakfast the next day, Letitia's announcement that they would be spending a few days in London as soon as things could be arranged was greeted by some very ungenteel squeals of excitement, though the reaction of Miss Edina Strachan was quite the opposite. With one look of sheer horror, she pushed back her chair, begged to be excused, and rushed out of the room before anyone could ask her about the problem.

Maura and Lucille, the other two boarders, appeared to have run out of sympathy for their Scottish friend. 'Oh, she *cannot* still be homesick,' said Lucille. 'Not after all this time.'

'It's only been a term and a bit,' said Maura, more reasonably. 'Does she not like the idea of London? I wish she'd tell us what the matter is.'

'I'll go to her,' said Mrs Quayle. 'But don't you two go off to Mrs Price's without me. I want to take another look at her satins, and I have a mind to that brown grosgrain, too. It's just my colour.'

By mid-morning, the Saturday shopping spree into Richmond, one of the week's highlights, resulted in a small mountain of parcels and boxes, each one opened to smiles of approval and admiration: silk stockings at twelve shillings the pair, pink satin evening shoes at five and sixpence, a blue pelisse at seventeen shillings, though the fur trim had cost an extra ten, a matching velvet hat with a turned-up brim, a length of best Lyon velveteen at fourteen shillings a yard, and some of the pretty Pekin striped silk. Edina, who had consented to go, too, could not be persuaded to spend more than one shilling of her weekly allowance. Mrs Nest, the milliner, had been the main source of ribbons and lace, artificial flowers, feathers and beads with which to remodel and beautify bonnets and, as soon as the chocolate pot and cups were returned to the kitchen, the three girls arranged themselves around the parlour table with the contents of workboxes spilled across it.

Letitia left them with the two ladies. She had asked Mr Waverley to call on her to explain why Mr Lake, her publisher at Mercury Press, still had not paid her what she thought was her due. This had been an irritant to her for well over a month for, having begun her third novel, no contract had been sent, nor any sales money for the second.

'What's the problem, Bart?' she asked, waving him to the chair beside hers at the dining-room table. 'Is he losing interest?'

Mr Waverley's good-natured smile was meant to reassure her, but lately Letitia had begun to wonder whether he was negotiating firmly enough with Mr Lake or whether he was simply accepting whatever the man proposed on the basis that she was fortunate to be in print at all. Sitting down, he spread out a sheaf of papers before her. 'No, of course he's not,' he said, 'but the longer he can hold on to any money, the better he likes it. Any business is the same. I've brought the new contract that I collected yesterday, and I'll take it back to him next week to be countersigned. But I have to warn you, Lettie, that his costs have increased.'

'What, without any warning? Poppycock!'

'I'm afraid it's true. The sales from *Waynethorpe Manor* are very healthy, but out of that you have to pay for—'

'For paper, printing, advertising, and anything else he can think of. Yes, I know that, Bart. Have *all* those costs gone up?'

'That's what he tells me. Not including his ten-per-cent commission, which he says, as a goodwill gesture, he will hold down just for you.'

'Hah! How very kind. And what kind of profit is *he* raking in from my success?'

'I don't know. But he reminded me that you'll be liable for any shortfall if the income from sales doesn't cover the production costs of the next one.'

'Well, I *know* that. Does he think it might not, next time?'

'He didn't suggest as much. I think he wants to remind you not to spend all your profits, in case…well, in case it's needed.'

'Typically patronising. What's the man playing at? I think we should go elsewhere if he's going to be difficult.'

'Don't fly off the handle, Lettie. Look, I've brought you the new contract to sign.'

'More to the point, I want to see a list of these higher expenses so that I can see exactly what he's deducted. He did pay you, I suppose?'

'He did, at last.' Producing a brown paper parcel tied with string, he laid it upon the table with a smile. 'Two hundred pounds for one thousand copies. That's a very tidy sum, Lettie, by anybody's standards.'

'If it had been two hundred and fifty, I'd have been more

impressed. Personally, I think he's making a tidy sum out of it, too.'

'Doesn't he deserve to?'

'No,' she said, indignantly, 'he doesn't. And I shall not be signing this immediately, either. I'll read it first and then decide. After my success, I can sell my new one to anyone I choose. He can simmer for a while.'

'Phew!' Blinking like an owl, Bart dipped his head to study her from beneath his brows. 'This is a newly sharpened Lettie Boyce indeed. Who's been coaching you? Rayne, is it?'

Her first impulse was to deny any such thing, but Bart was a good friend, and more than once she had wondered if he might offer to introduce her to some of the tender moments she would like to have experienced. He was clean, well presented and attractive, good-natured and obviously fond of her, yet never once had he given her the kind of look that made her heart beat loud and fast, as Rayne had done, nor had he ever spoken a private word of affection. Now, she felt the inclination to try him out. 'Would you mind if it *was* Rayne?' she asked.

To her relief, he did not pretend to misunderstand her meaning, but nor did he pretend to flirt, as she had given him the chance to do. 'We are good friends, Lettie,' he said, 'and I like Rayne. Always have done, even at school. But you and he make a much better pair that you and I would. Don't take it the wrong way, but you'll always be like a sister to me, nothing more.' He spoke with such sincere gentleness that Lettie was neither surprised nor embarrassed when he picked up her hand, took it to his lips and placed a kiss upon her fingers in a gesture of simple chivalry.

A brisk knock at the door gave no warning, no time to say either enter or wait, and as Lettie snatched her hand away, her snappy retort for the overeager young footman reached the ears of the man close on his heels.

'I *told* you we were not to be disturbed, Sam. Oh...Fin! Good morning.' As she rose to meet her cousin, Mr Waverley hurriedly gathered together the papers and then stood, hugging them close to his chest.

At the same time, it was clear that Lieutenant Fingal Gaddestone had witnessed the tender looks, the hand being snatched away, and the private nature of some business between them. 'I beg your pardon. I am intruding,' he said with no obvious intention of withdrawing. His startled frown quickly changed to a smile by which he hoped to lessen the seriousness of the interruption. Lettie was more concerned that her private papers should be collected than with welcoming him.

'Do come in,' she said, frowning. 'Mr Waverley is just about to leave. Have you two met?'

The introduction was brief and already suffering from the construction put upon Mr Waverley's friendship by her cousin. In the circumstances, Letitia was relieved to see that Uncle Aspinall and her sisters were entering the hall as Mr Waverley left, their noisy greetings soon covering her confusion. She was also relieved to see that Mr Waverley had the presence of mind to take with him the brown paper package.

Assuming that Cousin Fin had come primarily to visit his sister, she detached Miss Gaddestone from the amateur milliners and left them alone to walk round the garden, arm in arm. Uncle Aspinall's intention was to visit the stables. 'Talk to you later,' he whispered to Letitia, with an added wink.

Smiling, she squeezed his hand. 'After lunch?'

'Something light, Lettie. No shellfish. My gout is bad today.'

'I'm sorry, love. Shouldn't you be resting?'

'Yes,' he said, twinkling, 'but your mother thinks you have too many horses, so I'm going to take a look, then I can tell her she's talking rubbish.'

'What does Mama know about my horses? Has she been snooping? Three of the hacks belong to the girls, anyway. She's never shown much interest in my finances before.'

'Don't be hard on her, Lettie. She cares for you, in her own way.'

Letitia's refined grunt implied that she remained unconvinced. But the thought of her mama remaining completely ignorant about her elder daughter's tidy income soothed the irritation of the continuous interference. She joined her sisters in the sunny garden where their murmurs of delight at the planting made her realise how much she had missed their company. Hugging them both, she came close to tears, thanking them for liking her attempts at homemaking.

They laughed, of course. 'Why d'ye think we keep on turning up like bad pennies most weekends?' they said. 'We love it. If only Mama would redecorate in this style, Lettie. Chesterfield House is so *heavy* compared to this lightness.'

Laughing with them, she drew them towards safer ground. 'Now tell me about the latest beaux,' she said. 'Who are they this time?'

She had not expected to elicit anything particularly new on this subject, but in the space of two weeks it appeared that the twins had put Lord Rayne out of mind and replaced him with two extremely handsome, well-connected, well-bred, wealthy and available young men only recently returned from the Peninsular Wars ahead of Marquess Wellington. Amidst giggles, expostulations, descriptions and contradictions, Letitia gained the impression that the twins, already madly in love, had been in their company every day and every evening, and that Mama thought they were quite heavenly, their manners perfect, their credentials faultless, at least in England.

With some understandable trepidation, Letitia asked, 'So you've not seen much of Lord Rayne?'

'Rayne doesn't get a look in,' said Garnet, dismissively.

'To be more accurate,' said Persephone, 'we haven't seen him at any of the assemblies for ages. Mama insists that his interest is still on us, but we know it isn't at all. He's only ever been a friend, never a serious contender. He's never been known to keep a woman for very long, so it's silly of her to get up hopes for us. We never did.' For Persephone, the quieter of the two, that was quite a long explanation. So long, in fact, that it left both her sisters temporarily without words.

Letitia took a deep breath, her fingers pulling at the fringe on the edge of her shawl. 'Then if that's really the way of things,' she said, 'I have an admission to make.'

'Oh, we know about *that*,' said Garnet, kindly, removing the fringe from her sister's fingers. 'We were not going to speak of it until you did because we know how annoying you must find it to be told you must not show any interest in him. As if Mama could insist on *that*, indeed.'

'Mama told you not to speak of him?'

The twins nodded, but Persephone went on. 'We both know Rayne is more interested in you, so if you think you may be treading on our toes, you can take it from us that you're not. You may be treading on Mama's, but—'

'But that wouldn't be difficult, would it?' said Garnet, giggling. 'You are in the safest place here, Lettie dearest, where she can't get at you.'

Letitia understood by that, that the twins knew nothing of

their mother's controversial visit last Sunday, so she said nothing to contradict their belief. She saw no harm, however, in telling them how Lord Rayne had taken her up in his curricle, how she found him good company, how she was on friendly terms with his Richmond family and how, if she were to stay with his parents in Berkeley Square quite soon, they must not take it amiss, in view of Mama's opposition.

'Not a bit of it,' Persephone assured her. 'That would be further than *we* got with him. He never invited *us* to Berkeley Square.'

'Is he going to ask you to be his mistress, Lettie?' said Garnet, unable to keep the excitement out of her voice.

'You've been reading too many novels, love,' said Letitia, laughing. 'But what would you say if he did? Would you be shocked?'

'Envious!' said the twins in one voice. 'Is he going to? Will you accept him? Will he buy you another house? Do tell us. Mama would *explode*!'

'That's what bothers me,' whispered Letitia.

There was a pause. 'He's asked you?' said Garnet.

'No. Mentioned it, that's all. Just a mention.'

With affection, they watched the blush creep into her cheeks, brightening her eyes. Garnet leaned forward, speaking intensely. 'What we said just now about him not staying with any woman for long, well…forget it. He'll be looking for a wife at his age. That's our guess. And he's not stupid enough to let someone as good as you slip through his fingers, Lettie. Men must play the field, you know, before they find what they're looking for, and if Rayne wants you, take no notice of Mama. We are bound to toe the line because we're still under her wing—'

'Who's mixing her metaphors?' murmured Persephone.

'But you're not. You can please yourself. We'd just *love* to be somebody's mistresses, but it's not likely to happen.'

'Not with two of us.'

'Unless we shared,' said Garnet, dolefully.

'So,' said Letitia, 'if I were to rent a place in London for my tutors and pupils, and Gaddy and Mrs Quayle, would you come out with us?'

'Of course. Anywhere you like. Is that why they're remaking their bonnets? For a London visit?'

Letitia nodded.

'Then you should tell Uncle Aspinall. He'll find you a place, but you'll have to hurry, with all the celebrations planned for summer. The rentable properties will soon be snapped up if you don't get a move on.'

It occurred to Letitia then that perhaps she ought not to have spoken so soon about her plans, for now Gaddy would be sure to tell her brother, who would mention it to Aunt Minnie, who would rush to Lady Boyce with the news. And then Mama would not only wonder how she was able to afford all her horses and carriages but also how she was able to purchase the lease on a house in the middle of town at a time when everyone else was doing the same. Could she look forward to yet another meddlesome visit?

Although the twins knew nothing about Lady Boyce's visit to Richmond, her elder brother Penfold Aspinall certainly did. After checking her horses and stables as her father would have done, and after a lunch of cold tongue, baked ham, pigeon pie and salad, he took Letitia into the garden for a private chat. Telling her she must not take too seriously any of her mother's threats concerning Sapphire Melborough or the seminary, he reminded her of how his sister made a great deal of fuss and noise to get her own way. She had been that way from birth, he told her, adding that he should know about that better than anyone.

Having been on the receiving end of the set-down, Letitia was not wholly persuaded by his encouragement. How could he be so sure?

'The real reason she doesn't want you seeing Rayne is because of his reputation with women, and you being here on your own, unprotected and—'

'Independent, you mean.'

'No, unprotected, love. That's what concerns her. She still looks on you as a green girl, unfamiliar with men's ways.'

'Then why has she encouraged him to see the twins so often?'

'Tolerated, not encouraged. Because they're there with her, under her eye. And because there are two of them, Lettie, each looking after the other. She knows he can't have them both, and you know how they stick together like glue. They're safe enough. She also knows that the louder she shouts about Rayne being close to making one of them an offer, the quicker he'll back off. You're not safe, in her eyes. She doesn't want what happened to her to happen to you, too.'

'What? What *did* happen to her?'

'Oh, Lord, I've said too much, as usual.'

'No, you haven't. Tell me. I need to know.'

'Well, keep this under your bonnet, Lettie,' he said, lifting a straggling briar for her to pass beneath. 'It was while she was engaged to your father. I took her to a house party at the Listermans' down in Sussex, and she was miffed that your father had not gone with her. Some excuse or other...'

'He hated house parties.'

'Well, she jumped the gate and got into another man's bed. That's just like her. Cut off her nose to spite her face. She was a virgin, too.'

'Mama took a *lover*? To spite my father?'

'Not exactly to spite him. He knew nothing about it. But you know what she's like. Acts first, thinks later. I didn't know exactly what had happened until afterwards when the man began to pester her for more. Then she asked me to go and keep him quiet. So I did. Peacekeeper Penfold. I took with me a pretty young lass of very good lineage who is now the present Lady Melborough. Diverted his attention, you see.'

'The one who lives here, up on the hill?'

'The very same, love. Sir Francis is quite a bit older than her. More your mother's age. He's still frisky, too, by all accounts. Anyway, Euphemia married your father soon afterwards, so no one was any the wiser except Sir Francis Melborough. Certainly not Sir Leo Boyce.'

'So you don't think…?'

'Ah, I know what you're thinking. But, no, love.' He stopped beside the large cold-frames and stared inside. 'No, you were born a full year later. No connection whatever.'

'I see. Then could that be the reason why she doesn't care to visit Richmond, for fear of a chance meeting?'

'It sounds a bit extreme, but it could be. Her first visit was on a Sunday morning while everyone in Richmond was at church, wasn't it?'

'Except the Melboroughs, as it happened. But it might explain why she refused to attend our concert at their house.'

'And why she was *so* furious with the Melborough girl.'

'She told you what she'd said to her?'

'Yes, and expected me to agree. But I didn't. I reminded

her instead of a certain young lady at a house party in Sussex. And I told her it was your business and that of the Melboroughs, not hers.'

'Thank you, Uncle.'

'Cucumbers are doing nicely, Lettie.'

'Yes, we're growing tomatoes, too. Somewhere. Is what you've told me the reason she doesn't want me to live here, Uncle Aspinall?'

'Aye, lass. That, and living without proper protection.'

'And I suppose she would not regard Lord Rayne as proper protection?'

'You're old enough to know your own mind,' he said, 'and that's what I've told her. There's nothing wrong with Rayne that a good wife won't put right. Show me these tomatoes of yours, Lettie.'

'Over here,' she said, thinking that what he'd divulged to her about Sir Francis Melborough might help to explain why he'd been foolish enough to put his arm around Euphemia Boyce's daughter.

Before they rejoined the others, Letitia sounded her uncle out about available properties in London to rent for the summer season. He promised to help, though it was his lack of curiosity about who was to pay for an establishment large enough for upwards of fourteen people that made Letitia suspect that he must have come to his own conclusions. She saw no reason to query them, whatever they were.

Her conversation with Lieutenant Gaddestone, however much she had hoped to keep it both public and brief, was more to be endured than enjoyed. His untimely, and unnecessary, interruption that morning had confirmed a sneaking suspicion that he had returned from naval duties more full of himself than when she had known him as a youth, and this was not a side of him with which she felt comfortable. Nor did she appreciate it when he assumed the role of elder brother to a rather unworldly orphan.

She tried to curb her impatience, not to let it show. 'Mr Waverley,' she told him in answer to his remark, 'is our accounts and mathematics tutor as well as being my good friend. In those capacities we often have private business matters to discuss.'

'Oh, don't for one moment think that I disapprove of a young lady in your position accepting help when it's offered, Lettie. But one must observe the proprieties even *more* strictly when there are other young ladies in your care, and—'

'Cousin Fin, thank you for your concern, but I assure you it is entirely unnecessary. I am perfectly familiar with the proprieties, as all my staff are, and I have not given a single thought to your approval or disapproval of what I do. Now, shall we return to the others?'

'Oh dear, I see I have offended you.'

'Not at all, cousin. I shall not be in the least offended as long as we both respect each other's need to conduct our own affairs as we please. I am not quite the green girl I once was, you see.'

'Nevertheless, I would be failing in my duty if I did not try to warn you about single young men who try to make themselves indispensable…'

'To people like me? Then consider me warned, Fin. There, now you've done your duty. Feel better?'

'It pleases you to make light of my concerns, Lettie, but I would feel better if you were to come to me for help.'

'I don't need any more help, thank you, cousin. Uncle

Aspinall is the one to whom I turn for advice, and I shall continue to do so.'

'And Lord Rayne?'

'What about him?'

'Is he in your confidence, too?'

'Cousin Fin, I don't know what the navy years have done to you, but they seem to have given you leave to probe into matters that are not your concern. Now, if you're ready, we'll go and join the others. Uncle Aspinall will want to be going soon. He and Aunt Minnie are expecting guests this weekend.'

'I'm sorry you see it that way, Lettie. I have only your best interests at heart, and I have seen something of the world, you know.' When he saw that she was not about to reply to that, he continued. 'Before we rejoin the others, may I ask a favour of you on behalf of my sister?'

'Of course. Whatever can it be? Does she require a holiday?'

'Not that. It's her room, Lettie. I believe she has only one.'

'She has a bedroom, and free access to all the other rooms, as I do.'

'Yes, that's what I thought. Then I wonder if I might ask if she could be given a private room for her own personal use. Her own parlour, you understand. It would make such a difference if she could have a space to call her own. To entertain a guest, perhaps?'

'Has Gaddy asked you to speak to me?'

'No, indeed she has not. She would never complain.'

'Probably because she has so little to complain of, cousin. Sadly, I do not have any spare rooms, since we use them all every day. Of course, if you were to feel the need to contribute something towards Gaddy's upkeep, or help her with a little pin-money, perhaps? That would be much appreciated, and I'm sure she'd not refuse a small donation from time to time. Nor would I, as soon as you're in funds.'

'Ahem! Er...yes, indeed. As soon as my prize money is made available to me, I shall certainly begin to contribute towards her expenses. Gladly. You may depend on that, Cousin Lettie.'

Yes, she thought, you were not left penniless, either, when your parents died, and dear Gaddy would not be in need of my charity if you had made better provision for her before you went away.

Given a captive audience for the better part of an hour, Lieutenant Gaddestone relieved his failure with Letitia by regaling them all with an account of his successes, promotions, commendations, and future plans to buy a house here in Richmond for himself, his servants, horses and carriages *and*, he assured them, looking directly at Miss Gaddestone, for his dear sister, too.

Gaddy beamed back at him with gratitude and continued to stroke the lace edging on her sleeve. Letitia, on the other hand, was not inclined to join in the polite applause that greeted this announcement, being suddenly overtaken by the uncharitable thought that an extra room for Gaddy might easily be used for an entirely different purpose whenever the worldly Lieutenant Gaddestone needed a bed in Richmond. The more she thought about it, the more she was convinced that there could be more to his request than Gaddy's comfort, especially when he had shown so little interest in her welfare until now. As for expecting him to make a financial contribution, she was just as highly sceptical, and the small crease in her brow that had watched the departure of the carriage down Paradise Road took quite some time to disappear.

* * *

As if by arrangement, a diversion occurred to steer her thoughts away from the serious business of the morning when Lord Rayne arrived to say that two new riding horses were waiting at Sheen Court for the approval of Miss Lucille Ballantyne and Miss Maura Derwent. Already dressed in preparation for an afternoon ride, the four ladies accompanied Lord Rayne across the park, with Miss Edina Strachan looking distinctly out of sorts. Assuming that this might be because her old mount was not to be replaced by a more showy creature, Letitia had lent her the hunter to ride, though she was still visibly subdued.

The two new horses had arrived only that morning. One chestnut mare of fourteen hands, the other a dark bay gelding, both with excellent manners and breeding, as well as an interest in discovering whether their new owners would be as overweight as their previous one. 'Lady Enslack is an excellent horsewoman,' Lord Rayne told them, 'and these two are very well schooled. But they're not up to her weight, so she's letting them go. I thought you might like to try them out in the paddock. My brother and his family are eager to see how you like each other.'

Rarely had a trial passed so amicably as in those next two hours when the Elyot family joined in, and Edina, too, to practise over small jumps in the parkland beyond Sheen Court, to gallop and canter, and to accept all the help they were offered by two masters of the art. Not entirely to her liking, Letitia was guarded zealously by Lord Rayne for, without her spectacles, she was not aware of dangers in time to avoid them. Although she understood the reasons for his cautions as she leapt over hurdles and logs only a stride or two behind him, she found it both unusual and galling to be given constant warnings. What was worse, the three young Elyot children, all of them good riders, were beginning to think she was inexperienced, which was far from the case. Five-year-old Augusta loudly commiserated, having only recently been freed from the indignities of a leading-rein.

While Lord and Lady Elyot took the three young ladies back to the house for refreshments, Rayne escorted Letitia towards the stable where the two redundant mounts had been unsaddled. Stable lads and grooms carried buckets and rugs across the yard with only cursory glances in her direction, turning deaf ears to the snappy exchanges between the two as if they'd heard it often enough from Lord and Lady Elyot.

Holding her palm level with the ground, Letitia scolded. 'I've been riding since I was *so* high and I can count the times on the fingers of one hand when I've fallen off at a jump. There was simply no need for…what…where?'

Wasting no words on an answer, Rayne guided her without ceremony into the deep straw of the nearest loose box, closing the door upon the scene outside, enclosing them in the warm aroma of horses and the shadows of high barriers. She swayed against him, her feet hampered by the straw, her eyes straining to find any detail that would help her to focus before she was pulled roughly into his arms, her next spate of protests stopped.

Her mind whirled and steadied, then slowly closed down, sinking into the deep sensual place inside her that responded like fire on dry tinder at the first touch of his lips. It was not like that first time, fraught with anger and discomfort, nor was it like last night's kisses in the summerhouse, carefully regulated towards her inexperience. This time, it was as if both of them recognised the spontaneous and uncontrollable hunger for which the quarrelling was no more than a temporary release, a need that had perhaps grown during the night, directing every moment since then towards an excuse, any excuse at all, to satisfy it.

No explanations were asked or given, nor was there any time for pretence of maidenly reticence, the tenderness of the summerhouse kisses having wakened her to a vision waiting just beyond her reach, and now she was willing to be led to it without delay. But delay was inevitable in the meagre time allowed to them, and both felt the seething frustration of wanting more when their lips parted at last, leaving them trembling with the shock.

Letitia, to whom nothing like this had ever happened before, was ready to believe that Rayne would think little of it. But as in so much else regarding her knowledge of men, she was mistaken in this, too. And if she had expected some sort of flippant remark to put her at her ease, she was to make the surprising discovery that their fiercely passionate encounter had done nothing to moderate his impatience with her. Quite the contrary. Taking her by the wrists, he held her back against the high side of the loose box in an unnecessary show of restraint, as if she were an adversary instead of a lover.

'Saints alive, woman!' he whispered, harshly. 'You bring out the worst in me as well as the best. Heaven knows, I could put you across my knee. I was trying my damnedest to protect you out there, to keep you from injuring yourself. Little goose-cap!'

'I know,' she whispered. 'I know. I'm sorry.'

'And now I want to…no…no! That won't do.' Releasing his grip on her wrists, he drew them to his chest. 'That won't do at all. I'm losing my head, Lettie Boyce, and it's all your fault.'

'Tell me,' she said. 'Tell me what you wanted to do.'

His reply was slow to emerge, seeking a way. 'No, I cannot. It would not be fit talk for an innocent young lady's ears. You'd be disgusted.'

'Would I? I think I've moved on in the last few days, you know. But then, if you think I would not like it much, you're probably right, my lord. You know so much more about this kind of thing than me.' Even in the dim light, her coyness did not escape him; the tilt and turn of her head, the flutter of lashes and the untypically meek tone of voice.

'Yes, I do, minx. And when I share my *boundless* store of knowledge with you, it will not be in a stable or a summer-house, nor will there be a time limit. It will be in a bed. A large bed. And I did not say that you would not like it much, I said you would not approve of the *talk*. Once I have you in my bed, we shall be doing very little of that.'

'Oh, I see. May I be allowed to put my hat straight, please?'

Taking a step away, he watched the sinuous curve of her back and the outline of her high breasts under the habit, the reflection of light on the silvery hair resting on the collar, the graceful hands adjusting and pinning. Reaching out, he took her narrow waist in his hand, drawing her close again. 'Wayward, top-lofty creature,' he said. 'Still balking at my attempts to help, aren't you? Eh? Could you be a little less intense about protecting your independence now, do you think? You'll lose nothing by it. I want to be seen as your pro-tector, and I want *you* to be seen as my woman. Is that too much to ask?'

'No, my lord. I must try a little harder. Forgive me, I'm unused to it. And I *would* like to be seen as your woman. In fact, I think I may quite get used to the idea, in time.'

'Do you mean that?'

'Yes, really. Shall we begin again?' Meekly, she placed her hands upon his shoulders, learning to bend herself like a bow.

In view of the readjusted hat, his kiss this time was gentler. Yet in that short space of time, Letitia realised once again that the behaviour of the romantic heroes in her novels was based on imaginings with no more relevance to fact than fairy-tales, and that perhaps the reason for their success was because of her understanding of women's emotions and her ability to express them convincingly. Men, it seemed, were not as straightforward or predictable as she had believed them to be, if Lord Rayne was anything to go by.

After taking tea with the Elyots and riding back to Paradise Road with Rayne and the girls, Letitia's demeanour was so compliant and appreciative in every respect that he suspected her of intentionally overdoing it. Which she was. She had not, she told him on parting, quite got the hang of it yet. To which his reply fell some way short of the gentlemanly or the indulgent lover, though Letitia was quick to hide her smile.

Her writing that evening flowed as never before. Page after page was covered like parched ground after rain, soaking up her newest experiences, luscious with words and emotions as if her heart had slowly begun to blossom, promising fruit for the future and making her more eagerly impatient for the harvest; the next episode.

Sunday morning brought her back to earth with a crash and its usual measure of drama from Mrs Quayle next door, who came rushing round to Number 24 before Letitia had finished dressing to say that one of her charges was missing. It was Miss Edina Strachan.

'Her clothes and portmanteau are gone,' she wailed, 'without a word to anyone. How could she *do* such a thing?'

'Has her bed been slept in?' said Letitia, pushing her bare feet into slippers.

'She put a pillow into it,' said the plump little lady. 'Everything else is tidy. She's taken all her allowance, too. Where would she have gone?'

'She may have decided to go home.'

'To Guildford? To her grandparents? Oh, I don't know about that, Lettie. Why could she not have said?' Mrs Quayle's white lace morning-cap bobbed and fluttered, her face crinkled in distress as she took the artful deception as a personal affront to her hospitality.

The additional arrival of Lucille and Maura, with hair hanging loose, went some way to solving the vexed question of Edina's whereabouts. Clutching a small grey square of newsprint, they laid it down upon Letitia's counterpane and smoothed out its folds. 'We found it down by the side of her bed,' said Lucille. 'On the floor.'

'Torn out of Friday's *Morning Post*,' said Maura, with finality.

'We think it may be where—'

'Yes,' said Letitia, frowning at it. 'Thank you, girls, but we're—'

'Please read it, ma'am. We think it's quite possible she's gone to Portsmouth. Look, it gives a list of the ships that have returned to harbour in the last few days, and those that are expected.'

'And one of them is underlined. There, see? The frigate, *Centaur.*'

'Edina knows about frigates, ma'am. She told us.'

'Lots of times,' added Maura, under her breath.

Letitia took up the scrap and read it closely, her face visibly paling. 'To Portsmouth?' she whispered. 'Does she have a brother in the navy?'

Lucille was convinced otherwise. 'No, ma'am. A *lover.*'

'Oh, don't be…*what*? Would she? Could she? Surely not.'

'She doesn't have a brother,' said Mrs Quayle, 'but this could be why she's been so upset recently. Someone in the navy?'

'Yes,' said Maura, 'and she's gone to find the *Centaur*…'

'To seek the man she loves…'

'And then they'll have to elope, and…'

The story was moving too fast for Letitia. 'Thank you, girls. You've provided us with some good information here. Now you go and finish dressing for church, have your breakfast, and Mrs Quayle will join you in a few moments. Thank you for your help. We'll soon find her.'

The door closed upon the two satisfied sleuths, and the echoes of their excited chatter floated downstairs, leaving Letitia and Mrs Quayle to stare blankly at each other in some astonishment for the second consecutive Sunday.

'What's happening here?' Letitia said. 'Are we going to start losing one pupil a week? What's the matter with them? First Sapphire, now Edina. I'm not doing terribly well at keeping them, am I?'

For all her initial fluster, Mrs Quayle could see how much her friend was affected and was quick to assume her more usual practicality. 'Nonsense, dear,' she said, 'they're young girls with heads full of romance, aren't they? Now let's just sit down and think this through.' Settling herself upon Letitia's *chaise longue*, she took a deep breath. 'Today is Sunday, so she's not going to be on a stagecoach to anywhere, is she? Even if it passed through Richmond, which it doesn't. So the only thing she *could* have caught is last night's mail that picks up at Number 9 King Street after dark. That'll be the long-distance that goes from London down to Portsmouth, you know. Edina went up to bed early last night, complaining of a head. You know how off-colour she was all day yesterday. I was not too surprised. She took a cup of hot chocolate with her.' Her wide eyes expressed concern as the events began to link up.

'You didn't look in on her later?'

'Yes, I peeped in. It was dark. I saw the lump in her bed.'

'And you heard no sound? No door closing?'

'Nothing.' Mrs Quayle's lace cap flapped as she shook her head.

'Then if that's what's happened, she must have bought her ticket beforehand. As you go downstairs, tell Sam to run down to the posting office and find out who got aboard the mail to Portsmouth last night, and get them to look in the ledger for her name. I want to know what time it arrives, and the route it took.' The last few words were called out as Mrs Quayle disappeared onto the landing. 'Orla, we're going down to Portsmouth. Find us both something suitably grand and comfortable to travel in, and pack our portmanteaux for overnight.'

'Yes, ma'am.'

'But first, run down to the stables and tell Mr Benjamin that I need to speak to him immediately, if you please.'

'Yes, ma'am.'

'I'd better tell Mrs Brewster, too. See if Miss Gaddestone is about.'

'Yes, ma'am.'

'She'd better *not* be eloping,' Letitia muttered, kicking off the slippers. 'Underage and without her parents' consent. Little idiot.'

Chapter Ten

Tucking the torn-out square of newsprint into her reticule, Letitia heaved a small sigh of annoyance and turned for relief to the window of the coach where trees and hedges flew past, and approaching coaches seemed to disappear before she could see them. At least, she thought with a guilty satisfaction, this was sure to be a more comfortable ride than the one poor Edina must have endured in the mailcoach, squashed between two others, faced by three more, all probably snoring, grumbling or chattering noisily. In the darkness, there would have been nothing for her to see and only the briefest of stops to change horses.

Her own reticule, a kid bag with long straps for security, bulged with five- and one-pound notes, sovereigns and crowns, for every journey had its price. Edina's saved weekly allowances would be scarcely enough to see her through this adventure. Was that what it was? Just an adventure?

No, whatever Edina was, thought Letitia, no one could call her adventurous. Quiet and introverted, obviously unhappy, she had performed well at the concert, playing a medley of haunting Scottish airs to do with love, and the loss of it. Why had none of them seen the problem? Who was this naval man she was expecting to join? And where in Portsmouth would they be now? Or would they already have moved on? That she herself ought to have taken time to talk to Edina gave her no room for complacency, for she had been bound up in her own affairs to the detriment of her pupils. She had not noticed the smallest signs in Sapphire, either, to her shame.

'Why are we stopping?' she said to Orla.

'It's a tollgate, ma'am.'

A small thatched building appeared by the side of the road where a stout gate barred the way. Touching his cap in deference, the tollgate keeper approached the window. This was a superior conveyance, its occupants sure to be gentry with a pair of high-stepping greys like those.

Letitia let the window down. 'Good morning. How much?'

'For a town coach and pair, m'lady,' said the man, casting an eye over the gleaming panels and shining brass lamps, 'that'll be ninepence.'

'That will take us through the next one, too, will it?'

'Through the next two, m'lady,' he said, scribbling the details of the transaction on to his pad of tickets. 'Going far, are ye?'

'To Portsmouth,' she replied, passing him a handful of coins. 'Give the ticket to my groom on the rumble-seat, if you please.'

'Very good, m'lady. Not a lot of traffic today. Pleasant journey to ye.' With a wink at Letitia's pretty maid, he passed the ticket to the groom and went to open the gate, watching in admiration as the chariot swept past at a smart trot.

Letitia sat back against the soft upholstered seat and packed a cushion under her elbow while Orla pulled the window up with the leather strap. There were no seats opposite, only a slatted blind through which they could just make out the shape of the coachman's high box-seat. The large side-windows were curtained, fringed and tasselled, the floor carpeted and clean, a far cry from the functional crowded mailcoach. With so light a load, the pair of greys would make better speed than the team of six needed to draw the heavy mail with its many passengers and all their luggage. Although it would pay no toll, its horses were changed every ten miles or so. Edina's man, whoever he was, must be worth it for her to suffer willingly so much discomfort for his sake, Letitia thought.

Earlier, Sam had returned from the posting office in Richmond bearing the news that Miss Strachan's name was in the ledger and that her ticket to Portsmouth, bought on Saturday morning, had cost her twenty-five shillings, which she must have saved for weeks, if not months. How, Mrs Quayle had asked, was Edina going to pay for any accommodation except of the meanest sort? Miss Gaddestone did not think Edina would have thought that far ahead. Nor did Letitia.

Nevertheless, in spite of the concern, the guilt, and the sympathy that invaded Letitia's peace of mind, there remained the more unsentimental prospect of being able to observe Edina's determination and courage to join the man she loved at any price, and to use those observations in Perdita's story. One way or another, Letitia did not intend this experience to be entirely wasted on a wild goose chase to rescue a young lady who would probably not thank them for rescuing her.

A large part of the journey was taken up with thoughts about her own gradually mellowing relationship with Lord Rayne, the man she had been quite adamant she could never grow to like. There was no doubt that she was playing a very dangerous game by allowing herself to respond to him, for although she had intended it to be a device by which she might regain control of a difficult situation, the truth of the matter was that her heart had already begun to take the lead, leaving her head to catch up as best it may.

Asked if she was becoming addicted to the need of him, she would have refuted the suggestion hotly. Asked if she was falling in love, she would have scoffed at the idea. Wasn't love supposed to be deliciously comfortable, and weren't lovers supposed to be starry-eyed and agreeable? No, this thinking of him, past, present and future, could not be love, for the two of them had rarely agreed on anything except during those magically intimate moments.

The journey that would have taken the mail about six hours took the competent Mr Benjamin less than five, including two stops to change horses and to refresh herself and Orla. The first stop was at the Kings Arms at Godalming where Mr Moon the proprietor bowed and scraped, giving orders that only the soundest pair be put to the splendid town coach with the black-and-yellow wheels. Likewise at the Dolphin at Petersfield where the ostlers vied for the honour of harnessing the new pair and for pocketing Letitia's generous tip.

The long five-mile drag to the top of Butser Hill was fatiguing even for fresh horses, and Letitia insisted on a rest at the top from where they could see beyond the steep sloping sides as far as Portsmouth harbour, the Isle of Wight, and the open silver sea in the furthest distance. Ten more miles took them downhill to Horndean and another rest before the last eight miles to Portsmouth itself by mid-afternoon.

Larger by far than Richmond, the town had expanded as a port and naval base beyond the old fortifications that surrounded the old parts like a girdle. In the town centre, the narrow streets thronged with navy men of every rank, with merchants and suppliers, dock labourers and shrieking women, rumbling wagons, yapping dogs and the incessant cry of seagulls wheeling over masts and rooftops.

Mr Benjamin drove the coach straight down the High Street to the town's best hotel, the George, where Lord Nelson had stayed briefly in 1805. Hardly had Letitia's feet touched the cobbled courtyard before the innkeeper and his white-aproned wife were there to greet her, offering their best room and a private parlour, and a meal as soon as she was ready. One glance at the equipage, at her fur-trimmed pelisse and matching grey silk bonnet, not to mention the liveried groom and pretty maid, told them all they needed to know about the status of their guest.

The enclosed yard swarmed with ostlers and stable boys, horses and carriages, echoing with the clank of buckets, shouts and whistles, the clatter of hooves. Inside the comfortable low-beamed inn, the warmth was heavy with wood and tobacco smoke. The aroma of roast beef reminded the two women that they had missed Sunday lunch at Paradise Road that day. Housemaids and bootboys scurried past, doors opened and closed, bells rang, voices called, porters staggered over luggage and waiters swayed under trays held above their heads. Up a flight of polished stairs, they were led along a creaking passage to the door of a sizeable panelled bedroom, where mullioned windows looked out across the peaceful vegetable garden at the rear of the house next door.

'It's much too noisy at the front, ma'am,' said the landlord's wife, opening a small door in the corner of the room that gave them a glimpse of a small chamber with a narrow bed by the wall. 'Here's your maid's room and a closet for your clothes,' she said, beaming, proud of the extra facility. 'Your parlour is downstairs, ma'am, and the lad will be here with your bags at any moment. Shall I have a tea-tray sent up?' Nothing, it seemed, was going to be too much trouble.

A cup of tea was all there was time for, however, Letitia being determined not to waste a moment on creature comforts while Edina was adrift in a place like Portsmouth at the weekend, with dangers from every quarter. It was one thing, she said to Orla between sips, for them to be snugly protected in the town's best hotel, but it would be quite a different story for a lone young woman with very little money in her reticule.

Edina's parents and grandparents would have been frantic with worry, if they had known, but Letitia had decided that for them to be told at this stage would not help matters, since there was nothing that either set of relatives could do that she herself could not do more efficiently. Besides, it would take days for a message to reach her parents in Scotland.

Their first duty, she said, was to go out and search while there was still enough light before sunset, and a message was sent to Jamie, the groom, to meet them downstairs. He was a Portsmouth lad and would know where to go. He also had a soft spot for Orla.

Letitia had anticipated this moment, if not with dread, then with no pleasure, either, never having put a foot over the threshold of a tavern in her life, but having a fair idea of what to expect. With this in mind, she saw an advantage in changing from her elegant fur-trimmed pelisse to a very plain ser-viceable brown one with a straw poke-bonnet that would help to shield her face from insolent stares. Tying a long scarf round her bare neck, she regarded herself in the mirror, hoping to see nothing remarkable that would attract anyone's attention, yet respectable enough to show a woman of breeding with her maid and manservant. The plain gold spectacles, which would have been so useful to her on this occasion, went on and came off twice before being stowed away with most of the money she had brought. If she wished to avoid attracting attention, the spectacles were definitely not the accessory to wear.

The next two uncomfortable hours opened Letitia's eyes to the seamier side of Portsmouth life as she trawled through one inn after another, and some of the many boarding-houses, too, that were situated along the waterfront and in the narrow back streets. At this time of the weekend, the town appeared to be overflowing with guests come here to meet people off the ships or to deliver them, and although Orla and Jamie did much of the visual searching for her, the enquiries were left to her. But no one remembered seeing a young lady answering to Miss Edina Strachan's description, and while some replies were politely sympathetic, others were suspicious and rude, or asked a deal too many personal questions that had more to do with Letitia herself than with Edina. Verbally, she was well able to hold her own, but the relentless innuendo, intimidation and sly suggestions began to take the polished edge off her natural good manners, and she could hardly wait to sit a while and regain her temper.

After the first disappointing hour, Jamie had a suggestion to make. 'Do we know for certain whether the *Centaur* has arrived yet, ma'am? Has Miss Strachan's man actually signed off, or is he still expected?'

'I don't really know,' she replied, turning her head away

from the lewd remarks of a passing bunch of sailors. 'I'm assuming it will have docked. How do we find out for sure?'

The intrepid Jamie had the answer and, after disappearing into a noisily crowded tavern across the road, came bounding out a few minutes later with his hat in his hand and his hair ruffled. 'The *Centaur* came in last Thursday, ma'am. All the young midshipmen are in there.' He tipped his head towards the screams of laughter and the screech of a fiddle. 'But there's one who's gone off with a woman.'

'Gone? Missing, you mean? Absconded?'

'They won't know for certain until tomorrow, ma'am. But the woman he's with is a local lass, so he's probably not Miss Strachan's young man. Of course, her man might be a lieu-tenant or some other rank, but these chaps don't know much about what lieutenants get up to while they're ashore.'

'Then it looks as if we shall have to keep on searching, Jamie. Now, which of the inns have we not seen yet?'

'It's getting late, ma'am,' said Orla. 'Would you not prefer to eat and take a rest, and continue at first light tomorrow?'

'There's still some light left,' said Letitia, looking across at the dark shapes of boats and masts swaying gently on a mirror of apricot pink. Deeply troubled, she did not see how she could abandon the search knowing that Edina would face a night in this dreadful place, probably alone. 'Let's just walk up here. Where are we now, Jamie?'

'This is Broad Street, ma'am. It leads up to The Point.'

'One last try, then. We may just be lucky.'

Jamie and Orla exchanged a troubled glance, neither of them daring to suggest that Portsmouth Point was not the place for a respectable woman to be seen on a Sunday evening. Certain taverns were where men were paid their week's wages and, in spite of the laws against Sunday trading, those wages were all too easily liquefied, gambled away, stolen or paid to prostitutes. The Point was a curved spur of property-covered land from where the watermen ferried husbands and lovers to their ships after last farewells. To Letitia, it seemed to be worth her making another effort before darkness fell, for the idea of abandoning a genteel young woman to her fate might be the stuff of romantic novels, but had little to do with reality.

Predictably, the narrow street was already crowded, every door spilling out bawling women, children, dogs and drunks, rollicking and rolling towards the gap between buildings where could be seen the tall sails and the rigging of ships, rocking and rattling in the breeze. Small boats swarmed round them like flies, their occupants waving to children weeping in their mothers' arms and to women clutching at their bonnets.

'Surely this is not where she'll be, ma'am,' said Orla.

'She may be,' Letitia insisted. 'I have to go and see.'

The Ship Tavern was on one side, Moses Levy the Money-lender on the other, between the two an open space where a wooden-legged man scraped a fiddle for a jolly couple to dance to, porters heaved trunks, and a young woman was being carried out by two sailors in white trousers and blue jackets.

'That's her!' Letitia cried, making a dash towards the group.

But it was not her, only an unconscious girl of the same age.

'Where are you taking her?' she asked the one whose hands were hooked under the girl's limp arms.

'Home, ma'am,' he said. 'She's me sister.'

Letitia turned away, not knowing whether it was the truth or a lie. 'Will you take a look in there, Jamie? Or shall I go in? I will, if you prefer to stay here with Orla.'

'Lawks, no, ma'am, you ain't going in there. Here, you sit on this barrel, both of you, while I go inside.' Confidently, he strode off.

Sitting in the doorway of a fruit and vegetable shop, a woman smoking a clay pipe held their attention for a while before a loud burst of laughter from the door of the Ship made them turn in alarm. A crowd of sailors tumbled out on to the cobbles, each of them supported by women whose state of undress left Letitia and Orla in no doubt of their profession. Before either of them could move away, the boisterous mob surrounded the barrels, using them as convenient couches upon which to fall back with screams of delight, one couple landing across Letitia and using her lap as a pillow.

Furiously, she struggled to extricate herself, shouting in anger at the stinking half-naked woman and her cursing mate, tipping them off on to the floor in a tangle of limbs over which she had to clamber to be free. Sickened by the stink and obscenities, she kicked out at the grasping hands and turned to see Orla being wrestled backwards on to the barrel by a leering drunk whose stained white trousers were being hauled down by one of his mates. Hurling herself at the man, Letitia knocked him easily off balance, giving Orla just enough time to straighten up and roll away, clasping at the bodice of her gown. Then, holding hands, they hared down the street the way they had come, just as Jamie emerged from the tavern.

That experience was enough to convince them that their search would have to be resumed in daylight hours, for there was no more they could do that night. Edina was nowhere to be found on Portsmouth Point, nor did they encounter anyone who had seen her. It was hardly surprising in a town so packed with people intent on spending their Sunday in a state of self-induced forgetfulness.

By the time they reached the George Hotel, the shallow bay windows were ablaze with light, and the aroma of cooking and pipe smoke wafted out and mingled with the cool evening air. Even now, more guests were arriving, arguing over rooms, tripping over baggage, shouting orders, bumping into each other, some good-humouredly, others less so.

Exhausted and upset, despondent, hungry, worried and unsure about how best to proceed, Letitia was not even certain that Edina was actually in Portsmouth at all. Sending Jamie off with thanks and a hefty tip, she told him to go and eat with Mr Benjamin in their lodgings and to return in the morning for instructions, after which she followed Orla wearily up the stairs to their room, where the lure of a strange bed and an evening spent in her own sad company was strangely unappealing.

In the shadowy passageway opposite her door, a tall man stood with one shoulder leaning idly on the oak panelling, reading a newspaper. With a flutter of irritation, Letitia knew that they would have to speak to him to pass, and had just begun to wonder if they could sneak like children underneath the expanse of newspaper without setting fire to it when it began to lower, very slowly, revealing a tall beaver hat and then the face of the reader.

For one heart-stopping moment, she thought her eyes and the shadows must be playing tricks as a result of her tiredness. Disbelieving, she moved closer, seeing Orla dip a quick curtsy before unlocking the door, glance back at her mistress, and disappear inside. The shadowy face was exposed as the hat was lifted, his eyes lighting with laughter as the newspaper dropped to the floor, his arms reaching for her across one long ground-covering stride. 'Lettie!' he whispered.

'Oh! It *cannot* be. Can it?'

Without a single thought for either plans or propriety, she clung to his shoulders, curving into his hard comforting embrace as if he was the ultimate solution to every one of her cares, the one on to whom she could unload all she had carried since that morning, and before.

'Rayne…my lord…you're here,' was all she could manage to mumble as her mouth lifted to seek his, to take like a hungry fledgling all he had saved for that moment. Clinging, laughing, breathless with relief, they swayed gently like reeds, completely blocking the passage and quite oblivious to the clearing of throats that denoted a shocked disapproval. Eventually, Rayne's shoulder was tapped, turning him abruptly with an apology at the ready.

But this time the outraged expression behind them was too close for the shadows to hide, the tall feathers in the turban, the trembling feather boa around the shoulders too distinctive to cause any uncertainty. The voice yelped with malice.

'*Letitia!*'

'Aunt Minnie? Oh!' Letitia rested a hand on Rayne's arm for support.

Aunt Minnie yelped again, glaring at him, at her niece's possessive hand, then again at his face. 'Lord Rayne! What *am* I seeing here? Am I to believe my eyes?'

Coolly, with a slight lift of one eyebrow, Rayne placed a hand deliberately over Letitia's. 'Well now, Lady Aspinall, that would depend very much upon what your eyes have told you, wouldn't it? Are you staying at the George, too, or have you come especially to see us?'

Aunt Minnie gasped at the insolence. 'Young man,' she scolded, 'I did not come here to be questioned. You, however, have some answers to provide, and they had better be satisfactory, for it seems to me that this is just the kind of vulgar behaviour that only—'

'Aunt Minnie!' snapped Letitia. 'Lord Rayne and I have no intention of discussing anything with you in a passageway. If you will oblige us by stepping inside our room, we can perhaps speak in private. I've had a long and tiring day.'

The large hand squeezed hers, taking over. 'And Miss Boyce needs to rest and eat. After you, my lady.' Opening the door, he stepped aside and allowed her to sweep past him like a schooner in full sail. 'Leave it to me,' he whispered in Letitia's ear. 'You said *our* room.'

'I know I did,' she whispered back.

'She thinks we're…' He closed the door.

Aunt Minnie had not a moment to lose. Although turned fifty, she knew what she had seen, and heard. 'There can be absolutely no shadow of doubt,' she said, taking the centre of the room after a glance at the large double bed, 'that you have completely overstepped the bounds of common decency, Letitia, and you must now both—'

'Just a minute!' said Rayne in a voice that owed much to his years of commanding unruly young men. 'There is no one, I repeat, *no one* who will tell either of us what we must do. Or what we must not do. I hope that is clear, Lady Aspinall. Whatever you may think, we do not owe you an explanation for the greeting you saw just now. Miss Boyce is quite exhausted, having spent several hours looking round the town, and her relief at seeing me is perfectly understandable. It may not be what you are used to seeing, but times change.'

'And I suppose you are about to tell me that you're simply the best of friends, and there is no understanding between you.'

'None whatsoever,' said Rayne, emphatically.

'None whatsoever,' repeated Letitia, ignoring the quick squeeze on her captured hand. 'Between a mistress and her lover there is no requirement for an understanding of the kind you mean, Aunt Minnie. Lawks, but you're sadly out of time with such matters, you know. You'll be expecting me to wear a ring next, I suppose?' She felt Rayne's reaction through the briefest tightening of his fingers but, to his great credit, not even by the flicker of an eyelid did he betray the slightest astonishment at her unexpected announcement.

'You appear to be lost for words, Lady Aspinall,' he said. 'Is this a sudden affliction, or have we said something to cause you embarrassment? Surely there were such things as mistresses and their lovers amongst your ancestors, were there not? There are amongst my own, even in my generation. Let me see now, my brother *and* sister, father, mother, countless uncles and—'

'Stop! This is not a boasting matter, Lord Rayne. It's *outrageous*!'

'Of course it's not outrageous, Aunt Minnie,' said Letitia, crossly, finding that Rayne's solid presence beside her gave her the courage to speak her mind as she had never quite dared to do before, not even with Uncle Aspinall standing by. 'It's no good you telling me how different I am, how I never conform, how I don't fit in, and then getting all upset when I run true to form, is it? Will you and Mama never understand that you have forfeited any right to tell me how to run my life? When have *you* ever offered me support and approval instead of criticism and predictions of failure?

When have either of you ever sought my company just for the sake of it, as Lord Rayne has? Uncle Aspinall has, but not you, nor Mama, either. If ever I need any help, it will not be to you I turn, but to my lover, the only one apart from my sisters and a few others who would come to my aid even before I asked it.

'I didn't know Lord Rayne was coming, but he came, and I was overjoyed to see him. That was what you witnessed, Aunt. You would not know much about joy, would you? You would mistake it for outrageous behaviour. Well, call it what you like. I've had more kindnesses from Lord Rayne in one month than I've had from you since I was born. I had almost forgot how to tell kindness from interference, would you believe?' Her voice shook and wavered on a rising note close to hysteria that reflected the pressures of the day, the dreadful hours of searching, and now this. Suddenly, she felt weak and overcome by exhaustion, almost on the verge of tears.

'Enough, sweetheart,' said Rayne, placing an arm around her as only a lover would. 'Come and sit over here. Shall Orla order some dinner now? Is it not time we were eating?'

Letitia nodded, croaking a 'yes'. Orla curtsied and left the room.

'May I ask,' Rayne said to the dumbfounded aunt, 'whether Sir Penfold has accompanied you to Portsmouth, my lady?'

His question was redundant, for Orla had doubled back to knock on her mistress's door and to admit the gentleman in question. 'Sir Penfold Aspinall, ma'am,' she said, wishing she could stay to hear the rest.

The benevolent uncle took in the scene at a glance, his wife's high colour, her rigid posture, her most unusual silence and Letitia's sparkling eyes, a sure sign that she was up on the high ropes. 'Lettie, love,' he said. 'My lord, how d'ye do? Minnie, is it not time you were in our room preparing for dinner? I shall be ready to eat in a matter of minutes. Come on.'

Aunt Minnie thought there was something he should understand first. 'Aspinall,' she said. 'Letitia has had the impertinence to inform me that she is now Lord Rayne's mistress. There. What d'ye have to say to *that*?'

'What do you expect me to say, woman?' Holding out his hand to Rayne, he shook it in hearty congratulation. 'Well done, m'boy. Lettie needs a man of your ilk. Lettie, m'dear, you'll do well enough with Rayne. He's had plenty of practice. We'll talk tomorrow, eh?'

'Thank you, Uncle,' Letitia whispered, choosing not to comment on the practice Rayne had had, compared to her own. 'I'm glad *you're* not shocked.'

'Not a bit of it, love. Your aunt and I have to go and meet some friends off the *Primrose* tomorrow, as soon as she docks. They're coming back to London to stay with us a while, but we won't return home without seeing you again. Come on, Minnie lass. You're not needed here, and my stomach thinks my throat's been cut. Goodnight, you two.' Herding his very vexed wife like a stray sheep, he left as suddenly as he had arrived with a last smiling nod at his niece and a wink at her new lover.

Letitia discovered that she was trembling as she recalled the many times she had longed to speak to Aunt Minnie like that, but had never been able to summon enough courage. It would not have been worth the censure that would have come her way. With Rayne's support, that did not seem to matter.

'What have I done?' she whispered. 'What must you be thinking of me? That was a most unladylike thing to say.'

Rayne knew she was not talking about Lady Aspinall.

'You wonder what I think of you, Miss Boyce?' he said, moving away from the door. 'Well, first, that you are a never-ending source of delightful surprises, and second that you look all in. Come here, my splendid creature.' He leaned towards her and hooked his hands under her arms more lovingly than the sailor with his sister, easing her up to him, supporting her, feeling her unsteadiness in his arms. 'Straight from the heart,' he said, softly. 'There's nothing fake about you, is there, my beauty? Eh? You came straight to me like a bird, didn't you?'

'I've put you in a very difficult position,' she said, smoothing the lapel of his dark blue coat. 'It seemed to be the best way of avoiding all the dust she would have kicked up. But if you think I should not…'

'I think you should have said it sooner,' he said, laughing, 'but better late than never. I *did* mention it before, you know. Only two days ago.'

'Yes, I know.'

'And I said then that it was probably the most effective way of keeping the relatives quiet. Look what happened to your aunt just now. She was struck dumb. Have you ever seen that before?'

'Only with you there. Do you know, I think it might work. Would it be too much of a nuisance to you, my lord? You don't have to *be* my lover in every sense, you know, just because I said that. I really didn't mean… Oh, dear, this is so indelicate.'

'Lettie Boyce, listen to me. Between a man and his mistress there is nothing too indelicate to talk about. That's one of the advantages. There are no obligations or constraints that cannot be discussed, and I'm certainly not about to throw you on the bed and make violent love to you. That's for when you tell me you're ready, in your own good time. It was my recommendation, remember, that we should place you on a different level of society where you can be yourself more fully. And that's exactly what this will do. What's more, I'm going to enjoy helping you to stay there. We're going to see a more confident Miss Boyce, a woman of distinction. That's what I've been searching for, for years. A woman of distinction.'

As fleet as a hare in the night, the thought crossed her mind that this was what she also had been searching for since she began writing, not only for a way to rejoin society without her mother's constant carping to spoil it, but also to provide her with the kind of intimate experience that the heroines of novels acquire when they take lovers. Which they always do. Whether she agreed with him about wanting to make love at that precise moment was a question that caused a slight hesitation. She had never seen him more handsomely dressed in skin-tight doeskins and matching waistcoat, and his hands warmly encircling her bodice left a memory behind of how once, just once, they had strayed to more private places.

'Then that is what I shall endeavour to be, my lord, since you have been good enough to come to my aid more than once. It was true, you know, what I said to her.'

'About the kindnesses? Then she must have been excessively uncivil to her lovely niece. But no matter. We don't need her.' Taking her by the hand, he led her to the window-seat and sat beside her. 'Now, I think you'd better tell me all about this pupil of yours who is so eager to escape. Where have you searched?'

As concisely as she could, she told him of the fruitless enquiries, omitting the fracas outside the Ship, which she knew would only earn her a scolding. She might have known that he would look for her at church, and that Gaddy would tell him, but she had not expected him to follow her in his own post-chaise, or to find her so quickly. He really was, she thought, proving to be the kind of stuff of which romantic heroes are made, even if the rather excessive dominance was more comfortable on the written page than in reality.

An hour later, with Orla's help, Letitia was refreshed, clean, and looking more her usual self in a pretty white muslin gown under a pale blue sleeveless pelisse for extra warmth. A Paisley shawl was thrown around her shoulders as she went down to the private parlour, which she had offered to share with Lord Rayne.

'Do mistresses float about in dressing gowns?' she said, mischievously. 'If so, I shall be a sad disappointment to you. I've rarely had any cause to float.'

Rayne led her to the table and pulled out a chair. 'Invariably,' he said. 'Floating while in a state of undress is one of the prime requirements of a mistress. You have my word on it. I shall overlook it on this occasion, however, since the new position has taken us both unawares, but I shall expect you to practise your floating, in or out of a negligee, as soon as we return.'

'Very well, my lord,' she said, demurely. 'What's for dinner?'

He reached across the white linen tablecloth to take her hand, making her look at him and to see in his eyes a very personal answer to her question. Roaming over her, they rested on the pile of pale hair bound with blue ribbons and caressed the creamy skin of her neck and bosom, returning to her own flint-grey eyes framed with long lashes, the perfect half-moon lids, the fine arch of her brows. She could hardly fail to understand his silence or the gentle pressure of his fingers.

But he knew, as she had expected him to, how concerned

she was for her missing pupil and the dangers she would be facing, and that for them to rest here in comfort while Edina was still at large was not why they had come. They had already agreed on that.

'I shall take no more than a bite before I go into town. You will stay here and finish your meal and, if it grows late and I have still not returned, you will go to bed. When I find her, I'll bring her straight to you, whatever time it is. Don't wait up for me.'

'Come and tell me when you return, even if you return alone.'

'If it will make you more comfortable, I will.'

'Thank you. We can start looking again tomorrow.'

He smiled. 'Talking about looking....' He reached for a package that lay on the table. 'I think you may find this useful.'

It was wrapped in brown paper. 'A telescope? Like Lord Nelson's?'

'Not a telescope. Better than that.'

Inside the wrapping were two cases, one of engraved silver and mother-of-pearl, the other of green snakeskin edged with bands of gold. She knew instantly what they contained, for they were just of the size to hold folding spectacles, one pair of silver oblong-framed glasses with adjustable sliding arms, the other pair of gold with folding arms and diamonds set on the outer edges. Both of them were pretty enough to be worn with evening dress, delicate, modish and expensive.

'Oh, my lord! These are truly the most *beautiful*, the prettiest...'

'For the new Lettie Boyce. For indoors and out.'

'Yes, oh, yes *indeed*.' Putting on the silver pair, she stared at him with an innocent twinkle in her bright eyes. 'Is this distinctive enough?'

'Stunning. Are they going to fit? I can have them altered.'

'They fit perfectly. Now the others.'

The gold pair were oval and, with a movement of her head, caught a flash of blue-white light across the diamonds, creating the opposite effect from the plain steel frames she had worn before in public. These were quite unique, speaking of high fashion that only a few would be able to emulate.

'They're *very* good,' she said. 'I can see much better than with my others. I shall wear them all the time. Thank you, my lord. You are the kindest of men.'

'Not odious now?'

They rose and came round the table to meet each other and to melt in an embrace, which appeared to be all he wanted by way of thanks, though Letitia suffered a pang of guilt at the strangeness of it all. 'No one has ever given me anything like this before. Ought I to be accepting gifts of this nature?'

'If my mistress wants to see what she's doing,' he said, 'I would say she ought. Otherwise she's going to miss half the fun.'

'And if she wants to see what her lover is doing?'

'Then of course she should remove them and place them somewhere safe, until later. And while we're about it, I remember that we were rudely interrupted.'

Their kiss, continued from the one in the passageway, was destined not to be allowed to run its course, for the knock on the door had to be answered, and the waiters had to set the steaming dishes upon the dinner table.

Chapter Eleven

It was well past midnight when Letitia heard the tap on her door for which every nerve had been straining for the last six hours. She was at the door in one bound, tying her robe and peering into the dim passageway with a gasp of relief. 'Come inside,' she whispered to the two dark figures, one swathed in a pale greatcoat, the other leaning heavily on his arm, wearing a shawl over her crumpled day dress and spencer.

She might still have been taken for a young lady of quality, but the ravages of the last twenty-four hours were easily definable, especially on the drawn face. Even so, a glance from the expressive brown eyes showed how much she had longed for this moment.

'You should not have waited up,' Rayne said, closing the door.

'I had to. Where did you find her?' Letitia drew Edina forward and untied her bonnet. 'Come over here, love. Orla, go down to the kitchen and have a bowl of soup sent up. Some bread, too. And a jug of hot water. Is there any luggage?'

'I have her portmanteau here, luckily. Two women were trying to part her from it. I had to pay them to let it go.'

'Sorry,' Edina's voice wavered. 'I never meant this to happen.' Her eyes welled with tears, and Letitia felt the exhausted weight of her in the homecoming embrace. Then, remembering her dignity and Lord Rayne's presence in a lady's room, Edina turned and held out her hand to him. 'Thank you, my lord. I shall pay—'

'Miss Strachan, I *am* paid back, just to see you safe again. I shall leave you to tell Miss Boyce what happened, but first you should allow her to tend you. This is the moment she's waited for all day. I shall see you downstairs at breakfast, ma'am.' The candle flame shone across his features, showing Letitia the rather impudent lift of one eyebrow and the smile mingled with tiredness, the meaning of which went far beyond the formalities. 'Goodnight, Miss Boyce,' he said.

'Goodnight, Lord Rayne. We are both so very grateful to you.'

'Glad to have been of service, ma'am.'

'Eight o'clock breakfast?'

He bowed, catching her eye with a smile before he left.

Aware that a volley of questions would be inappropriate, nevertheless she allowed herself just two. 'Where were you?' she said, removing Edina's bonnet. 'Did you find a place to stay?'

'When Lord Rayne found me, I was at the Dolphin just a few yards up the High Street. I didn't have a room there. I was looking for…' The explanation faltered as a sob caught in her throat.

'The Dolphin? But that's a respectable inn.' Quickly, Letitia realised that the surprise in her voice was giving the wrong impression. 'I mean, did you expect to find somebody there?'

'It was a last resort,' Edina sobbed, with tears rolling freely down her face. 'I'd looked everywhere else. I found his mates in one of the taverns. They said he'd gone off with a local girl. I couldn't believe it. He must have known I'd be here to meet him. It's been six months, ma'am. So I went looking for him. All day, all night.' She seemed to assume Letitia would know that a young man was involved.

'Even though he'd found someone else?' Letitia knelt in front of her, taking the cold hands into hers. 'You wanted to find both of them together?'

'Yes, I wanted to see what she had that I lack. It's just as well that I didn't, or I might have torn her to *pieces*! Him, too.' The Scottish burr seemed somehow appropriate to the unlady-like threat of mutilation on such a scale, the rolling R's and the cutting *pieces*, the fierce Scottish passion. The poor girl, whoever she was, would have stood little chance against Edina in this mood.

To Letitia, this was a revelation. The quietly mannered Miss Strachan had not whimpered off like a scolded pup, but had scoured the town from end to end, angry, unhappy, and not willing to let go without a fight. All that, after weeks of despair. How terrible was this thing called love. What pain it could cause. Taking Edina into her arms, she rocked her like a mother and was mildly surprised to find how she softened before the storm of weeping overtook her, shaking the sixteen-year-old body with rasping sobs. 'Hush now, shh...!' she crooned. 'You're safe and unharmed, and what's done is done. We'll talk more about it later. Have you eaten?'

'Not since the last coach-stop. My money ran out.'

'And no sleep last night, I suppose. Come on, love. Take off these clothes. We'll soon have you comfortable again.'

Hot water and clean clothes, food, warmth and rest were plied within the next hour, at the end of which Edina lay like a child deep within half of the great bed, fast falling into sleep. Instead of adding to her wardrobe as the others had done, she had saved her allowance week by week, with this scheme in mind. During the previous hour, it had emerged that the errant young man was a naval recruit she had met while staying at Guildford with her grandparents. On parting, they had promised to write and eventually to go across to France where they could be married without parental consent, apparently not seeing England's hostilities with France as any barrier to this plan. It was this illicit correspondence that had kept Edina's spirits up, but when it was discovered, she was sent off to Richmond to get over her infatuation.

Letitia was slow to fall asleep, her mind buzzing uncomfortably with thoughts of Edina's unhappiness and how it ought to have been recognised before it came to this. On a more positive note, she had not understood until now how such a tangle could affect a young woman of Edina's calibre, a sturdy no-nonsense Scot whose heart was both wounded and insulted by a man's treachery, who could turn that affection so immediately into a furious energy great enough to sustain her through hours of humiliation and searching. She had shown a passion and courage none of them had thought her capable of, and now it remained to be seen whether she would stumble into John Bunyan's 'slough of despond'. Meanwhile, Letitia decided on some therapy.

* * *

Over breakfast in the cosy parlour, Lord Rayne supplied more details of his search that had taken him into every stinking tavern, only to end at the upper-class Dolphin Inn because, like Edina, he believed it to be a last resort.

Removing the top off her boiled egg, Letitia dipped a finger of toast into the yolk. 'I wonder if we might stay another day here,' she said. 'I have a mind to take Edina and Orla shopping for a few things.' The winsome smile indicated that this would include a tour of the local haberdashers and milliners.

'Of course. We can return tomorrow, if you wish.'

'What about your obligations at the barracks?'

'That's not a concern. There are others to take over while I'm away. I saw your uncle just now. He asked me to go with him to the Crown this morning. It's known here as the Navy House because the officers go to eat there. It's where he's arranged to meet his friends.'

'Aunt Minnie will probably spend the morning in her room. Do you know, I think we've shocked her so badly she may never recover.'

'Your uncle, on the other hand, feels quite the reverse. He thinks I am exactly what you need.'

'Uncle Aspinall is *usually* right,' she said, frowning at the toast before she bit at it, 'but not *invariably*. Still, I have his approval so I shall not be too concerned about anyone else's. Particularly now that I can see what I'm doing.'

'They look enchanting, Miss Boyce.'

'Thank you, sir. Orla likes them, too. And Miss Strachan.' She had already received several admiring stares on the way down to breakfast, and the thought of being able to see the

entire contents of a shop instead of a blur of colours made her
as excited as a child at Christmas.

After taking her breakfast in bed and borrowing some of
Letitia's clothes, Edina and her two chaperons stepped out of
the George into the High Street. Her parents and grandparents,
she told Letitia, would have punished her severely instead of
taking her out shopping. Although her pride had taken a bat-
tering, the previous day's fury had abated and, after some discussion, she was ready to accept that plans made at sixteen
were not always the most permanent.

With her heroine Perdita in mind, Letitia observed with
some interest the phases of emotion through which her pupil
passed, noting how they were never far from the surface even
while out shopping. Walking out of the Fabric Emporium
after choosing dress lengths for all three of them, Letitia was
stopped abruptly by Edina's hand on her arm. 'There...look,
ma'am! Over there. Those two at the back.'

Through her new spectacles, Letitia could see across the
promenade to where a young sailor was running to join a
chastened group of midshipmen being jollied along by two
lieutenants towards the place where a boat was moored at
the wall steps. The sailor was trying to fend off a dishevelled
girl, who clearly had not appreciated that her role had
become redundant at the Monday-morning round-up. The
young man bawled at her and she fell back, and Letitia saw
the anguish on Edina's face at the public rebuff, as if it had
happened to her, too.

The girl appeared to be the same age as Edina, and as
pretty. 'That's him, ma'am. Shall I go to her?' Edina whispered, clutching at Letitia's arm, the previous intention to

tear her limb from limb having, in that single moment, changed to compassion. Now, her only thought was to comfort her.

'I think it might be best,' Letitia said, 'if you did not. She may be even more hurt to know that there was someone else, or that she's being pitied. She will have friends somewhere. Look there. Behind. Two others are going to her.'

'Yes, but I wonder if—'

'Let it go, Miss Strachan,' said Orla from her other side. 'She'll not thank you for interfering. And there's better young men than that.'

It was not the usual way of things for a lady's maid of Orla's years to offer advice unasked, but nor was the relationship in the usual way of things, either, and Letitia was glad of her maid's support at a time like this. 'Shall we go to that art emporium next to our hotel?' Letitia said, gently drawing Edina away. 'You need some more brushes and paints, and that place is much better stocked than the little one in Richmond.'

Half an hour later, they emerged with smiles of satisfaction and several parcels carried by Jamie, for Letitia knew that Edina's watercolour box was a shabby old hand-me-down, not one to be proud of. Finding one with compartments for everything, wrapped cakes of paint, squirrel-hair brushes, pencils, palettes and water-bottles, Letitia bought it for her grateful pupil with a brief show of tears that were for pleasure, as well as pain and pity. Guilt, too, on Letitia's part, for she knew that this indulgence was partly to make amends for her previous neglect. In addition to that, Edina's artistic ability was superior to any of the others.

* * *

That evening, when Edina was in bed, Letitia and Lord Rayne were able to spend some time together in the parlour where they could decide what to do about her. 'She has pleaded not to be sent home,' Letitia said, snuggling into the angle of his arm. 'What am I to do?'

'Respect her wishes. It's hardly likely to happen again, is it?'

'The mailcoach ride alone was enough to determine that.'

'And neither parents nor grandparents are likely to find out.'

'No.'

'And she doesn't want to call at Guildford on the way back?'

'No, that would invite questions. She wants to return to Richmond.'

'With her box of paints and dress lengths and heaven knows what else. Was that a reward for her, or conscience gifts for you?'

She plucked at the black hairs on the back of his wrist before answering. 'Oh, you're right. I should take them off her and put her on bread and water for a week. Then I should be amazed if she doesn't run off again next weekend.'

'Minx,' he said, laying a hand over her wrist. 'I'm not suggesting you should punish the lass, but nor is there any need for you to fall over backwards to admit that you've failed her. You haven't. She appears to have begun this correspondence well before she came to your seminary, so she's been planning to make a run for it for months. What's more, she *chose* to save her allowance rather than spend it. She can't have it both ways. And what kind of message is this going to give to the others? Are you going to do the same for Miss Melborough, too?'

'Are you quite devoid of compassion, my lord?'

'No, nor am I quite devoid of common sense, either. You're getting emotionally involved in this and there's no need to. Miss Strachan is not a china doll, she's a—'

'She's a young lady of *sixteen*, which is beyond your experience, I might add. You think the rejection will do her no
harm. Well, you may be right, but at this moment she feels
the pain very acutely, as I have seen for myself, and since her
parents are not on hand to help, I'm doing what I can to ease
it. A lot is happening to her, my lord, and I believe she's
feeling rejection from all sides, not only from the young
scamp who promised her friendship. A few gifts are not going
to turn her head.'

'You think not, eh?' he said, softly.

Then, before she could decide what he might mean by
that, his arms swung her sideways, placing her across his lap,
unable to move. Scooping her legs up, he set them on the cushioned seat and held them until she had stopped protesting,
finally taking her wrist in his grip. 'So,' he said, 'if a few gifts
are not going to turn her head, Miss Mother Hen Boyce, what
will? In my experience, it usually works quite well.'

'That's not what I mean, my lord. You know it's not. Your
gift to me was not given for that purpose, was it? Because you
feel sorry for me?'

'Miss Boyce, I may feel some exasperation from time to
time. I may even feel like taking you in hand, but pity for you
has never been on my list, as it happens. To feel sorry for a
woman who has everything, as you appear to do, would be a
complete waste of time. I don't even feel sorry that you need
to see better. Irritation, perhaps, that you have steered yourself
on to the wrong social track, but that's something we can
rectify, between us. The gift of spectacles was merely to begin
that process.'

'Then why should you think differently of my gifts to
Edina? She has a talent for painting, yet her parents have

equipped her ill for it. I wanted to begin her healing. It was neither a bribe nor a reward.'

He studied the rebellious eyes, dark in the candlelit room and showing a trace of fear for her vulnerable position. Her lips had trembled as she spoke of healing. 'You feel her pain, too, don't you? That's it, isn't it? The rejection?' He traced an outline of her pointed chin with one finger. 'Caring woman.'

Tears rushed behind her eyes and brimmed over into the corners. ''Tis what all women feel,' she said.

'No lass. Not all women. Some would feel nothing, believe me. You feel things very deeply, don't you? Too deeply for your own comfort.'

'Too *fast* for my own comfort. I think I may have galloped into something I had not prepared for. This must be the first time you have ever been *told* by a woman that she's your newest mistress instead of waiting to be asked. But it's not too late to undo what I said last night, my lord, if you feel you've been rushed…'

'Oh, yes, it is,' he said, bending his head closer. 'Don't imagine you can wriggle your way out of it now, my beauty. I'm not letting go. You're netted, Lettie Boyce. Well and truly netted.' Releasing her wrist, he slipped his hand possessively into her underarm to fit snugly against her breast while his lips closed over hers, preventing any further discussion.

Letitia did not expect him to accept her offer, having already gone so far down a road of no return. Intuitively, she had sensed that it was her innocence that attracted him, and a kind of artlessness he was not used to. Fresh, responsive and smart, she was eager to learn and to bring to it a piquancy that previous amours had not. What other motive could he have for wanting her to be his mistress? To a man like him, what could be more enticing than that? she wondered.

His voice was thick with desire as the kiss ended. 'If we had privacy here,' he said, 'I'd be tempted to go further, but we cannot risk being discovered like this, sweetheart. Besides, as I've already said, I want you in bed for your first time. With all the trimmings.'

She could not resist a smile at the image, for she liked the idea of being in a more romantic place than this. It would fit more happily into her story, for one thing and, when the time came for them to part, he would be just as gentlemanly and considerate, she was sure. Men so hated it when women made a fuss.

After a fond farewell to Uncle Aspinall, the journey back to Richmond next morning was taken in convoy with Rayne's smart post-chaise leading the way, the front window of which gave them a view of the road ahead, and the liveried postilion. 'Tell me,' Letitia said, looking down at the gloved hand holding hers upon her lap, 'what did you and Uncle Aspinall do at the Crown yesterday morning?' Her shoulder was tucked warmly beneath his, though there was plenty of room for two on the seat with padded elbow-rests.

'Waited for Sir Penfold's guests to arrive. Chatted to several captains and admirals. One of them, a Captain Blair, knows your cousin, Lieutenant Gaddestone. He was surprised to find that Gaddestone was Sir Penfold's nephew, and staying with him.'

'Well, there's a coincidence. Did the captain like Fin?'

There was a slight hesitation before he replied. 'Oh, I don't know that captains and lieutenants need to *like* each other, exactly. But your uncle was very interested to hear what the captain had to say about him.'

'He would be. He'd be able to compare it with what Fin himself has to say, which is a great deal too much. Did I tell you he's asked me to give Gaddy an extra room? I'm convinced he'll ask to use it for himself.'

'You must not allow it, sweetheart. Not under any circumstances.'

'The only spare room I have is below stairs.'

'Keep it like that. I intend to be around more, Lettie. The plans for the Allied celebrations are being finalised, and I've done all I need to do for the present. The recruits are being sent to their regiments, and that leaves me free until the next batch arrives in the autumn. I'm ready to take some leave.'

'That means you'll be more…available?'

'From now on, I shall be very…available.'

'But I shall not. Have you given any thought about how this is going to work? It will be several weeks before we can go and stay in London.'

Rayne's voice was impassive, his eyes focussed straight ahead as if he knew she was stalling. 'It will work. Leave it to me.' When she made no reply, he looked down at her. 'Afraid?' he whispered.

'No. Of course not.'

Smiling, he squeezed her hand and turned his attention to the view.

Edina's homecoming on Tuesday afternoon was similar in many respects to that of the prodigal son without the fatted calf. Happy to see her back home, the girls bore her away, expecting to be given all the details of the adventure. But the discovery that Mr Waverley had not turned up for his usual mathematics lesson that morning was most disturbing, as was

Miss Gaddestone's news direct from his housekeeper. 'Attacked by highwaymen yesterday on the London Road,' she said once the girls had disappeared upstairs. 'I sent round a nice piece of beefsteak for him, so he can put it on his cuts and bruises or eat it, whichever he prefers. Poor Mr Waverley. She said he was quite poorly.'

'Highwaymen?' said Rayne, with barely concealed scepticism. 'In broad daylight? I'd be very surprised. I'll go round and see him, Lettie.'

'I'll come,' she said. 'Bart is a personal friend.'

'I suppose it's no good me telling you you can't, is it?'

'None at all. Shall we walk?'

'Very well. Might as well let the gossip start sooner as later.'

'Gossip?' said Miss Gaddestone. 'What gossip would that be, dear?'

'I don't know what Lord Rayne is talking about. Won't be long.'

Immaculately preserved, Mr Waverley's beautiful early Georgian house on The Green, almost next to the theatre, was a reflection of Bart himself: rose-toned carpets and walls, white and gilded woodwork, and delicate pieces of furniture perfectly arranged.

The housekeeper led them up the pale polished staircase, her worried frown preparing them for a disconsolate patient, but not for the sorry sight that lay swathed in bandages upon the ghost-white sheets of a four-poster bed. His upper head was turbaned with bandages, one arm was bound inside a sling, the other was covered with weals and bruises, his chest strapped across revealing triangles of mottled skin. One eye was completely closed, the other open just wide enough for him to see.

His mouth was cut and badly swollen, making it difficult for him to speak or to show his pleasure at seeing them.

Mr Thomas, the Welsh elocution teacher, rose to his feet as they entered, touching Bart's hand to say farewell. 'I'll call in later,' he said, articulating musically. 'Miss Boyce…my lord…'tis a sad business.'

Letitia went to kiss Bart's cheek.

Rayne wanted to know, 'Were you with him, Mr Thomas?'

'Monday morning, my lord, is when I'm at Number 24 with the pupils. Mr Waverley was riding on his own. One should not ride alone on the London Road, you know. I never do. Good day to you.'

They sat beside him, talking low, listening to his difficult whispers. He had been going to London, quite early, intending to take some papers to Mr Lake on Leadenhall Street. He had been set upon only a few miles out while the road was still deserted except for three men riding towards him. They had returned his greeting, then had turned and dragged him off his horse, beat him up, kicked him senseless and left him in the ditch. His horse had run off, but had been caught by a passer-by and brought back to him, and that was how he'd returned to Richmond, more dead than alive. Yes, he had told his housekeeper and doctor they were highwaymen, but of course they were not. He looked at Rayne with great sadness at that point, his swollen bloodshot eyes filling with tears.

'It's all right, old chap,' Rayne said, gently. 'Don't grieve. This kind of thing happens, and at least you're alive, fit and healthy. You'll make a good recovery. You have good friends and, in future, you won't go out alone. Were you not wearing your sword?'

'No.'

'Then you must. You know how to use it. Were the papers stolen?'

'No. In my saddle-bag. Safe.'

'Money taken?'

'No, nothing.'

'*Nothing*? Did you recognise any of them?'

Bart shook his head. 'Hired, I expect.'

'For what?' Letitia asked. 'To kill Bart? Why? Who would want to?'

Rayne laid a hand over hers. 'Perhaps we'll go into that when he feels a bit stronger.' He made as if to leave, but Bart signalled him to stay.

'Need to see Lake,' he whispered. 'Important.'

'Who is this Lake on Leadenhall Street?' Rayne said, giving nothing away. 'Can I help? I know where it is.'

Bart and Letitia looked at each other, sharing the secret, but not knowing how to proceed. It was time, Letitia thought, to accept some help; if that meant letting Rayne into it, then they must trust him. 'It's for me,' she said. 'The papers are mine. Mr Lake is a publisher. Mercury Press.'

'A publisher. I see. And you have papers for him. Well, that should be easy enough, if you will trust me with them.'

'It's a contract,' said Letitia. 'It needs to be discussed. Bart was going to bargain with him.'

'I see. You want him to publish something for you.'

Bart made a sound of impatience. 'Lettie,' he croaked, 'is an *author*, Rayne.' His mouth worked his swollen lips around the words, '*The Infidel*.'

'Good grief!' Rayne stared at Letitia, but found her eyes hostile, even suspicious. 'That's very interesting. Are you really? Those best-sellers that my mother reads? Well, then,

I'd be glad to help. I'll go and bargain with your Mr Lake. I'm quite good at that.'

Letitia frowned at him. 'You're not shocked?'

'No. Just tell me what you want from him and I'll fix it in no time.'

'It's not as easy as that. Bart has already spoken to him once. He's making things difficult. He doesn't know me. We've never met. That's the problem.'

'Nego…tia…ting through an inter…' Bart mumbled.

'Through an intermediary, yes. But it's always best if you can talk to these people personally, I think,' said Rayne.

'I can't do that,' said Letitia. 'That's why Bart does it for me.'

'Of course you can. You can come with me, can't you?'

Bart mumbled again. 'Are you and Lettie…?'

'Yes, old chap. We've come to an arrangement. D'ye mind?'

'Course not. Glad.'

'Good. I'll take care of her. I'll take her to Lake. He'll not get anything past me. Of course, I may not do as good a job as you, but I reckon it's time he spoke to the author herself now, don't you? This is a good opportunity.'

'We shall come and see you again before we go, Bart dear. And thank you for going. I'm so *very* sorry it's cost you this.' Letitia put a hand over his.

''Tis nothing,' Bart whispered. 'You go with Rayne, Lettie.'

'Yes, love, but while we're here, may I take the papers and that package with me?'

He pointed to a desk over by the far wall. 'In there.'

Lifting the veneered lid, she removed the contract and money and gave them to Rayne. 'Will you carry it for me, my lord, if you please?' She kissed Bart again before they left, holding back the tears for his dreadful injuries as the housekeeper showed them out. A few steps further on, however, she stopped.

'Forgotten something?' said Rayne, stopping with her.

'No. You're not such a good actor, are you, my lord?'

'What?'

'In there. You knew, didn't you? Don't deny it. You couldn't act the dunce to save your life. I could *tell* that you knew. "Good grief! That's very interesting,"' she mimicked. '"Are you really?" As if he was telling you I have two arms and two legs. You're supposed to be utterly *astonished*, not mildly surprised.'

'Oh, dear,' he said, attempting a look of remorse. 'I don't do astonishment very well, do I?'

'No, you don't. That's what comes of being one of the worldly "I've-seen-it-all" types, I suppose. How did you find out? Have you made enquiries?'

'Not at all, Miss Boyce. I found out quite by accident, though I don't think it was very clever of you to use your own initials for a pseudonym.'

'That was Bart's idea.'

'That doesn't surprise me. I don't know why you need a pseudonym at all. What's wrong with your own name?'

'Do you really need to ask that, after knowing my mother?'

'Take my arm. We can't stand here arguing. There, now let's get this straight. You are my responsibility now, and anything you want to do, you can do without seeking anyone's approval but mine. And I say you should be proud of your achievements and put your name to them.'

'It's not done.'

'It *is* done. Miss Austen lets it be known that she writes for a living. Maria Edgeworth does. So should you, as part of your new image. In fact, that would be a perfect way to re-invent yourself when we take London by storm.'

'Yes. Right. Have you actually *read* my novels?'

'Yes. Both of them. I could hardly qualify for the title of Worldly-I've-seen-it-all if I had not, could I?'

'And do you seriously believe that I would be accepted in polite society as the author of *that* kind of novel? It's not exactly Miss Austen's cup of tea, you know. Nor Maria Edgeworth's.'

Rayne halted as they reached the black railings outside Number 24 Paradise Road. 'Are you ashamed of them?' he said, turning her to face him.

'No, of course I'm not.'

'I should hope not. With the kind of success you're having, you should be proud to own them, not determined to remain anonymous. They're good.'

'You liked them?'

'I liked them, yes. And I can see why they're so popular, but it's quite clear that the author is inexperienced. If she's going to write a third, she'll have to think up something a bit more convincing and adventurous for the bedroom than the first two. All very nice, but not quite accurate, you know.'

'Not…accurate?'

'No. Imaginative, romantic, but lacking authenticity. She needs some first-hand experience.'

'Who does?'

'Well, the heroine for one, and the author for another. Quite soon, I would say.' They passed into the front hall, aware that this was hardly the kind of conversation to hold in front of young Sam. Nevertheless, the disguising of the topic was something that afforded them both a frisson of excitement.

'What kind of time did you have in mind, my lord? Within months? Or weeks, perhaps?'

Rayne handed his gloves and silver-topped cane to Sam and removed his hat, raking his fingers through his hair with a glance at the mirror. 'Hours,' he said.

Miss Gaddestone came gliding into the hall to meet them. 'Ah, you're back. How is dear Mr Waverley? Why, Lettie dear, the walk has put a bloom in your cheeks.'

Letitia swept past her. 'Shall we have tea and cakes in the drawing room?' she said, holding a hand to her neck.

The surprises of that day were not over, however. Taking Mrs Quayle with her in the town-coach, Letitia drove up Richmond Hill to the gracious home of Sir Francis and Lady Melborough, neither of whom had been far from her thoughts since the revelation that her mother's high-flown morals were not as pure as she pretended. For her to put pressure on both Sapphire and herself to toe her line was, Letitia thought, extremely hypocritical. It was time to put matters straight.

Unsure of the reception she would receive, she was glad of Mrs Quayle's bright bird-like chatter that complemented Lady Melborough's delight at seeing them. Within moments of hearing their voices echoing in the hall, Miss Sapphire Melborough herself came down the winding staircase, her arms open wide in greeting, her expression bright with joy. With a yelp, she flung herself into Letitia's arms in a manner not taught at the seminary for young daughters of gentlefolk, but which affirmed the news that Letitia had been hoping for without a single question being asked.

As soon as she was sure—only a matter of days—as it turned out, Sapphire had thanked her Cheltenham relatives for their kind hospitality, borrowed their old carriage and dismissed herself, and now she was ready to be given a second chance, if only Miss Boyce would allow it. Which was exactly why Letitia and Mrs Quayle had come.

With a certain knowledge on her side, Letitia's meeting with Sapphire's father was by no means as strained as it had been before she knew the reason for his previous over-familiarity. Now, she could put it into context, and the man was no longer a threat, and she could forgive his effusiveness instead of being offended by it. The meeting went better than expected. Sapphire would rejoin her friends at the seminary, having already forgiven Lady Boyce for her harshness on that particular Sunday. It was, Letitia told them, the overreaction of a mother to the foolishness of a daughter. Catching Sir Francis's eye at this point, she was reasonably sure that he understood the message: Miss Letitia Boyce was not another Miss Euphemia Aspinall.

Excusing herself immediately after dinner, Letitia went to her room to catch up with her writing, eager to commit to paper all that had happened to herself, to Orla and Edina and, indirectly, to Bart, too. At frequent intervals, the writing was suspended, pictures and words overpowered by other more personal developments and their significance to her future as a headmistress, as a writer, and as Lord Rayne's mistress. Was it all moving too fast for her? Had he already guessed her purpose in accepting the latter position with much less resistance than he might have expected, given her earlier hostility? Had his offer of help, both off the page and on it, been made in the knowledge that this was a role for which she had already selected him? He had, after all, gone straight to the heart of the matter during their walk home from Bart's house. He was no fool. Yet hardly had a day passed when she had not needed his help in some way, and not an hour had passed without thinking of him, and now a new question sneaked under the others about whether she needed him for her own sake or for Perdita's. Her eyes closed. The ink on the pen dried, and Perdita was left to her own devices as the wick burned lower.

On Wednesday morning, while the girls were upstairs in a French lesson, Mrs Brewster the housekeeper took delivery of a large item brought by the Ackermann's wagon from London to Miss Letitia Boyce. The white-aproned delivery man who carried it into the hall could not tell them the name of the donor. He accepted his tip and went on his way. Taking scissors to the string and copious brown paper, Letitia and Orla unravelled the mysterious package to find that it contained an exquisite portable writing-desk, the kind of thing she had promised to buy for herself as soon as she could justify the expense.

By its silver handle, Orla carried it into the dining room and laid it upon the table where Letitia smoothed its sides of tulipwood inlaid with ivory, running her hands over the silver mounts and hinges. 'Who is it from, ma'am?' said Orla. 'There's no card nor message, nothing except Ackermann's Repository, Strand, London.'

'There might be a message inside,' said Letitia, turning the key in the tiny lock. The lid opened out to make a velvet-covered writing surface that sloped towards cut-glass containers for ink and pounce, a place for pens, letters and papers, compartments, secret drawers, a space beneath for a manuscript book that closed with a conspiratorial click. But there was no clue as to who had sent it.

Letitia left it upon the table to be admired. Naturally, it caused a lot of interest.

Later in the morning, while she was arranging a vase of flowers, she heard someone enter the hall through the front door with a very loud and cheery greeting for Miss Gaddestone, followed by an imperious command for Sam to bring a bottle of wine from Miss Boyce's cellar. Then, marching towards the garden room while throwing over his shoulder the information that the phaeton was back in the—

The visitor didn't finish the sentence. 'Lettie! Good God! You're…you're back!' Lieutenant Gaddestone stopped in the doorway as if struck by a thunderbolt.

With hands fluttering like moths, his sister appeared behind him. 'I tried to tell you, Fin,' she whispered. 'Lettie came home yesterday.'

Poised like a miniature javelin in Letitia's hand, the sharp stem of a rose hovered over the vase. 'Good morning to you, too, Cousin Fin. The phaeton is back where? In the coach house, is it? My very expensive bay, too, I hope? Sam!' she called. 'We shall not need the wine, I thank you.'

'Er…well, you see…' he said, clinging to the brass doorknob.

'No, I don't think I do. Did someone give you permission to take my phaeton?'

'I didn't think you'd mind, Lettie. I came by on Monday morning to ask you, and Rosie said—'

'No, I did *not* say it would be all right, Fin,' protested his sister. '*You* said it would be all right and that you'd bring it back before Lettie returned.'

'Which you hoped would be later rather than sooner,' said Letitia, dropping the rose-stem into the water. 'So now you've brought it back in the hope that I shall be none the wiser, and you walk into my house as if it were your own, and then you order my servant to supply you with my wine. Is there anything else you would like to take advantage of, while you're here?'

'Oh, Lettie, don't go off into a pet about it. I wanted to ask you—'

'Like you asked about the wine? Really, cousin, are these the manners the navy has taught you?'

'I'm sorry, Lettie. I really didn't think you'd mind.'

'Unfortunately, I do. You could have hired a phaeton in London if you needed one so badly.'

'Short of funds, Lettie. That's the long and short of it. Pockets to let until they send me my pay and prize money. Shouldn't be long now, then I can buy my own. Sorry, old girl. Forgive me?' His boyishly handsome face relaxed into a winsome smile that had doubtless been tried on many a woman with unqualified success. This time proved to be an exception. His Cousin Lettie was furious. Not that this prevented him from asking a favour of her. 'You couldn't lend me a bit o' blunt, could you, Lettie? Just until it arrives? Pay you back, of course.'

'Will you excuse me for one moment? I've forgotten to ask Sam something.' Letitia went into the hall where Sam was straightening the pink Axminster. Straightening up, he received his mistress's message and went off to the stables as fast as his legs could carry him.

Curious, Lieutenant Gaddestone followed Letitia into the dining room. 'Are you going to ask me to stay to lunch, now

I'm here, Lettie? I had thought of taking my sister out strutting for an hour this afternoon.'

'I thought you understood, Cousin Fin, that Gaddy lives here in return for chaperon duties. This is a seminary, you know. Some of my tutors are gentlemen, and your sister stays in the room at all times. Quite often Mrs Quayle and I do the same. This afternoon, she will be with Mr Dimmock's class.'

'Can't you do it instead, this time?' His eyes were drawn to the portable writing-desk on the table. 'Oh, this is nice. Just arrived?'

Anxious to pour oil on troubled waters, Miss Gaddestone saw the change of subject as a godsend. 'Yes,' she twittered, 'half an hour ago, from an unknown admirer.' Her hands patted it lovingly.

'Oh, Gaddy! What nonsense,' said Letitia.

'Well, it *must* be, dear. Who else would do such a thing with no message to say who sent it? Isn't it a lovely mystery, Fin?'

There was a gleam of mischief in his eyes as his hand wiped across his mouth, pinching his nose as it passed. 'It is, *indeed*, sister dear. Now you know why I'm skint. Stumped the last of my pewter on gifts.'

His sister and cousin stared at him, open-mouthed. 'You?' they said in unison.

He swung his head like a pendulum, smiling broadly. 'Why not? Lettie's always been keen on writing, hasn't she? Just a token of my regard.'

'But, cousin, this must have cost a fortune. Is this really what you've spent the last of your money on? And now you're asking me to help you out? That doesn't make much sense, does it?'

'Trying to stay in your good books, Lettie. Thought this

might help to oil the wheels. By the way, I like the eyeglasses. They new? Must have cost a pretty penny.'

Angry and deflated, Letitia felt the joy drain from her. She had harboured her own thoughts about who the gift might be from, especially since he'd known for some time that she was a writer and that, for a stay in London, she would need to take her work with her. But for her *cousin* to spend money he did not have on such a thing was quite out of the question. It must be returned. 'It must go back,' she said. 'Gaddy, be a dear and ask Mrs Brewster for that wrapping paper, will you?'

Miss Gaddestone knew better than to argue. For her brother to buy gifts for his cousin was not at all the thing. Turning to go, she almost bumped into the tall gentleman who was just entering the room. 'Oh! Good morning, my lord.'

'Good morning, Miss Gaddestone, Miss Boyce, Lieu-tenant. Of course it must be returned,' said Rayne, looking sternly at the desk. 'Tell us where you bought it, sir, and we'll pack it up again.'

'Oh, you! Bought it…er…in London. If you think it was not a good idea, Lettie, I'll take it back myself. Look here, I never meant to embarrass you. My lord, are you not being a little high-handed here?'

Letitia breathed a very quiet sigh of relief, for Rayne had obviously heard the previous exchange and would know how to handle it. What was more, she now had a suspicion that Cousin Fin was not telling the truth.

'No, I don't think I am, my friend,' Rayne said, good-na-turedly. 'But it's interesting to see that our tastes are so very similar. So similar, in fact, that I bought one exactly like this only last week, thinking that it was unique. I must say I'm not best pleased to find that there are others like it. Where did you say you bought it?'

Cousin Fin frowned. 'Oh, it was some time ago. I cannot quite remember.'

'Ah, of course. So many gifts. Confusing, isn't it? Well, Miss Boyce, we can soon settle the problem. If you were to lift up the little wafer compartment next to the pounce jar, you may find the answer. That's it, lift it right out and look underneath.'

'There's a card. One of yours, my lord.'

'Turn it over, if you please.'

'It says, "With highest regards from Seton Rayne to Lettie Boyce." There, I don't think there can be any doubt about that, can there?' She smiled, shyly.

'A mistake,' Lieutenant Gaddestone muttered, turning very red. 'Easily made. Must have forgotten…meant to…thought I had done…lot on my mind, you know. Yes, saw one just like it….lovely piece…ah, well, I suppose I'd better be making tracks. Has Rosie gone? I wonder if I might have a quick word with her? Er, you couldn't let me have the use of one of your horses, could you, Lettie?' The request was given in a hushed tone, which he hoped would not catch Rayne's ear while that gentleman studied the hinges of the desk.

Rayne's ears, however, were in good working order. He straightened, favouring Lieutenant Gaddestone with a long hard stare. 'That would put Miss Boyce in a difficult position, sir,' he said. 'The horses in her stable belong to the young ladies here, except for the carriage horses. You surely didn't have the grey Arab in mind, did you?'

Cousin Fin coloured even deeper. 'I can see my timing is at fault, Lettie. I shall take my leave of you. Where will I find my sister?'

From the open door came the sound of voices and the patter of slippers on the staircase as the French lesson ended and laughter was released like a peal of bells. The girls would want her attention. Letitia knew that Cousin Fin would ask his sister for money for his return to London on the mailcoach. She also knew that, if she had not been here, he would have helped himself to one of the horses without Mr Benjamin to prevent him.

'Come with me, cousin,' she said, with a glance at Rayne. 'Don't go, my lord. I shall only be a moment. Please excuse me.'

Chapter Twelve

'Yes, you're quite right,' said Letitia, closing the dining-room door. 'I know I shouldn't have lent him anything, but the alternative was quite unacceptable, my lord. I could not have him taking money off Gaddy, nor could I allow him to walk all the way to London. Even though I do have a spare horse in my stable, I would not let him use it after he took my...' She sighed, walking over to the window to look out upon Paradise Road.

'Your what? What's he helped himself to?'

'To my phaeton and the bay.'

'Without your permission? The man's a bounder.'

'It was Monday morning and we were still in Portsmouth, and so was Uncle Aspinall. Poor Gaddy, she's so cut up about it. But thank you for coming so quickly to answer my call.'

'I was only at the end of the road. I'd been to see Bart. He's quite poorly. I told him I'd take you to see Lake tomorrow. I thought we could stay at Berkeley Square with my parents. Will it be convenient?'

'Yes, I believe so, but it means two more nights away.'

'You needn't be concerned. I've taken the liberty of hiring a butler for you.'

'But I've got Sam.'

'As a footman, yes, but he won't manage to keep the likes of Gaddestone out, will he? You need a large imposing adult butler, sweetheart, especially when there are young ladies to be protected. Parents will appreciate it.'

That small detail had escaped her. 'Right again,' she whispered.

'I'll never get used to it. Come here, woman.' He opened his arms, enclosing her with warm hands on her back.

'No,' she said, pressing herself against him, 'it cannot be good for a man, can it? Shall you be getting devilish righteous now, my lord?'

'Unless you can suggest a better reward.'

'Thank you for the beautiful desk. I could not have accepted it from anyone else, and I *did* so want to. It's the loveliest, most perfect thing I've ever seen. Shall we take it to London with us?'

'It can go anywhere with you, so I cannot be accused of taking you away from your writing.'

'Expensive gifts. I am already indebted to you.' She raised her head to meet his lips, drawing from him both comfort and excitement.

'And I intend to make sure it stays that way. Now, later today the new butler will arrive. His name is Mr Beck, and he knows exactly what his duties are. Perhaps you'll get Mrs Bruin to—'

'Mrs Brewster.'

'To show him round, have his room ready. Tell him who you want kept out, then be ready for me to pick you up at about ten tomorrow, and have your papers ready for Lake so that you can tell me about it on the way. We'll go straight to

Leadenhall Street. Then there's an evening soirée at the Misses Berry. They'd like us to go. Shall we? After dinner?'

'My lord, you think of everything,' she said, caressing his cheek.

'Yes, and there is one particular everything I think about almost non-stop. But now I must go, and you must tend your flock. Don't allow thoughts of your cousin to disturb you. I have his measure.'

'Do you, my lord?'

'Oh, yes, I most certainly do.'

No sooner had he taken his leave of her than she went straight away to find Miss Gaddestone, whose pretty room overlooked the garden, though it was obvious from the red and watery eyes that the view was not the occupant's focus of attention. Letitia took the frail creature in her arms. 'Oh, dear, please don't weep, dear Gaddy. I don't blame you in the slightest. Not in the *slightest.*'

'I should have told you, but he told me not to, that he'd get the phaeton back before you knew it and that I was not to worry. It was very wicked of him to put me in such a position, Lettie, because he must *know* how much I owe you, and how loyal I am, and now he's spoiling it by this *dreadful* behaviour, and lies about the desk, too. Oh, how *could* he do that? So…so humiliating, Lettie.'

'Gaddy dearest, you don't have to change one bit. I know how loyal you are. Fin is in a difficult position until his pay arrives.'

'Well, I don't know how he's going to make an offer for Number 20 when he has no idea how much he'll be getting.'

The hair along Letitia's arms stood on end. 'Gaddy dear, what did you say about Number 20? That's where old Mrs Sawbridge and her King Charles's spaniels live.'

Gaddy's hand flew to her mouth, her red-rimmed eyes like saucers. 'Oh, good heavens!' she said. 'He told me not to say anything about that, too. I'm not very good at deception, Lettie. I never have been, have I?'

'Thank goodness you're not. Please tell me. I think I ought to know.'

'That's what I said, too, but Fin said he'd tell you himself. Old Mrs Sawbridge is looking for a private buyer, Fin says, because she doesn't want people traipsing all over the house and upsetting the dogs, and she's going to live with her sister in Mortlake. She has a huge place by the—'

'Yes, love. I'm sure that will be best, but has Fin made her an offer?'

'He wants to look round it first, and that's why he was going to suggest to you that, while we're in London next month, you might let him stay here to look after things for you.'

'So he can pester Mrs Sawbridge to sell it to him? But as you said, he doesn't have any money yet. Is he expecting Uncle Aspinall to help him out, until he's in funds again?'

'I don't know, dear. He was in a rush to get your phaeton and go. He asked about Mr Waverley and then dashed off.'

'Just a moment. This was on Monday. Did you know then about Mr Waverley's accident?'

'No, not until Tuesday when he didn't turn up for his mathematics lesson. I was surprised Fin should have asked me about him, because they're not particular friends, are they? I just told him he was well, as far as I knew.'

'Did he ask you anything else about Mr Waverley, or me?'

'Only how long you'd known each other. I said several years, but I didn't think it was any of his business, and I have to say, Lettie dear, that I'm not too happy about him wanting to stay here while we're away, or about him buying Number 20. Do we want him living so close? And do I *really* want to live with him? He'll have his navy friends to stay, you know, and expect me to keep house for him, and then he'll get himself a wife and I shall be a nuisance to her, and...oh!' The tears spilled down her cheeks as the future spread itself before her like a bleak landscape full of pitfalls.

Once again, Letitia comforted her, telling her that she need never live anywhere she didn't want to. Besides, she was very much needed. How else would they manage? And, by the way, Lord Rayne had appointed himself their champion.

Gaddy sniffed and dabbed. 'That's not really a surprise, Lettie dear. I knew you and he were getting on well when I heard raised voices. That's always an indication of high regard, isn't it?'

If that was heartening news, Gaddy's disclosure about her brother's plans was quite the opposite, as was the news that Number 20 was up for sale. The ideal solution would be for Letitia herself to bid for it, to expand the seminary, but if the girls' parents objected to the idea of her writing books and being someone's mistress, the future would take a more unexpected turn. Ideally, she would like to take in more boarders and give Gaddy more space, but of such things were dreams made.

Taking written messages from the girls, flowers, a freshly caught trout, some new spinach from the garden, a book of poetry and an embroidered bookmark, Letitia paid a visit to Mr Waverley and stayed with him half an hour to tell him of her plans to go to London with Rayne. Not wishing to disturb him with Cousin Fin's devious activities, she kept well away from that subject, but told him instead of Edina's happy return to the fold and of the courage she had shown, and how she herself had made good use of the experience at second-hand for Perdita's story, which, she said, was likely to be the best of the three. Although Bart's attempt to smile was rather grotesque, it showed that he knew why she expected to improve.

By the time they reached London on Thursday morning, Rayne was in full possession of the facts about Letitia's writing and Mr William Lake's publishing of it, including the price of every volume, the number printed, the costs incurred and the fee paid, which he said was derisory in view of her success. If necessary, Rayne told her, they would give Lake the unsigned contract back and tell him that, in future, Miss Letitia Boyce's books would be offered to Egerton, Miss Austen's publisher, or John Murray in Albemarle Street. There were others, he said, who would jump at the opportunity.

But Rayne was in determined mood, and once Mr Lake had recovered from his initial astonishment at seeing, after two years, what his most famous author looked like, not to mention the aristocrat who brought her to his offices, he seemed not to resemble Mr Waverley's description of hard-bitten businessman as closely as all that. On the contrary, though Letitia said very little on her own account, Mr Lake responded to Rayne's amazingly fluent grasp of the business with obvious admiration.

While not for one moment implying that Mr Lake had been exploiting the anonymous author and her gentle well-bred mediator, Rayne picked up and renegotiated every single clause in the brief contract, including publication at Lake's own expense, a larger print run with a doubled cover price of six shillings for each volume, and a much increased payment for the copyright of the third book, to be renegotiated for subsequent ones. This, Rayne said, Miss Boyce would prefer to receive in advance. She would also want a bigger percentage of all sales and, for Mr Lake to make the best of these new arrangements, he would have to increase his subscription list to defray costs, find some more prestigious sponsors and employ some better marketing techniques. It was a pity, Rayne said, that one had to chase all round the London libraries to get copies of Miss Boyce's novels when they ought to be available from every bookshop. Libraries and borrowing from friends did not bring in the money.

However, Mr Lake brightened considerably when Rayne told him that, from now on, the author's name would appear on the book, for the name of Boyce would undoubtedly be good for publicity and, it went without saying, for Mercury Press. A new contract would be drawn up immediately, said Lake.

'To be delivered, by hand, to Number 24 Paradise Road, Richmond, within seven days, if you please,' said Rayne, 'for my client to check the details, and sign.'

'Of course.' Mr Lake blinked like an owl at Letitia, who smiled.

'It will be returned to you for your counter-signature within the next seven days, after which you will promptly return her copy and her fee. By hand. We do not expect to have to traipse all the way to London to collect any monies due to my client in future. This is to be written into the contract, sir.'

Again, Mr Lake blinked and scribbled furiously, slightly reddening around the jowls. 'As you say, my lord. We shall not delay. Anything else?'

'Miss Boyce?' said Rayne. 'Does that cover everything?'

'My two free copies to be increased to six?' she said, trying not to laugh.

Lake scribbled again. 'Certainly,' he mumbled. 'Six free copies.'

'And I would like the quality of the paper to be the same as the others, if you please, Mr Lake, and the covers, too. I like the gold tooling. Could we have blue covers this time, do you think?'

At last he smiled. 'I don't see why not, Miss Boyce. What will it be called, so that I may enter it in the contract?'

'*Perdita*, sir.'

'Ah, the lost one. And is she lost, this young lady?'

'She starts off lost, but…' she glanced at Rayne, feeling his eyes upon her '…she then begins to find herself. With help. Quite a lot of help, really.'

Lake nodded as if he understood perfectly. 'I look forward to seeing the manuscript. Do you have a date in mind, Miss Boyce?' He dipped his quill in the inkpot, ready to write.

'Probably the end of July. Shall we say July the thirty-first?'

Laying the quill down, Lane sat back to look at her over the top of his steel-rimmed spectacles. '*This* year? You have already started it, then?'

'Yes, it's well under way.'

'Splendid! Perdita will be found by July thirty-first. Excellent.'

By the way he looked at her, Letitia was left with the notion that Mr Lake believed Perdita's story to be vaguely autobiographical. But he was far too astute to say so.

Walking down the dingy wooden stairs from the office into the bookshop-library, Rayne made the remark for her ears only that, if he had anything to do with it, Perdita would be found well before the end of July.

It was no wonder that Lake was impressed, for Letitia had donned her most fashionable day dress and a three-quarter-length midnight-blue velvet pelisse with silver buttons and some very clever lattice work on the sleeves, the collar and around the crown of the matching brimmed hat. This might have been a severe ensemble but for the elaborate frill on the hem of the white dress that appeared also on the cuffs and neckline. If she had been concerned by the reception of Lord Rayne's parents, however, she need not have been for, although she had met them once or twice as a girl, they could not be expected to remember her as Lady Boyce's eldest blue-stocking daughter. Nor did they know from one month to the next who their youngest son's current mistress was, though their welcome was warmer by far than anything Letitia's mother offered her, these days.

'We've been in Berkeley Square only three years,' the Marchioness told her as they walked past portraits of ancestors in their best clothes. 'St. James's Square was becoming a little down at heel, and a bit too close to the high-class bawdy houses,' she confided with a grin. 'Some of them even spread into the square.'

Having met Lady Dorna Elwick several times, there could be no possible doubt about the relationship, for not only did mother and daughter share the same blonde prettiness, but their taste in clothes was remarkably similar, too, glamorous, diaphanous and cut daringly low over voluptuous curves, yet entirely suited to their characters, concealing little except their age. It was hard to guess how old Lady Sheen might be, though Rayne had told her that she had been the Duke of Ashen's mistress before she met his father, but had still been only twenty when she had had Nicholas. As he had said, mistresses were not new to the Sheens.

In the huge house, Letitia's room was along a gold-carpeted corridor hung with oak-garland wallpaper punctuated by white-painted doors. A green-liveried footman held one of them open. 'Here we are,' said Lady Sheen, passing through in a cloud of silk chiffon and swansdown. 'Seton says you must have the best Blue Room, and I can see that it's your colour, my dear. Your maid can have the little closet next door, and I've instructed mine to look after her, so if there's anything you require, she will get it for you.'

'You are so kind, my lady. Thank you. I didn't know quite how you would receive me when my own home is only a walk away. It must look rather…'

'Mothers and daughters don't always get on as well as they might,' said Lady Sheen, taking Letitia's hand. 'I'm fortunate, but I dare say if Dorna and I lived any nearer, we'd fight like terriers. Too much the same, you know. I don't think anything about you being here instead of with your mama, but I *do* want to hear all about this exclusive seminary of yours at Richmond. Ah, here's your maid and the luggage. Come down when you're ready. I think Seton wants to take you shopping.'

Seton, she discovered moments later, was more like his father and elder brother with the same lean fitness and graceful bearing, the Marquess's snow-white hair predicting how theirs might look in another thirty years. Letitia had dreaded some remark about her appearance as Rayne's lady friend, but the elegant Lord Sheen greeted her only with a genuine interest in the eldest daughter of the late Sir Leo

Boyce, the architect, who had flown the nest at such an early age. That showed courage. If you knew what you wanted from life, you should go and get it, he said. Then, laughing at his own moralising, he added, 'And it helps to know what you *don't* want, too. Eh, my lad?'

'Yes, sir,' said Rayne, pulling out Letitia's chair. 'Indeed it does.'

'As long as you don't spend all your best years finding that out,' said Letitia, 'before discovering that your standards were perhaps a little too unrealistic.'

'Then I must be one of the fortunate ones,' he replied, seating himself beside her, 'to have my high standards met before I reach my dotage.'

'Well said, lad,' said his father. 'You certainly aimed high this time. Now, my dear Lady Sheen, do you want me to carve this ham, or shall we see what a mess young Seton makes of it?'

Rayne stood up again. 'It is well known that no one but yourself can make a mess of a ham, sir. Pass me the carvers and I'll show you how to cut it into slices instead of doorsteps.'

'Tch!' said Lord Sheen. 'I was carving ham before you were born, lad. But here you are. You'd better get some practice in before you have your own lunch table. Eh, Miss Boyce?' He winked at her, fatherly.

Letitia smiled at her plate, at the gold rim and the crest upon it.

Replacing the smooth lid of her writing-desk, Letitia locked it. She had decided that, despite her good intentions, her thoughts on the past hours would have to wait until daylight. Now, it was time to prepare for a completely new experience, one which had not been far from her mind all day, as she knew it had not been from Rayne's, either. He had complimented her on her appearance, and she knew it had been meant, for his eyes had hardly left her. Others had done the same, people she knew at the Misses Berry's soirée who had not seen her for months, making her feel welcome and special, and somehow distinguished by being in Rayne's company. Nothing had been remarked, of course, about her new position, but everyone seemed to understand the nature of it. Nor had the two of them stuck together all evening, for that would not have been quite the thing, but their arrival, supper and departure together had been quite enough. As for the silver spectacles, she could hardly count the times she'd been begged to reveal which glasses-maker had supplied them.

Now, she removed them and placed them in their case, recalling the pleasure she had felt at being able to see at last the shelves of merchandise at the Exeter Exchange and the brilliant bolts of fabric at Wilding and Kent's. Faces she was able to recognise from across the street had smiled and called greetings. Men's heads had turned and the occasional whistle had been ignored, but inwardly relished. She also recalled the times when she had told herself how little these things mattered to her, how unnecessary to one's well-being. But she had been mistaken, for never had she felt so proud to be handed in and out of Lord Rayne's curricle, or to fly past with a wave and a smile. This unusual sense of elation had remained with her throughout the evening like a girl at her first ball, even though she was on familiar ground. Rayne had said very little to her on the short journey home, but had held her hand very firmly all the way, escorted her to the door of her room and asked her if she would keep it unlocked for him. What a question, she had thought, nodding her assent. What a shameless thing to do for Perdita's sake. Or was it?

Orla was dismissed, her evening clothes put away, her jewels, her papers, her hair plaited and hanging down her back. What were mistresses supposed to do at such times? Pretend to be reading? Asleep? Standing? Waiting demurely? In a pretty muslin house-gown she stood by the four-poster bed, thinking that no lovelier setting could have been devised for a seduction, nowhere more sumptuously comfortable, velvet and brocade curtained, white and gold painted, shaded with blue like summer cornflowers. There was a blue-and-white patterned *chaise longue* on which she would perch in the morning, and an ingenious washstand with a container to catch the water, brass taps, scented soap, white towels.

She was halfway across the room before the sound of the knock had died. Then she took a deep breath, waited three seconds, and opened it. 'Why, Lord Rayne!' she whispered. 'What a pleasant surprise. Will you come in?'

He caught the ruse immediately. 'Miss Boyce?' he said. 'Miss Letitia Boyce, author of *The Infidel* and others too numerous to mention?'

'The same,' she said, closing the door behind him.

'This is an honour, ma'am. I know it's rather late, but I wonder if you'd write a short dedication in the first eight I've brought with me, and the other twenty-four in the morning. I have them stacked up outside the door.'

'That might take some time, sir. Besides, when I'm told that my characters are not quite credible, or some such, I tend not to write dedications for them until they—'

'I did not say they were not credible, Miss Boyce, I said

that what they did *together* lacked authenticity. That's not the same thing.'

She felt the laughter welling up inside her as his hand took hers and led her gently over to the *chaise longue*, which she had not thought to use until tomorrow. He wore a long dark-green gown with a small leaf-pattern on it that caught the sheen of the candlelight as he moved. On his feet he wore leather mules that made no sound on the carpet, and she suspected that, by the exposed V of bare neck, he wore very little else except the faint aroma of sandalwood.

'Well,' she pouted, 'I have a moment. You could explain exactly what you mean, I suppose, though I can't promise to write…how many dedications?'

'Thirty-two.'

'Do you profess to be an authority on what people do together, sir?'

Wedging himself into the soft bolstered end of the *chaise longue*, he caught her by the waist and pulled her backwards against him, enclosing her with his legs and arms, nestling her against his chest as she had never been before. 'I have made something of a study of it, Miss Boyce,' he said in a voice that imitated exactly one of Miss Berry's guests who had brought along a working model of a beam-engine for discussion. 'I think I may say, with all due modesty, that I am a leading exponent of water pumps, pistons and steam-power, and just about everything else.'

'Is this what you were thinking of, sir, when you appeared to be listening so raptly?'

He sighed, dropping his voice to a chastened whisper. 'I admit, Miss Boyce, that I was not thinking of pounds per square inch in quite the same way that he was. There, now you have the truth of it. I went there only to gaze upon you, as I saw everyone else doing.'

'Now you *are* talking nonsense, sir. They were not gazing at me.'

'Yes, they were. All except Mr Beam-Engine. They all envied me, too, knowing that I'd have you like this before the night was out. In my arms.'

'Doing what people do together?'

'Which was something missing from your stories, Miss Boyce. Your characters don't talk to each other enough. It all happens far too quickly. Could you slow them down a bit and get them to enjoy it? It isn't about what *he* does to *her*, you know, it's about what lovers do *together*.'

Without a shred of awkwardness, he had gentled her into his close embrace where both her mind and body waited to be taught, for now his fingertips played over the inside of her wrists and along her arms and, because it was his touch and no one else's, part of her body was melting with desire. Turning her head against his chest, she whispered, 'Didn't you say once that you wouldn't be doing much talking, sir?'

'Later,' he said, 'neither will you.' He took the candlestick and moved it away to one side so that it no longer shone into her eyes. 'But most lessons begin with a resumé of what's already known, don't they? Take the kiss, for instance.'

Whatever ideas she'd had about learning the mysteries of lovemaking, the timing of it, the range, the depth of the heroine's involvement and the consummation, these were in danger from the very beginning of becoming changed by emotions she had not expected to feel. Her analytical mind had rarely let her down before, but this time it stood no chance against Rayne's skilful teaching for, whether he was using her stories as an excuse or not, it took only one kiss to confuse her organised list of questions.

She thought she knew about kisses, though now she found that those others had been chaste compared to the travelling variety that moved from her lips to cover her face, her neck and throat, then down towards her shoulders. His warm knowing hands preceded them, smoothing the way, slipping her loose gown off her shoulders until the neckline rested on the swell of her breasts, tantalising them both.

But by now the playfulness had changed to something more intent, for he would not make a game of this, her first time. She was a woman, not a child, and this was not a patronising lesson she needed, but a sensitive celebration of new womanhood to be remembered for all time. What was more, the love scenes in her stories, while lacking in reality, were beautifully imaginative, and Rayne knew that she would expect to find out from him, without disgust, what she could hardly visualise for herself. He did not suppose her mother would have been much help to her in this.

She lay quietly in the crook of his arm, all facetiousness gone, her eyes wide, dark with longing and apprehension, looking into his face to find the next move. Her neck had come alive with his kisses, waiting for more. 'You have a most beautiful mouth,' she whispered, touching the corner of it with one finger. 'Beautiful teeth, too.' Her eyes said more. Then, as if she had already learnt something, she reached up to draw his head down to hers, to feel his skin with her lips over his cheeks and eyelids, chin and ears, tasting the male scent of him. She felt waves of heat ripple through her as he breathed out in a rush, half-laugh, half-gasp, his closeness and the gentle male pressure of him alone making her weak with want. Her fingers trembled.

Rayne responded. Gathering her up in his arms and swinging them both off the *chaise longue*, he strode across to the bed where he held her, poised above the linen sheets with her robe slipped down to expose one breast, pushed by his arm to form an exquisite peak. Already aroused by his roving kisses, the nipple stood firm like a bead of dark coral upon a mound of cream velvet.

She saw his lips part and his chest heave under the deep breath. 'My lord?' she whispered, suddenly fearful. 'You are having second thoughts?'

Slowly, he shook his head. 'No, my beauty. I'm wondering how I've managed to keep my hands off you for so long. I'm also wondering how I'm going to show you what you hope for, taking time, making it last as I said it should. You are sensational, Lettie Boyce, yet you are still virgin and I dare not rush through this.'

'I think I understand. But surely we could compromise? You have no experience of virgins?'

'Only once, when I was fifteen. I don't think she enjoyed it much. I've learned a lot since then.'

'Nor do I expect to learn everything in one experience. A little at a time will do quite well, I think. I would not offer myself to anyone but you.'

He swayed her in his arms, smiling at a thought. 'I think we both knew, didn't we? Even then, when I was at my most boorish and you fuming with anger.'

Covering her exposed breast with one hand, she scolded him gently. 'I shall not tell you what I knew then, my lord. It would go to your head.'

Huskily, he laughed, lowering her to the bed. 'Then I shall return the compliment, sweetheart, and take your gift of virginity with as much care as I can, given that you are enough to send a man crazy with desire.' Shrugging off his robe, he was careful, she noticed, not to let her see all of him, but to rest beside her on one elbow, looking down into her eyes, though now it was a world of deep shadows and specks of light upon the gilded bed-posts and the canopy above them.

His hand sought her plait and began to undo it, combing through the long tresses to free the silver cascade and to arrange veils of it over her breasts, not knowing how every slight touch of his fingertips upon her skin sent shockwaves into her thighs. Pushing the rest of her robe away and sweeping her hair, he touched her nipples and, when she responded with a cry, he stopped it with a deep kiss while his hand continued its torment, raking and fondling, kindling and stoking the deepest fires within her as nothing in her imagination had ever done.

She felt herself being swept along a path completely unknown to her like a leaf in a whirlwind, giving him control of every move. Rayne was strong and beautifully made, bulging with muscle and sinew under her hands, surprising her with the hardness of him, the touch of smooth skin, the width of shoulder and deep curve of spine, the soft fuzz along his arms and chest and the feel of it next to her body, exciting her still more. Pushing her fingers deep into his hair, she felt its silkiness like water before his head moved away, bending to her breast, taking her hands with it.

Her cry became a low moan that did nothing to check him or the sensation wrought by his mouth. His hand captured her breast as if to hold all her desire in that one place while he took his fill, though long before he had finished his mouth had explored the surrounding areas, too, keeping her on the edge of an excitement that promised even more delights before returning to the piercing sweetness of his suckling.

Visiting her mouth again, he played tenderly with her lips while his hand smoothed over her stomach and hips as if purposely to take her mind in two directions, giving her the chance to protest. She did, half-heartedly catching at his hand as it slid downwards to the soft mound between her legs. His kiss deepened and, at last, her grip on his wrist slackened, letting it move on to explore the tender folds, which would be the last to yield to his courteous intrusion.

His stroking plunging fingers were, at first, a source of indescribable delight, for this was a sensation so unique that no one ever spoke of it, let alone wrote about it. But then came a sharp and distant pain that was more surprising for its unexpectedness than for its severity, making Letitia yelp even as his kiss came to comfort her, and she clung to his wrist again, nipping at his chin with her teeth in retaliation.

She heard his huff of laughter as he slipped an arm beneath her back, placing himself over her so that for a few delicious seconds she felt his weight, his nudging legs against hers, and it was all so quickly done that she had no time to argue about it. She sensed the change in him as his body hardened above her like a great buttress, his hold on her urgent and sure, guiding himself into her, pulling her close with his arm so smoothly that she was hardly aware of his possession except by the amazing sensation of completeness now replacing the one before it. He waited, pushing the loose hair away from her face, kissing her eyelids.

'Did I hurt you, my beauty? I'm sorry. I tried not to.'

'I don't…think…so. It's all right. Go on. It's wonderful.'

Slowly he began to move, deeper and deeper, filling her

entirely until she was rocked by each tender thrust, his magnificent body sending waves of warmth over her and a presence of domination that had less to do with submission than with a kind of intimate partnership, a binding contract between herself and him that, no matter what happened, would remain for ever. She was his woman. He was telling her so. She felt the primitive message through every part of her body.

It was not what she had intended to happen to her mind, however, for she had not believed it would be engaged on this scale, or that she would feel for him anything more than she had before, though that had grown of late. But how could she remain the same, having taken him into herself, to share the same delight? She was discovering what she had wanted to know, and far more than that, but now she was also discovering things about herself that were not on her list, like a heart that was not as impregnable as she'd thought, for instance. Like a burning bright desire that might not be quenched at her command.

She found no answers, for Rayne knew how to close a woman's mind to everything except the incredible plunging rhythm that brought with it a wondrous comfort and then, with his bold, earthy whispers, a growing excitement. She clung to him, moaning, tossing her silver hair upon the pillow. The fires intensified, and she was lost inside them. She heard herself cry out in a long sighing wail of ecstasy as he moved fast into her, and the whirlwind took her breath for its own, holding it beyond reach as the fire raged and consumed, making her call out again, softly, into his ear.

As if from a distance came the muffled sound of Rayne's deep groan, then the final thrust as he convulsed and relaxed, covering her with his warmth. She knew then with a compelling certainty that what had happened between them just now was not the usual way of things, otherwise the married women of her acquaintance would have spoken of it with more joy than long sufferance. They had provided no details, naturally, but all the implications were that the once-a-month respite was the best part of a husband's attentions. What she had just experienced was beyond anything in her fantasies, something to be accepted whenever it was offered. Perhaps oftener.

Rolling aside, he pulled her into his arms, spilling her hair out across his shoulder, kissing the top of her head and murmuring endearments she had never heard before about how she was now his woman, for all time.

Caressing his face, she pushed the damp locks out of his eyes and let her fingers wander over his mouth. 'You're smiling, my lord. I think you're pleased with yourself, are you not?'

His voice was a deep chuckling rumble that vibrated beneath her hand. 'I certainly am, my beautiful amazing woman, and I'm even more pleased with you. That was something I never thought would happen for years. Some women never experience that at all, you know.'

She knew what he referred to. He should take the credit for it. 'I have little to compare it to, but if I gave you pleasure, it was because you showed me how. My concern now is that once is not going to be enough. My memory—'

With a laugh, he reared up above her. 'Who said anything about *once*? Did you think to be my mistress for a day? A week? I'm keeping you, woman, and even when you think your characters know all they need to know, you'll still be mine. Don't think I don't know what this is all about.' His kiss drew her mind back to the experience they had shared, to its fierce beauty and the violence of their passion, to sensations of which she had known nothing until now.

'No,' she whispered, when his kiss finished, 'that's not what this is all about. I admit that was my original thought, but I am not so cynical that I can pretend to be unaffected by what's just happened, and before. Perhaps we should keep my characters out of the bedroom. They have no place here. Let them fend for themselves, my lord. They're undeserving.'

'They've had their uses,' he said, easing her back into his embrace, 'but it pleases me more than I can say that you want more, sweetheart. Was I too rough with you?'

'Wonderfully so, thank you, my lord.'

His arm tightened as they laughed together. Resting her leg over the top of his, she smoothed the sole of her foot along his skin, thinking that this must be the nearest thing to paradise she would ever come.

Chapter Thirteen

Although the new writing-desk had travelled to London with them, there was hardly any time for writing except for a few notes on their whereabouts, the emotions and sensations remaining in Letitia's mind as being rather too fragile to commit to words until she had time to understand them better.

Rayne had remained with her all night, jubilant that she wanted more of his loving. She was, he thought, a truly remarkable woman, an opinion that was apparently endorsed by his parents and those they had met in town, reminding him of the way people took second glances at Amelie, his brother's wife. Now it was happening to him, too, and, to show her off even more, he borrowed horses from his father's fine stable for a morning ride in Hyde Park, which he had seldom done with other women. Miss Boyce was superb on horseback in her pale grey and silver habit and, with her by his side, Rayne felt more proud and complete than he had ever done.

They returned to Berkeley Square for a light lunch before a walk in St James's Park to see the pagoda and Chinese bridge. When asked if she would not rather go shopping, her reply was that she could do that any time, but now she would rather walk with him and enjoy his company without interference. 'Is that selfish of me?' she asked him, pulling on her cream kid gloves.

'It's the first time in years anyone has preferred a walk in my company to a shopping expedition,' he replied. 'I'm truly flattered.'

'I know very little about you, my lord. I think it's time I did.'

The walk was taken at a sedate pace, neither of them realising how the hours flew as they talked and looked, and by the time they had strolled all round the park and back to Berkeley Square, Letitia had made another discovery that, far from being arrogant, affected, odious, or any of the other epithets she had once used on him, he was in fact very unassuming, knowledgeable and interesting to listen to. Which, if she had not been so prejudiced, she might have been able to see before.

That evening, the Marchioness of Sheen held a dinner party for eighteen guests, never a favourite entertainment with Letitia, who preferred intimate meals. This time, she discovered that the conversation round the great table was quite unlike the shallow isolating chatter at her mother's parties, for the Sheens and their guests were interesting and pleasantly easy-going people.

'My parents,' Rayne told her, 'are enchanted by you, Miss Boyce. In fact, they all were. My father tells me to be quick and snap you up before someone else does.'

She laid her palms upon his chest, trying to appear demure. 'But I thought you *had* snapped me up, my lord. Haven't you?'

'What he means, sweetheart, is that eldest daughters are

quite often snapped up by eldest sons. And I am not an eldest son. I shall have a modest inheritance, but nothing like the property that Nick will have. A little pile in Hampshire is all.'

'Are you telling me that, as a mistress, I don't get a Marble Hill House like Mrs Fitzherbert, or a fleet of carriages like the Duke of Cumberland's mistress did?'

''Fraid not.'

'Oh, dear. No flunkeys, servants, cottage in the country?'

'Nope.'

'Tch! Huh! Well, what am I doing here then?'

With a laugh and a swoop too fast for her to avoid, he swept her up into his arms and carried her across to the bed, holding her on to it before she could roll off. 'This,' he said, 'is what you're doing here, woman. It's what I've waited all day for. Now, shall you submit to me?'

The laughter stopped and he looked down at her in the candlelight with eyes darkly serious, watching the tiny pinpoints of light filter through her long lashes. Her full lips parted for him, and he bent his head to hers, tasting them gently before releasing the longings of the day.

Staying so close to home had reminded Letitia yet again that her mother's threat to publicise Sapphire Melborough's lapse from grace was still a very real one. The damage to her own career was also never far from her mind, though she found it hard to imagine that Mama would go to the lengths of discrediting her own daughter. Uncle Aspinall had been of the same mind.

Upon her return to Number 24 Paradise Road, it appeared that at least one set of parents were showing their disapproval by withdrawing their daughter from the seminary. The formally worded letter from the Reverend Miles Nolan and

Mrs Nolan begged to inform her of their reluctant decision to find a ladies' seminary holding stricter Christian principles than hers for Miss Verity Nolan whose character, at sixteen, was particularly impressionable.

'Well, I'm glad they think so,' Letitia said to Mr Waverley, later that day. 'Personally, I never believed Verity's character was anything like as impressionable as it ought to be, at her age. She meanders through life as if it were a dream, so I doubt very much if she'd even notice what I was doing with mine.'

Mr Waverley's grin was by now more comfortable. Sitting up against the pillows, his multi-coloured face made an interesting contrast with the white cotton, and Letitia was pleased to see that his nose and teeth were undamaged. He tapped the pile of letters she had brought. 'Never mind the vicar,' he said. 'It was to be expected. Look at these, though. Four more applicants. All you need now is more rooms.'

Smiling, she had to agree on all counts. 'That would be ideal, Bart. I have a mind to make old Mrs Sawbridge an offer for Number 20, but I've no idea how much she's expecting.'

'Go round and find out.'

'That would not be improper, would it?'

'Not at all. She may even prefer to sell it to her neighbour rather than to a stranger. Now, tell me how you fared with Mr Lake. Was Rayne businesslike?'

The news that she had a new contract seemed to cheer him and, as she left, she heard the sound of laughter through the open window as two more friends joined him. Dear Bart was on the mend.

But while Letitia had been visiting Mr Waverley, she had missed her own visitor. Miss Gaddestone was eager to give her the rather garbled message that Lady Elyot would call again soon but, meanwhile, Letitia might like to know that her niece, the one who was now Lady Boston living in the other northern Richmond, was to come to take up residence at Number 18 for a period of several weeks.

'When?' said Letitia, taking off her bonnet.

'Next Tuesday, I think. Well, Lady Elyot thinks. With all her family.'

'That's wonderful.'

Miss Gaddestone looked sideways at her cousin, aware of some reserve. 'Are you not pleased? Lady Elyot says you'll like her.'

'Yes, I'm sure I shall. I believe she has a fine voice.'

'Well, that's the other thing. Lady Elyot wants to hold a concert for them at Sheen House like the one at the Melboroughs.' Miss Gaddestone trotted in front of Letitia, spilling out snippets of information like the hare in a paper-chase.

'What?'

There was almost a collision. 'Er…a concert. With the Bostons. They're all musical. And our girls, too, like before. And she wants Lady Boyce to stay with them at Sheen Court, and Uncle Aspinall and Aunt Minnie, too.'

'*Stay* with them? She won't do that. Not Mama.'

'She will, Lettie. I've never known Aunt Euphemia pass up an invitation to hob-nob with the aristocrats, have you? All the families, Lady Elyot said. And that means theirs, as well as ours and the girls' families.'

'Well, we can't. We shall be in London by then.'

'No, we won't, Lettie. Not in ten days' time.'

'Ten…ten *days*? Gaddy, you didn't say we would, did you?'

'Yes, love. I told her… Oh, dear.'

'What did you tell her?'

'That we'd be delighted to meet Lady Boston and her family. Caterina, she called her. Such a pretty name. And that we'd be honoured to help with the concert. Well, we will, won't we, Lettie?'

'Yes, Gaddy dear. Honoured, thrilled, delighted. Is that tea still hot?'

That same evening, Letitia dressed with exceptional care for a private dinner with Rayne before going on to the Richmond Theatre to see a production of *The Duchess of Malfi*, which she afterwards wished she had not, so tragic was it. Later, in her own bed, she made love to him with an intensity that only an experienced lover would identify with fear and a growing jealousy, which he knew how to alleviate with a passion of his own and with assurances that she was all he wanted. Understanding the reason for it, he would hardly have been human not to feel a secret pleasure at the strength of her feelings.

Early on Sunday morning, he took his leave of her, promising to return by nightfall if it was at all possible. Otherwise, it would be Monday.

She had tried all day, to no avail, to place those feelings behind her. They were unfair, prejudiced and unworthy, too. What right did she have to claim all of his heart when it had never been offered to her, when she had not offered hers in return? Of course he had had affairs, many of them. That was no secret to Perdita. But this one involved a member of the family, one who would never quietly disappear like the others, and how could she expect to attain the same position in his heart as one who had been there for years already?

Had she not become his lover, she supposed her heart might have remained intact and proof against such anguish as this, but she had lain in his arms and become one with him, and his loving was like a drug. He excited and moved her as she had never been moved before. She had felt whole, replete and womanly, and there was little she could do for him that others had not done before. Perhaps better.

Perdita lowered her head into her hands, refusing the tears that threatened, determined not to give him up before she had even seen them together. Then she would know. Then she would decide...what...to turn off this thing called love? Impossible. It was a pain she would have to learn to live with.

Letitia laid the quill upon the writing-desk and stared at the page, starting a little at the faint sound below that would surely be him, come to share the night with her as they'd hoped. He had been at Hampton Court Palace all day with his brother, for the Prince Regent's favourite filly was foaling for the first time, an unpredictable business. The page was left upon the slope as she folded the lid on top of it, trapped safely between the wood.

Almost silently, the door opened to let the tall shadowy figure through with barely enough time to close it before one arm came across her shoulders, pulling her close, taking the greeting from her lips, hungrily.

'I'm late, sweetheart.'

'I thought you were not coming.'

'I said I would.'

'Your hair is wet.'

'It's raining.'

'You rode, in the rain? Was there no carriage for you?'

'Riding's quicker. I'm steamy and smelly. Will you still have me?'

'You need never ask that, my lord. Sit over here and let me pull your boots off.'

'This is not quite what you bargained for when you took me on.'

'I think,' she said, looking at her muddy hands, 'we are both getting rather more than we bargained for. Lift the other one.'

'Is this what they call indecent haste?' He grinned.

'Yes, I believe so. Come, give me your coat.'

A week ago, she would have been shamed at her urgent participation, to be undressing a man in her own room for such a purpose. Yet now she felt no modesty or unease, only the same desire as he to give and take the longed-for comforts of body and mind, to wrap him in her arms, to be protected against the world. She had never felt so safe.

Her cry of surrender came sooner than he'd expected, telling him how she'd missed him and needed him by her side. Now, she whispered fierce words in his ear, 'Go on, Seton, go on…do it now…I need you…I want you…quickly!'

'That's my beauty,' he replied. 'You've come to my hand at last.'

'You're gloating.'

'Yes, sweetheart, I'm gloating and you're mine. Mine.' With the last forceful word, he took possession of her, flying like eagles in a storm, softly buffeted, calling to each other, lifted high above the world until, spent and breathless, they came to rest, exhilarated and safe.

The new bond they had forged together was too precious and fragile for Letitia to tell him of her concerns about her perceived rival, nor was Rayne foolish enough to broach the subject before she did. Nevertheless, he sensed as before her need for reassurance, which, he told himself, she was much in want of, despite her seeming confidence in so many other matters. She was, he thought, a delightful mixture of self-reliance and vulnerability.

She was up before him next morning, for Monday was one of her busiest days. Rayne took a more leisurely approach to dressing, his breakfast brought up on a tray by Mr Beck, the new butler. Without the help of his valet, he would have the dubious pleasure of tying his own neckcloth.

Standing before the mirror, his eye was caught by the writing-desk that had given Letitia so much pleasure. Its lid and base were not sitting flush with each other, as if something was caught between them. Lifting the lid by just an inch to see where the problem lay, he was unable to prevent the quick release of a paper to the floor. He let go of his cravat and stooped to pick the page up, but before he could slide it back inside, the elegant writing made him pause, arresting his attention with its beautiful pattern. He turned it and read her last entry.

A sound escaped him, made deep in his chest. 'Oh, sweet lass,' he whispered, staring at the words. 'Is that how it is? Such pain?'

Then he read it again, finally slipping it back into the desk and finishing his cravat with an unusual lack of concentration.

Sure that they'd seen the last of Lieutenant Gaddestone for a while after the last uncomfortable fiasco, Letitia was surprised to see him ride towards her across The Green as she left Mr Waverley's house.

'Cousin Lettie!' he called. 'Good afternoon. I was coming to see you.'

'Cousin Fin? Coming to see me, or your sister?'

'You, of course.' Dismounting, he threw the reins over the horse's head and led it beside her. Steam rose from its flanks and flecks of foam fell from the bit, the nostrils distended and trembling. 'Something I need to discuss with you.'

Guessing what that might be, Letitia steeled herself against anger. 'If it's a question of helping you out again,' she began, 'I don't think—'

'No, it's about the house next-door-but-one to yours. It's up for sale, you know, and I'm interested in it. Just what I've been looking for.'

'How on earth did you hear of it? I've only just heard myself.'

He ignored her question. 'Thought I'd get my bid in first, but I need you to come with me, Lettie. It'll look better if I'm with you, won't it?'

'So the money problem is resolved, is it? That's a relief, Fin.'

'Yes, it's an ideal place. I could give my sister her own suite of rooms, and both of us nearby to help whenever you need us. Just the ticket. We could call now, if you like. On the way home.'

There was something strange about this, Letitia thought, which she could not define. He had ridden hard to get here, but The Green was not *en route* to Paradise Road. She wanted to ask about the prize money, but this was hardly the place to discuss it.

'How *did* you hear about it?' she said.

'Happened to be in the Crickett Players having a drink. There was a young chap there called Ted who does her garden. He told me.'

'Ted?'

'Yes. You know him?'

'Slightly. His father works for me.'

'He seems to know everything that's going on around here. Just seen him again, as a matter of fact, in the Cricketers.'

So that's why Fin was on The Green. Brewer's Lane, with the Crickett Players public house, was just to one side. His drink must have been taken in haste, for his horse had barely recovered. Caution warned her to go back to Number 24, to speak to him in private. 'I have these books,' she said, indicating the two volumes she had just brought from Bart's beside. 'I should take them home first.'

'We're nearly there, Lettie. You need not carry them round. Oh, look, something's happening at Number 18 today.'

'That's Sir Chase and Lady Boston's house. They're expected.'

Boxes, trunks and hampers were being carried up the steps to where an elderly servant stood protesting that they should have gone round to the back, and when Lieutenant Gaddestone tied his horse to the railings only a little further on, it was hardly noticeable amongst the clutter.

It seemed a pity not to take the opportunity to look round Mrs Sawbridge's house, having intended to do so as soon as she could. Now she could safely let Fin ask the questions.

But the ear-splitting yapping of four white-and-brown spaniels was louder by far than the clanging bell, and though old Mrs Sawbridge was very hard of hearing, it was the demented behaviour of the dogs that alerted her to visitors. It was as Lieutenant Gaddestone had said, Letitia's presence and interest in the house prompting the owner to let them look round at their own pace. 'My legs,' Mrs Sawbridge shouted, patting her hip, 'don't work too well up all those stairs. My bed is down here now. Too large…can't keep it up. Yes, you take Mr Ganston round, dear. You know where the rooms are.' This to the accompaniment of hysterical yelps.

Letitia did not think it would be possible to discuss the price, in the circumstances, though this was what she most needed to know. So she took her cousin through one room after the other, stepping over small oddments of the old lady's life while noting the similarities and differences. 'Do we need to go upstairs?' she asked, dubiously.

'Just a quick look, to get the size. It'll need decorating.' There was a musty smell of stale air and old clothes after years of disuse. 'There's probably a good-sized attic up here, too. Is yours like this?'

'Almost identical,' she said, following him.

The attic, however, which in Lettie's renovated house was divided into light well-furnished rooms for the servants, was a shabby dingy place with an old bedstead and mattress in one corner, boxes and furniture thick with dust.

Lieutenant Gaddestone went to inspect the windows. 'Stuck,' he said. 'Well and truly stuck. She's not used this place for years.'

'Ugh! I've seen enough. It'll need some money spending on it, Fin. Am I to congratulate you at last? You've received your prize money and pay?' She turned to go, but Fin had closed the door and was leaning against it.

'Er, no. That's what I want to talk to you about, dear cousin.'

'No? So how are you going to make an offer? Have you borrowed from Uncle Aspinall? Is that it?'

'No, I hoped *you* would help me out.' The boyish grin was gone. The affability with it. Here was a young man of powerful build and serious mien who had lured her into this ghastly, foul-smelling place for the sole purpose of getting her to do something she had already said she preferred not to. He was not going to let her go without an argument.

She decided that to scold him would show him her fear, so she walked to the front window from where, down below, she could see the tops of carriages pass along Paradise Road. 'No, Fin. It's out of the question,' she said.

'Not only that, Lettie. I hoped you'd agree to marry me. We've always been close, haven't we? Remember? It's not too late. Even though Rayne has got to you first, I'm still willing to have you. He'll not want you much longer, you know. Once he's had a woman, he—'

'That's enough! *Enough!* What I do in my private life has nothing to do with you, nor will it *ever.* Now stand away from that door and let me go home. I have duties to perform.' Forgetting her intention not to scold, she felt the waves of anger and fear surge upwards, past the irritation, the exasperation and sheer annoyance at falling into this trap, ignoring the warnings any fool would have seen.

'Not before you've heard my proposal, Lettie. You cannot pretend to be surprised by it, you know. All I need is a little family help.'

'*Have* you asked Uncle Aspinall?'

'Him? Hah! Some hope. He's told me to find my own place within the next two weeks, but he's not in line for a loan. Oh, no.'

'No, I don't suppose you could get him into a disused attic very well, could you, and then bully him?'

'Oh, come, Lettie. We can never talk at your home with my sister flapping about. And Rayne, too, with his superior airs. I had to find a way of getting you to listen, and the old girl will sell it to me if you're with me. All I need is a loan, Lettie. I shall be able to refund you as soon as my—'

'As soon as your pay arrives? Haven't we heard that rather too often now, cousin? It's not *going* to arrive, is it? What you want is for me to finance your purchase so that you can take your sister on as your unpaid housekeeper. Don't think we have not seen through your plan.'

'Wrong, Lettie. You've missed out the bit that concerns you.'

'Forget it, Fin. We may once have been good friends, but that was years ago and we've both changed. I shall not even *think* of being your wife.'

'Why ever not? I wouldn't beat you. I'm as good as Rayne in bed.'

'Is that so? Thank you for showing me so clearly the workings of your mind. I must say I'm hardly surprised that you know so little about women after being at sea for years. You have a lot of catching up to do.'

'Then who better to help me than our family blue-stocking? You run the school for wealthy daughters and we'll have this place for our home, with Rosie to run it for us. What a cosy family we'll make. Now come on, it's the best offer *you're* going to get. Mistresses are never permanent, you know. Especially not with Rayne.'

'Your interest in Lord Rayne does you credit, but I can tell you one thing. He would not stoop to do what you're doing now, asking a lady to lend him money. That is simply not done, you know. Nor would he hold a lady against her will, or force a marriage proposal upon her. Did you really think to win me by such methods?'

'Oh, not *win* you, exactly. Call it what you like, but you'll stay up here until you agree to fall in with my plans.' Slipping a hand into his pocket, he pulled out a key. 'Now, let's just see how long it takes, shall we? The old girl is not going to hear a thing. The windows don't open. I should imagine it gets a bit chilly up here at night, but I'll be back in a day or two, and by that time you'll be talking.'

'And have you thought how you're going to explain my disappearance? I do have a tongue in my head, Fin. I can tell everyone what's happened.'

He smiled and waved the key at her, fluttering the label upon it like a flag. 'Ah, here's the next trick up my sleeve, dear cousin. The young man called Ted, who does the old lady's garden.'

Letitia's heart lurched, uncomfortably. 'What about him?'

'He's eager to make your acquaintance again. He seems to think you owe him some kind of favour.' Deliberately, he glanced towards the bed piled with dusty blankets. 'You've spread your favours for Rayne and he thinks you might be persuaded to do the same for him, now. He had this made for me,' he said, still waving the key. 'He's good with his hands.'

A hot surge of nausea made her breathless with fear. 'That makes no sense at all, Fin. You're talking about loans, favours, marriage, abduction and assault all in one breath and you think I shall say nothing about it? You must be *mad* if you think to persuade me by any of those means. And Mrs Sawbridge may be deaf, but she's not blind as well. She can see that two people came in and that only one went out. She knows me well enough.'

'Yes, I shall say that you went out of the back door, the one that Ted uses. And while everybody is searching for you, I'll do my best to look distraught, comfort my sister, poke about in your rooms, find some money, too, I dare say. That's really what it all boils down to, Lettie, isn't it? Money. I lost mine and you kept yours. Well, now I want *your* share in return for husbandly duties.'

From the distance of the dirty attic floor that lay between them, she tried to read from his face something of the old Fin she had once known, but there was little for her to recognise except bravado. He had always had more than his share of that. 'I'm not afraid of you, cousin,' she said. 'I dare say you would like me to be, but I feel only pity and sadness, because I used to like you.'

'Don't,' he snapped.

She had touched a nerve. 'We were good friends once, but you've changed. Is it the navy? The brutality? I've heard of what happens.'

'*You'd* change. Anybody would, if they'd seen what I've seen. Beatings, lashings, deprivation, starvation. You cannot imagine. No one can. Don't talk to me of *sadness*. They've taken my best years and left me with nothing, so now it's up to me to seek out the weakest and take what I can get. And that means you, Cousin Lettie. Come on, it won't be so very bad. Give me what I want, and we can settle this between us now without...' Pocketing the key again, he moved slowly towards her, shrugging his coat off his shoulders, slipping his arms out of the sleeves while watching to see how she would evade him.

'Without what, Fin? Without hard feelings? Is that what you were going to say?' Fear caught at her throat, drying it, pounding a tight beat into her chest, making her look round in desperation for something to throw, as she had done with Ted in the garden shed. There was nothing to hand but, behind him, the door upon which he had leaned had begun to open, inch by inch, silently, and Letitia knew that she must keep her eyes locked with his, not to mirror what she could almost see, not to reveal her hope even by the widening of an eyelid.

'Hah!' Fin laughed, tossing his coat across to the bed. 'Hard feelings? No, I was going to say without any broken bones.'

'Then, my friend,' said a deep voice from the doorway, 'you had better stop there, unless you want a broken neck.'

Fin wheeled round to face the intruder, his face aghast, his whole body tensed to launch himself upon the man whose voice he recognised. But the intended attack was halted by the sight of not one man but three, one of whom was, apparently, even less welcome than the other two.

'You…you *bastard*!' he snarled at Ted. 'You filthy lying scoundrel. Whose side are *you* on when it comes to the share-out? How much did they pay you?'

'Not on your side, matey,' said Ted. 'Not the way *you* do things.'

'Put your coat back on,' snapped Rayne, 'and lay one finger on Miss Boyce and I'll kill you. You're not fit even to *look* at her. Do as I say.'

For a moment, while Fin went to collect his coat, it looked as if he'd given in. But none of the three believed it, and no sooner had he picked it up than his hand delved deep into the pocket, lifting it to aim the concealed weapon through the fabric at the three men. The most terrifying explosion Letitia had ever heard filled every corner of the room, a flash, a billow of smoke, and a crash as Fin staggered backwards and fell hard against the wall. His yelp as he clutched at his groin was like that of a wounded animal.

'Nice little thing, this,' said the man with the pistol, examining its polished handle and brass mountings. 'Where d'ye get it, Rayne?'

'Bath, last year. A boxed pair of Mantons. Cost me an arm and a leg.' Lord Rayne walked over to Letitia by stepping over the victim's legs. 'Come on, sweet lass. It's all over. Come.' Gently, he removed her hands from her ears and pulled her into his arms, supporting her, smoothing her back.

'Is he dead?' she said into his cravat. She felt his head turn to look.

'Nah! Squawks like a rabbit, so he ain't dead. If it'd been me, I'd have aimed two inches to the left, Chase, but I'm not grumbling. If I carry Miss Boyce, can you two manhandle him downstairs?'

'Carry me? What rubbish…what…oh, heavens…I'm not the swooning kind, my lord, as I told you before but…may I…just…sit?'

'D'ye want me to carry her?' said the man called Chase, grinning. 'I've not carried a blonde for quite a while.'

'You go and carry your own wife,' Rayne said. 'This one's mine. Ted!' he called to the gardener's son. 'I'll catch up with you downstairs, if you can take this great lummock with you. I have a bit of unfinished business to attend to up here first.'

'Aye, m'lord. But I don't want no payment, mind. I just didn't want to see any harm come to Miss Boyce. Scum like him should be… Begging your pardon, ma'am. You all right?'

'Yes, thank you, Ted. I don't know what you did, but I'm more grateful than I can say.'

'It were nothing, ma'am. Nasty character, this,' he said without pausing for breath as he heaved Lieutenant Gadde-stone over his shoulder like a bag of garden rubbish. 'A bit o' fun's one thing, but not this kind o' skulduggery. No thanks, Sir Chase. I can manage him. If you'll follow me down, sir?'

'Sir Chase?' whispered Letitia. 'Is that…your friend next

door? Already in, are they?' The sound of footsteps faded with
the voices.

'That's him. Sir Chase Boston.'

'You're still friends, then?'

'One of my closest. Why should we not be?'

'Oh…well, I thought…oh, never mind. You're looking as
if I'm about to get a scolding.'

'Very bad English but yes, in a nutshell, I *did* wonder how
an otherwise intelligent woman could get herself into an attic
with a bad penny like Gaddestone who you *must* know by now
to be as nicked in the knob as anyone on two legs.'

'I *didn't* know,' she said, 'or I would not have—'

'Then you should have done!' Picking her up before she
could struggle out of his arms, he carried her over to the old
bed, which was the only place to sit. 'This is going to ruin my
coat, and probably my breeches, too, but when a wife has to
be chastised it's best to do it promptly, or they forget, like
horses do.'

'Like a horse? Like a wife? What are you talking about?'

'Well, it's quite obvious what I'm talking about, little nin-
nyhammer. How many more times am I going to have to get
you out of these scrapes? Eh? Are you going to spend your
life being cornered in libraries, garden sheds and attics by all
the bedazzled males in Richmond?'

'Not to mention the back-rooms of Hampton Court Pal—'

The furious retort was cut short by his mouth hard upon
hers, and no matter that she was not feeling quite herself, his
kiss made no concessions to her fragility. When she was able,
she mumbled, 'That's hardly fair, my lord.'

'Listen to me, Lettie Boyce. I know this was not part of
your plan, and I know it's probably not what you want, but

it's what you *need*. And you're going to have to agree, or I shall lock you up in this attic with only bread and water until you *do* agree. If your dastardly cousin can do it, so can I.'

'Do what?' she said, nudging his cheek with her nose.

'Damn it, Lettie. Marry me. For pity's sake marry me and put me out of my misery. I cannot have you as my mistress. I thought I could, but I can't. I want you for more than that. I want you for life, waking and sleeping. You see what happens when I let you out of my sight? This. It won't do, I tell you. You'll have to accept me because I can't live without you. So there.'

'Well, if the alternative is to be locked in here with only bread and water, which I've never liked…'

'Marry me, dammit! How many proposals take place in filthy attics? D'ye want me to go down on my knees?'

'Dearest lord…dearest, most wonderful lord.'

'Lettie, you're crying. Nay, don't cry, lass. Just say yes.'

'Yes. Yes. Yes…oh, sweetest man. Yes.'

Other convincing words were lost as Rayne celebrated the sweet harmony of two minds and hearts that laughed and wept, kissing her damp lips and eyelids, in accord at last upon every vexed question, even who should be first to say the momentous word. Love.

'Learn to give way to your husband, my lady, if you please,' he whispered, rocking her in his arms. 'I shall tell you first, because it was I who *knew* it first when you rode onto my parade ground. And you didn't. I've loved you every moment since then, dearest heart. I've never known a feeling like this for *any* woman, the way I do for you. I never want to let you out of my sight. Heaven only knows what'll happen to you, if I do.'

'Then I shall try to stay where we can see each other, beloved. Thank you, my hero, for coming to my rescue yet again. I never felt so afraid in my life, nor so relieved to see the man I love. Have I told you how I adore you? How much I'm in love with you?'

'No,' he said with a smile, kissing the tip of her nose. 'Never.'

'Well, I am. I have been for…well…' she put on her spectacles again and looked at him over the top rim '…for quite a long time. I found that it hurts badly at first, but now…'

'Now?'

'Now it's like paradise, my love. Safe and exciting at the same time. Will you take me home now? I've had enough of this place.'

'Yes, I will, but we shall certainly have to spend some money making it as habitable as your seminary. A month or two of work, at least.'

'Pardon? What are you saying? You haven't *bought* it?'

'A week ago, my love. And she may be as deaf as a post, but she knows how to drive a hard bargain. It cost almost as much as yours, in the end.'

'Oh, Seton…darling man!' Throwing her arms around his neck with astonishing energy for one so shaken, she showered kisses over his face. 'You've *bought* it! It's yours, after all. So why did she let *us* in?'

'Because I asked her to say nothing. I knew *he'd* come nosing round in time.'

'And young Ted? He doesn't bear you a grudge, as Fin said?'

'Not in the slightest, sweetheart. Men don't, usually. He accepts that he overstepped the mark and got a facer for it. No grudges. He came to find me as soon as he realised what Gaddestone was up to, and fortunately I was at your house waiting

for you to return. I met Chase outside and he offered to come
and help, so I collected my pistol from the curricle and Ted led
the way. Yes, he'd talked in the pub once or twice to Gaddestone, and he'd had a key made. He left it on the hall table this
morning, but it was for Mrs Sawbridge, not for your cousin.'

'Oh, dearest one, how could Fin do such a thing? He never
used to be like that. Never deceitful. I feel so sorry.'

'Service in the navy and army changes people, my love. I
could feel it changing me, too, but I was fortunate to be offered
a job afterwards. But now we can put all that behind us,
expand your seminary, have a room for your writing, a
nursery, a suite for Gaddy, too.'

'You mean, you won't mind if I carry on working?'

'On the contrary, sweetheart, I shall expect you to. I cannot
have a wife who floats about in a state of undress all day as
mistresses are supposed to do.'

She sighed, rather gustily. 'Ah, no, indeed. But I've hardly
had chance to do any of that.'

'Tch! Oh, all right,' he said, lifting her into his arms and
striding across to the door. 'A week or two of floating, a month
of showing off in London, a splendid wedding after that, then
a honeymoon abroad. And *then* I shall expect you to buckle
down and plan your next novel and redesign this shabby place.
And then, if there's any time left over, we'll make some little
Honourable Raynes, shall we?'

Letitia hid her face in his lapel. 'Yes, my lord, if you wish.
But how am I to meet Perdita's deadline, I wonder?'

'Isn't she married yet?'

'Not yet.'

'Well, then, lock her in an attic until she agrees,' he said,
callously, manoeuvring her round the banisters.

Mrs Sawbridge was in the hall with a messy pile of chewed book covers and pages in her hands, looking rather worried. 'Are these yours, Miss Boyce?' she shouted. 'I should have warned you, the dogs like nothing more than a good book.'

Chapter Fourteen

Having heard from her husband something of the drama enacted that afternoon at Number 20, Lady Boston would not be satisfied until they had both called on Miss Boyce to see if she had recovered from the ordeal.

Lowering his newspaper to treat his wife to a look of mock-reprimand, Sir Chase said, 'You can hardly wait to get a look at Seton's woman, can you? It will be rather obvious, don't you think?'

Caterina did not think anything of the kind. 'Would it be *too* difficult for you to see it as a neighbourly act of concern, Chase Boston, instead of nosey-parkering? It doesn't matter to me whose woman she is, I can still enquire about her poor nerves, can't I?'

The newspaper was dropped into a heap as Sir Chase unfurled his tall powerful frame to stand before her. 'I can see I shall get no peace, Lady Boston, until you've met her. I suppose it serves me right for telling you she's a stunner. Rayne always knew how to pick 'em.'

'Must you be so coarse?' Caterina retorted, pulling the bell-cord.

Even so, she put up no resistance when he pulled her to him with one arm and held her close to his side. 'Only with you, sweetheart,' he said, kissing her.

The meeting both women had anticipated for some time with varying degrees of curiosity took place, after all, in an atmosphere so informal and spontaneous that it was as if they'd known each other for years instead of minutes. From the start, Letitia could hold no doubts that Sir Chase and Lady Boston's infatuation with each other was total and exclusive, their love still shining, new and untarnished by anything resembling jealousy. They had an infant named Charles, and by vague references to their time in Richmond, it sounded as if their wooing had been every bit as turbulent as that of Rayne and Letitia.

As for Rayne, any thoughts Letitia harboured about the exact nature of his relationship with the beautiful, dark-haired and talented Caterina were quickly untangled by seeing them now, sharing the kind of bickering disrespect of siblings, teasing and laughing. At the same time, Rayne made no secret of the fact that Letitia was the only woman in whom he was interested, or could ever be. So it was entirely by coincidence that Sir Chase and Lady Boston were the first to congratulate them on their engagement, and to stay until the early hours of the morning talking like old friends over supper, and discussing next week's family concert.

Miss Gaddestone had spent most of the evening at the surgeon's house where her brother was being tended. But when Lieutenant Gaddestone's failure to return to London caused his uncle some alarm, the Aspinall carriage brought the elderly gentleman to the steps of Number 24 Paradise Road before breakfast was cleared off the table and Wednesday's lessons begun.

Rayne had intended to return to Sheen Court early, to inform his brother of the news. But now seemed like the ideal time to air the problems that had affected Gaddestone and, by association, the rest of them, too, for Rayne had not yet shared with Letitia what he and Sir Penfold had learned while in Portsmouth. That kind of news, he thought, was best coming from family.

'At the place you called the Navy House?' Letitia said. 'Where you talked with the captain who knew Fin?'

'That's it, love,' said Uncle Aspinall. 'What he told us was a bit shocking, but by then I'd begun to have my doubts about my nephew and his many commendations. They turned out to be fictitious, like the prize money.'

'Then what really happened, Uncle?'

'Debt and drunkenness is what happened. He managed to gamble away all his money, couldn't pay his debts, and the punishment for that is to be discharged. He was taken on by another ship via the good offices of a friend, but unfortunately it started again, drunkenness and disobedience, throwing his weight about. He was ordered to apply for discharge, again. That was last month. The rest you know. His pay and prize money all went to pay his debts. It's no wonder he was desperate. Does anybody want that last muffin, Lettie?'

'It's yours, love,' she said, passing him the plate. 'But I wonder why you didn't think to tell me all this. It might have spared me some embarrassment.'

'Yes,' Rayne said, 'in hindsight, it might have done. We both thought your cousin would find a way of making a living, somehow.'

'But he preferred to use mine instead.'

'And there were two other contenders getting in his way.'

'Two? You mean he saw Bart as a threat as well as you?'

'I'm afraid he did, sweetheart.'

'Oh!' Letitia's hand flew to her mouth. 'That dreadful attack…?'

'Was Fin's doing. He paid three men to put him out of the picture.'

'Then he must have heard Bart telling me he'd be going to London early the next Monday, just as he was leaving. Oh, I'll never forgive him for that. Never!' She stood up, leaving the table abruptly and going over to the window. 'What he threatened to do to me was bad enough, but to drag my personal friends into it is *despicable*!'

'Well,' said Uncle Aspinall, munching, 'he'll be out of action for quite some time now. I'm going to send him to a gardener I know down in Cornwall. He'll keep him busy. Now, Lettie, love, come over here and hear this. The news from your mama and sisters is that they've accepted Lady Elyot's invitation to the concert next Thursday. Your Aunt Minnie and me, too. She took some persuading, mind, but she'll get used to it eventually.'

'Then if you were to tell them that Lord Rayne has asked me to be his wife, Uncle, Mama might feel happier about it, do you think?'

The last mouthful of muffin was helped down with a hasty gulp of coffee, the cup crashed to the saucer, and Uncle Aspinall's arms opened like wings to embrace her, his jolly face reddening with pleasure. 'I guessed it would not be long,' he laughed. 'Mistress, indeed! What a *fudge*!'

He did not, of course, see the lift of Rayne's eyebrow and the lazy glance that caught his beloved's blush.

* * *

The concert was, in the end, exactly the kind of glittering family occasion that Lady Elyot had planned, and more, for now there were several other events to celebrate, apart from the visit of the Bostons to their home on Paradise Road. One of them was the betrothal of Lady Adorna Elwick to Captain Ben Rankin who had been kept dangling quite long enough, they all said, the other being the appearance of Lady Boyce, though no one was impertinent enough to question her tactics out loud as they had done with Dorna.

She had arrived at Sheen Court with Garnet and Persephone only minutes ahead of her brother and his wife, still vacillating between pique at having her predictions overturned, satisfaction at having a daughter so well connected, and annoyance at having to moderate her strong opinions in an entire company of Letitia's most ardent admirers. Not least of her qualms was the certainty that she would be obliged to meet Sir Francis Melborough and his family, who had no reason whatever to remember her with any fondness.

Her well-honed acting skills, though usually standing her in good stead, were this time quite overpowered by the warmth of the greetings she received from her hosts, their family and from Letitia also, who shed a tear of relief and joy, and appreciation, too, at the effort her mother had made to be there. She, more than any other, knew what it had cost her to swallow her pride, even if the taste of it was sweetened by her reception. Resplendent in feathery plumes from her hair, Lady Boyce put on her warmest smile to embrace Letitia and, for the first time, to congratulate her on her happiness, turning to Rayne with a lie as great as any she had ever told with a conviction that would have rivalled the actress Mrs Siddons.

'And my *dear* Lord Rayne…yes, I always *knew* you'd be the one.'

Dutifully, he received her kiss to both cheeks. 'Really, my lady?'

'Oh, silly boy,' she said, tapping his arm. 'Of *course* I did. A mother always knows these things. Is that not so, Lady Sheen?'

The marchioness smiled and agreed, drawing her towards all those friends she could have met months ago if she'd not been so intransigent. But if Lady Boyce had hoped to delay her meeting with the Melboroughs, Sapphire had a way of demonstrating her complete lack of resentment and, in a gown of embroidered muslin, white and virginal, she ushered her parents forward. 'Do come and meet her,' she was saying to them. 'This is Miss Boyce's mama. Lady Boyce, do allow me to introduce my parents. They *long* to meet the mother of our most famous author. They're both great admirers of hers, you know. Mama has just finished reading *Waynethorpe Manor*, have you not, dearest? And now Papa has got it. *So* wicked!' She laughed merrily, blinking at Lady Boyce's perplexity. 'Surely you're one of Miss Boyce's dedicated readers, too, are you not?'

Standing nearby, Letitia felt the disbelieving stare of her sisters, the quick shifting blink of her mother and the uncomprehending frown of Aunt Minnie all at the same time, but it was Sir Francis who stepped into the breach as if he sensed what was happening. 'Well, of course she is, dear child, but you can hardly expect Lady Boyce to admit keeping up with the racy exploits of her daughter's characters. What mothers *do*, and what they *admit* to doing, are two quite different things. Don't you agree, Lady Boyce?' He held out his hand to her, smiling. 'Francis Melborough at your service, m'lady. And my good wife. You are fortunate indeed to have such a multitalented daughter. Sapphire has the greatest admiration for her, you know. Cannot wait to tell all her friends that she is taught by the author of *The Infidel*. You should see their faces.'

Lady Boyce's recovery was a marvel of improvisation. Caressing Letitia's face with a smile of motherly pride, she accepted Sir Francis's outstretched hand and allowed it to be taken to his lips. 'Yes,' she cooed with all due modesty, 'we tried to keep it to ourselves for a while, but these things have a way of rising to the top, don't they? I have to admit to borrowing my twins' copies, and they don't always get them back.' She sent another smile over to the twins with a silent demand for them to change their shocked expressions forthwith. Aunt Minnie was less responsive. 'And,' she told her audience, 'she's had *such* a success with the seminary. Always been a talented gel, you know, and so brave to strike out on her own without her mama's protection. Yes, I always knew she'd do well. And, Lady Melborough, you have a lovely daughter who is going to sing for us, I hope?' Linking arms, Lady Boyce strolled away, trailing a pile of black Chantilly lace behind her over the chequered marble floor of the hall, her black ostrich feathers nodding in agreement.

'Shall we play chess with her, sweetheart?' Rayne whispered in Letitia's ear. 'Black Queen in trouble, d'ye think?'

'Did you *ever* hear such dissembling in your life?' she said.

'It was a tricky situation. She got herself out of it rather well, didn't she? Keep your nerve, here are your sisters.'

There was no such pretence for Garnet and Persephone, only praise and compliments and a lot of questions that begged for answers, excitement, incredulity and a mountain of wonderment, which she scarce knew what to do with. They went off to tell Uncle Aspinall and to deal with Aunt Minnie's confusion.

'Where is Sapphire?' Letitia said, looking round. 'I have to find out how she knew, before we begin. Did she do this on purpose?'

'She's here. Ask her. But I doubt it. She's not malicious.'

Sapphire had noticed nothing amiss. Her explanation was simple. 'Oh, I didn't think it was a secret, Miss Boyce. You left your writing on your table, you see, and I had absolutely nothing else to do but read it until Lady Boyce had gone. I could easily tell the writing was the same as the other two because we've done about styles in our writing class. You have that lovely way of telling how your heroines are suffering. I can hardly *wait* till it's published.'

'Just one moment, Sapphire dear. Are you actually saying that you read my manuscript that day...?'

'Yes, ma'am. That dreadful day. You told me to stay in your room, and it helped to take my mind off things. It was the best four hours I'd spent for ages, except for the riding, of course.' Her blue eyes peeped up mischievously at Lord Rayne, quite unaware of the stir she had caused by her disclosure.

'Then I suppose all the girls know, do they?' said Letitia, wearily.

Sapphire's eyes sparkled again. 'Oh, yes, and they're all so proud of you, Miss Boyce. We're all going to give the performance of our lives tonight, to show everyone what a *brilliant* seminary we attend. But I must go and speak to poor Mr Waverley. He's not looking at all well, is he?'

In fact, Mr Waverley was looking better that evening than he had for a week, though he was still confined to a chair and his face was mottled with every colour of the rainbow. He was also receiving an inordinate amount of attention from the pupils, who had missed him greatly.

But the attention that evening was divided evenly between the performers, all of whom excelled themselves, and their headmistress who had brought them to such a high standard, who was now Lord Rayne's intended wife, and who was also the author of the novels few in the audience had not read, either from cover to cover or in a more probing manner. It seemed to Letitia, as she sat beside the man she adored, that her world had moved on into an entirely new phase, for now she had one more bonus to make her evening perfect. The approbation of her mother. Why it should matter so much to her when she had everything else she could have wished for, was not something she tried to analyse, for it went deeper than she cared to delve.

Lady Boyce sought her daughter out in the supper room during the interval, when the crowd around Letitia parted, knowing that this was to be a private moment. She took Letitia's hands and held them tightly, slightly trembling, her eyes awash with tears even before a word was spoken, her smile struggling against the things she felt but could not begin to say.

'Mama,' Letitia whispered.

'Lettie.' The hands shook, then loosened, sliding up her arms to hold her close, and Letitia knew that it was not for show, for her mother would never have wept in public for any reason other than genuine emotion. 'You've done well, dearest,' Lady Boyce croaked. 'I'm so proud. I didn't...'

'Shh! Hush, love. Say no more. We've missed a few months, that's all. We can soon make it up. No harm done.'

'Yes, we'll make up for it. Perhaps you could come and do this at Chesterfield House? You'll all be in London next month, won't you?'

Letitia's embrace was garnished with a laugh. 'Of course we will, Mama. We'll do it all over again for your friends.'

'I shall start planning for it straight away. And before we go home tomorrow, I want you to show me round your Paradise Road house, will you? I have one or two friends with daughters...' Lady Boyce wiped beneath her eye with the tip of one gloved finger '...who really ought to see *your* gels.'

'Of course, Mama. Come, I believe Lady Boston is about to give us another song. She *is* lovely, isn't she?'

Until that evening, Lady Boyce would hardly have heard any other meaning behind her daughter's observation, yet now it was as if she'd tuned herself to a higher frequency. They had been about to move off, but she lay a hand over Letitia's arm, sensing her concern. 'Lettie,' she said, 'I believe Lord Rayne has found in you something he's been looking for, for many years. I know what a fuss I made about it at first, because I was afraid for you, on your own. But I see that I need not have been. I've been watching the way he looks at you, even when you're not standing together, and there's no doubt at all in my mind that you are the only woman he sees. Don't allow doubts to cloud your relationship. They can, you know.'

If Letitia had not known of her mama's liaison before her marriage, she might have accepted the advice as no more than kindly platitudes. But she did, and the significance was unmistakable. Later, as she sat beside her betrothed, she looked across the vast room to see her mama sitting beside Sir Francis in close conversation, like two good friends.

'What's the smile for, sweetheart?' Rayne said. 'Your mama?'

'For the deepest happiness I've ever known,' she said, sharing the smile with him, 'and for the most wonderful man this side of paradise. That's where I first saw you, you know. On Paradise Road. Looking superior.'

'Then I shall take you back there tonight, some time before dawn, and show you how excessively superior I can be, my beauty.'

'Will you, my lord? And shall we not delay the making of the Honourable Little Raynes until we're quite settled? Please?'

'Oh, I think we may put some practice in, certainly. Where better than a ladies' seminary, after all?'

The sound of sweet music-making filled the hall, heads swayed, fingers tapped, and the applause reached the goddesses sailing on clouds across the ceiling.

It was a night to be remembered, especially later in the comparative peace of Letitia's bed where the two lovers pressed themselves along every warm surface with the music still echoing in their heads.

'Perdita is being sadly neglected,' said Letitia, drowsily.

Rayne's hand moved silkily over her buttock. 'Mmm…? So what else does she need to know?'

'What it feels like to make love when she's half-asleep.'

'And is that part of the story?'

'It could be. If the author knew something about it.'

'Well, then, perhaps she'd better find out. I take it her pains have been dealt with by now?'

'Oh, quite. Utterly. How did *you* know of her pains?'

'Don't all heroines go through anguish and torment?' His hand moved to the tender inside of her thigh, resting in the valley of her groin.

'Mine seem to, yes.' She yawned, noisily. 'Usually unnecessarily. Silly, really.'

Lifting himself on to one elbow, he lay above her, smiling at the double-talk. 'Then let's celebrate Perdita's discoveries, shall we, sweetheart?'

Her arms wrapped softly around his neck. 'And Letitia's,' she said.

Epilogue

In the circumstances, Letitia found it difficult to complete the manuscript on time, but complete it she did, even in the middle of the celebrations meant to mark the end of hostilities with France. It was the busiest time of Letitia's life, and the most successful and enjoyable, for she became all the rage at a time when it seemed that uniqueness must have run its course. Even without the wonderful entourage of scholarly pupils and tutors, even without the charming spectacles and superb costumes, the revelation that she was the *author*, eldest daughter of Lady Boyce and soon to be Lady Rayne, was enough to set a new standard that few of her contemporaries could reach. Not that she was aware of it; she was far too busy with domestic standards to concern herself with the ideals of society.

The seminary at Number 24 expanded in the following year into Number 20, which also became the Richmond home of the Rayne family, all six of them. Letitia's seminary was to develop, many years later, into Richmond's first National School on the site of what is now Eton House, 18–24 Paradise

Road, the address of the publisher of this book, Harlequin Mills & Boon, who still specialise in romantic fiction. As Letitia did.

* * * * *

Author's Note

For those who would like to know more about Lady Elyot, her story is told in *A Scandalous Mistress*. Her niece Caterina's story—i.e., Lady Boston—is told in *Dishonour and Desire*. The story of Lady Dorna's ancestor, the Adorna Pickering of the Elizabethan era, is told in *One Night in Paradise*.

Marrying the Mistress

Prologue

It was hardly more than two miles from the centre of York to the racecourse at Knavesmire, a distance that only a few months ago, the Honourable Linas Monkton would have been happy to ride on horseback without the least discomfort. On this occasion, however, his young mistress, Miss Helene Follet, had put her foot down and ordered the barouche to be made available, for nowadays Linas's cough left him weak, sweating with pain and gasping for breath. She dared not allow it, although she would have liked to ride her own black mare that weekend.

'I feel sure we're in for some showers,' she said, noting the bending tree-tops as they passed out of Micklegate, 'and I don't fancy getting soaked as we watch your brother's horses go through their paces. If it turns out fine, I'm sure he'll lend us two of his hacks to ride. Did you remember to pack the new linctus?'

'I expect Nairn did. You look very nice, my dear.'

Linas's compliments rarely went beyond 'nice' or 'smart', which Helene thought more appropriate for soldiers. 'Thank you.' She smiled. She had made the outfit herself, including the beaded panel down the front and the frilled chemisette that showed inside the neckline. The matching bonnet of ruched blue-grey silk had been made by her, too, after the latest French styles.

Linas himself ought to have been tucked up warmly in his Stonegate home on such a raw April day, but it was the start of the York racing season and nothing would have persuaded him to refuse his twin brother's invitation to stay the weekend at Abbots Mere, so close to the racecourse. The invitation had been to stay for a week, but Helene had balked at that and Linas, aware of a certain tension between his mistress and his brother, had not insisted on more than two nights.

Helene would rather not have gone at all. Although she enjoyed the races and the sight of horses in a herd at full gallop, bright with silks and shine, she could not look forward with anything like the same enthusiasm to meeting the Abbots Mere set, which, as like as not, would include a similar herd of Lord Winterson's mistresses, past, present and hopeful.

The twins were unlike each other in most respects, Linas being far from robust but still trying to emulate his brother in so many ways, by taking a mistress, for instance, and by trying to prove his fitness when it was plain to see, to Helene at least, that he grew weaker with each passing season. Lord Winterson's rude health needed no proof, for one look at his powerful physique was enough to convince any critic that his parents' recipe had favoured the first of the two to emerge with good looks, intelligence, and enough charm to ladle out whenever he felt he could spare the effort. At other times he could be insufferably proud and offhand, and it was said that one of Winterson's set-downs could cause a recipient's disappearance for as long as a six-month.

Linas had never indulged in that kind of high-handedness except occasionally to the servants, and it was this brand of gentle courtesy that had won Helene over. After insisting that she would never again become intimate with a man for money, however high-born, she had relented and become Linas Monkton's mistress, companion and nurse. That had been two years ago when she was still seventeen, two years in which there had been no sign of pregnancy, in spite of her desire to bear his child before it was too late.

Perhaps it was already too late, for Linas had not visited her bed once in the last two months on the pretext that any physical exercise brought on his coughing spasms. Tomorrow would be her nineteenth birthday. She hoped he might visit her, if only to be held in her arms.

It was unproductive to speculate on the welcome they would receive, Helene having no reason to suppose that they would be treated with anything but courtesy and, in her lover's case, with affection too. The brothers were very fond of each other, and although no obvious favour was offered to Linas when taking part in the usual manly activities, Helene nevertheless suspected that Lord Winterson kept a very careful eye on his brother, stopping within his limits or suggesting an easier route, ostensibly for his own benefit. Visiting Linas's home on Stonegate, Winterson never stayed long enough to tire him, nor was anything ever said in her presence about the array of medicines at Linas's elbow.

Helene hoped it was obvious to Winterson that she was taking every conceivable care of his brother without molly-coddling him, but the feeling persisted that he thought her a young social-climbing nobody on the look-out for a wealthy patron who would feather her nest for as long as possible. If he had taken the trouble to find out, she thought, he might have discovered the truth of the matter, that Miss Helene Follet was in fact a certain Miss Helen Follethorpe of Bridlington, only thirty miles or so away on the Yorkshire coast, where her father had once been mayor. Had it not been for Leonard Follethorpe's unfortunate experience, she would still be living with her family in comfort instead of selling herself to support those of her family who remained. Five years ago, taking a lover had been the very last thing on her mind, but she could be of little help to her family on the pittance she had earned as a York mantua-maker's assistant, and one could not be too finicky when near-starvation was a real alternative.

To say she resented Winterson's thinly veiled contempt would not have been an exaggeration. His manner was correct and as icy as if she'd been a crusty old dowager of fifty instead of a sleek raven-haired beauty of nineteen, giving her no opportunity to be as sisterly as she was with her own two young brothers. Not even for Linas's sake did Lord Winterson do anything to endear himself to her, and now as he strode out of the great Tudor porchway of Abbots Mere with three gigantic wolfhounds at his heels, his smile skimmed over her as if she were merely the house-keeper or Linas's nurse. The hand he extended came just a little too late to help her out of the barouche.

'Miss Follet,' he said, keeping the hand out so that she was obliged to accept it. 'Welcome to Abbots Mere.' The greeting was formal, and not particularly convinc-ing.

She had tried to ignore the ambiguous emotions that bedevilled her, but the contrast between Linas and his twin was so transparent, and she herself so receptive to all the differences between one man in the prime of his life and one whose prime had never quite materialised, that she now found it easier to accept it than question it. Winterson did not have his brother's lanky loping frame of a tired racehorse, but the deep-chested, well-toned solidness of a hunter.

Helene watched him move gracefully aside, her eyes taking their own wayward course over the broad smooth line of his riding coat, the bulge in his tight breeches, the tan-cuffed riding boots with spurs, and the muscled calves. Reprimanding herself, she refused to acknowledge the stark truth that she might have wished this man's physical endowments upon his sibling, forcing herself instead to smile at the brotherly embrace and the genuine laughter accompanying it. The stifling, insistent beat of her heart, so long starved of its own special excitement, was quelled with some effort as she diverted her thoughts towards Linas's pleasure and what she could do to maintain it.

Noting how Linas caressed the ears of the nearest

wolfhound, she could see how happy he was to be here and to spend time in the stone-built rambling place where he'd been born. As a concession to his asthma, he kept no animals except horses, but any excuse to visit his brother's racing stable was worth the sneezing fits and the itchy rash on his wrists that Helene cooled with witch-hazel and chamomile. The prospect of sleeping in his old room at Abbots Mere brought back the laugh lines to his pale winter face and lit up the sombre darkness of his eyes, as did the appearance of Somerton, the elderly butler.

Linas took Helene by the hand. 'Good to see you again, Somerton,' he said, creasing his papery skin with deep folds.

'And you also, Mr Linas, sir. M'lord Burl here has had us all up since dawn to get everything ship-shape. We've even polished the hounds' collars. Welcome, Miss Follet,' he said to Helene, courteously.

'Thank you, Mr Somerton.'

Perhaps being made aware by his butler that something more was being required of him, Winterson turned back to her to offer his arm, taking both her and Linas through a panelled passageway into the Great Hall. Again, the differences returned with the memory of that first meeting at the York Assembly Rooms when they had danced together just before she and Linas had first met, when she had seen the fear in Linas's eyes that she would surely prefer his brother Burl, as any woman would. But she had never been seriously attracted to men like Winterson with reputations for breaking hearts, nor could she afford the indulgence of falling in love. If Winterson had ever suspected that she was more interested in a long-term relationship, then he would have been correct. She was. But her affection for the Honourable Linas Monkton was none the less genuine, for all that, and her good care of him had grown into a kind of love far beyond convenience.

The company that weekend was exactly as Helene had expected it to be, noisy, good-natured and gossipy, flirtatious and with an air of competition she felt no need to be a part of, since she was unavailable. Not that she was entirely safe from the attentions of the men, but her status and devotion were sufficient to keep all dalliance at a very superficial level. And because she posed no threat to the women, they sought her friendship and asked her advice about even the most personal matters, especially about fashion. Yet they were not the kind of people she would have chosen to spend a weekend with, and she wondered why Lord Winterson enjoyed their company so much, unless it was to watch them compete for his attention.

Although Winterson must have known about Helene's previous employment as a seamstress, she had told neither of the brothers the full story of her transformation from well-brought-up mayor's daughter to mantua-maker's assistant. If either of them ever wondered how she had acquired such singular style and elegance, how she came to be fluent in French, or why she spoke English with only the odd vowel sound to betray her northern roots, they were either too uninterested to ask, or too well bred.

But the mantua-maker herself, once she saw what a gem she had taken on, had put those accomplishments to good use, transferring her from the workroom to front of shop, using her as a mannequin to model her creations and to suggest other ways of using accessories and fabrics with the kind of flair the older woman could only dream of. When Helene borrowed an evening dress now and again to attend the nearby Assembly Rooms with a beau, this was seen as a cheaper way of rewarding her than with money, for she was sure to tell admirers where such a beautiful gown could be made. Those years had been for Helene a time of intense learning in which she had absorbed every skill of the dressmaking trade, since then she had designed and made all her own garments, including her bonnets.

Despite her undeniable fashion ability, her popularity with Winterson's guests could not be called complete as long as Lady Veronique Slatterly was on hand to shoot down any woman perceived to be receiving more than her fair share of attention from the men, particularly from Winterson himself. Her envy of Miss Helene Follet was out of all proportion to her influence with anyone except Linas. But according to Lady Slatterly, Helene was almost one of the family whereas she herself had not yet achieved that status, nor had she any guarantee of success. Helene's superior position was too close for comfort, and the consequent trivial and ungenerous remarks that Lady Slatterly rained upon her, almost unceasingly, eventually drew even mild Linas's displeasure at dinner.

Handing Lady Slatterly a silver dish of sugary things, he told her, 'Take a few, Veronique dear. Chew them slowly to grind your teeth down.'

Frowning, she took the dish from him. 'What are they?' she said.

'Little sweet things, dear. Keep them by you. You need them.'

Damned if she did, and equally damned if she declined, she glared at Linas as everyone around them laughed, but the caustic remarks stopped for the rest of the evening.

This personal sniping would not in itself have caused Helene too much concern had she not already been feeling vulnerable, vaguely insecure and unsettled by not knowing how to relate to a host who treated her with such polite indifference as if it was no possible concern of his that she was caring so well for his ailing brother. As if she was doing it more for her own benefit, rather than his. Not that she expected their undying gratitude at every end and turn, nor even their thanks. Men only rarely went in for that kind of appreciation. But nor did she appreciate being taken for granted in the offhand way these brothers had. Linas was a very dear man, but he appeared to suppose that what Helene was doing for him was no more than he deserved after what he was doing for her. And since the question of the future was a subject he particularly wished to avoid discussing, it seemed not to occur to him that Helene would have benefited from some clarity on the issue. She had a house, servants, a horse and enough money to pay her bills, but presumably those would all disappear one day, unless she could make some other arrangement.

Had relations between Helene and Lord Winterson been more cordial, she might have broached the subject to him. But not the way things stood. There was a younger brother who also lived on the outskirts of York, a new country parson named Medworth whose profession and family kept him totally occupied. No doubt he was relieved to know that his brother was being cared for, but his absence showed that he had his hands full enough without involving himself in Miss Follet's problems.

Mindful of Linas's enjoyment, Helene made every effort to enter into the excitement of the first day, during which two of Winterson's racing thoroughbreds were competing. The day had begun with an earlier-than-usual breakfast and, since the weather was blustery but dry, Helene and Linas borrowed two of his brother's hacks to ride with the others, she in her habit of nut-brown velvet and matching plumed hat that drew many a compliment. Linas had retired early the previous night, well before the others, and had fallen asleep even before Helene could go in to wish him goodnight. His valet had told her that his master had been too tired even to take his usual night-cap of port, sharing with her a look of concern that did not bode well for the busy day ahead.

So it did not surprise her that no reference had been made to her birthday on the morrow, and it seemed to her inappropriate to mention it when all the attention was focused on the races, the guests, the winners and owners, the sumptuous feast, the meeting of old friends and the excitement of Winterson's successes. Linas had completely forgotten, and Helene had already decided that his guilt would serve no good purpose. Even so, there were moments during the day when her lovely expressive eyes must have revealed something of her hurt and disappointment, the ache to be at home with her family on this special day, enjoying their warmth and love instead of maintaining a position for which she had no real appetite, which she would once have reviled before she lost her innocence.

Turning to look at Linas, she checked that he was comfortable on the well-mannered hack, heaved a sigh, and looked away into the distance to where the newly white-painted grandstand swarmed with racegoers. A large horse and rider moved up beside her, blocking her view of Linas. It was his brother. At first his eyes followed where hers had been and then, returning to find that she was looking down at her hands as if deliberating whether to go or stay, said, 'No, don't go. We have not spoken all day.'

'To each other, you mean? What is there to be said, except congratulations?'

'Oh, dear. You're angry.' His voice was deep and apologetic.

'Not at all. But you must not be seen talking to me, my lord. That would look *very* odd, wouldn't it? See, we're being remarked already.'

'What is it, Miss Follet? You *are* angry. With me? Linas? Has he been flirting with someone?'

'I don't know *what* he's doing. Does it matter?'

His horse stretched its neck, pulling his hand forwards as it shook its head and jangled its bit, keeping its rider occupied with its sidling before he brought it back, almost touching her leg with his. She watched as he humoured the great beast with patience, as if he enjoyed controlling its movements, his face strong, impassive, astonishingly regular, for a man. His dark hair was too long, she thought, noting how it curled over his cravat at the back.

He had obviously been thinking of what she said. 'Or what he's *not* doing? Is that it? He's forgotten your birthday?' he ventured.

She knew it to be a stab in the dark. It must be. Yet the sudden surprise in her velvet-brown eyes escaped before she could hide it, and the denial that followed was worse than useless. 'Of course he hasn't. He...'

'He has, hasn't he? He was never any good at birthdays, Miss Follet. He rarely remembers ours, either. Shall I remind him for you?'

'No!' The word shot out, compounding the earlier denial. 'No, please don't.'

'Ah! You mean you'd rather remind him yourself in a week's time? Or you'd rather he didn't know at all?'

'I mean, my lord, that it's of no possible concern to anyone but me. Please say no more about it.'

'If that's your wish, then I must obey. But you're wrong to think it concerns only you. You are my guest and you're not entirely enjoying the experience. That concerns me. What can I do to put it right?'

'Nothing at all. Your hospitality is the finest, and if Linas is content then that is all I ask for.' She heard the emptiness of her reply and was not proud of its insincerity. She could hardly expect him to believe her.

'Fine unselfish sentiments, ma'am. But I fear I'm too cynical to be taken in by them. To say that my brother's contentment is all you desire, a woman of your age, is moonshine. Have you not thought ahead a little, to the time when you might wish for more?'

Like a ball of slow fire, a sob of pain rose into her throat to sear her with a longing so intense that she had once cried out in the night with it, soaking her pillow with tears, for it seemed at times that her thoughts were of little else. Before she could take herself in hand, her eyes had begun to flood with scalding tears, showing him what was in her heart as clearly as if she held its doors wide open. This man, of all men, to see her weakness, a man who had rarely condescended to speak to her until now.

She would have wheeled her horse away, blindly, but he caught at her bridle before she could do so, leading it away from the Abbots Mere crowd towards a deserted area of long grass where both mounts dropped their heads to snatch at a juicy mouthful. He held her reins and waited, keeping their backs to everyone but making no comment.

'I'm all right,' she whispered. 'Do forgive me. I had no wish to embarrass you, my lord.'

'I am not in the least embarrassed, Miss Follet. I tend to be outspoken, and I have touched a raw spot. I am concerned, but not embarrassed.'

'Yes, my lord, you have. Shall we say no more about it, if you please?'

'Of course. Are you quite recovered?'

'Yes. Quite.'

'Then we shall return.' Handing her the reins, he took stock of her smooth curvaceous lines under the habit, the neat waist and long back, the white lace at her throat. Black glossy hair was bundled into a gold net under her saucily feathered hat, and the deep reproachful eyes spiked with long black lashes were like pools to drown a man. Her full lips were mobile upon a skin of peach that he knew his brother had begun to abandon as his illness progressed and that this, as much as anything else, was a prime source of her distress.

Their return to the others, side by side, did not escape the notice of Lady Veronique Slatterly, whose displeasure bordered on extreme folly. 'Where have you two been?' she demanded, wheeling her grey mare round in circles ahead of them. Her blue eyes were cold and hard upon Helene.

Winterson's reply did nothing to thaw them, though her skin turned a healthy pink. 'I have not had to account for my whereabouts since I was fourteen, Lady Slatterly, and I don't intend to start again now. Nor, I imagine, does Miss Follet owe you an explanation.'

Snubbed in no uncertain terms, the astonished woman hauled her mare savagely away and, though Helene caught sight of her several times during the afternoon, she did not approach.

It was Linas himself who answered Helene's query about the exact nature of Lady Slatterly's relationship with his brother. Was she his mistress, or merely one of the hopefuls?

'He has no official mistress,' Linas told her on the way back to Abbots Mere. 'Veronique believes she stands a good chance, but she'll have to toe the line and curb her sharp tongue if she wants to get anywhere with Burl. He doesn't like the controlling kind of woman. Not even our mother had much success there.'

The parents, Lord and Lady Stillingfleete, had never exercised much control over any of their three sons, and had left the family home at Abbots Mere to live in a smaller Georgian house in Harrogate, within reach of the healing baths. Their large estate was now in Winterson's capable hands, visited only once or twice a year by the owners when they wanted a change of scenery.

* * *

As a result of Winterson's reprimand, Lady Slatterly's rudeness seemed to abate on the second evening, giving Helene some respite from the woman's jealousy. It also seemed to Helene that Winterson's manner had changed too, even if she was the only one to notice that, this time, he took part in her conversations instead of distancing himself, showing more of an interest in her well-being.

Linas was exhausted after missing his afternoon rest, and at dinner Helene could see how he fought against his fatigue. Not wishing to prevent him from drinking more wine than usual while so many were there to see, she was obliged to watch in dismay as his glass was refilled time and again. His speech began to slur, and his pale skin became unhealthily mottled.

Unable to hide the concern in her eyes, she found her looks intercepted by Winterson's equally worried frown. It was getting late, yet no one had deserted the gaming tables or the chatting groups arranged on couches and floor cushions. She shook her head at the young footman holding a tray of filled glasses in front of Linas, but too late to prevent one being removed, clumsily, sloshing the contents over white knee breeches and carpet.

She went to him, hoping to offer some unobtrusive help, but Winterson was there before her, lifting his brother under each armpit and good-naturedly ignoring his protests. 'Come on up, old chap. Enough for one day.'

'Stay with your guests, my lord,' Helene said. 'I'll go up with him.'

'No, you stay here. I'll see to him myself. Nairn is
on his way.'

'He'll be at his supper.'

'I sent for him. Leave him to us.'

His commands offered her a certain comfort for,
although she had not wanted to stay amongst the guests
for much longer, the alternative was even less appeal-
ing. To hand control over to his authoritative twin would
be no great sacrifice.

She stayed in the drawing room for another hour,
managing to convince all except one that she was as
light-hearted as the rest of them. Winterson reappeared
to lead a silly game of charades, but the pace slackened
and, two by two, the ladies withdrew to their rooms to
prepare for the night, still giggling and flirting. Helene
was relieved that she and Linas would be returning to
York in the morning. She would leave him at his
spacious Stonegate home to rest and recover, and she
would go to her well-ordered house on Blake Street,
which was not really hers but Linas's. She would
pretend to be its mistress when the reality was that she
could stay only as long as Linas was alive.

If she could have given him an heir, her future would
be more assured, but that was unlikely to happen, for both
of them had realised some time ago that one of them must
be infertile. Having as much pride as he, Helene preferred to believe that the fault must lay with him, but Winterson's wounding enquiry about her future had inflamed
a painful truth that was never far from her darkest
thoughts that, no matter which of them was responsible
for their childlessness, the outlook remained bleak.

Deep in thought, she allowed her maid to undress her and to lock away the few jewels Linas had given her since their first Christmas together. He had never thought it necessary to shower her with gifts, but now her birthday had come and gone without a word, and the thought re-occurred yet again that their relationship must be on the wane. Ought she to leave him now, before he did? Should she find another lover, and be passed from one to the next until…until what? Had his brother anticipated the end of the partnership? Was that another reason for his coolness?

With a pang of guilt, she decided not to go to Linas's room, knowing how the scene would do nothing to lighten her spirits. His brother and valet had tended him, and now he would be snoring heavily under a mountain of extra blankets with all the windows tightly shuttered and a lamp left burning next to the mahogany commode. The air would be heavy with the odour of medications and sweat. It was no place for lovers.

For a few moments longer she watched the rain beat upon the night-blackened window and run down the glass, parting and joining, lashed sideways by fitful gusts of wind. Then, drawing the curtains to shut out the sight of her distorted naked reflection, she parted the cool sheets and slipped between them, gasping at the sting of freshness upon her skin, her feet seeking the places where the warming-pan had recently been. The maid tiptoed across to the candlestick and blew out the flame, leaving her mistress to her rest.

Not for many weeks had Linas stayed overnight at her Blake Street house, nor had he invited her to stay

at his, and so it was with an immediate sense of consolation that, in unthinking half-sleep, she accepted the
gentle movement of the sheets behind her and the slight
dip of the feather mattress as his weight tipped her
against him. She had been asleep, that much she knew,
for the wind had whipped itself into a howling spring
gale that rattled the old casement windows, and
drowsily she wondered whether it was that which had
disturbed him or the sudden remembrance of her
birthday. With a grunt of contentment she snuggled
deeper into his warm body and took the weight of his
arm upon her hip, expecting that he would straight
away resume his sleep.

But the weeks of abstinence were testimony to the
way her senses remembered him, for instead of the
tang of friars' balsam, laudanum or linctus, there was
a fresh moorland smell of heather and larch trees after
rain, and instead of the heavy limpness of his arm, this
one was thick and prickly with fuzz, moving over her
skin with a purpose, his fingers spread wide to cover
hers.

Her breathing behaved strangely as she struggled to
bring back to her sluggish mind some memory of what
she'd been used to, yet even with her back to him she could
not reconcile those vague familiarities with the pulsing
firmness that now pressed against her. Could she be
dreaming? Had her tiredness, resentment and yearnings
taken her too far? Reaching backwards, she took hold of
the hand to feel for the signet ring he never removed.

But the hand slipped away quickly to grasp her wrist
and hold it immobile, and as she turned to him in sudden
alarm, he moved faster than she could ever remember

him doing without stopping to cough and regain his breath. She found herself under him, pressed softly by wide shoulders that covered her, arms that enclosed her, and a large head of thick hair that touched her face with its softness, imparting a scent of new-washed linen. His lips found hers with none of the usual tentative pecking by way of introduction that was Linas's way, but with the assured and competant kisses of one who knew how to suspend a woman's protests in a limbo of delight, and it was not until he had taken his fill of her lips that her terrible doubts were able to surface and demand verification.

Pushing at his shoulders, she struggled against him as her body tried to recognise the deception, her mind still trying to persuade her not to delve too closely for fear of discovering the truth. Wordlessly, so as not to shatter the dream entirely with accusations and denials, she put up a fight that was disadvantaged in every way, which he countered in silence and with ease, and ultimately with the potency of his kisses that she allowed with nothing like the opposition she ought to have offered. Once, holding his head between her hands, she traced his features with sensitive fingertips over broad forehead and brows, over closed eyelids, cheeks and nose, firm mouth and chin, wider than the one she was used to. He kissed her fingers as they passed across, and she melted at that small tenderness before exploring the depth of his hair and the deeply muscled neck that led her on over the contours of his shoulders, down and down.

It occurred to her that he might have mistaken her room for that of another, but he would surely know where his guests were being accommodated. If any other thoughts of reason or common sense sneaked into her mind that night, they stood no chance of being heard against the deeply urgent need that sedated her fears like a potent drug, a need borne of starvation and a sense of waste that had dogged the last year with her lover. Gradually closing the doors of her mind, she began again to lose herself in the lure of his closeness, in the touch of his hand exploring the full roundness of her breasts. Perversely, she joined him in the treachery, forbidding herself to think about the consequences or to seek answers to a host of questions that were sure to follow. She would take what he was offering her, on her birthday, the only gift of comfort she was likely to receive.

Whatever reasons he had for doing this, he was not inclined to share them with her, nor did she ask him to, for she knew this would never happen again. Ever. He was making use of her and she would do the same with him, just this once. She might have pretended it was against her will, but she knew it was not, her token struggles having lacked any conviction against his gentle but determined restraint.

Savouring every moment as never to be repeated, excited by his mastery, she refused to allow the lack of endearment or word of comfort such as lovers use to detract anything from the fleeting glimpses of heaven she saw that night for the first time. Her unlikely lover-of-one-night was not a man she could ever want except for this, for he had never done anything to court her favour, and an exchange of tender words between them would have been meaningless as well as hypocritical.

It was her experience alone that told her of his pleasure in her body, his delight and satisfaction with her loving. At the same time, he was a careful lover, taking time with her as had never happened for her before, bringing her to a state of ecstasy again and again, taking pleasure from her wonderment and indicating by his lips and hands the journey they would take. Yet each time was different, his energy and eagerness phenomenal.

He stayed with her until dawn to take full advantage of her newly awakened passion, feeding from her willingness and giving generously to satisfy her hunger. And as the light crept between the curtains, he disappeared as silently as he'd come, thinking that she was asleep, and she had let him go because the time for words was past. She knew it to be one of those rare events that happened without rhyme or reason to change one's life for ever, and that the experience was worth the heavy guilt she would have to bear as long as her relationship with Linas lasted. Although Linas was not faultless, he had never been disloyal to her in the way she had been to him. She could only hope he would never discover it. The worst part would be having to pretend that nothing *had* happened.

In the months that followed, that pretence was shattered when she found herself to be with child. Then, because she could not keep the information from Linas, she broke the news to him, expecting that he would put an end to their association and reclaim everything that was his, including her home. To her utter astonishment, he did not, preferring to accept the unborn child as his own along with the congratulations of his friends and family, even though he must have known it could not be. Helene had assumed that pride in his manhood was more important to him than the truth, for he asked no questions, nor would he allow her to offer any explanation and, when the child was born, Linas's joy was as great as hers. At last, he had the heir he wanted.

The boy seemed to provide Linas with a renewed lease of life and, for the next three years he hung on as if to escort the lad through his first formative contacts with the world. But the effort could not be maintained, his hold began to slacken and, just after his son's third birthday, Linas was taken to Abbots Mere to end his days where they had begun, with his twin.

By that time, Helene had begun to suspect how adroitly she had been used by the two brothers. Now, she was sure of it.

Chapter One

York—January 1806

It would usually have taken me only a few minutes to walk from the workrooms of Follet and Sanders on Blake Street to Linas's house, but that day was an exception. That day, I was wearing my pretty fur-lined bootees, not designed for three inches of snow that had fallen in flakes the size of halfpennies since mid-morning, and by the time I reached the corner of Blake Street and Stonegate, where Linas's house was, the freezing wet had reached my toes and I was dizzy with slithering over a bed of snow-covered ice. I'm a tough northern lass, I reminded myself, clutching my thick woollen shawl tighter round my shoulders. I've been in many a snow storm before. The scolding did little to ease the situation.

The steps up to Linas's front door were thickly packed with the stuff, the shoe-scraper at the side piled with it, which should have warned me that someone had entered quite recently. But my hood was falling wetly over my face as I went inside, sending a shower of snow on to the already puddled black-and-white chequered tiles, and it was only when I threw my furry hood back that I saw more of Mr Brierley than his serviceable boots. Mr Brierley was Linas's lawyer who had, I suppose, as much right as me to be standing in the hall of his late client.

His greying forelock was plastered across his head, his spectacles speckled with snow, catching the light of the single lamp, and his attempted smile was cooled by the unusually low temperature. Linas had always maintained an uncomfortable warmth in all his rooms. Now, they were uncomfortably cold. But then, nothing was going to be usual for Linas any more after yesterday's funeral and today's thick white blanket being gently laid over him.

'Mr Brierley,' I said, returning his half-smile, 'I didn't expect to see you here so soon. Not for weeks. Well, days, anyway.' Shaking the hem of my pelisse, I showered his toes with snowflakes and saw him step back. My glance at the hall table verified what I feared: two grey beaver hats, two pairs of gloves, one antler-topped cane and a riding whip that I recognised. Silver-mounted. It was not what I had expected, or wanted, so soon after yesterday. I ought to go, I thought, before he appears. We shall only bicker.

The lawyer must have recognised the hint of unwelcome in my greeting, which, I admit, was not as fawning as it might have been from a client's mistress. Client's mistresses usually have expectations. 'No, indeed, ma'am,' he said. 'We lawyers are not known for speeding things up, I agree, but Lord Winterson asked me to meet him here, to—'

'To take a look round? Yes, I quite understand, Mr Brierley. Shall I leave you to it? Is that your inventory?' There was a black leather notebook tucked under his arm, and my accusatory tone drew it from its pigeonhole to prove itself.

'Er…no. Not to take an inventory. It was Lord Winterson's wish to attend to other pressing matters before the snow delays things. Perhaps that is also why you are here, Miss Follet?'

Yes, I suppose he was entitled to ask my business now. 'The snow will make no difference to me. I come here every day, sir. The servants need direction at a time like this.'

'Which is exactly why we're here. To help re-settle them. I have here some contacts…' he tapped the notebook with white fingertips '…and they'll need the references Mr Monkton prepared for them.'

Ah, yes. References. Linas would have discussed the futures of all his employees with his lawyer and brother. Mine too, I hoped. What a pity he had found it so difficult to take me into his confidence at the same time, to spare me the worry of how I would manage on my own. I had made plans, as far as I was able, but it would have lightened my heart if he had shown as much concern for my future as he had for the rest of his household. My repeated promptings, gentle or insistent, had brought no response except irritability and fits of coughing, and finally I had stopped probing for any kind of assurances concerning me and Jamie.

'Of course,' I said. 'Then I shall bid you a good afternoon.'

My feet were wet, my fingers inside my woolly gloves frozen, the hall was bare and gloomy, and I did not want to see Linas's brother that day. Or any day. I reached back to pull up my hood, numb fingers fumbling with an edge of wet fur, icy water running up to my elbows.

'I believe,' said Mr Brierley, 'Lord Winterson would like you to be present at the reading of his brother's last will and testament tomorrow, Miss Follet.'

The shake of my head was hidden from him. 'No, I think not,' I mumbled. 'That will be no place for a man's mistress, sir. Please excuse me.' But my fumbling had obscured the quiet entrance of the one I hoped to avoid, and suddenly he appeared in the corner of my eye through the wet points of fur.

In almost six years there had never been a time when I'd been able to control my heartbeats at the sight of him. In the last four years—almost—there had hardly been a day when some detail of that night had failed to appear, or the wounding deceit of it fail to hurt. Between them, they had used me and I intended to make *him* aware of my anger as I had not been able to do with Linas. I could hardly bite the hand that fed me and my child, but I could and would refuse Winterson's attempts, such as they were, to make me see him in a better light. And who could blame me?

The day before, with so many people there, I had done my best not to look at him. Or not to be *seen* looking at him. Now I did, and was astonished to see the shadows of deep sadness around his eyes, the unease of his mouth and the sagging tiredness of his shoulders that leaned against the doorframe into the study. Like me, he had kept his coat on, a long buff-coloured caped affair that barely cleared the floor, hanging loose over charcoal-grey riding coat and breeches, black waistcoat with a row of gold-figured buttons and watch-chain. His neckcloth, as always, was immaculate. His hair, as always, needed cutting.

I am ashamed to say that, in my own grief at the loss of my lover, I had spared too little thought for how he must be feeling at the loss of his twin, having to watch him fade away like a candle flame, burn low and finally extinguish. I had no cause to grumble that I was excluded, for Winterson sent a carriage for me at the end so that I too could be there for Linas's last moments when it seemed, perhaps for the first and last time, that the three of us had shared a special tenderness and compassion, putting aside the complexities of our re-lationship. He had even allowed me some time alone with Linas at the end, which was remarkable when his parents were waiting to do the same. I was grateful to him for that. Returning home afterwards, my life seemed to be suspended and without cause, except for little Jamie. The funeral had upset me and I had slept badly, and I suppose it must have showed in my manner.

'Miss Follet?' he said. 'Could you spare me a moment of your time?'

'I told Jamie I would not be long.'

'Please? Just a moment?' He moved to one side, holding his hand out as if he was sure I would comply.

I left my hood up. And I left Mr Brierley in no doubt

about my reticence as I swept past them both into the green book-lined study that had been Linas's retreat during his last, most painful year. The once cosy room, always littered with books and papers, was now unnaturally tidy and distressingly naked. Incomplete. I turned the wick up in the oil lamp on his desk before going to stand by the white marble fireplace, putting some distance between us, hitching up my woolly scarf against a sudden chill. 'My lord?' I said, to convince him of my impatience.

'Miss Follet…Helene…' he said, wearily. 'Brierley and I had…' he sighed and looked away as if the room was affecting him too '…had hoped to have the will read here at Stonegate tomorrow. But, as you see, that may be prevented by the weather. If it carries on like this, those who ought to be here will be unable to manage it, or even get home again. I think we shall have to postpone it till it clears. I don't know how you're fixed for funds, to put it bluntly, but since Linas's accounts are frozen for the time being, I wondered if you might need some help until we discover what arrangements have been made for you.'

'How kind,' I said. 'If I had not chanced to see you here today, you might still be wondering.'

'It was not chance. I know you still visit daily. Such habits are hard to break. I called at your home, but you were not there, so I came here to meet Brierley and to wait for you.'

'You called…home? You saw Jamie?'

'Yes,' he said, raising an eyebrow at my tone. 'Is there some reason why I should not? He's grown in the last few weeks.'

'I should have been there. He's already missing his father.'

Unthinking, I stepped straight into the bag of worms. There was a crackling silence broken by the loud ticking of the bracket clock.

'Then this may be the best time to remind you, Miss Follet, that his *father* has just made contact with him, which you have so far been at pains to prevent by every means known to you. I could hardly have said so while Linas was with us, but now we must both try to accept the truth of the matter and do whatever is best for the child. You surely cannot be too surprised that Linas wished me to be Jamie's legal guardian?'

'That is probably the one thing that will *not* surprise me, my lord. It's well known that a child's guardian must always be male, you being the obvious choice, but that does not alter the fact that I am Jamie's mother and, as such, it is I who will decide where he will go and what he will do. And who he'll do it with.'

'Which is why I want you to hear Linas's will at first hand.'

'So you know the details of it, do you?'

'Yes, I know more details than you. That's only natural. We discussed it as brothers do.'

All too eager to display my wounds while I had the chance, I could not resist putting another slant on it. 'Oh you *did*, didn't you? Four years ago you discussed it. In some detail. Linas wanted an heir. You obliged. And I fell for it like an idiot. Like a resentful birthday-gift-starved fool. I paid for it, too.'

'You got Jamie. He was what you wanted. Don't deny it.'

'But one does like to have a say, nowadays, in who the father is to be. Even mistresses appreciate some warning of *that* event.'

'Think about it,' he snapped. 'Had you been *warned*, as you put it, there'd have been no Jamie, would there?'

'No, my lord. There most certainly would not.' I had to admit defeat on that brief skirmish, and I had no stomach for a prolonged argument on the topic. I closed my eyes with a sigh, holding a gloved hand to my forehead. 'This will not do,' I whispered. 'It's too soon for recriminations. Or too late. I'm tired. It's time I went home.'

He watched me, saying nothing as I recovered.

'I know there will be changes,' I said. 'I've had time to prepare for them, whatever they are. And thank you for your offer of a loan, but I think we shall manage for the time being. I also owe you thanks for allowing me access to Linas at the end. That was generous too, and…and appreciated…' My voice wavered and caught at the back of my throat, dissolving the last word. I took some deep breaths to steady it.

'It was no more than you deserve. It was your careful nursing that kept him alive longer than his doctors had predicted.'

'I think it's more likely to be Jamie who did that.'

'Yes, that too. Jamie was your other gift to him. Linas was a very fortunate man. He told me so more than once.'

'Did he?' I remarked, tonelessly, wistfully.

'Did he never tell you so?'

'No. Not even at the end. I think the pain made him forgetful. Or perhaps he thought I was the fortunate one. I don't know. It doesn't really matter now, does it? But I mean what I say about not hearing the will read, my lord. I would be out of place. I am not family and I have few expectations, except for Jamie, having fulfilled the role I was employed to do, to everyone's satisfaction.'

'You were not *employed* in any capacity, Miss Follet. You were my brother's partner. It was his decision not to marry when he discovered he had so few years to live, and our family agreed that for him to do so would serve no useful purpose.'

'Rather like good farm management, I suppose. You see, I am well able to think it out for myself, Lord Winterson. Having a mistress to support for just a few years was safer than taking on a wife. Linas preferred an illegitimate heir able to legally inherit and keep his estate intact, to a widow who would remarry and siphon it off into another man's pockets. But don't tell me that I was not employed, for that is certainly what I was, and I shall not sit with you round a table to be told that my golden goose has gone and left me nothing except my bastard child to care for. You may be very sure I shall guard my only treasure against any attempt to siphon *him* off into another man's pocket. He may be the Monkton heir, but he is also my only legacy. *Mine*, my lord.'

I should not have said it, not then when emotions were so raw, Linas barely out of earshot, and both of us so tired. But my resentments were begging for release, freeing up words that I should have kept tightly controlled, as I had always done. I could have blamed my outspokenness on my northern roots, but that was too easy an excuse. So I held my breath and waited for him to retaliate in the usual Winterson fashion, with a set-down meant to silence me for months. Which he had every right to do.

His reply, when it emerged, was a calm reiteration of his claim. 'And he is mine too, Helene. Linas has made me his legal guardian and you will have to get used to the idea, like it or not.'

'I *don't* like it.'

'But I think Jamie will. He needs an active father, now he's growing up. He needs more to do than walks with his nurse.'

'He's still only a babe. He needs only me.'

'So let's wait till we've heard what provisions Linas has made for you, then we shall know better what his needs are, shan't we? You are exhausted, and so am I. It's time you were home. Come. I have to get back to Abbots Mere before the snow gets deeper.'

'What about the servants?' I said, relieved to have been let off so lightly. 'You came here to—'

'Brierley can stay to deal with that. He lives on Petergate. You should trust him. He's an honest man.'

'I'm sure he is. He'll have your interests at heart.'

'And Jamie's. Is that such a bad thing?'

Still, I could not help myself. Perhaps I wanted to provoke him, to make him react, in spite of his courtesy to me. Perhaps I was a little mad that day. 'If I was retaining him,' I said, 'it would not be such a bad thing. But I'm not, am I?'

We had reached the door where his hand rested upon the large brass knob but, as my stupidly caustic remark stung him into action, he turned to me with characteristic speed, taking me by the shoulders with hands that bit through all my woollen layers. Holding me back against the deeply carved doorcase, he bent his head to look inside my hood and, whatever anger he saw on my face, it could have been nothing to the fury on his.

'Stop it, woman!' he snarled. 'You think you're the only loser in this damned business? You think you've had the thin end of the wedge, do you? Well, *do* you? Forget it. He was my brother. You had him for the best part of six years. I had him for thirty. We both…you and me…did what *he* wanted us to do, and if you had less choice in the matter than you'd have liked, well, I had just as little. I did it for him, and you believed I did it for you, didn't you? That's why you're so angry. D'ye think I make a habit of creeping into my lady guests' beds while they're asleep?'

Since he was being kind enough to ask my opinion on that, I'd like to have said that he must have had a fair bit of practice at it. But, no, I said nothing of the kind. Nothing at all, in fact. I simply shook my head, which made my hood fall off. I noticed two new hairline creases from his nose to his mouth. I noticed that his eyelids were puffy, as if he'd been weeping. I noticed a sprinkling of silver hairs in that luxurious dark mop, just above his ears.

'I'm sorry,' I whispered. 'I'm overwrought. We both need to rest.'

He sighed through his nose with lips compressed, and I thought he was going to say more because his eyes held mine, letting me read the sadness written there more eloquently than words. Then he released me, and I felt the tingling where his hands had been, and I stood still while he pulled up my hood and settled it round my face. I was under no illusions; he would do the same for any of his closer woman friends, I was sure. Perhaps their minds would empty too, just for those few seconds.

'Calm down,' he said, gruffly. 'Go home and get warm. Come on.'

Outside on the pavement, the lamplighter clambered down his ladder into the horizontal white blizzard, having cast a halo of light dancing across the ghostly snow-covered figures below. Lord Winterson's groom emerged from the narrow alley that led to Linas's courtyard and stables, riding one horse and leading the mighty grey hunter that blew clouds of white into the freezing air. 'Follow on,' Winterson called to him, taking my arm and linking it through his.

'I can manage,' I said, ready to pull away. 'Really I can.'

But he clamped my hand with his elbow and, bending his head into the snowstorm, began to escort me home, not far, but far enough for us both to struggle against the conditions. His only conversation was, 'Mind...take care...hold on...you all right?'

Standing under the porch before the door, I thanked him.

'Stay at home till it clears,' he said. 'I'll contact you as soon as I can get through. See Brierley if you need anything. He'll help.'

I nodded and watched his effortless leap into the saddle, wheeling away as if the snow was no more than a mild shower. Across on the other side of Blake Street, the lights in the workroom, more properly known as Follet and Sanders, Mantua-maker, Milliner and Fabric

Emporium, had been extinguished earlier than usual to allow the girls to get home, though I knew that Prue Sanders would still be working at the back of the shop on the new year's orders, the alterations on ballgowns, fur trims and muffs. The cold weather had swept in from the north-east with a vengeance that year, and I had ordered that the fire in the sewing room should be kept burning constantly to keep the place warm. It was an expensive luxury I had not budgeted for, and my recent assurances that I could manage were not nearly as certain as I'd made them sound. But not for any reason would I have accepted a penny from him. Prue and I would have to manage on what the business earned.

That evening, however, my thoughts were in turmoil, for although my contacts with Lord Winterson had always been as brief as I could make them, this was the first time he and I had spoken about what had gone before, about his claim to Jamie, or about my feelings on the matter. As long as Linas lived, the subject had been studiously avoided, and now the impromptu unveiling had shaken me, if only because I had believed until then that he and Linas were alike in refusing to discuss things they found too uncomfortable. I had been proved wrong.

Only a day after his brother's funeral, Winterson had brought out our shameful secret for its first airing, along with the reason for it and the well-planned result of it. My Jamie. He was right: I *was* angry, not because I was mistaken about his motives—for those I knew by then—but because *he* had known how easily I would give myself to him that night, repeatedly, willingly, and with little conscience. He had known, and my pride was wounded to the quick that all our mutual antagonism had been so easily suspended in the face of a temptation like that. How shallow he must think me. How disloyal. How easy.

What he would never know, though, was that I had fed off that experience since it happened, savouring it every night through each amazing phase, knowing that it would never be mine again. And since he had been unconvinced of my dislike of him *before* the event, I must of necessity try harder to convince him of it afterwards. His accusation about keeping Jamie at a distance from him was a part of my strategy but, with him now as Jamie's guardian, I would find that more difficult, thanks to Linas.

Chapter Two

Thanks also to the weather, that part of my plan held up well when all the traffic in and out of the city was stopped for more than a week until men could shovel paths through the deep drifts, allowing access to the suburbs. We heard reports of farmers losing sheep, of snow burying hedges and cottages, trapping the mail-coach miles away with all its passengers, and the drowning of some young lads who had played upon frozen ponds. Fresh falls of snow added more depth to the fields each morning and broke branches off trees, the dropping temperatures killing everything that was too old, frail or poor to keep warm. The thermometer in Linas's hall registered thirty degrees Fahrenheit, and a few days later we had twenty degrees of frost. I had never experienced such cold.

All through the freeze, my daily visits to Stonegate continued, partly to check on the remaining servants and partly to mentally mop up what was left of the essence pervading each room. In one way I had to be thankful that his suffering had ended at last, for I had not found it easy to watch him die and know that there was no way of stopping it happening. Jamie's birth had done more than anything to extend the reprieve, but Winterson had been right to suggest that, when his brother's illness began to distress the little fellow, a move to Abbots Mere would be best.

So I'd had a chance, at the end, to spend more time with Jamie, to begin some small rearrangements of our life in preparation for the future, to involve myself more with the thriving dressmaking business, to make another buying trip to Manchester and to pay an extended visit to my family without having to account for our absence.

Even so, I felt the gaping hole in my life where my Linas had been for, although we had not been lovers in the true sense for years, we had shared a real need for each other that was not wholly material, but emotional and spiritual as well. We never actually spoke of it: he was not good at speaking of love, and any attempt on my part only embarrassed him. But we were aware of our need for each other, especially so since Jamie's appearance, and I was not foolish enough to end that prematurely when I knew the end would come soon enough. Had I remained childless, I might have thought differently, but I could not take a gamble when there was the son of a noble house to care for.

The River Ouse that brings boats up to the York warehouses froze all river traffic to a standstill, offering a quicker way to cross without using the bridge or the ferry. Those who could skate had a merry time of it, and Jamie's nurse and I took him there, astonished by his pluck and persistence.

While Linas was alive, the natural tendency had been for everyone to compare him to the one he called papa, but by three years old his sturdy little frame and bold wilful nature, dark eyes and thick curly hair indicated characteristics that I was able to identify only too easily. Fortunately, my own dark colouring disguised the truth, but then, that must also have been taken into account at the outset, I supposed. It was so clever of them.

The nine seamstresses in the sewing room were loath to return home each evening during the freeze when the conditions at work were so much more comfortable than their own. Remembering how I too had been one of them, fourteen years old with only my clothes to my name, how Prue had sheltered and fed me, I tried to do the same for them, many of whom had worked there longer than me. Oh, she had worked me harder than hard to make it worth her while, being a canny Yorkshire woman, but I had not resented it, nor did the girls appear to resent me moving up the ladder rather faster, so to speak. Now, Prue Sanders and I were partners in the business, having expanded sideways into the house next door to the Assembly Rooms. A perfect situation, if ever there was one.

My own house was placed diagonally across the road, so convenient for us both especially during those exceptionally cold weeks when the ice seemed to creep into our veins. All our stores of potatoes froze solid. Few people could reach the mill for flour, nor could the miller use his wheel, sending up the price of bread accordingly. Fish was locked under the ice and people had to delve earlier than usual into their reserves of dried and pickled foods, feeding cattle with precious hay.

I did better than most in that respect, for as soon as a narrow passage was cut through the drifts, two pack-ponies and men arrived at my kitchen door having trekked from Abbots Mere at their master's command. Into the kitchen were carried sacks of flour, oats and barley, chickens and geese, a brace each of pheasant and grouse, rabbits and a hare, baskets of apples, pears and plums, butter and cheeses, eggs and half-frozen milk, a half-carcass of lamb, hams, and trout packed in ice, all piled on to the table while cook stood with jaw dropping. I saw this gift as an answer to my refusal to accept a loan. For all our sakes, I was bound to accept this.

Gulping down beakers of mulled ale and wedges of fruit cake, the men would give no more information than, 'Compliments of Lord Winterson, ma'am. And ye're to let him know when you want some more. He hunts most days.'

'What, on horseback? In this snow?'

'Usually on foot, ma'am.'

Jamie jumped up and down at the end of my hand. 'Oh, can I go too? I go on foot with Uncaburl?'

'Nay, little 'un,' said one of the men, replacing his woollen hood, 'tha'd be mistekken fer a rabbit.'

'Would I, Mama?' said Jamie, looking worried.

I lifted him into my arms. 'No, sweetheart. Your ears are much too short to be mistaken for a rabbit. But the snow is too deep. Now we must say thank you to the men and let them go. It's starting to snow again.'

I sent my thanks to 'Uncaburl', thinking how ironic it was that food was more available to him out in the country than it was to me here in the town. Winterson's revolutionary farming methods would see him through any crisis. According to Linas, Abbots Mere had never produced so much since his brother took it over. In truth, I had started to worry about what my own family would suffer if the freeze continued much longer, living several miles from York and completely cut off from supplies.

Perhaps I exaggerate. No, they were not *completely* cut off, only in the sense that they were invisible to all intents and purposes, living in hiding in a deserted village between York and our old home town of Bridlington on the east coast. There, the North Sea hurls itself at the cliffs in easily provoked anger.

For several years, my perceptive partner, Prue Sanders, withheld all questions about my family and why I was cut adrift from them. When the time was ripe, she knew I would take her into my confidence. So it was after I had borne Jamie and gone into partnership with her, extending the shop to twice its size, that I felt she was owed some kind of explanation as to why a woman like me had had to look for work as a lowly seamstress in York.

She was not the kind of woman to express astonishment; it was as if she had already guessed parts of the story, reversals of fortune being no new thing in those uncertain war years. When I told her my father had been mayor of Bridlington, she simply nodded and carried on pinning a gathered skirt on to a bodice. 'Mm…m. Wealthy?' she mumbled, without looking up.

'He was a merchant. A ship owner, and Customs Collector.'

'Oh, yes,' she said in the kind of voice that expects

the Customs Collector to be up to some shady business, as a matter of course. 'Smuggling, was he?'

Her assumption was correct, of course, for every villager along the North Sea coastline had a hand in the 'Free Trade', and few could afford not to be involved in the carrying, the hiding, the converting of boats, the warning systems, not to mention the putting-up of money to buy the goods from northern France and Flanders. The new French aristocracy led European fashions, and all things French were much in demand, imports that were taxed so highly by the English government that smuggling became a kind of protest against the unaffordable import duties.

'Yes,' I said. 'He got caught. Informed on by a so-called friend.'

'Nothing new there, then,' she said, pinning. 'Good rewards.'

'Yes, it was the Customs Controller who shopped him for half the value of the contraband and five hundred pounds extra. Father wouldn't accept the man's offer to marry me, so that was how he took his revenge.'

'And did you want him?'

'Lord, no, Prue. I was fourteen and he was thirty-something.'

'So your father was arrested. He'd not be found guilty by a local jury. They never are.' She was so matter of fact. So dispassionate.

'No, but he used a firearm, Prue.'

The pinning stopped as she straightened up to look at me. 'Oh,' she said. 'That's serious. That's a hanging offence. Confiscation of property. The works. Is that how you came to be...?'

I remembered those weeks when the world turned upside down for our family, how my father was dragged off by the local militia to the gaol at York. 'Yes,' I said. 'More or less. But his friends from Brid rescued him and hustled him away to Foss Beck Common. My mother and the rest of us joined him there, but he died soon after.'

'Foss Beck?' Prue said, taking the last pin from between her lips. 'Is that where they are? I always thought...'

'Yes, I know you did. I'm sorry I deceived you, but it's not a story to boast of, is it? It's easier to call Brid home than a deserted village. Linas doesn't know about what happened. No one does.'

'Aye...lass!' she said, sitting down at last. It was unusual for her hands to be idle. 'Dear, oh dear! You lost your father too? And your home?'

'He was wounded, but he kept it quiet. It seems so absurd that, only weeks earlier, he could have afforded the best attention in England. My mother has never quite recovered from the shock of it all, so it fell to me and my two brothers to survive on what we could find. We have a French relative who lives with us too, and he's been very good. We have a few servants to help out, and friends from Brid brought us food and bedding and tools. Even hens and goats. We managed.'

'I didn't think any of the houses at Foss Beck were still habitable.'

'The manor house has been half-ruined for centuries since the plague killed everyone off, but we manage to live in half of it.'

'And there's no chance of returning to Brid?'

'My brothers were nine and eleven, and I was

fourteen when we went into hiding, old enough to be arrested as substitutes for my father's crimes. It's a risk we daren't take, Prue. Not even after all these years.'

'So that's when you came looking for work in York. I see.'

'While I still looked half-respectable. Sewing was one of the things I could do to earn money. You must have seen in me something you could use.'

'Yes. Your skills, and the fabrics you brought in each month.' Picking up a bobbin of tacking-cotton, she pulled off a length and snipped it with her teeth. 'I've never asked where it came from, Helene, and I don't intend to ask now. If I don't know, I can't tell any lies, can I? Where did I put my needle?'

'On your wrist.' She wore a piece of padded velvet like a pincushion around her wrist. With Pierre, our French *émigré* relative acting as a go-between, and me not asking any questions about the source of his merchandise, everything he obtained for us was passed straight into the dressmaking business, the only one in York at that time to sell fabrics and designs too. The money from the bales of muslins and lace made it a lucrative trade that allowed me to supplement the poor wage I had earned and to take money and goods back to my family. Had it not been for Pierre and his French connections, we would certainly have starved. Prue must have known how the precious goods were obtained, and our customers must have guessed. My only thought was how to keep myself and my family alive.

'Yes…well,' she went on, threading her needle in one quick move and rolling a knot between finger and thumb, 'you've been a godsend to me, Helene love. Not just the fabrics, though I'll not deny they've done a lot to help things along. Your business ability, for one thing. Your looks, for another. Your style. Your knowledge of French too. And I know how hard it's been for you, though I don't know what your ma would say about *how* hard you've had to work. Does she know?'

'That I've had to sell myself?'

'Mmm,' she said, rippling the needle through the gathers.

'No, Prue. She doesn't. The boys do, and Pierre. But beggars cannot be choosers, can they?'

'No, love. You've had to grow up rather fast, haven't you? But it's not made you bitter, has it?' The needle delved and pulled up, finding its own rhythm.

'Yes, it has,' I said.

The needle stopped in mid-air as she looked up at me. 'Then don't let it,' she said. 'Regretting is a waste of time. What's done is done. You have a man, and a child, and a partnership in this, and youth, beauty, and more common sense than most women of your age. So, you've got responsibilities.' The needle began again. 'Well, most of us have, one way or another. Nothing stays the same, Helene. Believe me.'

'I do believe you,' I whispered.

Things would *not* stay the same. For one thing, I was determined that my infant would not suffer the same deprivations I'd suffered. Little did I know then how his future would pass out of my hands with such finality, nor did I fully appreciate the wisdom of Prue's advice about my bitterness.

Lowering Jamie to the ground, I took him by the hand and led him back to the warm kitchen where the piles of food were being sorted by cook's eager hands. He stroked the hare's soft fur and spoke into its huge reproachful eyes. 'Sorry, hare,' he whispered. I showed him the intricate pattern of the pheasant's feathers and the long banded tail that I would save for the millinery girls. 'I want to see Uncaburl,' said Jamie, sadly.

'Yes, love. But you saw Uncle Burl only last week, and the snow is very deep. I don't think our horses would like it.'

He barely understood. 'We could go to see Nana Damzell, then?'

Damzell Follethorpe was my mother, who had not seen him for over a month and Jamie now able to talk so well, I dared not take the risk, with Winterson being a Justice of the Peace and Jamie so willing to chatter about all he knew. 'Soon, darling,' I said.

'She'd like some of this, wouldn't she, Mama?'

'Yes, love, she certainly would.' The same thought had passed through my mind too, but I could not see how to get it there.

Mrs Neape, my cook, understandably not wishing to see the supplies dwindle so soon, had the answer. 'Don't you worry, young man,' she said. 'This lot will stay frozen solid down in the cellar for weeks. Then you can take some of it to Bridlington to your Nana Damzell.'

It was where all my household believed my family to be living, about forty miles away on the coast. Foss Beck was less than half that distance, and the only person ever to accompany us there was Jamie's formidable nurse, Mrs Goode, who would not have disclosed the smallest detail of my secret. She had once been a man's mistress, too. 'As soon as the snow begins to melt,' I promised, 'we shall go. What shall we take her?'

'Eggs. She likes duck eggs, Mama.'

That would be like taking coals to Newcastle. They had hens, ducks and geese roaming freely, and no shortage of eggs. But bread would be a problem.

'Tell me when you're going and I'll make you some of my meat pies,' said Mrs Neape, hoisting the side of lamb on to her padded shoulder. She would not, however, see any need to send loaves of bread.

With little improvement in the weather, the reading of Linas's will was delayed for almost three weeks and, even then, several of the family were missing, so Mr Brierley told me, owing to the impassable roads. It was he who called to say that he hoped I would not mind hearing at second hand what concerned me, since that was how several of the others would receive news of their endowments too.

What they were endowed with I have no idea, never having shown much interest in what Linas owned, or whether he relied on his wealthy father for an allowance, as many sons did. Even when they were twins, second sons rarely prospered as well as their elder siblings in the property stakes, although I had no doubt that Linas would never have been left wanting. As his mistress, I was probably the most expensive of his few extravagances, albeit not as costly as some I've heard of. I had, after all, reorganised my own business after Jamie's birth, and thank heaven for my foresight, Mr Brierley having no outstandingly good news to offer me that day.

At first, I could hardly believe what I was hearing.

That Linas wanted me to continue living on Blake Street came as a great relief, though no real surprise. Mr Brierley's assurance was quite clear that the house would be made available to me for as long as I wanted it. But when he kept his balding head bent while unnecessarily sorting papers out across the polished table, I guessed that he was seeking not figures, but a kind way to break the news. It came very quietly and deliberately.

'As for pecuniary endowments, Miss Follet,' he said, glancing up at last, 'that's *money*, you understand...'

'Yes?'

'Mr Monkton has left you the sum of three hundred and fifty pounds per annum for the rest of your life.'

'Yes?'

'Er...yes. That's all.'

I stared at him, frowning, puzzled. 'All? Three *hundred* and fifty?'

His finger pointed at the yellow page. 'Yes. That was his wish.'

'But how am I supposed to manage on that? Has he left no provision for our son?'

'Certainly. Master James Frederick Linas Monkton has been left, you will be pleased to hear, a substantial trust fund, to remain in the hands and to be administered by his sole guardian, Lord Burl Winterson of Abbots—'

'Yes, I know where Winterson lives, but what else is there? Surely Linas left me something for Jamie's needs until he comes of age? I cannot raise him on three hundred and fifty pounds a year, Mr Brierley.'

'You are not supposed to, Miss Follet, if I may say so. The trust fund to be held by Lord Winterson is designed to cater for all your son's needs, as and when he needs them. This will include all his living expenses, his clothes and education and so on. All you will have to do is to apply to James's guardian for—'

'But that's ridiculous!' I yelped, jumping to my feet. 'Are you saying I shall have to request money for Jamie's food, but not for mine, candles and coal for Jamie, but not for me, his nurse's wages, a groom...'

'No...no, Miss Follet.' Mr Brierley smiled, waving a hand in my direction. 'I don't suppose it will come to that, will it? I'm sure Lord Winterson will see that you have what you need for young James. A kind of allowance? Monthly? Weekly? But Mr Monkton's wishes are quite clear that his brother shall have every say in his ward's upbringing, and I have Lord Winterson's assurance that he intends to exercise his guardianship with the authority of a father. It must surely be comforting for you to know that your son will have a guardian who is so committed to his immediate welfare.'

I stood by the window, stunned by the chilling austerity of Linas's tight-fistedness. I felt I deserved better than that, after almost six years of devotion. I wished then that my life had taken a different turning. Gripping the rose-velvet curtain, I spoke my thoughts out loud. 'The house will have to be sold,' I said. 'And I shall have to find a husband. Yes, that would be best for both Jamie and me. Even with a house to live in, it's going to take every last penny I can earn to keep it going.'

'Ahem!' Mr Brierley coughed, shuffling the papers again. 'I believe Mr Monkton did add a clause concerning that eventuality, Miss Follet, if I can find it somewhere. Ah...yes, here we are.' He adjusted his spectacles. 'Should Miss Helene Follet decide in the future to take a husband, then my son James Frederick Linas Monkton shall live permanently and exclusively in the home of his guardian at Abbots Mere in the county of York. There. He's saying that—'

'Yes, thank you. I believe I know what he's saying, Mr Brierley. In short, I shall lose Jamie if I marry.'

'Correct. You will also lose the use of the house too, I'm afraid.'

'What?'

He nodded, pursing his lips. 'Mmm. Well, you can see his point.'

My head reeled as I sat down with a thump upon the couch. Oh yes, I could see his point quite clearly. No wonder he'd been loath to discuss it with me. Not only had he decided by whom and when I should bear a child for him, but now he was asserting that he could take it away again if I did not conform to his wishes. How dictatorial was that? As for Winterson exercising his guardianship like a father, well, yes, he would. *Exactly* like a father.

'That is most unfair, Mr Brierley, and *highly* unethical. That is interfering with my right to take a husband and to keep my child.'

'Surely, Miss Follet, it is better for your son to have a guardian he knows and likes than to have a stepfather he doesn't know? I do believe Mr Monkton had this in mind when he made this wish.'

Did he? I struggled to think *what* Linas had in mind when he saw fit to interfere in my life even after he'd gone. Jamie was precious to him too, I understood that, but he could not realistically expect me to see eye to eye with his brother on any matter relating to Jamie's up-bringing, when Winterson had no experience whatever of children. I felt insulted that he could not have left matters in my hands and made funds available to me for Jamie's use. Did he think that, although I could manage a business, nurse him day and night, run my own household and care for a three-year-old, I could not be relied on to handle a trust fund? No, probably not. There had been times when I wondered whether Linas spared much thought for me at all. Now I knew the answer.

'This will have to be contested,' I muttered. 'It won't work.'

'Miss Follet,' said Mr Brierley, removing his spectacles and sitting back in his chair, 'one cannot contest a will simply on the basis that one thinks it might be difficult to put it into practice. There is nothing here that is unworkable. You may have found it disappointing, but the terms are not so very unusual. Mr Monkton's reasoning was sound at the time, and he does not state that you should not marry, only that his son shall live with his guardian if you do.'

'And you see nothing sinister in that, sir? Is it remotely likely that I would allow that to happen, do you think?'

'Ahem! I really cannot comment on that, Miss Follet, except to say that Mr Monkton's prime concern was for his son's well-being.'

'Which I find difficult to understand, sir. One would have thought that his son's well-being would be all the better for knowing that his mama was happy too. Oh, yes,' I said as he opened his mouth to speak, 'I know that wealth is not happiness, but how am I supposed to pay the servants' wages, keep the place warm and in good repair, and maintain the standard of living that Jamie is used to, I wonder, on three hundred and fifty pounds a year? Not to mention my own requirements. I shall be obliged to look for a little cottage to rent. That seems to be the only solution. Thank you for coming, Mr Brierley,' I said, holding out my hand. 'I think the best I can do now is to speak to Lord Winterson personally and see if we can come to a more sensible arrangement. Even he must realise what an impossible position this puts me in. Good day to you, sir.'

He shook my hand and gathered his papers together. 'Mr Monkton's servants will be gone from Stonegate by Friday,' he said. 'All of them except the top four have been paid and found new positions. The house will then be locked, prior to the new administration of the estate. If there is anything in the house that belongs to you, Miss Follet, I wonder if you would mind letting me have a list of the items so that I can isolate them. Oh... er...one more thing. If I may have your key to the Stonegate property?'

I took it from the drawer of my writing table and gave it to him. There were several things at Stonegate that belonged to me: a pair of miniature cameo portraits, my silver pill box that Linas used once, the embroidery workbox I kept there and a set of ivory combs, brushes and manicure tools. They were private, and I'd be damned if I'd make a list for him to hum and haw over.

It occurred to me much later that night as I lay sleepless, that Mr Brierley had not brought with him the title deeds to my house, or things to sign that would establish me as the new owner. Well, I must remember to mention it next time we met.

Chapter Three

Had I misunderstood? Had I not listened to him with enough attention? Had he *really* said the house would be mine? Mr Brierley had made no response to my angry comment that I would have to sell it and find a small cottage with fewer servants. Reduced circumstances I was familiar with, the fortunes of women in my position being notoriously unstable, but was that really what Linas had wanted for me and Jamie? I found it hard to believe.

My house on Blake Street was newer and more fashionable than our old family home had been, furnished with woods that shone like satin, hung with soft tones in velvet and silk, carpeted with Axminsters and matching Persian rugs, my bedroom patterned with birds and trees. My canopied bed was carved by George Reynoldson of York, no less. I had a family of loyal servants who gave me no trouble at all, and Linas had paid their wages without me ever having to worry about the cost. I kept a phaeton and two horses in his stable at Stonegate with no clear idea of whether they would still be mine to use. I ought to have asked Brierley at the interview, but perhaps he had given me enough bad news for one day.

My first call on the following day was to Follet and Sanders. Leaving Jamie at home with Goody, his nurse, I trudged over new layers of frozen snow. Every rooftop and ledge was capped with rounded pillows of white, blown like lace into every crevice and beyond where the great white minster reared its spiked towers, draped like a bride, silent and virginal.

The workroom door let in a fall of snow as I entered. Shivering in the chilled hallway, I met Prue with chattering teeth. 'It's as cold in here as it is outside,' I complained. 'We'll never attract any customers at this rate.'

Unmoved, she kissed me daintily on both cheeks, casting her eye over my black outfit with the grey squirrel fur up to my ears. For all her fair, petite, middle-aged looks and elfin ways, she was as tough and sensible a businesswoman as any in York, with the typically dour sense of humour that can poke fun at what is difficult to accept. 'No, dear,' she said, without a hint of levity, 'but we're selling fur muffs and knitted gloves like hot cakes, so we can't have our customers getting overheated, can we?'

'And fur-lined capes? Those fur hats, too?'

'Fur-edged handkerchiefs,' she replied, dead-pan.

'No!'

'No,' she agreed. 'Come and see.'

'It's not warm enough in here either,' I said, entering the large workroom where women sat at the oak table, each with a mound of fabric before her, reels of cotton on revolving stands, pincushions and tapes, scissors, lamps and lace edgings. They looked up and smiled, all of them swaddled in woollen shawls and fingerless mittens. The windows were white, patterned with ferns.

'No coal delivery this week,' Prue said. 'We're having to eke it out. I can't keep the fire going all night any more, and now the pump is frozen.'

'I'll send some coal across. Get cook to make some soup.'

'That all adds to the costs, you know.'

Faces looked up, grinning slyly. Prue never starved them.

She followed me into the fitting room, draped with discreet pale curtains and peopled by miniature figures on shelves wearing the latest Paris modes. In here, I paraded gowns before our best customers, where they called me 'Madame Helene', impressed by my French pronunciation and having no qualms about our poor relationship with France. War or no war, French modes were all the thing, and our supplies of silks and lace was wondered at, bought, but never queried.

'Brierley came about the will,' I told Prue, quietly.

I told her what had been said. She listened, unruffled.

'Then go to Stonegate and collect them,' she said. 'Go now. You don't need a key. Go in by the kitchen door. If you delay till Friday, it'll be too late.'

'Do I care enough to go and help myself?' I asked.

'Of course you do. Go! Mr Monkton's servants will let you in.'

She steered me through into the shop festooned with fabrics where customers were being attended at the long counter. 'Good morning, Mrs Barraclough. Miss Fairweather. Lady Bess, good morning to you.' She flicked a fair eyebrow at me and ushered me out into the snow, closing the door, setting the bell tinkling again.

At Stonegate, it was easy enough to pass through the ginnel into the courtyard and from there to the kitchen door. The cook, butler and coachman were there, huddled round the fire, surprised but not unwelcoming. I explained my mission and was led courteously up the back stairs into the echoing hall. 'Would you like some assistance, Miss Follet?' said the butler. 'Or would you prefer to be alone?'

'To be honest, Mr Treddle,' I said, 'I'm not even sure I ought to be doing this. Mr Brierley said to make a list, but I really don't... well, you know.'

'I understand perfectly, ma'am, and I feel sure Mr Monkton would too. May I suggest that you place your possessions on your bed, and I will personally wrap them and have them conveyed to Blake Street later on today. Would that do, do you think? That way, you'll not have removed them, will you?'

'Thank you, Mr Treddle. That will do perfectly.'

'Very good, ma'am.' He bowed, leaving me alone and feeling as strange as I had at my first entry, seventeen years old and on the cusp of something new. Yet again.

Upstairs, the sour smell of medication had gone and the tables had been cleared of the usual healing clutter. My silver pill box, brought from my old home, was still in his bedside drawer, yet even now I hesitated to take it. Smoothing the grey fur coverlet, I sat down on his bed as I had so often done to comfort him, to talk, to watch him sleep. Dear Linas.

The door, left open, gave on to a wide landing and the curve of polished elm, and if my eyes had not been closed by memories, I would have noticed, long before my return to the present, the tall great coated figure who had come to stand just inside the door frame.

I started with a gasp of shock, only half-believing.

'Miss Follet,' he said, softly.

I took a breath, summoning my matter-of-fact voice. 'Oh…you! You've saved me a journey. I was going to pay you a visit today.' He looked less weary, I thought, wishing my heart would not be so feckless.

'In this weather? I should hope not. Was it urgent?'

'Mr Brierley came. You must know, surely.'

'And?'

'There are things to be discussed.' Glancing at Linas's open drawer, I explained. 'He wanted me to give him a list. I don't do lists of possessions. I've lost too many possessions for that.'

'I don't blame you. Was there something in the drawer? Treddle told me why you're here.'

'Well…yes. That pill box. It was my father's.'

'Then take it.' When I did not, he walked over to the drawer, removed the pill box and gave it to me. 'There. Now, what else is there?'

'You don't mind?'

'Why should I?' he replied, wandering across the room with his hands clasped behind his back beneath the greatcoat. 'My staff are not going to know what belongs and what doesn't when they start next week.'

'What do you mean…*your* staff?'

He stopped his wandering and turned to face me with a searching look as if he was deliberating what to say. Yet again, I felt that this must be the prelude to some unwelcome news. 'Some of my staff from Abbots Mere. The house belongs to me now.' Then, as the shock dawned upon my face, he added, 'Oh, dear. Brierley didn't tell you? It was remiss of him to keep you in the dark. The staff you saw downstairs will remain, and the housekeeper too. I can use a house in the city as well as one outside it.'

What a fool I was. Why could I not have drawn more realistic conclusions about this? Guessing the answer to my next query, I asked it nevertheless. 'So who owns the one I live in on Blake Street? Mr Brierley said I would maintain the right to…'

'To live in it as long as you wish. Yes, that part was not in the will, but Linas and I agreed it between us. It belongs to me, you see. It always did. I lent it to Linas for your use.'

My guess had been correct. My arms prickled, but not with the cold. I stood up and closed the drawer with a snap. 'If I'd known *that*…'

'You'd what? Have refused to live in it?'

'I had thought…*hoped*…that Linas would provide me and his son with a roof over our heads, at the very least. Now, I cannot even sell it to make ends meet.' I could not deny that one of my main reasons for wanting to bear Linas's child was to do with the security it would bring. It had, as it happened, brought much more than that, not least being great happiness to his last few years. I had never regretted that part of the experience.

'You don't *need* to make ends meet, Miss Follet. I intend to continue paying all the running costs, as I have done since I lent it to my brother. You won't have any more expenses than you did before, except personal ones for which Linas has left you a modest sum.'

'You...*you* paid for its upkeep? And servants too?'

'Well, of course I did. Linas didn't have many extravagances, apart from...'

'Apart from *me*!'

'...from yourself, which I was quite content to finance. There was no sense of obligation, I assure you.'

'I've heard enough. No obligation, you say, when I was well and truly shared, wasn't I? You even *paid* for me. How do you expect me to feel about that, my lord? Grateful? Flattered? Slightly bewildered? Who exactly *have* I belonged to all these years, I wonder? All neatly contrived to live as the mistress of one twin whilst bearing the other one's child. Someone should write a play about it, shouldn't they? What a *comedy*!' Clutching the pill box, I strode past him, but was held back and swung round by his hand beneath my arm.

'Come back, Helene. You can't walk off in the middle of a discussion.'

'I'm not in the *middle* of it,' I snarled at him, pulling my arm away. 'And you can keep the other things I came for, since you probably paid for them too.'

'Listen to me, woman,' he growled, preventing my escape with his great bulk, legs apart, a black silhouette against the light. 'You're blinded by your anger because what Brierley told you was not what you expected. But be reasonable, will you? You want to continue living on Blake Street and you want the funds to maintain it properly, to give Jamie the stability he needs. And now when I tell you that's exactly what you *can* do, you fly off the handle and say it's *not* what you want. Well, make your mind up, but try to think what's best for Jamie instead of getting all hoity-toity about it. Does it matter *who* the house belongs to as long as you can both live there? Who else should pay the bills except me, I ask you? His guardian. Come down off your high horse for a moment. You'll have all you need.'

'What I need, my lord, is control of my life, for once. Control of Jamie's life, too. And that is still being denied me.'

'Then try being realistic. Sons remain in the control of their fathers or guardians and there's nothing you can do about that. You must have known as much. So, if you want to stay with him, you will have to accept the same constraints and try to regard them as benefits. Which they are. Linas knew that, and his will reflects it.'

'Is that so? Even to a ban on my marriage.'

'What marriage?'

I shrugged. 'Well, to a future husband, of course. Who else?'

'Do you have a candidate in mind for the position?'

'It would make no difference if I did. I stand to lose my son if I do.'

'Nonsense. You wouldn't lose him. He'd be with me.'

'That's the same thing, isn't it?'

'No. You know full well it isn't.'

There was something in his voice which I could not identify, but which I preferred not to enquire into too closely. Far from simplifying matters, our discussion had taken me further into obligations I would rather not have had, for while the crisis over costs appeared to have a solution, the acceptance of it for little Jamie's sake was not at all to my liking.

'Just the same,' I said, 'it's a risk I'm not prepared to take.'

'A risk? Is that how you see it? As risk? What on earth do you think I might do to the little chap?'

The risk, of course, was not about what he might do but what he might *not* do, namely to protect my son from the kind of racy lifestyle enjoyed by the Abbots Mere set, the foolish irresponsible blades and the Lady Slatterlys of society. She, for one, would enjoy finding my Achilles' heel in Jamie and, having found it, would twist the dart till it hurt. I was certain of it.

'The kind of life you lead is quite different from the one he's been used to with Linas and me,' I said, turning away. 'And you are not used to children.'

'I'm willing to learn. And he has a nurse. Anyway, you take him to see Medworth's family and to play with the animals there. He can do the same at Abbots Mere, and more. He'll have his own room, a pony to ride...'

'He's too young for that,' I objected, weakly.

'Of course he's not!' he scoffed. 'I learned to ride at three.'

'The question doesn't arise. Jamie will stay with me. A child of three needs his mother.' I hoped he would hear the finality in my tone.

'Nevertheless, Miss Follet, I think you will have to accept that Jamie will want to visit me, and that I shall want to see him. Often.'

'I have to, don't I? Perhaps one day a week, or al-
ternate—'

'No. My work doesn't run like clockwork. I have a
large estate, and I do things as and when they need
doing. When I send for Jamie I shall expect him to
come, and that will vary from week to week. I shall also
expect him to stay, sometimes. You too, if you wish. I
shall have rooms put aside for your personal use.'

Alarm bells rang. 'For my personal use. How
thoughtful. So tell me, my lord, what kind of signal that
will send to family and friends? Will your current
mistress vacate her rooms for my benefit? Shall I be
seen as the newest member of the harem? It could get
quite cosy.'

He didn't react, this time, as he'd done before, but
looked down his straight nose at me with his eyes
narrowed, his mouth beginning to lift at the corners.
'So…o, *that's* what's bothering you, is it? Ah, I see.'

Suddenly I was having to defend myself to him in a
way I'd never had to do for years. Linas seemed so very
far away, which was good, for I did not want him to hear
this conversation. 'Yes,' I snapped, heading for the door,
'that *is* what's bothering me. How *could* you be so insensitive as to think I would ever agree to stay there
after…' My cheeks flamed. Why had I brought that up
now, of all times?

I stalked off into the room next door that I had
always used, scarcely more inviting than Linas's, espe-
cially in the cold blue light of winter. 'You must know,'
I mumbled, 'that for me to be seen as one of the Abbots
Mere crowd is the last thing I ever wanted, even when
Linas was with me.' I started to rummage. 'I have a few

things to look for. Treddle said he'd send them on, but if you'd rather I left them, I shall quite understand.'

He caught up with me and perched on my delicate stool with the petit-point cushion, his greatcoat swamping it, his long booted legs looking very out of place in a lady's bedroom. I glared at him, bristling with hostility.

He held my glare with those supercilious brown eyes. 'I know,' he said. 'You wish me to hell. But some matters have to be tackled head on, and we're going to have this out whether it embarrasses you or not. You must have learned by now that you've met your match, Miss Follet.'

What I *had* learned was that Linas and his brother were even less alike than I thought, one refusing point-blank to discuss the future, even mine or his son's, the other one impatient to settle every detail. One, a prevaricator with no future to see into, the other with bountiful years ahead. Linas must have thought my future would take care of itself. I was not his wife. Why should he bother?

'Shall we postpone the debate about whether or not I have met my match, my lord? If you're asking whether I ever felt a certain imbalance in my relationship with your brother, then, yes, I cannot deny that. It could hardly be otherwise, could it, with Linas unable to see far ahead. Happily, I can see far enough for myself, so I shall not go hungry. You must tell me how to apply for Jamie's allowance each month, and perhaps arrange for Mr Brierley to make it available. I shall keep every receipt, naturally. I pride myself on being able to keep my own accounts.' It was immodest of me, but I thought he may as well know.

'Mother. Mistress. Businesswoman. Is there any-thing at which you are not proficient, Miss Follet?'

'Yes, I am not a good liar, my lord. The other day you were kind enough to remind me that your high-minded act of self-sacrifice was entirely for Linas's benefit, not mine. So I would be lying if I failed to point out, in case you should misunderstand, that I thought only of him too. I wonder you did not hear me call out his name, once or twice.'

'We spoke no words, as you well know.'

'Which only goes to show the limitations of your memory, my lord.'

'I'm flattered to know that yours is still sharp, Miss Follet.' He stood up, damn him, as if to claim the last word on the subject. 'And since you were also kind enough to point out the undesirable nature of what you call the Abbots Mere crowd, perhaps I may be allowed to voice similar concerns about your dubious connec-tions. Not quite the kind of thing Jamie ought to know about. You entertained young Solway for a few months, I believe, as well as Standish's middle son. What's his name? Bertrand, is it?'

'For money, my lord,' I snapped. 'I was obliged to sell myself.'

'Ah, of course. For money. Well then, you need hardly be too concerned about visiting Abbots Mere with my ward, since none of the women who stay there are ever paid a penny. They do it voluntarily.'

'In which case, then, one would expect to see the place swarming with your other little wards. *That* part must cost you a small fortune.'

'No!' he said, picking up a porcelain plate from the

mantelshelf and looking at the back. 'You and Jamie are the only ones to cost me anything.'

'How sad. That's something I can easily fix, my lord.' Boiling, churning, *seething* with anger at being outmanoeuvred, I gulped down the rest of my venom in a pointless threat that meant nothing at all, since there was no way in which I *could* fix it, except permanently.

Looking back on it later, I suppose that's what he thought I meant, for when I moved towards the door again, thinking only to get away from the haunting place, he slammed it shut before I could reach it, catching me like a silly sheep against the wall.

'Admit it or not, lady, as you please,' he said, but no more than that before he pushed my head on to his shoulder and brought his mouth down to cover mine, making me forget what it was I was not admitting, and a lot more besides.

He must have known…oh, yes…he *must* have known how much of that night I remembered. He must have known too how desperately I needed comfort instead of conflict and how much I would have preferred matters to go my way, for a change. He must have known, with Linas no longer to care or be cared for, that I felt both free and guilty, grieved and confused and not as well organised as I pretended to be. So I half-expected his kiss to taste of revenge after our session of deliberate wounding, our first close contact in all those difficult years. I thought he was about to put me, finally, in my place.

But it was not like that, not bitter, but meant, I think, to remind me of the magical beauty of that night without words, passionate but tender too, wanting, taking and giving. Predictable was not the way to describe Burl Winterson, yet I could taste the hunger in his kisses that roamed slowly across my lips, and I felt the desire in his hard arm across my shoulders, the soft hand holding my face. Feel, taste, scent…ah, yes…the scent was there too. Moorland. Fresh linen. Trees after rain. How could I not be reminded?

He must have heard the moan, faintly, in my throat.

'You're right,' he whispered, 'about not being a good liar. I think we'd both better stick to the truth in future. And let us get another thing straight before we leave. You and Jamie will continue to live under my protection on Blake Street without any more argument. You will bring him to visit me and you will both accept my authority as you did with Linas. I do not need to remind you again whose son he is.'

'And I suppose the next thing will be that you'll expect him to call you Papa, will it?' I said, trying to stiffen in his embrace, and failing.

'That'll come too. One thing at a time.'

Squirming out of his arms, I steadied myself against the blue-flocked wallpaper. 'I was being sarcastic,' I said, pettishly. 'I have no intention of giving you that satisfaction. And what is it I'm to admit, or not, as I please?'

'That you've met your match, at last. Now, where are these other things of yours? Come and show me.'

Chapter Four

No expectations, I had said, choosing not to hear the unreality of such a boast. But it was not true. I *had* expected, and yet again had failed to take into account the uncanny affinity between the twin brothers who, although unlike in many ways, had shared the same birth and the same life.

To hear that Linas had never owned my home on Blake Street had shocked me. To discover that he had not personally been responsible for its running costs, and mine too, had left me totally bewildered and very angry, making me revise my assumptions about why he had wanted an heir so much when he had so little to leave. A trust fund, yes, but no property. Linas had owned the Stonegate house, but Winterson had lent *his* property on Blake Street to Linas for my use, and Jamie's. And now, he was adamant that we should stay there while he made use of the larger one, as well as Abbots Mere. It was going to be difficult for me to escape him or to avoid his promised interference in our lives, our freedom being the one thing to which I had most looked forwards.

And the kiss? Well, no more than a reminder, a clever way of exposing my pathetic lie that had been intended to hurt him as he had hurt me. He said we should both start telling the truth, but I had no wish to tell him anything. To do that would be dangerous for a woman in my position. All the same, it was his kiss that kept me sleepless for most of the night.

Long before dawn, I had reached the decision not to delay any longer my visit to Foss Beck Common. My family's food situation must now be getting desperate, I thought, though there were other reasons for me to go too. They would not have heard of Linas's death, and I had to speak to them about the future. Mama would be suffering from the extreme cold, and I also needed to collect whatever Pierre had managed to acquire for my business. There was also money to be taken to him from the sales of my last consignment which, even when shared between us, was almost always a considerable amount. He never told me exactly how much it cost him to pay for these goods in the first place, or even whether he paid in kind and, if so, what kind. But I had recently felt that whatever he paid was nothing like as much as the returns we were getting.

So I had my horse saddled at daybreak, loading the packhorse with gifts and supplies and, wrapping myself thickly with extra shawls, set off along the snow-packed Roman road towards Bridlington. Jamie had not been pleased to be left behind: so unpleased, in fact, that his screaming tantrum was the last sound I heard as Goody hauled him away with both threats and promises. I knew what Jamie needed most, but my firmness was sometimes not enough, and nor was Mrs Goode's. Did he really need to see more of me, or less?

There had been no new falls during the night and, although the wind was still biting hard, the sky was blue and cloudless, the sun's rays bouncing off the dazzling white of moor and valley. I went alone, sure of the way, expecting to meet very few travellers, and certainly no coaches. Only a mile or so out of York, however, I realised what a big risk I was taking, for the road was treacherous with ice, the snow blown into drifts by the north-easterly against which the poor horses had to battle with heads down.

The sky was beginning to darken under a full moon by the time I reached Fridaythorpe and found the turn-off southwards to Foss Beck, another three miles of deep drifts and hidden tracks. Then, the land spread out before me like a laundered sheet stained with the dark shadows of trees, and I cursed myself for my impetuosity and foolhardiness while thinking of how I needed to see my family, and how they needed the food. It was quite dark before I made out the squared shapes of buildings ahead, before I rode, exhausted and chilled to the bone into the rambling desolate place, after a journey of less than twenty miles usually accomplished in three hours. Four, at the most.

The dogs picked up my shouts, baying with excitement when they heard my voice, yelping as the torches waved. My brothers ran out to take my bridle, catching me as I fell into their arms. Finch was nineteen, Greg seventeen, and as strong as young oxen. 'Sister! Are you *mad* to come here in this weather? Here, hold on to me. Can you stand? Shall we carry you?'

'I'll carry her,' called a deeper voice. 'Unload the horses, lads.'

'No one shall carry me,' I protested, hearing the authority in Pierre's command. Five years older than me, he had assumed the position as head of the house since my father's demise, which did not go down well with anyone except my mother. Careful not to add my approval to hers on that vexed question, I greeted Pierre as I had done my brothers, with a hug and a frozen smile that hurt my face. 'Yes, unload the horses and tend them. I'll go on up to Mama.' I staggered like a drunk towards the stone steps.

High waves of snow broke over the outbuildings in the courtyard where deep passages had been cut to the doorways, the paths marked out with straw. Now half-ruined, the large house had been built in the thirteenth century for the lord of the manor, with walls three feet thick and living quarters, as usual, on the floor above the undercroft. The place had been derelict until my family took possession of it, believing like everyone else that the abandoned village belonged to no one and that the land had reverted to common useage.

Carrying what I could manage up the flight of steps, I almost fell into the vast space that had once been the great hall. This had been my home too, though still a far cry from our grand house on the coast, as well as the one I used in York filled with polished wood, glass and fine paintings. Here, the massive beams under the thatch were thick with cobwebs, the bare walls flaking with centuries-old limewash.

'Helen! It cannot be…my lassie…my little Helen.'
My mother's wail, squeaking like an untuned spinet,
sounded to me like an angel choir. It might, I thought,
have been the real reason why I had to make that
dreadful journey, to hear her voice and find the warm,
eager, clinging welcome of her arms, her hands, her
lovely smile, her tear-filled eyes. We sobbed, laughed,
and sobbed again, rocking and cooing in wordless
mothering sounds.

Anxiously looking over my shoulder, she croaked,
'Ye've not brought the little one, have ye? Not in this
weather?'

'No, Mama. But he wanted to come to see Nana
Damzell.'

'Then what's wrong, lassie? Is it your man? He's
worsened?'

'Gone, Mama,' I sobbed. 'He's gone.'

'Aah! *Gone*.' The words were merely breaths of
sound as she studied me. 'Gone. Oh, my poor wee lass.
Tch! Oh, lassie. After all that you did.'

With our typical northern philosophy that sympathy
was best expressed in practicalities, she began to bustle
about, removing my frozen layers, drawing me to the
roaring log fire to seat me with a blanket round my
shoulders and a cushion beneath my numbed feet.
Croaking, she called to the two elderly family servants
to fetch bowls of broth, which they were already doing.
'Gone,' she kept whispering as her fingers wrapped and
tucked. 'Tch! Gone at last. So sad. Here, eat it up,
lassie. You're home now.'

That kind of care, and the exhaustion, was all it took
to release the flood, and for some time I could neither

hide my grief nor tell her about the events that had changed my life once more. Though I tasted nothing much, the warming broth began to send my blood back into my aching limbs, thawing my brain. Then, like a runaway child returned to the fold, I was quizzed about my eating, sleeping, monthly periods, keeping warm, exercise and rest, overwork, moods, mine and Jamie's. None of this did I resent. It was one thing to laugh at the banality of such an inquisition, but quite another to weep at the loving intent behind it. And if it was intrusive, it was the kind of intrusion I had missed and longed for.

Naturally, I had questions of a similar nature to ask Mama, though the state of her health had patently not improved since my last visit just before Christmas. Like her energy, her voice was fading away with each passing season, and I think she knew that the ailment that devoured her lungs would not be held back for her as it had been for Linas. Living in the fresh country air had its advantages, but the raw winds that scoured the Yorkshire Wolds that winter could be mightily unkind to all but the sturdiest beings. Some patients retired to nearby Scarborough to recuperate, but no doctor ever recommended an isolated place like Foss Beck Common. Yet when I suggested that she might consider coming back with me to York, her indignation flared like the protective mother she had always been.

'What? Leave the boys and Pierre?' she said in her hoarse whisper. 'I would not dream of it, love. They're making a grand little farmstead of this place, you know, and as soon as we can afford it, we shall rebuild the other half of the house so we can spread out a bit. We may do the same to one of the cottages too. It'd make more sense if you and young Jamie were to come and live with us now. Wouldn't it? You know how he loves the place.'

It was true that he did. As soon as he was old enough to travel, I had taken him to see them and to ask for their understanding. A bastard in the family was not something they had ever thought likely, but I need not have been concerned, for there was no criticism of the methods I had used to earn money for us all. Only Pierre was less than enthusiastic, never having made any secret of his hope that I would one day agree to be his wife. I suppose it must have irked him that others had been where he'd wanted to be first, but I had given him no promises or even the expectation of any. I looked upon him as one of my brothers, but never as a future husband.

Unpacking the goods I had brought, woollen clothes, medicines, new boots, Mrs Neape's pies, and at least half the food sent from Abbots Mere, I told them about Linas's will, about my plans and disappointments, my fears, and the unlikelihood of Jamie being allowed to live anywhere except York. It looked, they agreed, as if I might have to stay there too, at least for the foreseeable future.

If it was not what any of us wanted to hear, it was even less acceptable to Pierre, who took me to one side before we settled in for the night. Only an inch or so taller than me, he was yet strongly built and pleasant of face, and certainly the man my father had earmarked for me, when the time came. I cannot say that I was glad not to have my father there with us, but he would have put a very strong case for that connection, and I doubt if my unwillingness would have had much to do with it.

As a terrified twelve-year-old, Pierre had been smuggled out of Paris and across the English Channel, having lost both his aristocratic parents to the guillotine during the Revolution that put an end to France's royal family. Though that particular danger had passed, Pierre looked upon our family as his own so much so that, after my father's tragic end, he had taken much of the responsibility upon himself, for by that time he was a comely nineteen-year-old with a noble manner, unafraid of work or danger, assertive and enterprising. It was he who maintained the connection with the Bridlington smugglers, though he never volunteered any information about how exactly he was able to procure such large quantities of costly fabrics for me to sell in York. And I never asked him to. Yet it was due to Pierre's involvement with contraband that I had been able to take a partnership in Prue's thriving business on Blake Street.

Sometimes I would travel to Foss Beck to pick up whatever he had obtained for me; at other times Pierre would bring it to York on pack-ponies and leave it at Follet and Sanders. Occasionally he would call at the house on Blake Street as a distant relative from Bridlington, but never with the goods. The pack-ponies, it was assumed, were to take supplies back home from the shops and warehouses. There was never any question of him meeting Linas, and to Jamie he was 'Uncapare'. I was, of course, very careful not to be seen handing him any money, nor did I have any doubts about Pierre's honesty.

'Helene,' he said, speaking to me in French as he always did when we were together, 'I'm so glad to see you again. But you ought never to have made the journey alone. It's far too dangerous.'

'I had no choice, Pierre, if I'm to keep our family a secret.'

'Well, I shall ride with you tomorrow when you return. I can take the new goods to the shop. As it happens, I have some other business in York, so I can kill two birds with one stone.' His teeth shone even in the gloom, startlingly white against his healthy outdoor skin and black hair, like my own. 'Does one throw stones at birds?'

'Not nowadays. What business?'

'Oh, a message to pass on to friends, a contact to make, some purchases. Who is this brother-twin of Mr Monkton? The guardian. What's he like?'

'He's good to Jamie. He adores him.' I knew it was an ambiguous reply, intentionally so, for indeed it was a mutual adoration that I had done little to foster, to the frustration of them both. Jamie's strong will, having turned more recently to noisy tantrums, was never witnessed by Winterson for whom my beloved infant was a lamb, obedient and obliging, trotting after his idol and beaming with good nature when he was allowed to ride on Uncaburl's shoulders. To see them like that made my heart flip like a seaotter, and to ache for hours afterwards.

'And you?' said Pierre. 'You adore him too?'

'Pierre,' I replied, wearily, 'I have just lost the man I lived with and cared for. The father of my child. Except for Jamie, adoration has no place in my heart at the moment. I love my mother and brothers, and I am very fond of you as a brother, and I am grateful to you for your care of us. But things are not moving on for me in quite the direction I hoped for. Rather, they seem to have come to a standstill. Perhaps it's too soon to expect them to. Let's just see, shall we? I wish Mama would come to York where I can tend her. I'm very concerned about her.'

'She won't, Helene. Your father is still here, remember. She will not leave his grave. She wants to stay beside him.'

I nodded, aware that my tears, so recently shed, were by no means spent. 'Then I had better not mention it again. But try to understand my position, Pierre. Please. I'm being torn two ways at present.'

'My understanding matters to you?'

'Certainly it does. You are family. It will always matter to me.'

'Forgive me,' he whispered, touching my arm with a tentative forefinger before withdrawing it quickly. 'You're right, it's too soon for you to see ahead, and you are weary. It's only that…' he sighed '…that we meet so rarely and, when the chance arises, I must take it before you're gone again.'

'Then we shall talk more on the way home. Goodnight, Pierre.'

'Goodnight, Helene.'

I turned away, but not before I had caught the 'my love' whispered in my wake, which I pretended not to hear, dismissing it from my mind as one more complication I could do without. Even so, I had witnessed yet again the small signs of rebellion from Finch and Greg as they deliberately ignored Pierre's commands that ought to have been requests, and I prayed that, if only for my mother's sake, the boys would not cause any trouble.

* * *

I had slept that night in my underclothes upon a duck-down mattress with a feather pillow and thick furs to keep me warm. Yet I awoke with limbs that hurt as if I'd run all the way from York, and a splitting headache. Whatever my ailment, I dared not delay my return home, for the thought of Jamie missing me, being upset and refusing to eat was more than I could contemplate. Heaven only knows how I clambered up into the saddle, more thankful than I expected to be that Pierre was with me to lead the pack-pony. Tearful farewells were not my style, but knowing what I did of Mama's condition, I could not have said for certain whether she would still be there to welcome me on my next visit. And for some miles I was very poor company, wondering how and when I would be called upon to bear yet another loss.

Even with Pierre for companionship, the return to York was no more comfortable than before, as by that time I was feeling wretchedly unwell and not at all inclined to converse. With the wind at our backs for much of the way, we made marginally better progress, but the sky was again heavy with snow, darkening by the hour, and we reached York speechless with cold and tiredness. For me, it was another nightmare of a journey, but one that could not have been put off, all the signs being that reserve food supplies at Foss Beck had run drastically low.

With the light almost gone, Pierre was anxious to unload the goods and then to conduct at least some of his business before it was too late. So although I was desperate to see my Jamie again, we went first to deliver the much-needed stocks to Prue, and I took the pony and horse back to Linas's stable, grateful that Pierre had agreed without a quibble to leave me to myself. I was sure by then that I was coming down with something more than a cold, for my joints ached unbearably, and I was shaking like an aspen leaf. The walk back to Blake Street took all my last efforts.

Hoping for whoops of joy at my appearance, I encountered only my maid's anxious face as she dealt with my enquiries about Jamie. 'He's gone, ma'am,' she whispered, round-eyed. 'Mrs Goode and him.'

'Gone? What d'ye mean…gone?'

'Let me help you with your coats, ma'am, and I'll tell—'

'No! Tell me *now*, Debbie. Where *are* they?'

'At Abbots Mere, ma'am.'

'*What?*' It was one of those inane responses that only buys time to think up every dreadful reason and result, every terrible revenge and almighty row that will follow if the matter is not righted that same instant. There was to be no hope of that.

'Lord Winterson came yesterday after you'd gone, ma'am, and there was Master Jamie—' she pointed to the hall floor '—kicking his little heels and screaming and crying, and there was nurse trying to reason with him and could hardly make herself heard, ma'am. Rolling about, he was.'

My head swam; I had to sit. 'And Lord Winterson?'

'Strode through the door, ma'am, took one look and said, "Hoy! Enough!" And do you know, ma'am, Master Jamie just stopped and ran to him, just like that. He was sobbing his heart out, mind. Poor little soul.'

I held my head in my hands. I *thought* I had done the right thing, but clearly I had not. I was the worst mother in the world, at that moment. 'Then what?' I whispered.

'Well, Lord Winterson picked him up and talked to him, and told Mrs Goode that she should pack things, that they would go to stay with him at Abbots Mere till you returned from Bridlington.'

Where I had not been.

'Ma'am, you look terrible. Are you all right?'

I swayed unsteadily, holding my head before it fell off. 'Yes,' I said. 'I'm going over to Abbots Mere. I shall have to go back to Stonegate first to get a horse. You stay here, Debbie, and tell Mrs Neape where I've gone.'

'At this time of night, ma'am?'

'*Yes!*' I yelled. 'At *this* time of night, girl. I want my *son*!'

She was a Leeds lass, and not easily browbeaten. 'Then I'm coming too,' she said. 'Just wait till I get my coat and boots on, ma'am.'

'Debbie, I have no time to argue. You can't come.'

'I can, ma'am, and I will. You're not going on your own.'

'There's only one horse.'

'Then I'll walk it.'

I turned and went out. It had started to snow again, but Debbie caught me up before I reached Linas's stables. She was carrying a portmanteau. 'What's that for?' I asked.

'Things, ma'am. We might have to stay.'

What a treasure she was, that girl. I was wrong about there being only one horse; there were several, most of them newly arrived. I chose two of the heaviest, ordered them to be saddled and gave the worried groom a silver shilling when he told me Lord Winterson would probably kill him. 'He won't,' I said. 'Help me up.'

It was dark and snowing fast, laying a clean white cover upon what was already there. The two black, wet, agonising miles took us almost an hour, with me clinging to the saddle to stay upright and often my beast stopping when it felt me slip or slouch. Gritting my teeth against bouts of faintness, I forged ahead with Debbie calling and encouraging me to stay on. Then, at last, we passed through the old Tudor gatehouse and headed for the lights of the house and for the fearsome battle that would be raged within minutes of my arrival.

Being no rider, Debbie fell off her horse into the snow, picked herself up and ran to the door, hammering upon it with the heavy iron ring until it opened. The crashing noise in my head stopped; I heard her yelling at someone, echoing from a long way off, then shouts. My face was in the horse's snow-covered mane and I could not move it from the hot-cold sweat that beckoned me into its arms, to sleep. The horse tipped, throwing me sideways into a black gulf.

A deep voice rumbled against my ear. 'What in heaven's name possessed her to come…?'

'She would do it, my lord. I tried to reason, but she's unwell, and I could not let her come alone.'

'But at *this* time of night, in this weather?'

How many times had I heard 'in this weather' recently? 'In this weather,' I muttered, 'I've come for my son.' The world was still moving, swinging me this way and that. 'Jamie,' I said. 'I want Jamie.'

'You want for some common sense too, woman, coming out here in a blizzard, in the dark too. And how you managed to get to Bridlington and back in two days in this lot is going to take some explaining. Did you fly?'

I was being carried, and not expected to answer. Which was just as well for, at that point, I suppose I must have passed out again.

Chapter Five

Nights and days merged into a timeless blur during which I was fed like a fledgling without knowing whose nest I was in. Shadowy figures lifted and bathed me, tucking me into warm feathery layers, soothing my aching body, cooling my fever. I dreamed, but never managed to trawl them up from the depths. I wept, they said, but could not explain why. And at last the snow-white glare from the casement seeped into my eyelids and brought me back into the room I had sworn never again to occupy, for any reason. I think I felt then that this was one of those bizarre situations that could only have been engineered by Fate itself. It was only with hindsight that I was able to see how I had made Fate a convenient scapegoat.

My infant's delight at finding me silenced all my earlier fears that he would bear me a lifelong grudge for breaking my promise to take him to see Nana Damzell. Without a mention of that particular dilemma at Blake Street he bounced into my room, picking up the thread of his life from where he'd left it the moment before to tell me about the snowman, the ride with Uncaburl that morning, and the promise of a pony of his own. Of screaming tantrums, Mrs Goode assured me, there had been none, not even when he was opposed.

I saw nothing of my long-suffering host, however, until the fifth day of our visit when I was at last able to find the energy to walk a few steps. Winterson himself was allowed into my room to carry me downstairs, swathed in blankets, to the warm parlour where he placed me upon a long cushioned chair with eight legs and a woven rattan back. I had been in no position to appreciate the first carrying. With the second, however much I tried to hide the thrill of being helplessly buoyant, the closeness of his face and the memories it evoked must have shown in my eyes whenever he glanced down at me. Which he did several times.

Abbots Mere had once been the abbot's own guest house for visiting dignitaries to the great minster of York. Since the dissolution of the monasteries, the house had been sold off, enlarged and altered at the convenience of each successive owner, though no Georgian styles had been allowed to interfere with the sixteenth-century interior that still showed in every part of the building. The parlour was a large low-ceilinged room, exquisitely plastered and oak panelled, with brightly painted coats-of-arms around the plasterwork frieze. The walls were hung with lace-collared ancestors, the floor covered with mellowed pink-and-blue Persian carpets, furnished with dark oak tables, chairs with tall backs and barley-sugar legs. In the massive stone fire-place, a log fire crackled and blazed behind cast-iron firedogs, and silver oil-lamps were reflected in polished surfaces. I had been in this room many times before, but always it had been Linas who lounged on the long chair, and never had I been here alone with his brother. I had always seen to that.

He sat opposite me in a red upholstered wing-chair with his face partly shadowed so that I could not tell his expression, though he rarely allowed one to know what he was thinking at the best of times. 'Inscrutable' sounds like a cliché, but it suited him well. A long-case clock chimed softly, musically, and his three great hounds flopped quietly behind his chair.

'I've sent for some tea,' he said. 'Will you join me?'

'Thank you. I hope Jamie and I have not been an imposition. I really had no intention of...well...' I thought he might interrupt me with a polite denial, but he did not, and when I couldn't think of what to say, he was unhelpful.

'No intention of...taking a fever? Coming all this way in a blizzard to rescue your child from my clutches? Well, you can see he's suffered very little from the experience.'

Being in no mood for an argument, not then, I sighed my annoyance and looked pointedly towards the window. 'Has the snow stopped?' I asked, hoping he would catch my meaning.

'If you mean, can you escape, then I'm afraid the answer is no. You've missed three days of snowstorms and now all the roads are impassable, according to my information. I hear that the road to Brid has been blocked beyond Fridaythorpe since the snow started. No one's been either in or out.'

'That's annoying,' I said, ignoring his reference to Bridlington. 'I had hoped to go home tomorrow.'

'You'll do no such thing,' he said, quietly dismissive. 'You've been ill. My bailiff forecasts a thaw before long, so you'll have to be patient until you're stronger and the roads are dug out.'

'I have a business to run. Anyway, I'm not ill. It's only a chill.'

'Yes, and I dare say you've been too busy chasing about the countryside in the snow to give any thought to your own needs. Perhaps it's time you began to think of them, unless you want pneumonia too. If I were you, Miss Follet, I'd take this as an indication that you need some rest, after all that's happened.'

That made me angry. Take a rest? How like a man. Ignore everything that needs attention and everyone who depends on you and take a rest. How *could* I rest?

Winterson's housekeeper, Mrs Murgatroyd, came in with a silver tray of tea things and, while she set it out and poured the steaming amber liquid into fine Queen Anne teacups, I was able surreptitiously to knuckle away a tear of impotent fury and to mop my nose on the back of my hand. Very unladylike. My hand shook as I accepted the teacup, rattling it on the saucer, so she removed it with a smile and set it on the table beside me. Then, bobbing a curtsy, she withdrew.

'How *can* I?' I said. 'Customers still need new clothes, even in midwinter.'

He plopped a lump of sugar into his tea. 'Well, for a start, you can allow Jamie to spend more time here.

Mrs Goode is a very sensible woman and I'm perfectly willing to share the duties of caring for him. Medworth and his wife are too. Their eldest is just about Jamie's age, you know, and there's nothing more respectable than to be related to a country parson's family. He enjoys his visits there, I believe?'

I nodded. 'Yes, very much, but…'

'But what? Too countrified for you?'

'I am a countrywoman too, my lord. Mr and Mrs Medworth Monkton are delightful and charming, and so is little Claude. But Linas was never very happy to see pigs and geese, hens and goats wandering through the house, especially when there are small children and babies about. Last time we were there, the goat chewed the baby's layette; when the donkey wandered into the dining-room, they allowed Claude to feed it with his own bread. I'm used to animals, but I would never go quite that far.'

'No, I wouldn't feed good bread to a donkey, either. It's far too rich. But you know Linas's attitude to animals, Miss Follet. He could never see the need for them except as food or transport, or inside a kennel. It would be a pity, wouldn't it, if our Jamie adopted the same indifference to them. He's quite fearless with them, you know.'

Our Jamie. *Our* Jamie. 'Yes,' I replied, stepping gingerly over the implications. 'I do know. He has a little temper, too.'

His voice dropped, soft and indulgent. 'That's not temper, lass, it's sheer frustration at not being able to express himself, to tell you how he feels. You offered him the alternative of twiddling his thumbs at home

with his nurse while I offered him the chance to ride in
the snow, without you. There's no magic in that. He's
a lively little lad, bright and bursting with energy and
curiosity. He doesn't always want velvet suits and silk
shirts. He's not a puppet. He needs coveralls and some
muck to stamp in, and things to climb.'

'You make it sound as if you know about such
things.'

'I do. I've *been* a three-year-old boy. You have not.'

I had brothers. I knew he was right, but how could I
offer Jamie those more alluring alternatives while
keeping to my intention not to get involved, more than
I must, in Winterson's life?

My silence prompted him to ask, 'Does he enjoy
seeing your family? He was very disappointed not to
go.'

'Yes, he loves it. I promised to take him, then I
couldn't.'

'Because of the snow?'

'Yes, it was too dangerous.'

'But you had to go, did you?'

'Yes, I *had* to go. My mother is ailing. The same
as Linas. I knew they'd be snowbound and running
low on food.'

'But they were not snowbound, if you got through
to them.'

'They were, almost. My brothers knew that, if they
got away, they'd probably not get back again and, as it
was, I only just managed to find them, knowing that I
could stay overnight. They told me I was mad, but I'm
the eldest and I have a responsibility to them. My
mother needs medicines. I cannot let a snowfall stop

me, but nor could I have taken Jamie and his nurse. I tried to make him understand—' I stopped and held a hand to my face.

'You're not the monster-mother you thought you were, you know. He was as right as rain, once I picked him up.'

He was trying to reassure me, I knew, telling me that there was no magic in it. But Jamie would run to him without any promise of rewards or alternatives, but simply to be noticed by his hero. It had been the same when Linas was alive. Jamie doted on him.

'Who is Nana Damzell? Your mother?' he said.

I nodded.

'I see. And there are animals there too. They have a farm?'

'Yes. Please don't ask me any more, my lord. I cannot tell you.'

'Why? Are they outlaws, like Robin Hood?'

'Not at all like Robin Hood,' I said, glancing at my cooling cup of tea. My hand still shook, but I managed not to spill while I drank, wondering how much my chatterbox son had divulged about his uncles and their isolated home. I suspected that Winterson would have liked to ask me about the Bridlington connection, but he apparently thought that enough had been said for one day, for he did not pursue the question of why anyone living in a town the size of Brid should run out of food. Or indeed how I had managed to get there. Or not.

'Miss Follet,' he said, after a pause.

'My lord?'

'I wouldn't like you to think that I shall make a point of asking Jamie about his maternal family. I shall not. I can see that you'd rather not talk about them, so I'll wait until you do. But neither do I want *you* to use Jamie's inclination to chatter as an excuse to keep him away from me. You're entitled to your privacy, and I shall respect it. That's what Linas did, I believe.'

The truth was more stark than that. Linas had not the slightest curiosity about my family. Not only did he never ask me about them, but even when I visited them for two days at a time, with Jamie, he didn't ask where, who, or how they were, whether they had what they needed or what had happened to their former lives. I didn't complain, for I was able to share my earnings with them and that was all that mattered. But I often found it strange how Linas's life revolved only around himself, until Jamie came.

'As you know,' I said, very quietly, 'Linas was a very private kind of person, and I sometimes think that he tended to ignore the possibility that I had a family in case I brought them into the life we shared. I would never...ever...have done that, but I think he believed it was a risk. Some mistresses' families can be quite demanding, as I'm sure you've heard.'

He smiled at that. Lady Emma Hamilton had recently lost her beloved Lord Nelson and, anticipating that he would leave her substantial wealth, the poor woman's relatives were already hounding her day and night. That, at least, would not be happening to me. 'Well,' he said, 'now you see how differently Linas and I view matters. I can accept that you have a responsibility to your family whose privacy you wish to protect and who you need to visit from time to time. But to take Jamie all that way without a proper escort is a risk I do not want you to run. In the future, you must take at least two men with you. Either my men, or your own.'

While we were on the subject, I thought I might as well tell him, though I could easily foresee the reaction. 'When I told them about Linas, there was some discussion that I might go and live with them again. With Jamie.'

'Who suggested that?'

'My mother would like it. She wants me to look after my brothers.'

'Yes, I can understand the reasoning, Miss Follet, and you must do whatever you can for them, but I would not allow Jamie to live so far away. He will be either at Blake Street with you, or here with me.'

'I told her that I could not do so. I have my business to attend to, you see, and I need to be on hand. It brings me an income, and, if that were to go, *they* would be much the poorer.'

'Oh, so your business supports them, does it? I thought…'

'You thought it was another way for me to line my pockets? Yes, well, that is what mistresses often do, I believe. They usually move on when the going gets rough, and I didn't do that either, my lord. Nor did I shirk from telling Linas that I was pregnant, even when I feared he would surely turn me out. *That* was a risk, I can tell you. A very uncomfortable one.'

'I can see why you are bitter, Miss Follet.'

'At the way I was used, and still *am* being used? As Jamie's mother, being told what I must and must not do, as if I were married? Which I cannot do either?'

'Have there been no compensations?' he asked from

the depths of his chair. His long legs crossed and re-crossed, and I saw the pinpoints of fire reflected in his eyes as they turned again in my direction.

'Jamie. And a place to live in comfort, and a thriving business and good friends to work with. Yes, and I still have *some* freedom left, which I shall fight tooth and claw to keep.'

His tone sharpened to match mine. 'You have no need to fight tooth and claw, lass. We're on the same side.'

I swung my legs off the long chair, ready to go. 'Correction,' I said. 'We have *never* been on the same side, my lord. Not even before I became your brother's mistress, when you tried to warn him off me. Too un-reliable, you told him.'

'Is that what he told you?'

'That's what he told me. We laughed about it. We shall never be on the same side, except where Jamie's welfare is concerned. Now, if you will excuse me, I'm getting rather tired.' I tried to stand, but the room swayed dangerously and I had to sit down again with an ungainly thud, my hands clutching to keep me upright. 'Oh!' I said. 'Oh, dear.'

He was beside me instantly. 'Steady…steady, lass. God's truth, but I've never known a woman fly up into the boughs so fast. Now wait. I'll take you back, but I shall not allow you to walk. It's time you were taken in hand.'

I let the remark go, for he was justified in thinking that I was on edge, snapping and snarling as if I was being threatened. 'I'm all right,' I said. 'It's just dizzi-ness, that's all.'

'No, you're not.' Busily re-wrapping me, his hands came to rest upon my shoulders where the blanket pinned my arms to my body. Holding it tightly so that I could not protest, he swung me once more into his arms where I lay with my head upon his shoulder, utterly powerless. Wordless, too.

'Now, my beauty,' he said, sternly, 'let's get one more thing straight, shall we? It will be better for Jamie if we both try to show him that we're friends, not rivals. I shall not use him to score points, nor should you do that. If you want to fight me, we'll do it in private, not in front of him. Agreed?'

'Yes.'

His eyes narrowed and his lips moved, and I knew there was more to come. 'Fierce woman,' he whispered. 'My God, but the lad has a warrior-mother to defend him, doesn't he? You don't have the physique to go with it, though, so don't even think about going home yet. You need some care and attention first. I expect someone can take care of the shop?'

'Yes.'

'And the house? I'll get a message to them as soon as I can.'

'Yes. Thank you.'

'Saints, lass. Have I silenced you at last? No, perhaps not. I remember there was another way to do that, wasn't there?'

'*Please!*'

'Hah!' Throwing back his head, he bellowed with laughter as the door opened, letting Jamie and his nurse into the room to make what they could of me in the arms of Jamie's guardian.

It could have been worse, as it happened, for Jamie was too young to think anything of it and Mrs Goode was one of those rare creatures whose experience of life runs just ahead of one's own. She was approaching middle age and still handsome, and the flash of interest in her eyes disappeared as she dealt with the scene with perfect composure. 'Oh, good,' she said. 'You just on your way up, ma'am?'

Jamie ran to Winterson's leg and clung, somewhere beneath me. 'Bring Mama, Uncaburl,' he said, 'to see snowman. He wants to say goodnight.'

I began to protest, but Winterson had other ideas. 'Right,' he said. 'So if you let go of my leg, young whipper-snapper, and hold the door open for us, we'll go. Come on, lead the way.'

So we did, followed by hounds, striding, trotting and sailing high along the stone passageways, across the great hall and out to the front porch that overlooked the snow-covered terrace. The formal garden lay beyond like a fairyland of blue shadows and heavy-laden trees, and the cold air filled my lungs, making my hair prickle and my eyes water.

'Not too cold for you?' said Winterson, softly.

'No, not at all. It's beautiful.'

Mrs Goode tucked the blanket deep into my neck, her expression suitably serious. Jamie ran to greet the snowman who stood twice his height, wearing an old beaver hat. 'See, Mama!' he called. 'He's got Uncaburl's best hat on.'

'It was either that or one of my neckcloths,' the donor explained. 'There was little choice in the matter, really. What d'ye think, ma'am?'

'He's a splendid snowman,' I called. 'Shall we say goodnight to him before we go in?' It was like being a family, I thought. Mother, father and child, so different from the previous artificial relationship of pseudo-father and pseudo-uncle with me somewhere between.

But close behind that thought came the warning. Beware. This is getting too dangerous. Held in his arms, safe and warm, assuming another ambiguous role, it's going to be so easy to forget the brothers' scheme, forged years ago without a by-your-leave. You owe this man no favours, the warning said, coldly, bitterly.

Back in my room upstairs, the blankets were peeled off.

'Whose nightgown is this?' I said, noticing for the first time the unfamiliar broderie-anglais yoke. I had made all my own night attire.

'Mrs Murgatroyd found it for me,' said Debbie, holding the sheet open. 'I only managed to pack one, and that's gone to the laundry.'

'Then get this thing off me,' I said. 'Heaven only knows who's worn it before me. I'll have my own back, if you please.' I could well imagine who had worn it, and who had been hurriedly slipped out of it, too. One of his mistresses.

Wrestling it over my head, Debbie treated me to some mutterings about the whims and fancies of con-valescents, but the enchantment of the previous hour had faded and, as Debbie opened the bedroom door to retrieve my gown, I heard the chimes of the long-case clock before the parlour door closed upon them. He would be in there thinking, no doubt, that he had won that round hands down.

My recovery took only a few days, since I was healthy and strong and eager to resume my life in York. I used those few days well, though, playing around Winterson's spacious house with Jamie and Mrs Goode, having snowball fights in the garden, playing hide and seek, watching the racehorses, walking in the snow and skating on the lake. Each night my beloved infant would fall asleep with apple cheeks, exhausted and happy in his own rosy paradise, and I fell asleep in the hope that the thaw would set in overnight while my heart was still my own.

I kept to my side of the agreement to assume a convincing friendship with our host, which was little different from what I had always done whenever Jamie was there to see. But as for sitting with him in private again, that I did not do, but found some excuse to be elsewhere. It was not so much that I wished to evade any future tactics he might be planning, but that I had a campaign of my own that did not include letting him think I was softening. Not one bit. Good manners I could manage when I had to, but pretend a sincere friendship I would not.

At last, after a day of shovelling, of dripping eaves and light sleety rain, the way was cleared between Abbots Mere and York, and I knew that Goody and I would have our work cut out convincing Jamie that going home could be better than staying. A coach ride being out of the question, Jamie rode with Uncaburl to lead the way, helping to ease the transition, while the rest of us followed behind with two grooms. Whether Uncaburl said anything to his ward about accepting the situation, far from ideal in Jamie's eyes, I do not know, but there were no tantrums.

Jamie was carried around the house, straddled across

Uncaburl's waist, to reacquaint him with his own room, his rocking horse and Noah's Ark. How they had missed him, his guardian said, promising him another visit to Abbots Mere before long.

'And a pony?' said Jamie. 'You did say a pony, Uncaburl.'

'When the winter has gone away, there will be a pony for you.'

'He's too young,' I whispered as we went downstairs. 'I told you.'

'I know you did, but he's desperate to learn and that's the best time to do it. Trust me. I'll find something suitable. He'll be safe with me.'

'What am I to do about my own transport, my lord? Am I allowed to borrow one of the horses from the stable at Stonegate, as I did before?'

Mrs Goode and Jamie had gone ahead to the kitchen, leaving Winterson and me in my pretty pale-green panelled dining room. I poured a glass of port and handed it to him, aware that I was occupying his house and beholden to him for everything in it, even my mode of transport. My question about the horses was meant to point to the fact.

He placed the glass upon the table and came to stand before me where I could breathe in the freshness of his skin. 'Miss Follet,' he said, 'you may borrow any of the horses from Stonegate at any time, but don't take your phaeton out yet. It's not safe. If you want to go visiting, send me a message and I'll have a carriage sent for you. And don't go too far.'

'I see,' I said, flatly.

'No, you don't see, do you? You think I'm trying to

curb you. But this is only while the roads are treacherous. There's twelve inches of snow underfoot, and when all that thaws there'll be floods everywhere and the Ouse will burst its banks. The ground is still frozen solid. The water will take weeks to drain away. So don't take any foolish risks.'

'Yes, I *do* see. I'm sorry. I shall be careful with Jamie.'

'I want you to be careful with you too, Miss Follet.'

'Yes, of course.' As Jamie's mother, I had to stay in one piece.

'Oh, for pity's sake, woman. Must you see everything I say in the wrong light? Could *you* not thaw, occasionally?'

I had no answer to that, none that I dared speak. But something in my face must have given me away just long enough for him to see beneath the ice and, before I could sidestep, his hands gripped my upper arms, pulling me to him and sliding round to my back like steel bands, bending me and knocking my breath away.

'I could thaw you,' he whispered. 'I did it before and I could do it again. You've done your best to keep a distance between us. Don't think I've not noticed. But the time will come…'

'No, it won't,' I whispered back, finding it hard to breathe. 'The time will never come, my lord. Now let me go before we're discovered.'

His arms dropped. He seemed to struggle against some emotion that closed his eyes and tilted his head back with a noisy sigh that made me long to comfort him, to touch his lips with my own. He turned away to the table, picked up his glass and downed the contents in one gulp. Then, smacking the glass down, he threw open the door into the hall and called for his coat with quite unnecessary loudness.

I should have felt well satisfied by that but, for some reason, I felt quite the opposite, strangely upset and subdued, and wondering how much longer I would be able to stay on course.

Chapter Six

Not for my own peace of mind, nor indeed for his, could I allow him to go like that. We were not sworn enemies and, although his own behaviour had been less than gentlemanly, I must try to learn how far to push him. It was something I had not needed to do with Linas.

Caring not what Mrs Goode or Debbie might think, I quickly threw on the outdoor clothes I had just shed and went out again, half-running along Blake Street to the corner of Stonegate where I believed he would have gone. I was right. His horses were still in the courtyard, his grooms surprised to see me so soon. One of them ran to open the kitchen door for me.

He was there, hatless, in conversation with Linas's housekeeper, the first to notice my entrance. She turned in surprise. 'Miss Follet! Good morning, ma'am.'

He came towards me at once, his eyes anxious. 'Is something wrong?'

I felt that my impulsiveness was getting me into as

big a mess as my long-held resentments, for even now I had not rehearsed what to say to him. 'Yes,' I said. 'I forgot something.' It would do for a beginning.

As if he felt something of my discomfort, he escorted me up to the hall where the smell of paint, the general mess of displaced furniture and bare flooring indicated that a grand spring clean was already under way. The changeover was as good a time as any, and already the new coats of white and pale grey paint had brought a clean light to the walls.

'In here,' he said, holding open the door to Linas's study. It too was in some disorder, the bookcases half emptied, the mantelshelf bare, the few chairs shrouded with holland covers. 'Will this do?' he said, closing the door behind us. 'What is it? What did you forget?'

'My manners,' I replied. 'I've come…well…to beg your pardon. It was unpardonable of me to allow you to leave my house without thanking you for your good care of us, and for the second load of supplies, and for your kindness to me and Jamie. Thank you, my lord. I am not as ungrateful as I appeared to be just now. Of course, your own manners leave much to be improved on, but I am the one who should apologise. Which I do.'

He listened attentively, though I saw his lips twitch as if a laughing protest was being held in check, though his acceptance was never in doubt. 'Let's face it,' he said, 'you've been under some considerable strain lately, Miss Follet, so I think an occasional bout of queer stirrups can easily be forgiven. Think no more of it. As for what you choose to call my kindness, it has given me pleasure to be where I was most needed. That's exactly how I hoped it would be, though without

the illness. My house is always open to you whenever
you need it, and for any reason. Or for no reason. It can
be your second home, if you wish it.'

This time, I would not allow my scepticism to spoil
his generosity, so I nodded and thanked him politely and
said I believed that's what Jamie already had in mind.
Which made us both smile. I felt we'd made some
progress.

His hand rested upon a pile of leather-bound
volumes too large for bedtime reading, his palm fondly
sweeping. He saw me watching, though thankfully
without being able to see into my mind. '*History of Arts
and Sciences*,' he said. 'I shall keep these, but I don't
know about this lot.' He patted a smaller pile of notebooks that had been well used. Linas had been an avid
note-taker. 'I don't have time to go through them.
Would you care to take them? They might be of interest,
or they might not.'

I had an obligation to do what I could. 'Yes, I'll take
them home. They're probably household accounts, in
which case they'll be helpful.'

'Anything else?'

'Er…else?'

Suddenly, we'd begun to talk more like friends
instead of fencers looking for an opening to make a hit.
He would be spending some time here, and perhaps I
ought to be making the most of that convenience instead
of bemoaning it. There had to be some advantages
somewhere. Perhaps, I thought, I'd been too hasty in my
determination to exclude him.

'Yes,' he said. 'I mean…things.' He cast an eye over
the piled-up desk. 'There must surely have been other

gifts apart from those few you mentioned before? You should have them. If you tell me where they are…?'

I hesitated, then decided he should know how things stood. Mistresses, after all, are not on the same footing as wives. 'The things I collected before were bought by me, my lord, not Linas. They were only here for my use when I stayed, that's all.'

'Oh. Not gifts?'

'No, not gifts. Linas rarely bothered with gifts, did he?'

'So…your black mare was not a gift?'

'The horses and the phaeton belonged to Linas, not to me. They go with the house. I'm not complaining, my lord. That's how he preferred it. I think he was never quite convinced that I would stay. Perhaps he was influenced by your opinion that I'm unreliable. Who knows? So thank you for the offer. I could say, this, this and this, but that would be grasping and dishonest. There is nothing here that belongs to me.'

He stood very still while I spoke, looking hard at me with eyes widening, then frowning with concern. It was clear he was both surprised and puzzled. 'And gifts from you to Linas? Was that the same?'

Since I was being scrupulously honest, it was not. I shrugged, trying to make light of it. 'Embroidered nightcaps, silk nightshirts made by me, silk evening shirts ditto, kid gloves, a tambour-embroidered red-wool dressing gown that I made for him, with matching slippers and cap, monogrammed handkerchiefs and satin embroidered braces, and that striped lustre waistcoat you admired. None of them will fit me, I'm afraid. The monogrammed table linen had better stay where it is.

And the cushions, too. And the chair-seats and fire-screen.'

'Good grief!'

'Oh, don't be concerned. That's just the way it was. Linas knew he didn't need to pay me in the way that mistresses are usually paid because for one thing I never asked him to. I had a house to live in and a way of earning a legitimate living, and that's all I ever wanted, and all *he* needed from me was affection and attention, and for me to nurse him. And Jamie, of course. It worked both ways, didn't it? I don't think I let him down, my lord.'

Slowly, his gaze swung away to rest lazily upon the white scene outside and on the dazzle of windows opposite. 'No,' he said, 'I don't think you did either. If anything, the shoe was on the other foot, Miss Follet.'

'Anyway,' I said, 'it's never much use going over old ground again and again, is it? It's too late. Linas was very poorly and he did what he could. I only tell you this to settle once and for all what belongs to whom. Fortunately, he didn't need to buy my clothes, or Jamie's either. That's one thing I could manage to pay for.'

'You are the best-dressed woman I know. You must have saved him hundreds, over the years.'

'Well, now that's gone to Jamie, hasn't it? But when I said it's no use going over old ground, I meant *our* old ground too. I've had my say about that now, and you have listened and I believe you understand my feelings better than you did before. But we must try to put it all behind us and move on, although I would not want anyone to assume that I am now one of your mistresses simply because I was your brother's, and because Jamie and I must visit you. That's never going to be the case, my lord.'

'I agree. It's never going to be the case because I shall never ask you to be my mistress, Miss Follet. You may be assured on that.'

'Oh, then we are agreed. What a relief. So now we can perhaps deal more comfortably together without all those strings attached. Like business partners for Jamie's welfare and no more embarrassing references to...well...you know.'

Again, he appeared to be having difficulty in hiding a smile, though I had not thought my proposal to be so very entertaining. 'Just put it out of our minds, eh?' he said, touching his nose with a knuckle.

'Completely and for ever. I am not a saint, so I cannot say that I have forgiveness in my heart, but nor do I intend to harp on the subject till the string breaks. It could become tedious.'

He turned back to the window, I think to hide his face. 'Well, then,' he said, 'I suppose I must be devoutly thankful for a thaw, if nothing else. I was afraid the big freeze might last well into the spring.'

There was barely enough time for me to appreciate the analogy before the door opened rather abruptly to the sound of a high voice preceding its owner as if in mid-conversation. 'Oh! And so *this* is the dreary study that needs...oh!' she squeaked. 'Miss Follet...er... I had *no* idea you were here. Am I interrupting something?'

'Yes,' said Winterson, coldly. 'You are.'

'No,' I said, 'not at all, Veronique *dear*. This *is* the dreary study that needs a lick of paint. I always used to knock before I entered.'

Credit where credit's due, I recovered myself superbly. Faster than she did from my reply. But I could see her great baby-blue eyes greedily taking in my dishevelled appearance, my hair straying over my ears, my unbuttoned pelisse-coat and woolly scarf, hardly a walking advertisement for Follet and Sanders. She, on the other hand, wore a well-tailored crimson thing that drained her milky complexion and clashed gaudily with her yellow hair.

Picking up Linas's notebooks, I glanced up to see Winterson's displeasure. 'Thank you for these,' I said, forcing my frosty smile into his eyes. 'I would not like them to fall into the wrong hands. He was always *most* fastidious about who he allowed into his study, wasn't he? Good day to you, *dear* Veronique. So good to see you looking…er…well.'

Winterson found his tongue. 'Miss Follet,' he said, following me to the door, 'I'll come with you—'

'No, thank you, my lord. You must stay and entertain your guest.'

He opened the front door for me, but I was out through the crack and down the watery steps too fast for him to protest, and I felt him watching me stalk through the slush without a backward glance like an offended black-headed gull.

To say that I had made a complete fool of myself was well short of the truth: proposing a truce, putting my gripes behind me, attempting to lift our fragile relationship on to a more level plane, thinking in my stupidity that perhaps I'd been a mite too harsh, after his faultless hospitality. What *could* I have been thinking about? Had I really expected things to change because I'd thought it was time they did?

I had never 'deared' Lady Veronique Slatterly before, but if she was going to insist on getting under my feet at every end and turn, as I had no doubt she would, then there would be no more 'ladyshipping' from my lips. The thought of her paddling about in Linas's house made me sad and angry, and the thought of Winterson entertaining her there, perhaps in the same bed that Linas and I had once shared, made me angrier still. She must, I thought, have been waiting for Winterson to arrive. Timed to perfection. And why had he tried to hide his cynical smile? Why had he not simply laughed out loud at my absurdity?

Of course I had no hard and fast evidence that Veronique Slatterly *was* his mistress; it was an assumption I made in view of her frequent appearances at Abbots Mere and her simpering, clinging possessiveness of Winterson as if she were already the lady in residence. It was hard to know for sure, his attitude to her being not quite lover-like enough to reveal any deep affection, nor was it *quite* dismissive enough to keep her away for good. However abrupt he was with her—and he could be very abrupt, when he chose—it did not stop her from returning for more of those periods when he seemed content to tolerate, if not actually enjoy, her company.

She had wealth and good connections, plenty of rakes and rattles for friends and a fond father who owned a very successful racing stable near York. His jockeys were drawn from a keen circle of well-born young men who swarmed around the fair and voluptuous Veronique with a view, I supposed, to taking a share of what was on offer. Yes, I had seen the kind of favours she allowed, intimacies she didn't bother to hide from me since she probably assumed I had done the same, at some stage. Such were the problems of being a man's mistress rather than his wife. I dare say she thought that that kind of behaviour would make Winterson all the keener.

However, she had a title and I was still, in her eyes, a mantua-maker's assistant with ideas beyond her station. But because I now had close ties to Winterson's family, which she did not, she saw me as a threat to her ambition to become his wife. I would like her to have understood, once and for all, how unnecessary her fears were, but the cool civility he had always extended to me was far from the uncertain reception she often had to put up with from him and, although that seemed not to deter her, it did little to help my cause either.

From a woman's point of view, I was not in the least afraid of her but, as a mother, I *was* afraid of what she might try to do to my darling innocent Jamie while he was staying with his guardian. She would continue to think what she liked about my place in the grand scheme of things, but without Linas to help me keep out of her way, I would now have to remove the gloves and reveal my claws. Fortunately, I have never been afraid of taking matters into my own hands.

After two weeks away from home I had plenty of catching up to do and so, following some soul-searching concerning my responsibilities to Jamie, the business, and myself, I put aside what had happened, determined to move on. It was not as easy as it sounds.

One of my first calls was to the shop on the other side of Blake Street where I had to leap over gushing streams of melt-water running along the gulleys. Prue never complained about my absences, but I could see she needed all the help she could get. 'Orders?' she said. 'I should say so. The St Valentine's Day ball is only one week away and we've got fittings every day until then, and one worker off ill. We shall have to take an apprentice if we're to be ready on time. We need more lace too. Would there be any in those bundles Mr Follet brought?'

'You've not opened them yet?'

'No, I was waiting for you. Look, they're over here.' With an effort, she pushed two very large bales across the table towards me, too heavy to carry. Wrapped in waxed canvas and tied with twine, they contained separate packages of fabric, none of them of the ordinary sort I bought from the Manchester warehouses, but the finest sheer jaconet muslins, silks shot with gold threads, printed calicoes from India, brocades and silken ribbons, gold and silver braids, priceless bales of Alençon, black Chantilly, blonde and Valenciennes laces. Here were the finest embroidered kid gloves by the dozen, furs and fans, silk stockings and velvets, Kashmir shawls and nets like cobwebs that English women hankered after. Forbidden fruits. Exotic and rare—its value was immense.

Lifting and sorting, gasping at each new revelation, we were both dumbstruck by the quantity and quality, for this was by far the most valuable consignment Pierre had ever brought us. 'Where on *earth* is he getting it all from?' I whispered, holding up a length of tulle. 'This is...*priceless*!'

Prue was a realist. 'Not exactly priceless,' she said,

lifting to one side a heap of narrow lace edgings. 'Lyons velvet will sell at fourteen shillings the yard, and we can get three shillings for this French merino. And look at these braids, Helene. Three and fourpence a yard for that one, four and sixpence for that.'

'But how is he paying for all this, Prue? That's what I need to know. The money we put aside from the last load couldn't possibly have bought so much, not even at French prices. Look at this. We've never had an ikat-dyed muslin like this before, have we?'

'Nor Russian sable either. This'll make a lovely collar and cuffs for that grey velvet pelisse of yours. And take a look at this grosgrain, and these Pekins.' She held up an armful of silk that shone with a seductive lustre; the pale stripes on a paler background was what our younger customers could not get enough of.

'I can't understand it,' I said, trying not to sound too critical. 'He's actually buying more goods than we've given him money for, Prue.'

She frowned at me. It was probably the first time we had ever discussed the whys and wherefores of our dealings with Pierre. He bought the goods, we sold them, and the money was shared between us with one share allocated for the next consignment. The profits so far had been generous, benefiting all of us although, in theory, he could only buy what the previous share would cover. 'Does he go over to France for them?' she said. 'Personally, I mean.'

'I have no idea. He may do, but I think it's more likely that he uses an agent to bargain with the suppliers in France and to have a cargo waiting to be picked up by an English boat. Somehow.'

'I thought it was the French boats that brought it across the Channel.'

'Well, you may be right. I don't really know. All I *do* know is that Pierre works on his own and appears to deal only in fabrics. My father used his own boats, but Pierre is not in that league now.'

'Who knows what a Frenchman will get up to?' She smiled. 'Perhaps the less we know about it, the better. We've never bothered before, so why should we start now? Where's my notebook? I must make a record of this before we use it. Shall you write a notice for the window?'

'Yes. I'll advertise for an apprentice, too.'

'You'll be wanting something for the Valentine ball too, Helene. We ought to have thought about that before now, you know.'

'It wouldn't look good, Prue. I'm in mourning. I shan't be going this year.'

There was something in the way she looked at me, standing stock-still as if I had caused the pain in her eyes. 'Not going?' she whispered. 'Can you afford not to go? You know what a difference it makes to our order book when you're seen wearing one of our gowns at the Assembly Rooms. And this is one of the most popular balls in the whole calendar.'

'I know that, Prue. But I've always had a respectable partner until now, haven't I? So how d'ye think it'll look, only weeks after Linas has gone, and me cavorting around without him? What d'ye think they'll say? That I'm already on the look out for a replacement? Have some sense, Prue.'

She took my rebuke like a friend. 'What about Mr

Monkton's brother? You've just spent two weeks at his home. Would he not oblige?'

'Obliging doesn't come into it,' I said, crossly. 'I would not ask him. And anyway, he's in mourning too, so he won't be going, so that's that. Nor do I relish the idea of being taken for *his* mistress, which is *exactly*,' I snapped as she rolled her eyes heavenwards, 'what would be said if he were to partner me. You know how people talk. They're probably talking already.'

'And *you* would not be so hot under the collar, Miss Helen Follet, if you didn't already think more about Lord Winterson than you let on. You may be able to cut a wheedle with some folk and bamboozle others into thinking that you hold him in aversion, young lady, but I haven't been a dressmaker all these years without discovering where women wear their hearts as well as their hats. But if you're quite determined to play the martyr, then don't let me stop you, only don't ask why we have so few orders from February until Easter, will you?'

'Oh, Prue!' I wailed, thoroughly exasperated. 'Do try to understand.'

'I do,' she said. 'Better than you think. Now be quick and write that notice for the window, then let's get some work done, shall we?'

So I wrote:

Madame Helene, of Follet and Sanders, Blake Street, begs to inform the Nobility, Gentry and Ladies visiting York that her Show Rooms are now open with a choice selection of Millinery from Paris, Gloves and Bonnets from one guinea.

Mechelin, Lisle and Valenciennes laces, Real Brussels lace, Bobbin net veils and squares, also satins, bombasins, velvets and sheer muslins. Dresses for Weddings and Mourning made in the first style and a perfect fit insured. Executed with dispatch.

An Indoor Apprentice Wanted.

Placing the notice inside the window, I wondered if we might have an application from a fourteen-year-old whose life had taken an unexpected turn, as mine had.

The day was busy with clients released by the thaw from the big freeze, all expecting their orders to be ready in record time as if we, not they, had time to make up. The 'Nelson Fashion' was all the rage since the victor's tragic death at Trafalgar in the previous October. Before that, it had been the Lady Hamilton style, an empire line in white satin, gauze and muslin with the hair cut close around the ears, and no hat. Now, the demand was for imitations of Emma's white satin trimmed with gold, silver or lace, and a turban embroidered with 'Nelson' topped with white plumes.

The newest February edition of *Bell's Court and Fashionable Magazine* showed the most recent 'Trafalgar Dress', which so far I had kept out of the shop. Our embroiderers were working day and night ornamenting every border with festoons and coronets, Nelson's name, ships and flags, anchors and badges, and even a newfangled stitch that took far too long. Black-edged fans, ribbons and shawls, handkerchiefs and headgear, reticules and gloves: one could dress from head to toe *à la Nelson*.

I took *Bell's Court* home with me, with Prue's last parting shot resounding in my conscience about the Valentine's ball and the renewed surge of patronage that would be ours as a result of my wearing one of her gowns. Always in the very latest mode, my ballgowns had been the best possible advertisement ever since I'd been allowed to wear them. Now, they were my own property, and who was I to complain when our wealthiest clients requested copies? To a provincial business like ours, that was worth much.

With little Jamie snuggling on my lap, we leafed through the pages of drawings, giving each of the toffee-nosed models an appropriate name. 'That one,' said the little fellow, wiping his nose on the sleeve of his night-shirt, 'is Miss Mooney. She's all in white. Mama, wear that one.' He tapped the long feather boa. 'Worm,' he said, yawning. He looked good enough to eat—warm, soft and sleepy-eyed.

'What does Goody think?' I said, glancing at his nurse. It was not the first time I had asked her opinion about such things, but on this occasion she appeared to see that it was not so much the style we were discussing as the propriety of me attending a ball.

'Mmm,' she said, smiling gently, confirming what I thought. 'It's tricky, isn't it, ma'am? A mourning ballgown for a function one is hardly expected to attend. *However*,' she continued, 'there's the obligation to one's business partner, for one thing. For another, a fashionable ballgown could be contrived to reflect mourning for *both* Lord Nelson *and* for a loved one. And for another, it is quite possible to attend a ball without taking part in the dancing. Many ladies go only to be seen and to socialise, ma'am, as I'm sure you're aware. It would not be remarked upon, in your case.'

'So,' I said. 'Is it to be black, or white?'

'Both,' she replied, smiling at my acceptance. 'Keep it ambiguous, I always say. Shall I take Master Jamie up now?'

I was glad, in a way, that the decision had almost been made for me. I say 'almost' because, in my heart, I welcomed a chance to dress up and spend an evening in good company, meeting old acquaintances and shedding my cares for a few glamorous hours. I could tell myself that I was doing Prue a favour, but the truth was that Linas's death had cut me adrift again, unsettling me in a way that nothing else had done, not even my father's sudden death. Could there have been something in what Prue said about wearing my heart for all to see? Was that *really* what I'd been doing?

Chapter Seven

In that first week of the thaw, I felt as if my concerns were quietly breeding, growing all the more irritating for my inability to decide what to do about them. It was not like me to be so undecided.

For my mother's progressive illness I could do little except visit her as often as I was able and hope to be there when she needed me. On the more immediate problem of Pierre, I would have welcomed some informed advice rather than the heavily biased opinion Prue had offered me. She was, quite naturally, in favour of leaving things as they were, but I could see all too clearly that to do so was running a serious risk not only to ourselves and our business, but also to Jamie. While Linas lived, the risk had somehow seemed less of a threat.

Smuggling was illegal, I knew that. Along with thousands of otherwise law-abiding people, I was breaking the law. But Pierre's last consignment had indicated what I had not suspected before, that he was dealing in more than exotic fabrics, and that perhaps he was doing it for my sake, hoping to place me in his debt. If that was so, now was the time to call a halt before it was too late.

If it had been left entirely to me, I would have dealt with the problem at a sedate pace, in my own time. But once again Fate took a hand in things, setting the machinery in motion and taking no account of the inappropriate timing. We were leaning over the stone balustrade of the Ouse Bridge, Jamie, Mrs Goode, Debbie and I, to watch the swollen brown waters shoot below us at an incredible speed, the swirling satin surface wrinkling only inches away from the top of each arch. All along the banks as far as we could see, the flood had reached across the staithes and the new tree-lined walk, pushing back into the lanes on both sides, flooding houses. Debris and boats piled up together with tree trunks tossed like matchsticks upon the roaring torrent. Jamie, clinging tightly to my neck, was fascinated. On the bridge behind us, horses and carriages splashed through the water and mud, some of them loaded with baggage and furniture. A voice broke through the general din. 'Miss Follet, this is too dangerous. The water is still rising.'

Contrarily, my emotions wavered between elation and defiance, for he was one of the concerns I didn't know what to do about. My small son, however, suffered from no such conflict. 'Uncaburl!' he yelped, struggling against me, leaning out heavily with arms like reaching tentacles. 'Uncaburl, hold me.' The changeover was happening, whether I liked it or not.

I watched Jamie cling to him with a look of triumph on his little face. 'We're in no danger,' I said, not best pleased at having to justify myself.

'No, of course not. But I think you should come away now.'

His calmness, I knew, was for Jamie's sake, but when he turned and strolled off with my child in his arms, knowing that I would follow come hell or high water, it was as if he knew exactly how to lead me in any direction without the slightest fear of argument, either now or in the future. 'Where are you going?' I called, beckoning to Mrs Goode and Debbie.

He had the grace to wait for me, then. And he was smiling. Both of them were. Conspiring. Father and son, as alike as two peas. My heart flipped and twisted, acknowledging the deep yearning of my womb to be filled with more babies, more warm, defenceless, soft pink creatures to suckle, to adore. His babies. More Jamies to replenish me and make me whole and fruitful, to depend on me alone. I am not usually so tearful, but at that moment he must have caught a quick watery flash along my lower eyelid before I could catch it with a finger.

His smile vanished. 'It's all right,' he said, very quietly. 'Just stay close. We'll keep to the higher ground, I think. Coney Street will soon be awash so we'll go along Davygate instead. I have some visitors who want to see you.'

'Who?' I croaked. 'The last visitor you had I didn't want to meet.'

'Mutual friends. They went to Blake Street first, then to me at Stonegate. So I came to find you.'

'You found us, Uncaburl!' Jamie cried, proudly.

'Yes, little one.'

There was no more conversation as we walked in

single file through the watery streets, slippery with slush and silt, we women picking up our skirts although it was too late to make much difference. Approaching the space known as Thursday Market where many lanes met, the aroma of roasting coffee wafted out through the open doors of coffee houses where men came and went. My eyes were on the conditions underfoot, but Jamie was like an eagle on a cliff. 'Uncapare!' he yelled. 'Mama, look! It's Uncapare!'

I looked up, sure of some mistake. I would have to apologise. Two men had just emerged from the Davygate Coffee House ahead of us and were walking in our direction, their heads bent, deep in conversation. One of them was unmistakably Pierre Follet. Here, in York. And I would be obliged to introduce him. This was just the kind of thing I could have done without.

Hearing his name, Pierre looked up, first in astonishment and then with indecision, then with a quick word to send his companion off hastily in the opposite direction. His eyes darted uncertainly over Jamie in the care of a stranger, changing to relief and warmth as he saw my smile. *Between us*, his answering smile said, *we can bluff this out*.

As usual, I greeted him with a kiss to both cheeks and was pleased when he placed a kiss gallantly upon my hand. I was even more pleased when he spoke in French, which I had no doubt Winterson would understand. Pierre's drab coat and grey knee-breeches reeked of tobacco smoke.

Leaning out of his nest, Jamie insisted on hugging Pierre's head, thereby enforcing some kind of informal introduction between the two 'uncas'. Knowing that I would be on safe ground here, I took the plunge. 'Will you allow me to introduce my cousin to you, my lord? Monsieur Follet lives with my family in Bridlington. Pierre, this is Lord Winterson, Mr Monkton's brother.' I saw no reason to go into detail about the exact relationship, using the term 'cousin' in its loosest form. My father's family had been known as Follethorpe for three generations, now.

'Monsieur,' said Winterson. Speaking in faultless French, he asked Pierre if he was staying in York long, how bad were the roads to Brid, and was there any better news of Miss Follet's mother? It was a catch, I knew, to see how Pierre would describe her health, though I resented Winterson using such a device to expose his doubts.

Pierre put on a grave face. 'Madame Follet has been very unwell for more than a year, my lord,' he said. 'I've come to call on her usual apothecary on Petergate. He's preparing something stronger to deal with the pain.'

'Did you intend to pay us a visit before you return?' I said.

'Not this time, *ma chère*. Forgive me. Time is short.'

Jamie pouted. 'Come with us, Uncapare,' he pleaded. 'We're going to Papa's house.'

Sitting aloft in Winterson's arms, their faces a few inches apart, only a blind man could have missed the likeness between father and son, even with that age difference. In one respect, it was unfortunate that Jamie still referred to Stonegate as 'Papa's house' for that would take some time to change. But for him to say it to Pierre, who knew that Winterson now owned it, was particularly ill fated and guaranteed to set the cat among the pigeons.

Pierre's eyes darted between them, comparing, recognising each similarity, for although he had never met Linas, he knew that the twin brothers were not identical. This was disastrous. His refusal came as no surprise. 'Ah...*petit Jamie*,' he said, 'I must take some medicine to Nana Damzell. She's waiting for it. Next time, yes?'

Jamie nodded. I took the cue, gratefully. 'Send me word, Pierre, won't you? Give her my love. And the boys too.'

'Indeed I will.' He bowed, but for me there was no smile, only a cool, guarded glint in his eyes that I recognised and felt deeply, like a reproach. For Jamie, he had a smile and a kiss to the tiny waving fingers. For Winterson, he had a brief nod and, 'My lord', before he turned away.

'Safe journey, *monsieur*,' called Winterson. 'You'll be home before dark, I hope?'

Waving a careless hand, Pierre slewed round. 'Oh...easily,' he called back. Instantly, he saw his mistake reflected in my eyes, but he could do nothing about it but shrug and walk on. It was already mid-day, and no one could have covered the forty miles to Brid before darkness fell, especially in those conditions. Foss Beck Common was a possibility. We watched him go, swinging away down the cobbled street and disappearing round the corner, ignoring Jamie's waves. I felt a cold chill grasp at my arms and shoulders.

'Well, well,' Winterson drawled. 'What an interesting family you have, Miss Follet.'

'Oh, not *now*,' I said, under my breath. 'Let's go and visit the visitors. One fiasco at a time, *please*.'

Even so, as we drew level with the coffee house from which Pierre had come, Winterson slowed down to take a long look through the bow window where, inside, a grey fog of smoke hung over the tables of bent heads poring over newspapers and broadsheets, pens and papers, copper coffee pots, cups and the inevitable clutter of plates and clay pipes. It was the kind of place I had never associated with Pierre, an outdoor man. Yet he had admitted to contacts in York and surely that was the kind of venue where he would pick up news of his homeland. In a coffee house, his nationality would arouse little comment when so many Frenchmen had fled to the safety of England in the pre-Napoleon years. Yet I would like to have known why he had time to spend there, and who was the companion he didn't want us to meet.

I would rather have gone back to Blake Street instead of the disorder of Stonegate, but I was pleasantly relieved to find that Winterson's visitors were high on Jamie's list of favourites. 'Uncamedith!' he cried, hurling himself at the young curate's black-stockinged legs, clinging like a limpet. 'Where's Aunt Cynthie?'

Effectively hobbled, Medworth Monkton picked the limpet off, laughing. 'Upstairs, young man, telling the workmen off for sitting down on the job. As usual.'

If Linas had been the worn-out racehorse and his twin the well-toned hunter, then the younger Medworth could have been compared to a sturdy northern fell-pony, strong and energetic and with a forelock of dark hair that had apparently refused all attempts to imitate Brutus. Pleasant looking he was, too, but lacking the heart-stopping masculine virility of his elder brother that riveted the eyes of women and made their minds wander off the subject, whatever that was. They stood together, the three of them, and though Medworth held Jamie, it was as obvious as night follows day which one was the father.

We stood in the dining room, breathing in the odour of new paint, where the walls had been lightened with spring tones of pale yellow and white, though the floor was still bare and the windows curtainless. Already, the improvement was startling, the room had expanded.

Medworth's wife, a merry motherly lady two or three years older than her husband, came down to join us with a sparkle in her eyes and the rosy cheeks of one who has just given someone else's workmen a dressing down. Warmly, she embraced me and told me how she had advised Winterson that a deep red carpet would be best in a dining room to absorb any spillages, a suggestion that appeared to meet with no particular enthusiasm. They were a happily outspoken pair, beloved by their parishoners as much for their kindness as for their lack of pretensions. Cynthia was expecting their third child, otherwise, she told us, they would have defied convention and bought tickets for the St Valentine's Day ball at the weekend. 'I may have been able to manage a stately gavotte,' she said rather wistfully, lifting a holland cover off one of the chairs, 'but not an eightsome reel. Oh, I *do* admire these seats, Burl dear. I wonder…?'

'Miss Follet's handiwork,' said Winterson. 'And no, dear sister-in-law, I shall not be replacing them. However, I *shall* take your place at the ball in order to accompany Miss Follet. You may sit on one in your delicate state, Cynthia. I have no objection to that.' He took the holland cover from her and threw it aside.

'Burl Winterson,' she giggled, sitting down.

He must have felt my stare, for he turned suddenly to catch my expression with an equally challenging one of his own, daring me to take issue with him, there and then, in front of his brother.

The truth was that Mrs Monkton's delicate state was a complete surprise to me, and instead of offering them my felicitations, I was once more overtaken by the yearning, now tinged with envy, and it was all I could do to keep my hands away from my flat belly to still the ache of emptiness. 'No,' I said, 'I don't think…I still have reservations…I'm not sure.'

'About…?' said Winterson.

'About whether it's the right thing for me to do.'

'Well, my dear,' said his brother, 'you must do whatever you feel is correct. But let me say this: Linas would not have wanted us all to go into months of mourning for him. For you to be seen in public at this time will not cause even the lift of an eyebrow from his family, and indeed, Burl's decision to accompany you will prevent comments from anyone.'

'Yes. Thank you. But I didn't think it would be seemly to dance.'

Looking across at his wife's nodding approval, Mr Monkton's beaming face softened even more. 'Wife,' he said, 'I don't know why we didn't think of that ourselves. We *could* go, for an hour or two, for a game of cribbage? A chat with friends? Just to be seen? How d'ye like that idea? No dancing?'

Cynthia was a farmer's daughter with the healthy

glow of a ripe apple and eyes like pips, her hair a curly mouse brown, her wide smile only one step away from laughter. 'We'll go and purchase tickets before we return home,' she said, 'and heaven only knows what I'm going to wear. I suppose it will have to be black?'

I assumed that she would want to talk of gowns, but I was mistaken. It was little Claude's third birthday the following week, and she wanted Jamie to spend the day with them at Osbaldswick. Would I take him and Goody over there after breakfast on Tuesday? Still, I could not help feeling relieved when they eventually departed, leaving a strained silence behind them.

It was almost lunch-time and Jamie would be hungry, and I could not keep him and the women waiting while Winterson and I hammered out the dents made to my family's façade by Pierre. Or tackled the vexed question of the ball and his sudden decision to escort me there.

'What d'ye think of the red-carpet idea?' he said as we returned to the dining room.

'Not much. Deep gold, perhaps, or pale green. That is, if you really intend to keep the chair covers as they are.'

'I wouldn't dream of changing them. Same for the curtains?'

'No. White brocade curtains with gold bobble-fringe, to match the gilding on the architrave.' I'd had years to think about it.

'White? Really?'

'Yes, really. Echoes the ceiling and frieze. Reflects the light. Widens the narrow windows. It's always been so dull in here. That's why I made the floral covers in pastel shades. But why not ask Lady Slatterly's opinion? She'll be the one dining in here most, surely?'

'Tch! You *have* got a bee in your bonnet about her, haven't you? There's really no need, you know.'

'The hem of my skirt is wet,' I returned. 'I must get Jamie and go.'

'I shall call round to see you later on.'

'I shall be in the workrooms all afternoon. I have clients to see.'

'Then I'll call round this evening.'

'You're staying in York tonight?'

'If need be. And no, the lady will not be here with me.'

A quick retort flew unbidden to my lips as if my heart felt the need to deny its caring. But the issue of beds, Linas's and mine, was too personal to discuss in the same breath as the Slatterly woman, and I dare not trust my voice to speak without revealing the unsoundness of my feelings. 'Perhaps tomorrow might be better,' I said, lamely, hoping he'd insist.

'This evening. After dinner.' His hand rested on the doorknob as he waited for me to reach him, though I could not meet his eyes. 'What is it?' he said, softly, deeply. 'Did she upset you?'

I knew he referred to his sister-in-law, yet there was no truthful answer to his query. With one hand on my forehead, I hid my eyes, shaking my head rather than give him an unconvincing no.

'Then what? Is it too soon for me to be making changes here? Does it distress you?'

'No, it's not that. Earlier…when Jamie and you were…together.' The words tumbled out, revealing what I ought to have kept to myself. It was foolish of me. It was not his problem, but mine, yet he appeared to understand without more being said.

'Well, yes. That small point did not escape your cousin, any more than it has escaped Medworth.'

My hand moved down to my mouth. Medworth too. 'Then Jamie must not be seen with you, my lord. You must see that,' I whispered.

'That's not the answer, is it? You know it isn't.'

'Then what is?'

Jamie's wail reached us through the door, and the brass knob in Winterson's hand began to vibrate urgently. Slowly, still looking at me, Winterson opened the door just enough to allow the angry little fellow to edge through, his face red with indignation. *'Uncaburl!'* he yelled.

'Whoa!' Winterson said, sternly. 'Manners, young man, if you please.'

On the very edge of a tantrum, Jamie stopped and looked up. 'Sorry, Uncaburl,' he wavered. 'Mama. I'm hungry. I'm *very* hungry.'

Holding out my arms, I enclosed and lifted him, feeling his warmth melt into me, and through half-closed eyes I was unable to hide the all-consuming craving for fulfilment that had been with me for days.

It had been a tiring but enjoyable afternoon spent in talk of little else but fabrics and designs, colours and styling details, the clients ranging from a dowager marchioness to the adolescent daughter of York's wealthy gentry attending her first ball. I was back home in time to tuck Jamie into bed and tell him a story, sending him to sleep before the happily-ever-after.

Finding no good reason to dress up for Winterson's informal visit, I changed into a loose gown of soft violet cloth with a frilled collar and wrists over which I wore a grey sleeveless waistcoat, floor-length and shadowy-patterned, my hair only just held up by a large tortoiseshell comb. He had recently called me 'my beauty' as if I were a horse being told to lift up its other hoof, but my disconcertingly honest mirror told me only that I had lost weight and looked rather tired. I was bound to agree.

He arrived well before I had finished picking at my cold supper on a tray, shrinking my small but pretty parlour even more, and settling himself upon my blue velvet couch that could seat three of us and only one of him. 'Would you prefer to use the drawing room?' I said, thinking more of the distance I could keep.

'No, it's cosier in here. Finish your supper, ma'am.'

Winterson had brought regular news of his ailing brother's progress to my drawing room, but there had never been a time when we'd discussed our relationship, or Jamie's future, or my relatives, or anything as ephemeral as a local ball. 'You could have given me some warning,' I said to his opening of the subject. 'It would have given me time to—'

'To cry off. Yes, that's what I thought. Thank you,' he said, receiving a glass of port and placing it on the small table. 'But I had no intention of allowing you to go without an escort. Linas would not have approved.'

'Shall we not bring Linas into everything?' I said. 'Have you given any thought to how it will look on Saturday when I arrive with you, his brother? Can you not anticipate the speculation, my lord?'

The slow blink, like an owl, then that deeply chilling

note of sarcasm he was so good at. 'From one who has suggested keeping Linas out of it, that is a singular question, Miss Follet. Have *you* thought how it will look for us to arrive separately on Saturday and have nothing whatever to do with each other? Jamie's mother and guardian not on speaking terms? What will be the conclusions drawn from that, do you imagine?'

My silence answered his question while I pondered on his ability to see further ahead than me, who specialised in looking backwards.

'Have you forgotten?' he said, more gently.

'No. I have not forgotten.'

The Valentine Ball at the Assembly Rooms here on Blake Street was where I had met, first him, then Linas. We had danced together, he and I, saying very little, but aware of a powerful charge between us that dear Linas had no means to rival. We had been the centre of attention that evening. Yet it was Linas who pursued me, and Linas that I chose to cleave to because he needed me most and because I was not in a position to refuse his offer. I was under no illusions, after that, about Winterson's fleeting interest in me, which was no more nor less, I suppose, than his interest in many another. But for me, the disturbance in my heart was more profound than anything that had gone before, and so painful that I could hardly have called it love when I was obliged to see him regularly, for Linas's sake, and to suffer his coolness. Now, he asked if I'd forgotten, as if I might as easily have forgotten my name.

'We need not dance,' he said, 'unless you wish it, but it's best for all of us, as a family, if we are seen to unite on these occasions. And it's quite out of the question for you to go alone, yet I think you *should* go. So I shall call for you at eight and I shall escort you home afterwards.'

'The Assembly Rooms are only four doors away.'

'I know. If it's very wet, I'll have a chair brought for you. Now, eat your supper, and then you can tell me about your French cousin who thinks he can reach Brid in three hours over flooded roads.'

'I think I'd rather not, thank you. There's little I can tell you. He's a distant cousin, and I have no idea what he was doing in a coffee house except drinking coffee and reading the newspapers.'

'Then perhaps I may be forgiven for constructing a few facts of my own. The apothecary on Petergate where Monsieur Follet obtained your mother's medication informs me that her name is Mrs Follethorpe and that the French gentleman calls in regularly, about once every month. Which begs the question, in my mind, whether you and the French cousin are more to each other than that.'

So, he had already made enquiries. 'The apothecary had no right to give you that information,' I said, angrily pushing the tray away.

'Perhaps not. But he's as open to persuasion as the next man.'

'Well, then, let me put you out of your misery, my inquisitive lord. I changed my name to Follet when I came to seek work in York for no other reason than to protect my father's name. If he'd lived, he'd probably not have objected, since he always saw Pierre and me as future partners. As it turned out, he died only a few weeks after we left Bridlington. And, yes, it's quite obvious that my family don't live there, for reasons which I cannot discuss with you. Pierre is no more or less to me than a devoted relative who has helped our family through difficult times.'

'That's the first time I've ever heard you speak of your father. Could he be, by any chance, the famed Leonard Follethorpe, one-time mayor of Bridlington? No need to look so surprised. I *am* a Justice of the Peace, remember, which requires me to know what's going on in the area.' When I made no reply, he continued. 'So, if my knowledge is correct, and I'm reasonably sure it is, may I offer you some advice? The notice appearing in your shop window advertising French laces and other forbidden things from across the Channel may not be the good idea you believe it to be. If I were you, ma'am, I would keep quiet about that kind of merchandise when there are men walking the streets of York whose job it is to winkle out receivers of Free Trade goods. If they were to suspect that you and Mrs Sanders were involved, you would be asked to provide some very explicit answers ranging back over several years. You are an unmarried mother, don't forget, and very vulnerable.'

'Jamie,' I whispered.

'Yes, our Jamie. You cannot afford to take risks, Helene. Can you?'

'I had already reached that conclusion.'

'Of course. I cannot believe you would do anything so dangerous unless there was a very good reason for it.'

'There is.'

'Yet it occurs to me, as it will also have done to you,

that if you are able to do so well from the sale of these
luxury goods, your family ought to be living in some
style by now. Are they?'

'No. Far from it.'

'Then perhaps it's time the business was looked into
and stopped.'

'I don't know how to stop it.'

'Simple. You say "stop".'

'It's *not* simple. Prue depends on it. My family
depend on it. And I depend on it. How d'ye think I've
been able to manage all these years?'

'I had already begun to wonder.'

'Well, now you know. I'm in deep trouble and, if I
were you, I'd have no more to do with me.'

'Too late,' he said, quietly. 'It's much too late for
that.'

Chapter Eight

We sat for some time without speaking although the silence was loud with sound, the crackling fire, the clock, the thud of my heart.

Reaching for his glass, he held it up to the lamplight, took a sip and replaced it on the table next to the pile of notebooks I'd still had no time to read. 'Mmm,' he said. 'What you need, Miss Follet, is some protection. It's not usual for a lady of your standing to live without a chaperon. When Linas was close I suppose it mattered less, but I think you should give the matter some thought.'

'I already have. I would have liked my mother to come here so that I could care for her, but she won't consider it.'

'That's not quite what I had in mind.'

'I have Mrs Goode, and Debbie.'

'Yet you went out alone to visit your family in atrocious conditions. You cannot continue to do that kind of thing. It's asking for trouble.'

'Then what am I to do? Advertise?'

Leaning forward, he extended one long arm towards me so that his forefinger just touched mine as it drooped over the arm of my chair. The shock of its tender impact caught at my mind and held it still. 'No,' he said, 'not yet. Not till we've explored the other possibilities. Next time you visit your family, I shall go with you. We'll take Jamie too, and show them what Monsieur Follet saw. You cannot keep that from them for ever, you know. And while we're there, we'll tackle the other problem too. Now don't start your objections too soon. You need some help in this, and I'm the one to do it. None of you can keep on living off illegal gains.'

I drew my hand away from the contact, too full of contradictions to accept whatever he was offering, too determined not to be won over at the touch of one finger. 'That's not possible,' I said. 'They'll think… well…'

'Yes, they *will* think. And as Jamie gets older, everybody else is going to think too. Surely your own family should be the first to know how things are between us, Helene. Not from gossip, but from us.'

'What d'ye mean? How *what* is between us? You're not suggesting telling them what happened, are you?'

'I'm suggesting telling them what's *going* to happen. They'll be able to see for themselves what's happened, won't they? Your French cousin, for instance, who has hopes of owning you, one day. Isn't it better he should know sooner rather than later that he doesn't stand a ghost of a chance? And your mother too? Isn't it best that she knows, before it's too late to tell her? It's time we began to put things in order, lass.'

If I was confused before, I was even more confused after his attempt at clarification. 'Pierre? My mother? Tell them what—that Jamie isn't Linas's?'

'That you are to marry Jamie's father and guardian. And if you don't want to tell them, then I will. Or would you prefer Jamie to discover what it means to be illegitimate? It won't be long now, the way he's chattering.'

'And that's what you call exploring the possibilities, is it?'

'Yes, Miss Follet, it is. So before you give me all the reasons why you can't accept that plan, consider instead the deep trouble you just mentioned. I'm offering you a respectable way out of it. I can take on the responsibility for your family without resorting to the illegal methods that are keeping you all in danger. You're playing with fire, and that's no way to conduct a business. Mrs Sanders will have to understand that.'

Naturally, I had my doubts whether either Pierre *or* Prue would understand, but Winterson knew nothing of Pierre's part in the smuggling, nor would I tell him. The talk of marriage, however, had taken me off guard, although I could appreciate that the offer was for Jamie's sake more than for any romantic reason. He put me right on that, too.

'Consider this also,' he said. 'If I'd chosen to go down on one knee and beg you to be my wife, you'd have stuck your neat little nose in the air and said not in a million years, wouldn't you? Eh?'

'Yes. Very likely.'

'So that's why I'm ignoring the romantic bit and *telling* you that you'd better start getting used to the idea. Fix any reason to it you like. Our son, illegitimacy, Linas, me, family likenesses, gossip, whatever.'

'Yes, whatever. But you've missed out an important snag, of course.'

'Which is?'

'That I am not good at sharing a man, my lord. Your kind of life and mine would not mix. You have mistresses, I believe? Well, I don't suppose anything would change there, would it? That would be asking too much of both of us.'

With a sigh, he leaned forwards again to rest his arms along his thighs as he looked at me with a frown of impatience at my recurring theme. Or so I thought. 'Then allow me to explain, my beauty, once and for all,' he said in a voice devoid of tenderness.

'Oh, there's really no need,' I snapped, nettled by the reading of my mind. 'I expect you used Linas's bed. Or did she prefer the one in my room?'

'Huh! Listen to me, Helene. In return for land, I train some of Lord Slatterly's racehorses. It's a reciprocal arrangement that benefits both of us, so he'd take it very hard if I told his beloved only daughter to keep away. She comes and goes, but I cannot stop her if she thinks she stands a chance with me. She doesn't, and she never has. Not once. Her friends all make use of her, but I prefer not to. In fact, I'm probably the only one who doesn't, and I only allow her to stay at my home when there's a party of friends there too. Never alone. No matter what she may say or imply, that's the truth of the matter. She's already wheedled her way through the back door of Stonegate, so I've given strict instructions that she must not be admitted while I'm out, under any circumstances. You, on the other hand, are always to be welcomed.

'But the day you saw her there was also the day you told me you were willing to put the past behind us and be friends, for Jamie's sake. Helene, I'm offering you more than that. I'm offering you both a new life. All together.'

'I didn't expect…that. It's further than I'm prepared to go, although I can see the advantages and I'm aware that a woman in my position can hardly afford to turn down such an offer without good cause. Especially when it comes from her child's father. But you see, my lord, ever since I discovered how you and your brother planned to make use of me as if I were a heifer of sound stock expected to produce a healthy bull-calf, the whole business of marriage has turned rather sour on me. My inclination now is to remain chaste until I can decide for myself when to continue my own breeding programme. I had not meant to keep harping on that string, but I seem not to have made it clear that I mean to stay as independent as I was when I first came to York. I find it suits me better. Yes, I know it may sound selfish, but I really cannot allow my three-year-old son to choose a husband for me.'

By the time I'd finished, I was trembling with the effort and with trepidation, too, for he was not a man to take a woman's snub lightly, having offered so much. So I rose rather quickly from my chair with the intention of putting myself beyond his reach. And his anger.

He moved much faster than I did, and I was caught under the arm and pulled back against him, off balance, my vision blurred by the lamplight and shadows, by the sharp conflict of wills and, in my case, by an explosion of petulance. 'Let go...let *go*!' I cried, struggling furiously inside his arms. 'I don't want...no...I don't *want* this! You're hurting. Let *go*!'

It was all the same, fighting him, loving him, wanting the hard pressure of his body against mine. Even the pain. Even his anger. But I could hear by his breathing, by his soft whispers and by the nudging gentleness of his lips that he was *not* angry, but enjoying my struggles. His hands restrained me, forcing me to be still while his forehead came to rest upon mine. We stood, head to head, me panting with vexation and he with eyes alight, amused to see my hair slowly slithering down my cheek, the tortoiseshell comb hanging on by a tooth.

His nose rested beside mine as he spoke, gentling me. 'That's my beauty. You think I wouldn't guess how you'd react to that? Eh? How you'd give me another roasting as soon as you had half a chance? Superb woman. Hush now. Not a heifer, sweetheart. Never a heifer. Nothing like. You were always a classy thoroughbred, temperamental, distrustful. You've not been handled well, have you? I shall have to remedy some wicked habits, but I can do it. I can make you sweet-tempered again, my lovely witch. And I shall get close to you again.'

'I shall not marry you.'

'Yes, you will. Of your own accord. You'll see.'

His hand raked through my hair to grasp a handful of it, tipping my face to fit against his mouth, closing my eyes as he did in my dreams, sinking me deep into the overlapping sensations that nightly craved consummation. I could not allow him to take me further, rendering worthless all I had striven for over the years. He had once called me unreliable, an insult that still rankled for, of all my copious faults, unreliability had never been one. Murmured so sweetly, his descriptions of me both excited and hardened my heart, for if anyone was responsible for my distrust of men, it was he. I would not make it easy for him, although my boast to choose my own time to breed was an empty threat he must have recognised. If I wanted to keep this roof over my head, I would be obliged to choose its owner above all others.

'Let me go,' I whispered. 'We are never going to agree on this.'

'You think not? Well, I can wait. You'll come to me.'

'Can you wait another four years, then?'

His head jerked back and he was once again the proud powerful hunter with eyes that glinted like polished jet. 'Don't play the waiting game,' he warned, 'unless you're prepared to damage yourself and our son while you revenge yourself on me. Time is too precious for that, Helene, and your heart is not really as hard as all that, is it?' As he answered me, his hand slipped beneath the grey waistcoat, pausing over my crazy heart to feel its beat before straying to one side, cupping my breast, reminding me once again how easily I had given myself to him that night.

Rather than try to find an answer, I prised his hand away, murmuring, 'Have we explored the other possibilities, my lord? Or is that it?'

'There were no others worth exploring, Helene. In spite of your cynicism, we *are* talking about Jamie's future here. Just remember, will you?'

'There was never any danger of me forgetting,' I said.

Again, it was the tone of my voice that betrayed my peevish heart that would have kept its wound for ever open, if need be, at whatever cost. But I was a mother first and foremost, beyond the anguish caused to my womanly pride, and I could no more have put Jamie's well-being in jeopardy at the expense of my self-esteem than expose him to a cage of lions. He was my life, and here was I, about to reject the best possible future for him, only to wreak vengeance for perceived wrongs. What was I about? Could I afford to ignore the olive branch he was offering to put things right between us? He had even tried to clear up my concerns about the Slatterly woman.

'Helene, look at me,' he said, lifting my chin.

I *did* look at him, and loved and hated him, wanted him, wanted to hurt him, wanted him to persist with me, to see my ritual objections for what they were and not to concede defeat. I wanted him to storm my barriers and crash through to the core that was his for the taking. I had always wanted him. I had lived, wanting him, for years with his brother and child. My body ached for him night and day without ceasing. So I looked up at him, not wanting to hear him accept one single word of my hostility. 'Don't speak,' I whispered, placing a finger upon his lips, 'until I've tried to excuse myself.'

'There's no need,' he said, behind my fingertip.

I wanted to kiss him. I wanted him to kiss me senseless.

'I know I've been breaking the law. It's a way of life for the people along our coast, and when I was given the chance to make some money for my family, I took it, just as I sold my body, and worked here in York, and scrounged to feed them and clothe myself. Now, you're offering me a respectable way out for which I am grateful. But they depend on me. The success of the shop has been built on it. You may forfeit Lord Slatterly's goodwill if you were to give his daughter the cold shoulder, but I shall certainly lose my partner's goodwill if I suddenly stop providing her with our most lucrative lines. You say you're willing to share the responsibility for my family, my lord, but they wouldn't allow it, and nor would I. Linas played no part in their lives, and nor must you. As for your offer of marriage… well, it's taken me unawares, and I must delay my answer to that. Jamie's birth certificate cannot be altered: he was born out of wedlock with Linas as his father, but I dare say memories will fade. At this moment, he needs a father more than ever he did.'

'He needs brothers and sisters, too,' he said, watching my eyes turn away, my lips part for the sigh that followed.

That was the last weapon left to me, after marriage, the one thing I could hold on to longest in my quest for retribution, though which of us would feel most pain was open to question. How long could I hold out against him? How long would his patience last? He was right about Jamie needing siblings, but one could not ignore the element of self-seeking that went with it. His kisses were telling me that.

He read my expression correctly. 'No, you're right,' he said. 'One thing at a time. We've made some progress, and I have to be content with that.' He lifted a fistful of my hair and held it on top of my head, with strands wandering into my eyes. 'Beautiful black witch,' he murmured. 'I lie. I'm not content, but it will have to do. As for your family and business, let me deal with that. Trust me?'

'I may not always agree with you, my lord, but I cannot fault *your* reliability.'

'*That* was taken out of context. One day, I'll explain it to you. The day after tomorrow is the ball and my parents will be over here for the weekend. Will you bring Jamie to see them on Sunday? For a family lunch?'

'Yes, we'll come. Thank you.'

'Good. Then I'll send a carriage for you.' Taking my hand from his chest, he touched my knuckles with his lips. 'Go to bed early and don't lose any more sleep over it. We had to come to an understanding sooner or later, did we not, Miss Follet?'

'For all our sakes,' I said.

But too much had happened for my thoughts to quit the future and lie quiet in the present, and sleep came nowhere near till the town-crier had called out the hour for the third time and Debbie had brought some warm milk to calm me. One thing that gave me some peace of mind, however, was that I had not shared his beautiful body with the Slatterly woman.

Next morning, with Winterson's caution still uppermost in my mind, I went straight to the shop to remove the incriminating notice from the window. Quite what had possessed me to put it there in the first place I will never understand—it was what we had always done without thinking of the possible consequences. Prue was not there, though she had been in.

'She's left a message for you, ma'am,' said Betty, the senior seamstress.

Propped up against a pile of calicoes was a hastily written note, very much to the point. *Mother v. ill. Father in a state. Dare not leave them. Sorry. Prue.*

It was bad timing. Perhaps the cold had affected them. Her unscheduled absence, however, made it easier for me to take some positive action in advance of any snooping visits from the Customs and Excise Men, a fear that had stayed with me since Winterson's call. With Prue out of the way I would do as I pleased and remove the damning evidence while there was still time, and none of the sewing-women making the least objection when I explained what we would do.

The unused cellar was ankle-deep in flood water from the street outside, but as each package was placed in the niches set into the darkest wall, this proved to be the safest of all places, the only one too uninviting to be investigated fully.

As if some supernatural clockwork had been set in motion, we were visited that same afternoon by two dour gentlemen who asked with the greatest courtesy if they might inspect our property in the name of His Brittanic Majesty King George III. As if we had any choice.

Well acquainted with Customs Officers, I found little that was unfamiliar about these two, and nothing that ought to have caused the alarm I felt, or the fear, the appalling guilt, the sickly terror of being just in time, and the dread that something relevant had been missed out. I could only pray that the women would answer any questions calmly, for I'd had little time to brief them. 'Do you seek anything in particular, gentlemen?' I said. 'Where would you like to begin?'

Their eyes darted, missing nothing, but they were uncommunicative. They fingered the fabrics, lifted rolls, drapes and boxes, but we could all see they didn't know a poplin from a kerseymere. One lifted a length of heavy Argentan lace attached to the dress Betty was stitching. 'Where's this from?' he said, rubbing it between finger and thumb.

Betty hardly paused. 'Nottingham,' she said. 'And Maudie's sewing Bedford, and over there is the Limerick, and that pile you've been looking at is Devon, and that bobbin lace is from Buckinghamshire. It's known as…Bucks…point…' But with a lift of his eyebrows, the man had moved on.

'You have a loft, ma'am?' said the other man.

'Yes, indeed we do. The ladder is over there in the corner.'

He clambered up, but came down again immediately. 'There's nothing there but chairs,' he said, pained.

'No, that's very true.'

'Why not?'

'Because we can't get up there, can we?' I replied with a hint of impatience. 'Everything we sell is on show to our customers, not in a loft.'

The pulling out of drawers, hampers and baskets went on, bolts of fabrics were toppled to expose walls that had to be tapped, with ears pressed against them. 'You have cellars?' the man said, frowning at the floor.

'Yes, the trapdoor is in the kitchen, but we don't keep anything down there. It's too damp.'

Nevertheless, they took one look down into the murky hole, saw their lamps reflected on the water and closed the lid with a grunt of acceptance. 'What's through there, ma'am?' said the man, indicating the fitting rooms.

'My customers, sir. By all means take a look, but please don't go into the fitting rooms without a warning, or I might never see them again.'

'So where do *these* fabrics come from, exactly?'

From the drawer of my desk I brought out a sheaf of receipts and pointed out to him the recent dates. 'Mostly from Manchester, but some from Sampson and Snape's warehouses in London, some from Paisley near Glasgow. Shawls, see? Some from Norwich, too, stockings from Leicester and Derby, gloves from Worcester...' I spread the receipts out before him '...and silks and muslins from...'

'Yes...yes, thank you, ma'am.'

'...Blackburn, and cottons from...'

'Thank you, yes. What about the bonnets?'

'The millinery is made to order, sir. To match an outfit. The Lord Nelson turban is very *à la mode*, at the moment.' I took one off the wooden stand and passed it to him.

Gingerly, he took it off me, pulled a face and passed it to his colleague. 'Nothing much Frenchified about that, Horace,' he muttered.

'Nah, c'mon, we've seen enough.' Horace passed the turban back, like a bucket. 'But you had a notice in your window saying something about these things being straight from Paris, didn't you?'

'Yes.' I smiled. 'Ladies always fall for that, sir. They

see the French modes in our fashion journals, so anything with a French name is bound to draw them in. A little deception, I know, but they understand.'

'Bit of a wild goose chase, Horace.'

Horace looked at me with—I thought—a trace of sympathy. 'I heard that Mr Linas Monkton passed on recently, ma'am. Very sad, that was. A lady such as yourself needs protection in these times. And a little lad, too, I believe. Pardon me, ma'am. No offence.'

'None taken, sir,' I said, indulging in a moment of relief that the dreaded inspection had passed without incident. 'But I *do* have some protection. Mr Monkton's family are very supportive. Lord Winterson is my son's guardian, and he keeps a very close eye on my business affairs.' It was a boast I never expected to make. I felt them both stiffen, heard them gulp, saw their eyes blink and widen with concern.

'Lor…ahem!…Lord Winterson?'

'Aye. He's a J.P., Horace, is Lord Winterson. Better be going, eh?'

'Thank you, gentlemen. I shall tell him you did your job thoroughly and with courtesy. Good day to you both.'

The light outside was fading and a fine rain was beginning to spatter against the glass as I closed the door and leaned my forehead on the cool wall. A dizziness passed over me, reminding me that I had eaten no lunch that day. The danger was gone, the goods were safe, and I had used Winterson's name to protect myself from further investigation, which, to be honest, I ought not to have done. But the blissful feeling of security I had experienced as I spoke the name out loud seemed to outweigh all other considerations.

Coming along the passage to meet me, Betty took me into her arms to quell my shaking. 'We all knew, ma'am,' she said. 'None of us ever said nowt, but we knew. Come and have a nice cup o' tea.'

There was a slightly hysterical edge to our giggles as we nibbled our biscuits, the tea being just as likely to be smuggled by the tea merchant as our fabrics were by us. And the sugar by the grocer, for that matter.

Underlying that light-heartedness, though, ran another thread of concern about how we should all manage without the goods that had kept us in business for so long. It was not a problem I could discuss in the workroom, yet our handling that morning of the consignment brought by Pierre had only strengthened my suspicions that he must be playing some secret game of his own that I was not being allowed to share. His appearance in York, ostensibly to purchase my mother's medication, was in itself unusual, for I had taken enough to last her a month on my last visit, some of which had been double-strength for emergencies.

And who was the furtive scruffy character he'd been with in the coffee house? And why, for the second occasion, had Pierre found no time to call on me at home? Was his excuse a genuine one? Recalling Winterson's decision to accompany me to Foss Beck to meet my family, I wondered whether that would solve any of the problems or simply create new ones, in the light of Pierre's attachment to me. Though the outcome was hardly in question, I was still unwilling to be the cause of any bitterness between them. Perhaps the best thing, I thought, would be for me to go there alone, despite Winterson's instructions.

Chapter Nine

The terrible floods that followed the thaw brought tragedy just as severe as the crippling cold, and now instead of freezing to death, people fell victim to diseases borne upon the waters that carried effluent from broken cesspits into even the most respectable houses. Tavern taprooms were awash, the Guildhall cellars were flooded and, on my Friday visit to Lop Lane to see how Prue was managing, I discovered that the rats escaping from the water had gnawed their way through her store cupboard, eating everything remotely toothsome. Both her father and mother had gone down with the sickness by the time I arrived, and Prue herself was at her wits' end with worry. It was not the time to tell her about the Customs and Excise Men.

The apothecary on Petergate was running low on the standard remedies for such a prevalent complaint and had quite sold out of mallow-root and seeds for a decoction that rarely failed, in my experience. All he could offer me was powdered bistort root, a syrup of dried roses, and distilled mint-water which, although soothing, were not what I would call out-standingly effective. I purchased all three and took them back to Lop Lane, then I set off to scour the other apothecaries, returning an hour later with a quantity of Dr James's Fever Powders, Analeptic Pills, and a bottle of Dr Benjamin Godfrey's Cordial that I'd seen advertised in the *York Mercury*, hoping that one of them would ease the distressing symptoms. I also sent round some candles and firewood, bread and milk, cheese, soup, clean bed linen and blankets in return for the soiled ones that poor Prue had been forced to use, underlining once again the difference in our circumstances.

She had once been my employer, but now I was reminded of how hard she must be finding it to care for two ailing parents in their dilapidated town house while keeping up the appearance of a thriving business. In some ways, my responsibilities were similar, but in my accommodation I was far more fortunate than Prue, and I longed to help her out instead of giving her the bad news about the smuggled goods that only waited to be told. Nor did it help my conscience much when Debbie assisted me with a final fitting of the ballgown I'd been making all week. If Prue had not insisted that I show it off for the sake of the business, I doubt I would have spent my time so indulgently.

Nevertheless, when Saturday came I could hardly contain a *frisson* of excitement as Debbie clipped a pair of small pearls on to my earlobes and then, finding little else for her fingers to adjust, she twisted long tendrils of my hair like corkscrews and arranged them in front of my ears. She had threaded ropes of seed pearls through my coiled hair, but I would wear no other jewellery except a small pearl and moonstone brooch to clasp the folds of my gown upon one shoulder.

I had made the dress of white crape, a sheer silk gauze with a crimped surface that produced a matte effect, underneath which the soft sheen of a white satin undergown showed through when I moved. Narrow black satin ribbons crossed over the short bodice to outline my breasts, tying at the back in a bunch, the same ribbons edging the skirt above a narrow hem of black lace. It was a plain easy-to-wear style to suit many shapes and sizes, its greatest extravagance being in the rich drape of silk over satin, like moonshine behind a film of clouds edged with the darkness of night. To add another touch of luxury, I carried a black lace fan edged with black feathers, one of two sent by Pierre in the latest consignment. White satin slippers with pearl-studded buckles, silk stockings, long white satin gloves and a reticule trimmed with black beads completed the ensemble.

Although I was more or less satisfied with my appearance, I was still apprehensive and unable to dismiss the memory of that time, years ago, when the enigmatic Burl Winterson had partnered me, living up to his reputation as a thief of women's hearts. We had met on subsequent occasions at the Assembly Rooms when I was with his brother, but never again had he stood up with me for more than one dance, which I thought more likely to be a duty than a pleasure.

* * *

He came at eight to collect me, waiting at the bottom of the staircase to watch me descend, his eyes showing the kind of appreciation he had never revealed previously, I suppose for Linas's sake. He held out a hand to support me down the last stair, not knowing how the steely strength of his arm imparted the kind of secure confidence I'd never drawn from his brother. Then, I had been the supporter. This time, he would be my protector.

'St Valentine's Day,' he said, quietly.

'Yes.'

'Six years ago, was it?'

'Yes, my lord. It's surprising how much can happen to people in that time, isn't it? We've both changed,' I said, hurriedly, in case he was about to suggest we might start again at the beginning.

But he agreed with me. 'We have indeed,' he said, 'in many respects, although six years may also confirm first impressions, Miss Follet. In your case, motherhood has made you even lovelier than you were before, to my mind.'

'For which I should offer you my thanks, my lord?'

His reply was a shade too prompt for civility. 'Yes, I think you should. What kind of thanks did you have in mind?'

He always took my sarcasm too literally. 'I'll think of something suitably momentous, if you give me time,' I said, looking round me. 'I have my pattens somewhere, to carry me over the mud.'

'You won't need them. I have a chair waiting outside.' Taking the black velvet cape from Debbie, he draped it over my shoulders, still smiling at my snappy retort, making my heart lurch at the closeness of his hands. If I had indeed been improved by motherhood, then fatherhood had brought him closer to physical perfection than ever, and the thought of walking into a ballroom beside such a handsome beast made me resolve to get the most out of the experience, not to spoil it with petty bickering.

I had seen him in evening dress many times before, always attracting attention by the perfect cut of his coat, skin-tight white knee-breeches and stockings, his neck swathed in a snow-white cravat that set off the healthy outdoor skin of his lean cheeks. His hair, I noticed, had been trimmed, though it still curled, thick and luxurious, over the white muslin. My fingers itched to sink into it. 'Thank you,' I said. 'That was thoughtful.'

'I would have had them bring it inside, but they'd have covered your hall floor with mud. So this is what we'll do.' So saying, he bade me place an arm around his neck, swooped me up into his arms and carried me down the steps to the sedan chair where I was placed in the cushioned interior without a speck of mud reaching the hem of my gown. Then, with the lid lowered and the door closed, I was swayed and jogged along the cobbles to the steps of the Assembly Rooms where a sea of colour dotted with black seethed upwards between the massive pillars into the portico, to the distant sound of a country dance in progress.

Chattering and squeals, shouts and giggles, wavings and trippings-up all contributed to the excitement of seeing and being seen, the promise of liaisons, the affirmation of connections, comparisons, flirtations. It rubbed off on me too, as my eyes singled out the most interesting fashions and a few I had personally designed, sometimes sadly disfigured by fussy accessories, others improved by slender bodies and graceful steps to give them life. Aventurine and crimson, claret and cherry, geranium, azure, citrus and cinnamon, rose, violet mingled with black and white, hairstyles *à la Grecque*, braided and wreathed *à la peruvienne* with ears of corn and feathers, turbans, lace caps and knots of hair like steeples. Sashes and shawls, sleeves of puckered net, necklines only a finger-width away from decency, bare shoulders and arms, looped trains and glimpses of silk-stockinged ankles all taken in by one sweeping glance as we followed the tide and waited to deposit our cloaks.

'Lady Osmotherly, lovely to see you looking so much recovered. Lady Percival, so delighted to see you again. Mrs Knopp, I hoped you'd be here.' I curtsied to the exact degree, endorsing their patronage of Follet and Sanders. They trusted me with their most intimate secrets and I was accepted by them as a friend. Here in York, as in many other provincial towns, the social structure was less rigid than in London, barriers between the great northern families with centuries of inherited wealth and the *nouveau riche* having often been breached in the unsettled years of war with our neighbouring France. I knew their daughters, had been on the receiving end of their ambitions and disappointments, and had been asked for advice along with hints on fashion, which, as often as not, placed me in the role of confidant. Shy smiles were exchanged across the jostling anteroom, smiles which then settled upon my well-known escort and back to me, approving or envying my choice. Little did they know what lay behind that choice.

After so many years of being held at a distance, it still came as something of a surprise to me that, when he wished it, Winterson could make me feel cherished and so necessary to his enjoyment. It was not what I was used to, nor was it what I'd seen of his offhand manner with other women and, although that never appeared to dampen their interest in him, it would certainly have inhibited mine if I'd been looking for a successor to Linas. What I had found acceptable in a lover six years ago and what I would accept now were two different things, small indefinable things like taking my cloak, offering me his arm, greeting my acquaintances and introducing me to his, none of which Linas had bothered with unless I prompted him.

Mr Medworth Monkton had been correct when he assured me that no one would remark on a show of solidarity in our ranks, he and Cynthia having arrived just ahead of us, already chatting animatedly to a group of friends who apparently saw nothing out of the ordinary in my being there with Linas's two brothers. Cynthia, wearing undiluted black from head to toe, was complimentary about my evening gown. 'I might have known,' she said, 'you'd create something out of the top drawer, Helene dear. That's a simply *glorious* gown. Do you not agree, my lord?'

'I always agree with you, dear sister-in-law,' he replied, gazing abstractedly over my shoulder into the assembly. 'Miss Follet is indeed a glorious creature.'

The last remark was made quietly as if half to himself and half to anyone who could catch the words and, as Cynthia's berry-eyes twinkled and widened, her husband drew her away with a hand on her elbow and a look of sheer mischief.

'A game of faro, m'dear, and perhaps a glass of iced water after the shock of hearing Burl wax lyrical, eh? Come, my love. It may be catching.' He winked at me, in parting.

'Shall we see you at supper?' I said.

'Of course. I'm already starving.' Cynthia laughed, moving off.

'I think you should be careful,' I murmured to Winterson.

'Of what?'

'Of where you direct your dry wit, my lord. Your sister-in-law is a dear lady and quite likely to take you seriously.'

'And you do not, Miss Follet?'

'I'm learning how to tell when you're talking moonshine.'

'Then keep learning. I was not talking moonshine, and that was not an example of what you choose to call my dry wit. And you had better refrain from talking cant while you're wearing that dress. The two don't mix. Come over here and watch the dancing for a while.' Squeezing my arm with his, he led me through the throng, nodding and smiling at friends till we stood behind the dancers. At the far end of the ballroom, the orchestra swayed and gently perspired, flanked by marbled pillars, the gold-topped Corinthian capitals of which clung to each side of the creamy-green room, lit by sparkling chandeliers that hung in crystal tiers above the moving pattern of figures.

Several times I moved away from him, but always found that he had come to rejoin me, and for an hour or so we were engaged in conversation with friends who accepted that neither of us intended to dance. But the talk returned again and again to the severe flooding that had devastated acres of good arable land, drowned many animals, ruined stores of hay and cut off entire villages for the second time in a month. The Vale of York with its wide river was now a disaster area, leaving few families untouched by its broken banks.

Prue, I was sure, would be happy to hear the compliments about the dress for, although it was not quite the done thing to comment, northern folk have fewer scruples about making known their likes and dislikes or issuing praise where they think it due. I didn't mind, sure we'd be seeing some new customers within the next week or two.

There was one, of course, whose compliments were less than direct. Lady Veronique Slatterly, looking like an overblown peony in a bright pink frilly creation and too much jewellery, wished to know more about the black lace fan. 'Now where on *earth* did you find that?' she said, looking me over as if I'd got it all wrong. 'It looks Parisian to me.'

'I didn't find it,' I said. 'It was given to me by my cousin Pierre. And it *is* Parisian.'

'Oh,' she said, looking dubious. 'You actually have French relatives, do you? I thought perhaps you used the name Follet only for professional purposes.' She glanced up at Winterson, who stepped in with an unexpected contribution.

'Miss Follet has no need of an assumed name. We met Monsieur Pierre Follet in York only a week ago, a generous man of about my own years, good looking, good breeding, still unattached and wealthy. Shall we introduce him to you, Veronique?'

Before she could hide it, a look passed across her eyes like a cloud that casts shadows across a hillside and moves on, and I sensed a desperation and a kind of loneliness that stems from having everything except the thing she most wants. Winterson's glib offer had hurt her, as did the patronising smiles of the group and, for once, she was stuck for an answer.

I put on my school-ma'am voice. 'If anyone offered to present such a paragon to me on the assumption that I would drop my handkerchief at any niffy-naffy fellow still on the shelf, and a Frenchman too, I would say he had maggots in his head, my lord. I'm sure Veronique would say the same. We're both more than capable of finding our own beaux, are we not?' I said, turning to her and placing my fingertips upon her arm.

'Yes,' she whispered. 'Indeed we are.' Her colour had heightened, and I felt she was close to tears.

I could not leave it at that. 'Shall we leave these coxcombs to their racing talk and repair to the supper room?' I said. 'I have an appetite.'

She nodded and turned away, missing my frown at Winterson and the hand I laid on his arm to prevent him from following.

Looking back over the past days, I could see how his recent account of Veronique's circumstances had affected the way I was beginning to respond to her, for I accepted his word that they had never been lovers, despite her wanting it to be so. Indeed, he had confirmed what his feelings were only a moment ago in that insensitive remark as he rushed to my defence with an unnecessary put-down. Perhaps, I thought, Veronique's intention had been merely to keep me on my toes with a few needling comments but, whatever the truth of the matter, she had revealed to me that there was more to her than the shallow golden-dolly. Here was a rather sad young woman searching for something that life was not providing her with. My theory, such as it was, was further strengthened in the supper room where we met Medworth and Cynthia Monkton still eating and socialising.

Standing sideways on to a lady dressed in violet and silver, Cynthia's profile accentuated her newly rounded shape clearly. Unlike others, she would never have attempted to disguise it. There was no need for introductions for they had met Veronique on many occasions at Abbots Mere, but her astonished glance at Cynthia's bulge brought back the cloud of discontent to her eyes that disappeared almost as quickly as before and, instead of the usual congratulations, she dithered as I myself had done only a few days earlier. Quickly averting her eyes, she stuttered something about the warmth, accepted a glass of punch from Medworth and gulped it down rather too quickly, pressing one hand beneath her bosom.

After some chatter, I drew Veronique aside in the hope that we might sit and talk together as friends, for once. But it was not to be, for we were joined by Winterson, who seemed determined to sit us down at a table and to share the food he had brought as if to make amends for his earlier tactlessness. If he saw anything unusual in our being together, he gave no sign of it.

Other things had begun to make more sense to me concerning Veronique's spite, her unconcealed jealousy of my position, especially while I'd been pregnant with Jamie. Did she share with me that yearning for a child? Had it become almost a sickness with her, as I well knew it could? Did she need some real friends? And would she accept me as one?

'I think,' I said to Winterson when she had been invited to dance, 'you might try a little more kindness. It wouldn't hurt, surely?'

Sitting back into the gilded chair, he crossed his long legs and treated me to one of those superior looks that tell a woman he'll humour her at the price of a brief skirmish. His eyes narrowed, cynical, amused, as if he enjoyed having to defend himself. 'Hurt whom?' he said.

'You. A gentle answer turneth away wrath, you know.'

Heads turned in our direction as he laughed out loud. 'Oh, don't go all biblical on me, Miss Follet,' he grinned. 'But to answer your question, yes, it *would* hurt, eventually. Give some people an inch and they'll take a yard. You be kind to the lady if you wish. It's in your nature. But if I did the same, she'd get the wrong end of the stick all over again, just when I think she's started to see that it's you I want, not her.'

'I shall pay no attention to that last remark.'

'Do as you please. It's true. I only dole out kindness as I do to my horses, as an inducement for something I want or as a reward for something I'm given, not as largesse to those who'd take advantage, as she most certainly would. So there you have it.'

It was not so much the sentiment alone that shocked me, for that was a typical response from the wealthy land-owning aristocracy who rarely saw the need to part with anything unless there was a sound reason for it. But to apply that to friendship did strike me as odd. 'Well,' I said, 'I never heard anything quite as cynical as that in all my born days, my lord. So am I to take it that the only reason you've ever had to offer *me* kindness is because you expected something in return? Never kindness for its own sake?'

'For both reasons I've just stated. You have what I want, and you've given me something too.'

'So if that were not the case, I take it you would have no other reason to offer me kindness.'

'But it *is* the case, Miss Follet. I cannot imagine seeing you without wanting you, nor can I forget what you once gave me.'

'This conversation is shocking,' I whispered, pushing it to its limits. 'And what happens when…if… you get what you want? You revert to unkindness, do you? Thank you for the warning.'

'No. When I've got what I want, I shall want more. I shall never stop wanting more.'

'How do you know that?'

'How do I know, woman? Do you need to ask? We—'

'Shh! No, don't say it. I *don't* need to ask. Nor do I need to ask you about charity, or compassion, or pity. Clearly you don't deal in those, either.'

'If we're talking about our mutual friend again,

charity she gets from her father by the cartload, compassion is for women to give, and pity she'd not thank
you for. Or me. I know what she needs, and she's
looking in the wrong direction for it. I offered to help,
just now.'

'Yes, by stepping on her pride, before her friends. By
being facetious at my expense. That was not well done,
my lord,' I said, angrily. 'She was hurt by it. You understand little of women's needs, in spite of what you say.'

His reply came after a long silence during which he
watched my anger simmer and my eyes avoid his. 'I
understand your needs,' he said, softly. 'But I was taken
once before in a direction I didn't want to go, and I'll
be damned if I'll do it again. Yes, I have grown cynical,
and perhaps unkind too. And I could have taken her at
any time these last six years, Miss Follet, and landed
myself high and dry for my kindness. For that's all it
would've been.'

'I didn't mean that sort of kindness,' I said. 'And what
do you mean about a direction you didn't want to go?'

'Remind me to tell you one day. It's a long story.'

I knew that it concerned me, but I would probe no
further. 'I think,' I said, 'that we are talking about two
different things. A woman's view of kindness has other
connotations. Men calculate the cost beforehand.
Women calculate afterwards, if at all.'

'By which time it's usually too late.'

'Yes. That's the nature of it.'

The strains of a gavotte from the ballroom signalled
the end of the interval and our eyes held, in remembrance of another time when we had lost ourselves in
our own and each other's needs as if differences did not

exist. He had become hardened, unsympathetic, and I had grown wary and resentful, and now we needed to find a way of moving on without causing more pain.

'Dance with me,' he whispered.

My eyes must have reflected my doubts, but he did not accept my refusal. Standing abruptly, he held out a hand and raised me to my feet, leading me like a sleep-walker into the ballroom where we joined the end of the line, moving into the steps as we went, turning, parting, closing, balancing.

If there were stares of disapproval, neither of us noticed, only the slow and stately steps that moved us apart and together again, our bodies and hands just touching, like those six years condensed into six minutes. His eyes were brazen with desire, and mine were speaking of I know not what, except too much of my feelings. He was a superb dancer, bending and graceful, concentrating totally on his partner as if she were the only one, while other dancers glanced through their eyelashes and turned pinkish after being held by him. I knew then that I was losing control, that I was showing him what was in my secret heart because, with his outspoken talk of wanting me, he had found a way in.

The slow seductive ritual ended and, after that, we seemed to be marking time until we could catch a mutual signal to end the charade and go home. We talked again with friends, we drank more punch and ate more apple pie and cream, we laughed at poor jokes and came together again with Medworth and his fecund wife, and the desire to be like her in that one respect burgeoned within me again, as I believe it had with

Veronique too. Inside me, I quivered and sobbed with the effort of constraint while outwardly I displayed the ice-cool front that deceived everyone. Everyone, I think, except him.

Finally, when my almost frantic glance connected with his lazy blink, he made our excuses, found my cloak and his hat, and carried me over the muddy cobbles to my home, ignoring the smiles and stares of those who passed by. His taciturn silence warned me of what was on his mind, but it was on mine too, and past the stage of discussion.

'Lock the door and go to bed,' I told the astonished footman.

'Yes, ma'am.'

Thinking I would be late, I had told Debbie not to wait up, but she had left a single candle burning in my room where chocolate-brown shadows wrapped us in a blanket as dark as the lust that spilled over, even before we had pressed the door closed with our bodies, our mouths and hands already seeking. The room was warmed by a low fire, but neither of us noticed it in the heat of our desire, in the relief of being alone with our craving where no polite preliminaries were expected.

I have no notion how long before we paused, but by then his hands were slipping softly over my gown, his mouth lifting from my bare shoulder to whisper commands against my face, and I knew by his tone not to expect the same restraint this time from one who had waited over-long for what he wanted. I would not plead for either gentleness or consideration after my own enforced celibacy, for I was no inexperienced girl with unrealistic dreams of tenderly sighing lovers. The desires of my heart owed nothing to all that.

My expectations were not far wrong.

'Take it off,' he growled.

'Help me.' I was breathless, trembling.

'Where...how?'

'At the back. Hooks and eyes. And a tape inside.'

Turning me round, he snapped the fastenings apart like the rattle of a drum, sliding it off my shoulders and over my feet, flinging aside my work of one week while shaking off his own tailcoat to keep it company. I have never in my life seen a man remove his own tailcoat so quickly.

I stood with my palms pressed to my breasts, a natural reaction, in the circumstances. But he took my wrists and slowly eased them apart, holding them wide against the door panel, and I could not help but turn my head aside as he leaned away to scrutinise my body, as a sculptor would. My eyes closed, and his lips awakened my breasts to his warm hungry wanderings until they closed over the nipples, engorging them, forcing a cry from deep in my throat.

'Untie my cravat,' he whispered.

'Let me go, then.'

His hands needed that excuse to explore my waist and hips, caressing while I struggled blindly with the knot at his throat. Eventually, my fumblings produced an end, which he pulled, throwing the long thing on to the growing heap with a laugh before taking my mouth in a kiss that made me reel, reminding me again of his words earlier that evening, uncompromising, almost vengeful. 'Look at me, Helene,' he whispered to my closed eyes.

High up on the chest the candle flame wavered beside us, illuminating his face like the setting sun on coastal rocks, deep shadows and rugged surfaces sloping to granite throat and shoulders. His eyes were more intense than ever I'd seen them, but when had he ever allowed me to see what he was thinking, until now?

'Don't hate me for this, as you did before,' he said. 'You were willing then, and you are willing now. But don't reward me with your hate.'

'I don't hate you,' I replied, taking his face between my hands. 'I'm being given the choice, this time. That's all I ask, to be given the right to choose. This night, I've chosen to take whatever you have to give, kindly or not, and to give as much in return. I shall not hate you for that.'

'Then that's all I dare hope for, sweetheart,' he said, blending the last word seamlessly into a searing kiss that sent me spinning into another kind of darkness. I felt myself being carried and laid upon the cool sheets of my bed where the long curtains blocked out the wavering light, but not the sight of a broad torso being revealed, like the muscle-bound marble of a Greek god. He was more perfect than my imagination had drawn him, more gracefully vigorous in movement, his bared legs more robust, his back rippling with manly strength, his deep chest just as my fingers remembered it, wide and downy in the centre. Half-intoxicated, I watched him blow out the candle flame, heard his soft movements, felt the mattress dip and then the wonderful soft warmth of him, setting me on fire with his first touch.

Somewhere at the back of my mind, I wondered if

he might intentionally be recreating the sightless sound-less anonymity of that first time when our senses had blended on another level. On that occasion, I recalled, I had tried to fight him off, though not with half the effort I might have done. Then, he had gentled me and led me, half-swooning, into hours of loving that had ebbed and flowed on a tide of sensations, dazzling and seducing me with skilful wooing. He had been pas-sionate then, but I had known nothing of his reasons except, perhaps, as a solace for my unhappiness. I learnt that it was not the case.

This time, knowing him just a little better, knowing myself even more, my desire for him had grown so great that I was ready to close my mind and to respond without the restraints of reason or preference. Even un-gentleness, I felt, would be preferable to the last four years of emptiness.

His hand swept over me from throat to groin and my body responded like a wild thing, uncontrolled, fiercely demanding the attention it had lacked, arching into him to know the touch of his skin upon every surface. My lips opened upon his face to feel with my teeth and tongue, to fill all my senses with his taste and scent. My fingers raked deep into his hair, letting the thick silk slip through them like water, and my thighs yearned and opened for him as his kisses reached my throat.

He made me wait, holding my pestering hands away with a deep laugh. 'Not yet, my beauty. Not yet,' he whispered. Tracking downwards, he nudged and licked, knowing that I would soften and wait, though I doubt he knew how his leisurely suckling would make me weep, and beg him to take me. He changed to the other breast, teasing the deserted one with tenderly milking fingers. But I could bear it no longer, letting out the wail held too long in my lungs. 'Burl…please!'

As if he'd been waiting only to hear me call his name, he placed an arm beneath my hips, holding me as he'd done that first time to feel the hard throbbing length of him before slipping wetly inside, dilating me with each slow and powerful thrust that changed my tears to panting sighs and moans of ecstasy. Then, I was neither Helen nor Helene, but the primitive spirit of womanhood, earth and growing things. My womb was greedy for him, inviting and fruitful. My hands caressed, urging on his teeming virility. He was everything I remembered. And more.

I think we had both expected…wanted…it to last longer, but we had failed to take into account the tensions of the evening and all that had gone before under cover of our animosity. Neither of us could delay the growing thunder that roared through our beautiful rhythm, and Burl's response owed something to that ungentleness I'd been prepared for which, when it came, brought quivers of delight from deep down in my roots.

'Sweetheart…hold on!' he gasped, thinking that I might protest.

My fingers dug into his back as he bent deeper into me, though I had not intended the damage to his skin to be as noticeable as it was, later. 'Yes,' I told him, 'yes…oh, yes! Go on!' Flying along with my body, my mind rode the storm, plunging and surfacing, clinging to the calm that followed, floating with him upon that delicious pulsing beat that always fades too soon.

Like babes, we slept in each other's arms, spooning

back to front with his hand between my breasts and his face in my loosened hair and a tangle of pearls. Hours later, I think, I woke to hear the wind howl and gust at the windows, to feel a warm body at my back just as it had been that first time. His hand was stroking my thigh, slipping down between them, fondling.

We might have recreated that original scene, but now we were strangers no more, our appetites renewed by sleep and no impediments of kinship to add guilt. He must have been awake some time for he was impatient, already pulling me roughly under him without preamble. I felt justified in making a sharp protest, feeling that some wooing would not come amiss at this stage, even from a lover hungry for consummation. So I bit the nearest part of him, which was his chin, making him rear back and give me a chance to roll away, squirming and flailing my arms, doing no damage whatever.

Following me across the bed, he swung his feet to the floor with a purposeful thud, swept me round by the legs to face him and placed himself between them, quite out of reach of my arms. Until then, I must admit it had not occurred to me that there were other ways of doing this, but he taught me something that night about how, if lovers are of the same mind, enjoyment can be taken how, when and where they will.

Naturally, I refused to make it easy for him at first, protesting that a February night calls for some form of covering if one is not to suffer from exposure. But that problem was soon solved and my protests curtailed, for it was the most exciting and unique experience that ended very suddenly in an explosion that left us both gasping and laughing. He pulled me upright, cradling and rocking me while he knelt between my knees with his head on my breast and my hair covering his face. 'My fierce beauty,' he whispered. 'I think I can just about handle you. Eh, lass? After a few battle scars.'

'Brute,' I murmured. 'Mannerless brute.'

His arms tightened, and I felt the deep chuckle within his chest.

But I was far from serious, for laughter was also new to me in this context. It had never been a laughing matter with his brother, a solemn, silent and usually hasty affair, more like, with politeness and reserve followed by instant sleep, no talk, no aftercare, no banter, compliments or approval. Now, in the space of one night, I had wept and laughed, retaliated with my own kind of manhandling, and experienced more joy and pleasure than in all those years as Linas's mistress.

Inevitably, in the langour that follows exhaustion, there was teasing mixed with the adulation; accusations from me of smugness, counter-accusations from him of impetuosity, then the half-expected mention of marriage which, he suggested, would tame me. Another bairn was what I needed, he said, yawning and pulling my hips closer to his.

We lay together, wrapped against the howling gale, me with my face beneath his chin. 'Is that what this is all about?' I said. 'Getting me with child again?'

'You are remarkably innocent, Miss Follet. What did you *think* this was all about? Not for our mutual enjoyment, surely?'

'You know what I mean. This night. Coercion, is it?'

'Don't spoil it, sweetheart.'

'All right. I agreed not to blame you. So three months from now I'll ask you again.'

'You won't need to. Three months from now you'll be my wife.'

'No, I won't.'

'Little goose. Go to sleep.'

I did not sleep immediately, as he did, but lay thinking how easy it had been for me to overturn all my intentions to keep him at a distance. Now, despite my impassioned contradiction, I knew that I was committed, that it was only a matter of time before I would be obliged to agree to his proposal, if one could call it that. The only card I had left to play concerned the timing, for I was sure that tonight's loving would be as potent as the last. Well, I would make the next few months spread out until I could keep him guessing no longer, having little reason to agree with him there and then.

Other concerns plagued me too. Although I realised that women married knowing much less about their husbands than I did about Burl Winterson, it was what I *knew* about him that made me think I was heading for disaster. The evening's talk about the way he limited his kindnesses should not have surprised me as it did, for until recently his uninterest in me had been a prime example of it, as had his visit to me that one night. He had wanted something, and got it. Now, he wanted Jamie and me to make an instant family, hence the sudden revival of interest of which this lovemaking was a part. He had admitted it without batting an eyelid. Was I supposed to feel flattered? Gratified? Piqued? Insulted? Would it all grind to a halt when it was accomplished, or would he keep on wanting more of me, as he'd said? It was a gamble, but was I really in a position to care as much as I did? If I had cared less for him, perhaps I would have reached a decision more easily.

The following morning I was woken before Jamie's habitual assault by a large figure in dark silhouette whose arms were braced on each side of me, his voice softly whispering. 'I don't want to leave you without a word, sweetheart, as I did before,' he was saying. 'Wake up and listen.' He was dressed and ready to go.

'Mmm? Yes?'

'I must go. My parents are at Abbots Mere and I want to be there before they're up. I'll send a carriage for you and Jamie.'

'No need. I can drive the phaeton.'

'It's blowing a gale. You can't ride out in this.'

'But I must go to Prue's first.'

'On a Sunday? Why?'

'She's in a fix. Both her parents have the dysentry.'

'For pity's sake, lass, keep away, then. It's contagious.'

'I must go. I shall not get too close.'

'Send one of the servants. Please. Think of Jamie.'

'Yes, if you insist. I'll send someone else.'

'Promise?'

'I promise. I'll be ready by mid-day.'

'Good. Wrap up warm. D'ye want to stay overnight?'

I smiled. 'Thank you, but no. I must be at the shop early tomorrow.'

His nod was curt, but understanding. For a short separation, his kiss was long and deep, and I felt my body stirring even before it was awake.

Moments later, Jamie came to join me, as usual. 'The bed's nice and warm, Mama,' he said, snuggling up. 'Did Debbie sleep with you?'

'No, darling. We're going to have lunch with Uncle Burl today.'

'Ooh, goodie! I wish Uncaburl was my papa. Shall we ask him?'

'No, darling. Not yet. It's too soon after Papa went, you see. We shall have to be content to have Uncle Burl as your guardian for a while. That's almost the same thing.'

'But I want to live with Uncaburl, Mama, like Claude lives with his papa. Claude's friend says I haven't got a papa.'

I could feel the little fellow's hurt and bewilderment. 'I'm sure Claude's friend didn't mean to be so ill mannered,' I whispered, stroking his dark curls. 'Perhaps he doesn't understand.'

'He does, Mama. He said I never had one. He said you were not Papa's wife. You were, weren't you, Mama?'

'It's no business of Claude's friend whether people's parents are married or not. If he mentions it again, I shall speak to Uncle Medworth.'

'Uncamedith knows.'

'He knows? About the rudeness? What did he say?'

'Said he had more 'portant things to think about.'

Chapter Ten

Much as I disliked sending a deputy to see how Prue and her parents were, I felt obliged to keep my promise, if only to avoid exposing Jamie to the infection, even at second hand. Debbie had no fear of catching anything, she assured me, though I insisted she tie a scarf over her face before she left the house. Having delivered the basket of food, she was back home inside the hour with the news that the old couple were still very poorly, the various potions having made little difference. Their growing weakness was a cause of serious worry, but Prue, she said, was managing well enough.

I had agreed to be ready for Winterson's coach by noon, and it was my desire not to disappoint Jamie or to keep the coachman and his horses waiting in the pelting rain that prevented me from listening to my conscience. Prue needed a doctor, yet I told myself that one more day might see an improvement. So it was with the firm intention of sending my own Dr Biggs round there first thing in the morning that I set off with Jamie and

Mrs Goode for Sunday lunch at Abbots Mere along roads that were, in parts, axle deep in water.

Jamie had no trouble pretending he was sailing a boat through lanes and past cottages while the rain clattered incessantly upon the roof of the coach and bounced off the horses' backs. Branches had been brought down during the night, and every dip of the land was reduced to a lake where seagulls wheeled, reflecting the leaden sky and rippled by the wind.

By contrast, Abbots Mere was a warm haven lit by oil lamps, candelabra and blazing log fires, with the tantalising aroma of roast beef and Yorkshire puddings reaching the stone-paved hall. The sound of laughter reached us too, and I felt the familiar shiver of apprehension before going in to meet Winterson's parents for the first time since the funeral.

I had taken care to dress appropriately in a charcoal-grey silk velvet sleeveless pelisse over a long-sleeved gown of silver grey sarsenet. No jewellery. No ornament. My hair tied up with black satin ribbons that hung down my back. Nothing to show how I felt after a night spent in the arms of their eldest son so soon after his twin's death. Nothing to betray the hypocrisy, either.

'You look beautiful, Miss Follet,' Winterson whispered. 'Are you well?'

I knew what he was asking. 'Yes, my lord, I thank you,' I replied demurely. 'I am indeed well, if a little fatigued.'

'Really?' he said. His eyes laughed into mine. 'Oh, dear. Unaccustomed exercise, is it?'

'Shh!' I said. 'Jamie dear, here's Claude come to find you.'

I followed on behind, using Jamie to interrupt the

conversation quite naturally before his grandparents turned to greet me. Not that they were in any sense an awe-inspiring couple. Far from it. But there had once been a reserve in their manner towards me, as mistress instead of wife, that had only recently been replaced by a genuine warmth and, I think, with some admiration and gratitude for my dedication to their son. According to him, they had been more than relieved by the appearance of a grandson, which had perhaps worked in my favour too, and now they had smiles for me as well as for Jamie.

Lord and Lady Stillingfleete were a handsome couple. He had been a major in a top cavalry regiment when he'd married Lady Frances Milton, the celebrated beauty. She was still lovely, stately, slender and white-haired with particularly brilliant dark brown eyes able to convey in one glance the precise degree of her approval. Although I had now no need to doubt that, I could not help but wonder if those discerning eyes would see behind my Sunday face to the previous night's lust that had spilled out with an unstoppable energy, or the tell-tale signs that might still linger upon me, somewhere. I hitched up the fur-trimmed collar of my pelisse to reach my earlobes, just in case, then wished I had not for, on rising from my curtsy, I saw Lord Stillingfleete's eyes leave his son's and return to mine. 'Miss Follet, come to the fire, m'dear,' he said, and I knew that he had interpreted the gesture correctly.

Heaven knows, I'd had plenty of practice, but I would never have made a first-rate actress. I did not go to the fire, but to Medworth and Cynthia, hiding my blush in their greeting and the duet of chatter about the perilous journey from Osbaldwick, all the while aware of how the grandparents watched my Jamie like a pair of eagles, linking his dark good looks to their eldest son, as anyone must. They had not seen him for several months, and he had changed with each passing week. Their expressions, shifting from child to father, were easy to read, and the realisation seemed to catch them unawares in a moment of rigidity. Immediately, they recovered themselves, transferring some of their attention to little Claude, who was attempting to ride one of Winterson's unwilling wolfhounds. To my mind, the child needed a firmer hand than Medworth's, who appeared to find something to applaud in every silly thing his son did.

Winterson lifted him off and dismissed the hounds from the room with one word, for Claude was over-weight as well as over-indulged. Fortunately, the youngest one had been left at home, or we might have been treated to more bids for attention.

In some ways, the Sunday lunch was an ordeal that demanded a greater-than-usual effort on my part. Winterson's family were never difficult to converse with, but I found myself having to work hard to keep my thoughts on track when my eyes were drawn like magnets to the one for whom I hungered much more than roast beef or pheasant, salmon or winter veg-etables. Having given no thought to how I might feel if that solo night should ever be repeated—for I had not believed it would—I was confused by the meld of emotions and by the way my body had not recovered from the hours of arousal after so many years of neglect. No matter how I tried to hold them back, the memories of his magnificent body lying warm upon me blanked out the middles and ends of so many of my sentences that it began to look as if I might be sickening for something. More than once did Winterson come to my rescue, smiling at my dreaminess and reading my eyes like a book.

Unusually, the children were allowed to eat at the table with the adults, a treat I approved of on occasions like this. It was gratifying to see how well my Jamie behaved compared to Claude, who messed about with his food and kept his mama so completely occupied with him that she was scarce able to eat her own lunch. Medworth seemed totally unaware of any problem.

Apple pie, creamy rice pudding with nutmeg, and spotted dick with custard was the perfect conclusion to a family meal on a day of such darkness and unrelenting rain, though we sat in the rosy glow of a fire that filled the room with the sweet aroma of burning apple boughs.

'I had the men clearing the ditches when you were last here,' I heard Winterson telling his father, 'but the snow, then the floods have filled them up completely. Some of the fields will take months to recover.'

'Then you may have to reclaim more of your wasteland.'

The two men took their glasses of port to the long window that overlooked the flooded terrace. Beyond, the swollen river had lost its banks, rushing and seething like a brown menacing monster across the field.

'I've already decided on that,' Winterson replied. 'Do you care to come and see what I intend? The plans are in the study.'

'Aye. I'll come and tell ye where ye're going wrong, lad.'

They smiled and sauntered off, leaving Cynthia to sink deeply into one of the leather sofas and Lady Stillingfleete to do the same in a high-backed chair, already halfway to a siesta. True to her name, Mrs Goode had taken the boys into a window-seat where they lounged against her knees and the book she was reading to them, and I was left with Medworth, who was already fretting about being home in time for his evening service. Pulling out a wad of papers from his coat pocket, he noisily smoothed them out upon the table, pulled a candlestick forwards, and began to read his sermon to himself.

I moved away, relieved by the suspension of polite exchanges across the dining table that had covered every topic from food to floods, fashion to farming. I was not myself, I realised, nor would I ever be the same again. Riddled by conflicts, my life was changing like the landscape by forces outside my control, and I would have to heed my intractable head or my vanquished heart, neither of which was reliable.

I had not intended to follow the one who monopolised my thoughts, and certainly not to snoop, but the sound of his voice and the need to be near him drew me along the panelled passageway towards the oak-lined study where he daily met his steward and bailiff to plan the estate work. The door remained open wide enough for me to see a table covered with maps, and over by the window stood Winterson and his father with their backs to me, hands clasped behind, their shoulders almost touching.

Lord Stillingfleete was speaking with some emphasis. 'You'll have to marry her, Burl. Damn it lad, I'm not blaming you one bit. She's a high-flyer, but it's as plain as a pikestaff and it'll be even plainer as Jamie gets older. *Then* you'll have some explaining to do. Better to put things on a legal footing now than hang about for more years. What's stopping you?'

'*She* is, Father. She's bitter about what happened. Linas gave her a raw deal, you know, and it's going to take me some time to win her trust.'

'Well, I cannot insist on knowing what you and he agreed, for it's none of my business, but time is what you don't have, Burl. Do something about it before the gossip starts. If your mother and I can see it, so will others.'

'I am doing, sir. But she'll come to me in her own time, not mine.'

'She's in love with you. We can see that, too.'

'Yes, I believe she may be.'

'Isn't that enough? The lad needs a father more than a guardian.'

'Yes, sir. She knows that, too. Give me time to…'

They turned away and I had to step well back into the passage and retrace my steps while my guilty heart thudded an angry rhythm of its own. *She's in love with you… Isn't that enough?… You'll have to marry her, Burl.* Standing with my back pressed against the panelling, I could feel each heartbeat rebelling against everything the two of them had said. They had no conception of how things stood with me, nor how many shades of grey came between their black and white. To his father, the matter was simple: marry her before people start to talk. I could almost taste the perversity that rose into my mouth, ready to shout my objections. Well, at least he appeared to understand that I would marry in my own good time and in no one else's.

Making a slight sound, a cough and an exclamation about the chill, I once again approached the open door, tapped, and entered. With shoulders hunched, they were braced over the maps on the table, looking up in surprise and with some questioning in their eyes. Women rarely visited men's offices. 'May I come in?' I said. 'I don't mean to disturb you.'

'Of course,' Winterson said, smiling. 'I'm showing my father where the worst of the floods are.' With one finger he drew an oval around the river and its surrounding plains. 'It'll be weeks before we can plough these fields again, and we've lost acres of grazing before the land will recover.'

I peered at the areas shaded with grey, land belonging to the Abbots Mere estate, other fields shaded a darker grey presumably belonging to Lord Slatterly which Winterson had the use of. A large area to the east was enclosed by a wide red line. 'And that?' I said, knowing the answer.

Lord Stillingfleete replied. 'Foss Beck. Been wasted ever since I can remember. No one goes there. It's time it was looked at, Burl.'

'Yes, as soon as I can reach it I'll go there. We can't afford to hang on to unused land any longer. I believe there are some ruined buildings on it.'

'They'll have to be demolished. You could use the stone for barns.'

The shock in my voice made them both look sharply at me. 'You...you *own* this place...Foss Beck?' I said.

'It's been part of the estate for centuries. It was a thriving village once with its own manor house and a priest for the church, but I believe it was hit by the plague more than once, so that was the end of it. There must be quite a few fields worth reclaiming.'

'But surely, if it's deserted, it must have reverted to common land where anyone can—'

'Not anyone, Miss Follet,' said Lord Stillingfleete. 'That might have been the case if it had once been legal common, but it never was. Over the years we've turned a blind eye to some land that was less profitable, or inaccessible, but at times like this we have to work them and make them yield again. New methods, you know. Fertilisers, crop rotation, new hardier strains of wheat. And new sheep breeds, too. Burl needs to get his hands on it, especially after a winter like this.'

I was staggered. Numbed with shock. My family had lived there in hiding since I was fourteen, expecting to renovate the buildings, dragging every ounce of goodness from their small crofts, eking out an existence. Where would they live if the old house was levelled, their garden ploughed over? Ought I to expose them now, before it was too late? Should I reveal their reason for living there, and who it *really* was who had borne the Stillingfleete heir, a criminal's daughter whose relatives lived illegally on the Abbots Mere estate, her father buried there?

But the two of them bent to the map again, the query dealt with, and I could say nothing of my dread as a sickness filled my lungs, blotting out each panic-stricken response as it arose. I would have to go and tell my family immediately. They must be warned of what was about to happen to their livelihood.

Though the rain had not abated all day, we were back home on Blake Street before darkness fell completely. Winterson had found the chance to speak a few words with me alone and had demanded to know what ailed me. Was it fatigue, or something more?

No more than that, I lied, wondering how convinced he was. It seemed to satisfy him. He would be in town in a day or two, he said, and I think when he kissed me that he expected some pleasurable response rather than the vague nod that was all I could manage. Perhaps if his parents had not been staying, I might have told him what a catastrophe he was planning but, as it was, his fierce kiss was accompanied by the distant howls and screams of his over-tired nephew, reminding me of my promise to take Jamie to his birthday party on Tuesday. Straight away, I saw that I could make that the day for my visit to Foss Beck while Jamie and his nurse were at Osbaldwick, which was fortunately in the same direction.

As Medworth's carriage moved off, I made sure that Winterson knew about the invitation. 'See you on Tuesday,' I called, waving.

It took what remained of my dwindling resolution not to change my mind about staying at Abbots Mere overnight when I could think of little else but wanting him. But to have done so would have convinced his parents that Winterson had already taken Linas's place as my lover, which was certainly not the cut-and-dried case it would appear to be, especially when I'd told him only recently that I would not allow that to happen. Yet it had not taken him long to find a way round my objections, and the last thing I wanted was for Lord and Lady Stillingfleete to label me as fickle.

For his father to recommend to Winterson that he

should marry me, a mere milliner and mantua-maker, was in itself remarkable when the pedigree of future daughters-in-law must be well documented and above reproach. Nothing so lofty could be said of mine, unfortunately, although Jamie's appearance had certainly helped in that respect. For one thing, he was the Stillingfleete heir and, for another, he was unmistakably Burl's offspring rather than Linas's, a fact that was unlikely to be admitted, but which could certainly be ignored, once his parents married. And for that event, I felt no immediate obligation to comply, after the way I'd been used by them.

I slept alone, and fitfully, plotting the course of the previous night's lovemaking while posing a hundred questions that could be answered in multiples, some of them concerning the fate of my family, who deserved better than poverty and obscurity and, on my part, denial.

My first duty next morning was to visit Prue with Debbie, carrying armfuls of clean bedding and food. But it was a doctor they needed most, and I called upon my own man, Dr Biggs, bidding him return with me, which he did, shaking his bald head sadly at the emaciated old couple too weak to move, and at the mess caused by the flood water in which they were obliged to remain. With all the stubborn pride of old folk, they refused even to consider accepting my offer to have them at Blake Street. Between us, we did what we could for them, yet I felt I was paying the good doctor for little else but a potion to ease their pain and a prognosis of only a few days more.

In Prue's absence, the shop continued to function just as if she was there, for now we had gained a very presentable young apprentice who had taken on many of the daily chores that used up precious time. She was a neat and willing girl, glad of the chance to join our company and so, with Betty as deputy manager and myself to keep an eye on our list of patrons, new designs and accounts, we were able to fulfil all our orders to everyone's satisfaction.

That evening I called at Stonegate to order the phaeton and pair to be brought round to Blake Street early next morning, come rain or shine. I also bade Goody prepare for an overnight stay at Medworth's house, since I would be unable to collect Jamie from the party before dark. What a nuisance those short days were. But looking back on those decisions, I can see how unclearly I was thinking, how desperately I was trying to juggle my responsibilities, and how spineless I was being by not explaining to my child that I was going to see Nana Damzell yet again, without him. I even chose not to tell him that he'd be staying overnight at Osbaldwick, sure that, between them, Cynthia and Goody would fill the gap left my by absence. Yes, I admit it; I was afraid of provoking another tantrum. We have a saying, in Yorkshire: 'What the eye doesn't see, the heart won't grieve over.' Applied to Jamie, it was patently nonsensical.

Cynthia's colourful description of the floods between York and the little village of Osbaldwick was not, for once, as exaggerated as I had thought. Although not of the high-perch design, the body of my phaeton was set well above the large back wheels and yet, even at that elevation, the water came within an inch of the floorboard, the horses wading belly-high through flooded tracks. Unusually, Goody was heard to comment that, if dear Mr Monkton could have bestirred himself to send his carriage for us, we would not be subjected to such danger, all for a birthday party. Personally, I was relieved he had not, since I was carrying hidden supplies for my family at Foss Beck.

As soon as I could politely excuse myself from those gathered for the party, and with Jamie too occupied to notice, I went on my way eastwards out of Osbaldwick. Cynthia, so easy going, assured me that he and Mrs Goode were welcome to stay until I could collect them some time before dark the next day. However, not having ventured in this direction since the snowfall, I had not appreciated how serious the flooding was, kicking myself for not paying closer attention to Winterson's maps. For mile after mile I drove the phaeton through the flooded lanes, even the higher ground being thick with mud and rubble, the ruts made by other wheels being too deep to get out of.

I became increasingly concerned, for the skies darkened menacingly as rain began to sleet across the open moors, forcing the hardy sheep to huddle together for shelter. From rocky outcrops, water poured in angry brown torrents into deep gulleys, then across the track, the underground culverts being unable to cope with the volume. Then, and only then, did it occur to me that the usual dainty trickle of water at Foss Beck into the trout stream below would certainly now be as swollen as these.

I was right. The whole mercy mission was a complete disaster, for when at last I managed to reach

Foss Beck Manor, the house was up to its second storey in water, completely cut off from the world, and from me. My shouts to the boys had to be conducted across a new lake while I dripped with rain, the phaeton leaning into the mud, the horses exhausted. The news from my brothers was that Pierre had left them, gone who knew where, after angry words. My instructions to make Mother and her companions ready to leave as soon as I could get a boat to them were greeted not with thanks, but with caution, my brothers unable to agree with me that she would go anywhere, even with me. At that, I grew angry and yelled at them to insist, telling them that I would be back the next day, though heaven only knew how I'd get back home that night in those dreadful conditions.

My journey home was no better, for the dark was falling and the horses were unable to find the road in the deepening water and, when the phaeton jolted to a standstill with a lurch to one side, I knew that to walk the rest of the way was my only option. Shivering with the cold, I began to unbuckle the horses from the phaeton. Then, through the howl of the wind, I heard a shout that made them whinny in reply, my own reaction being both joyful and concerned at some gruff traveller's annoyance that my phaeton was in the way. No one would want to turn back or wrestle with a broken vehicle, having got so far. Paralysed with cold and wet, I stood with my ankles locked into the mud and my shoes buried somewhere behind me, my teeth chattering like castanets.

Flickering lamps appeared, a coach-width apart. Two

large horses loomed up with a dumpling-shaped coachman above them, with doors beyond that opened on both sides discharging men who called instructions and waded towards the horses as if this was all in a day's work. One tall familiar figure strode forwards out of the grey wetness, leaving a wake to wash against the banks. His arms reached out, ready to catch me. 'Hell!' he called.

Hell, or Helene? I wondered. Either would do.

'I'm s-s-stuck,' I gasped, flapping my arms to keep my balance.

Grim and gloriously handsome, with rain dripping from his hair and face, he caught my wrist, bending towards me and ducking his head under my captured arm. 'Right,' he said. 'I want you to lie over my shoulder…go on…bend…that's it. I'm going to pull.'

I thought he meant the arm held hard upon his chest, but then I felt my feet move through the mud and my body hoisted high into the wind where I hung over the swirling water like a sea bird, a very limp and emotional sea bird that mewed with relief to be wrapped untidily around the neck of its beloved. 'Burl,' I sobbed into his broad back, 'you came for me.'

'Yes, and the sooner you stop galloping over here like an angel of mercy, woman, the better it will be for all of us. How the devil did you think you were going to reach Foss Beck when it's under water?'

'You knew?'

'Of *course* I knew,' he snapped. 'It's my property and it's my business to know who lives on it. I'm not as nicked in the nob as all that. There.' He lowered me carefully to the ground. 'Stand there and wait.' Pulling a rug from the carriage, he shook it out and parcelled me securely inside it, lifting me up on to the seat where the hollow patter of rain made a welcome break from the squall outside.

'I don't think you're nicked in the nob,' I muttered.

'Then you should try thinking with your head instead of your heart, little fool, or I might be performing this wild goose chase once a month.' The door closed, and I was too exhausted to be affronted, to answer back, or even to think of a snappy reply.

As I saw it, I'd had little choice when to go, or by what method. As for the angel-of-mercy bit, that was what a man *would* think, especially one who sees a kindness as a chance to bargain. I lay there helplessly with my head on the velvet armrest, shivering and dizzy, half-listening to the comings and goings outside, the thud and splash of hooves as the horses were released.

He grunted and closed the door, then quickly opened it again to cover my muddy feet with the rug. 'Leave the phaeton,' I heard him call. 'We'll come back for it tomorrow. Come on, lads. Let's be away. Jump on.'

My deliverance was made all the sweeter when he climbed in, lifting me into his arms to hold me across him with my legs along the seat and my head resting against his wet greatcoat. 'I can do nothing about the wet,' he murmured, 'but I'm sorely tempted to beat the hell out of you, one day.'

'Please don't,' I whispered.

I felt his warm lips touch my forehead, then the softness of his handkerchief wiping my eyes and cheeks, the tightening of his arms to snuggle me closer to him. Rocked and lurched, my aching limbs succumbed to the warm dampness of his embrace while my mind wrestled weakly with an ever-growing mountain of problems. 'I have to collect Jamie from Osbaldwick,' I mumbled. Already my plans had become confused.

'No, you don't. Jamie is at home with Mrs Goode.'

'Home? How did he get there? Did Medworth...?'

'No. I took them. Then I set out to look for you. Don't you ever tell anyone where you're going these days?'

'I told cook we wouldn't be home for dinner.'

'Extremely thoughtful of you. But that's not quite the same, is it?'

'It's the best I could do. I didn't know you'd be at Claude's party too.'

'Just as well I was,' he muttered under his breath.

But I heard, and sensed that there was more to this than a kindly lift home for my son and his nurse. 'Why?' I said, raising my head. 'What's happened?'

'Nothing,' he said, pressing me back onto his chest. 'Jamie is perfectly safe at home, and probably fast asleep. As I suspect you would like to be.'

I sighed. If Jamie was safe, that was all I could ask for. I knew, however, that once I was home and dry, I would have some explaining to do, for this amazing man was not only Jamie's guardian, but mine too, and he was taking the role very seriously indeed.

I have no recollection how long it took us to reach York, though I realised it could not have been as long as the outward journey. The rain had stopped by the time we reached Blake Street, and it was the regular rumble of cobblestones under the wheels and the hard clop-clop of hooves that woke me to the clammy warmth of my situation. Never had I been so thankful to be home, to be ministered to by my maid and house-keeper, to bathe in a hot tub, dress in warm robes and then to partake of soup and rolls by the fireside with my feet tucked into my best fur muff, mostly for effect. My hair was left loose to dry, the rainwater having done it no harm and probably some good.

My Jamie was indeed sleeping soundly and, on careful inspection, showed no signs of injury. Neverthe-less, as I sipped at my soup, I questioned Mrs Goode about their few hours at Osbaldwick, expecting to get no less than the full unadulterated female version rather than Winterson's, which would probably not suit me half so well. He had promised to return in a couple of hours. There was no time to lose.

'No, ma'am,' said Mrs Goode as soon as the door closed behind the footman, 'it was not exactly a tantrum, but Jamie has a little temper, as we both know, and he's taken rather a strong dislike to Claude's little friend.'

I groaned. 'Oh, not the *friend* again. What was it this time?'

'The same insult as before, ma'am. Only this time, Jamie was not in a mood to ignore it. They were all chasing the ducks over by the mill-pond, with Mr Monkton and a friend of his standing nearby, talking. Then, before we knew it, the two boys were wrestling and pummelling, rolling straight into the pond where the reeds are. It's flooded, you see. Personally, I would not have let them anywhere near it.'

My soup spoon hit the dish with a clatter. 'Oh, no!'

'I'm afraid so, ma'am. Mr Monkton and his friend didn't even notice what was happening. But Lord Winterson had just arrived in his carriage. I think he was expecting to see you and take you back home,' she added, coyly. 'His three hounds raced across the field to the mill-pond and took a flying leap into the water. It was Jamie's shouts they heard, I think.'

I whispered from between my fingers. 'What then? Didn't Mr Monkton see *anything*?'

'No, ma'am. It was the wolfhounds the boys clung to. They're so strong. They pulled them to the edge, barking like mad, and Lord Winterson went running full tilt, and climbed down into the water and lifted them out. I was there by that time, and Mrs Monkton too. I'm to blame, ma'am. I ought to have been there with them.'

'No, my dear. Don't blame yourself. Not when other adults were there, on the spot. Was he very upset?'

'Jamie? Only a little, and not hurt. The other child was very frightened. Jamie told us in the coach what it was all about.'

'Ah. So Lord Winterson knows?'

'I felt it best to tell him of the first incident too. I hope I did the right thing, ma'am. Jamie was getting a bit mixed up about his parentage. Oh, dear,' she said, turning a rosy pink. 'I *do* beg your pardon.'

'No need, dear Goody,' I said. 'It is confusing for a three-year-old, particularly when someone comes along to challenge what he's been told. Did Mrs Monkton suggest you should go home?'

'Oh, no. It was Lord Winterson who said we should go. I think he was rather annoyed with Mr Monkton, and no one protested when we left, not even Jamie. And

I certainly didn't. What a chaotic household, begging your pardon again, ma'am.'

'So did Jamie's guardian take him to task for brawling in company?'

Goody's tight-lipped disapproval changed to a fleeting smile before her sober reply. 'Er...no, not exactly,' she said. 'But he *did* promise to teach him how to swim, in summer. And how to hit with the fist closed instead of open, tucking the thumb down.'

'How to *hit* someone? God's truth! What kind of a guardian is *that*?'

From the doorway, a deep voice replied. 'A useful one, I hope. I did knock, but you didn't hear.'

'Do come in, my lord,' I said. 'We were discussing the day's events.'

'Which is what I hope to do too.'

Mrs Goode rose and bobbed a curtsy. 'Good evening, my lord. Will you please excuse me, ma'am? I have things to attend to upstairs.'

'Indeed I will. Thank you for all your help. Goodnight.'

Typically discreet, she left us with a smile. Even though Winterson knew she was totally in my confidence, he closed the door behind her without suggesting that she might stay. 'Well,' he said. 'Two half-drowned Folletts in one day. That must be some kind of record. Do I get a medal?'

Chapter Eleven

The way he looked at me across the cosy parlour, arrogance spiced with a trace of uncertainty, I would have given him anything he asked. But he had told me to think with my head instead of my heart, and my reply was guarded, taking into account his request for rewards after a kindness done. 'Not a medal, but perhaps an hour of my company, my lord, for what it's worth. Will that do from one half-drowned Follet? That, and my thanks for the rescue? I've heard about the mill-pond incident, and I'm most truly grateful to you.'

With arms folded, he lounged against the door looking down his straight nose at me with eyes that roamed, halted, and roamed again, sparing me no little confusion. '*How* grateful?' he said.

Yes, anything he asked. 'Oh, dear,' I said, looking down at my hands. 'Are we to talk of rewards so soon? Did you ask Jamie, too?'

'No, he's too young. I prefer to ask his mother instead.'

My heart was misbehaving badly under his scrutiny.

He'd been to Stonegate to change his clothes and to
clean up, for he was almost as soaked as I. Now, he was
perfectly dressed in a mid-grey tailcoat of smooth
superfine with an M-cut collar over a waistcoat, just
showing, of silver cut-velvet. It shone like pearls when
he moved. The broad shoulder upon which I'd been
hoisted only hours before was now unblemished by the
slightest wrinkle. His beautiful head appeared to be
supported by the white folds of his cravat, and the dark
hair showed ridges of dampness along finger-raked
waves. He was, in fact, heart-stoppingly desirable. He
was also in my room, alone with me, and expecting
something.

'His mother,' I said, 'has been advised to use more
common sense. Perhaps you could help her with that.
Will you be seated, sir?'

'I hoped you'd ask me.'

'Forgive me. I've only just begun to thaw.'

He pushed himself off the door and came forwards,
settling himself into the wing-chair that Mrs Goode had
just vacated. 'So, if it's too soon to discuss rewards,
Miss Follet, may I ask how you managed to reach your
family at Foss Beck? Is your lady mother improving?'

'I didn't manage to see her. I didn't actually achieve
anything I'd set out to achieve.'

'Which was?'

'You must be able to guess, after I'd heard how you
intend to reclaim the site. If I'd known it was so badly
flooded, I'd have taken help with me.'

'So why d'ya think I'd drawn a red line round it
on the map?'

'Well, to mark it out for reclamation, I suppose.'

'Yes, when the floods subside. The red line enclosed the worst areas, to show my father which part is ear-marked for the greatest attention.'

'Attention? You spoke of demolition as if no one lived there. If you knew my family lived there, why did you pretend not to?'

'Because, Miss Follet, I prefer my father not to know. Would you rather I told him? If I'd thought you intended to race there like a mad March hare without first discussing the problem with me, I'd have told you to wait till it was safe.'

'Much good the delay would have done when they're going to have to leave for one reason or another. The place is in a terrible state, and they're running short of food and fuel, animals drowned, hens stuck up on the roof. I promised my brothers I'd bring help tomorrow, so I *have* to make another attempt. Somehow. How long have you known?'

'About your family? Since your visit in the snow. I made enquiries. I knew someone was at Foss Beck, because my bailiff told me. He and my steward keep a close eye on all the estate.'

'My brothers intended to rebuild parts of it. They love the place.'

'Using the money from contraband?'

'Yes. They've saved and been thrifty. They work hard, too.'

'And the cousin, Pierre Follet? Is he to be rescued too?'

'Pierre has gone, so my brothers tell me.'

'Aah! Has he indeed? Where? Back to France?'

'Why do you say that?'

'I assumed, that's all.'

'I don't know. I shall find out when I get them here.'

'Where…here? In York? You mean, in this house?'

'Yes, if you'll allow it. It'll be a bit of a squash, but they'll be safe and dry, and well fed.'

'Tch! Angel of mercy on the rampage again?'

'I don't need your gibes, my lord. They're my family. We don't do rewards and bargains; we simply help each other for love's sake. You've done the same for yours.'

'Quite right, sweetheart. And I was not mocking you. Your principles are admirable. You put me to shame.'

Even so, I believed he *was* mocking me, but this was no time to make an issue of it when I needed his help.

'Would you care to tell me about them before we meet?' he said, gently.

'I can do better than that. If you were to help me rescue them tomorrow when you send men to retrieve the phaeton, you could meet them sooner.'

His promptness took me by surprise. 'That can be done. I will arrange to have them brought here, if that is what you wish.'

'Thank you. That would help. The floods are actually working in your favour, it seems. They've brought your plans forwards, haven't they?'

'Yes, that's about the size of it.'

'And since you have a policy of never doing anything for nothing, I suppose you'll expect them to pay you to be rescued.'

'You will be familiar, Miss Follet, with the Yorkshire adage, "Never do owt for nowt. And if tha ever does owt for nowt, do it for thi sen." Yes, I expect there'll be some kind of price to pay. After all, this is my house.'

'What kind of price do you have in mind, my lord?'

'I'll think of something. Leave it to me.'

'Gladly. But I hope it will be something they can afford. Once their livelihood is gone, they'll have few means, except for their savings.'

His fingertips pressed together, making a tall steeple. 'Then it will have to be something *you* can afford, won't it?' he said, quietly.

Inevitably, we had strayed on to dangerous ground. In a house of this size, it would be quite impossible for us all to live together for long, the three bedrooms being taken up by myself, Mrs Goode and Jamie, with servants' quarters for my cook, housekeeper, maid and footman, chambermaid and kitchen maid. My mother would need a room to share with her two old faithfuls, the two boys to share another. I had no idea where or how they would all fit in, unless I converted my parlour into a bedroom. But where was I going to find beds for them all? Where would I put all the stuff they would bring? If only Winterson would offer them the use of Stonegate. I could not ask him, but I needed more than a rescue for them. I needed another house.

'I don't suppose…?' I began, hesitantly.

'Yes?'

'That there's any chance…well…that they could be…er…re-housed somewhere? The boys are strong. They'll have to start earning. Somehow. I don't expect my mother to see the year out. She'll need my attention. Do you have a small property they could…er… borrow, until…?'

'Until?'

He was not about to make it easy for me. Why should

he? He had more than once suggested marriage and I had refused to consider it, expecting that he would keep trying. His father had urged him, only to be told that the final decision rested with me, to be made in my own time. Now, much sooner than I had intended, the time had come for me to offer myself as the price of my family's welfare. I would have to summon up the courage.

'Lord Winterson,' I said, watching his steepled fingers curl up cosily together, 'you once offered to marry me, for Jamie's sake. Do I take it that your offer still stands?'

'No,' he said, tonelessly.

'What?'

'I said no. I make no offer.'

'Oh, I see. Then you do not wish me to be your wife, after all.'

'I didn't say that.'

'Then what *did* you say?'

'I said that I make no offer, Miss Follet.'

'Isn't that the same thing?'

'Not at all. I have no objection to you making *me* an offer, nor does it stop me accepting it. After all, *you* are using marriage as a bargaining tool, are you not? So if you want that to be the price of my help to your family, then you must offer me that price and let us see if we can reach agreement.'

No doubt he caught something in my eye, some glance of controlled self-consciousness, for he continued before I could find a word to say. 'Yes, I know what you're thinking. You are recalling the time, only last weekend, when I said I shall never stop wanting you.

It's still true, but you must not confuse that sentiment with weakness. You see, you're just as bad as me when it comes to the price of a favour, are you not?'

'No,' I said, indignantly. 'We were talking then of kindnesses. Marriage is not a kindness.'

'You have experience of it, then?'

'No more than you, my lord.'

'Then we're both in the same wobbly boat. Do I take it that you're offering me your hand in marriage? Not for our own sakes, of course, but for more unselfish reasons.'

What deceits. What bickerings and bluff. Who did we hope to fool by this dissembling? I wondered. I adored him, and he must have known it, yet my pride was still unmended and I could not offer it to anyone in that condition. Only as an exchange of favours, so that we both knew what we were getting, this time. So that there was no talk of love, the superb abstract that cannot be weighed or valued. Nothing as fugitive or as fragile as love. No, nothing as dangerous as love that can be confused with so many other agonies. Yet there was a moment, a lull in the grand deception, when our eyes held as they had before, when our desires went naked and wanton into each other's souls, reaching in to dance madly, to mate, and to come as close to love as need be. His eyes darkened, and still I was too uncertain, too cautious to bare my heart to him in words.

'For those reasons, my lord, yes,' I lied. 'If you will find them somewhere suitable to live, with a patch of land where they can start again. They can stay with me until then, but I must keep my promise to rescue them tomorrow. Is it agreed between us?'

Leaning forward, he took both my trembling hands

into his. 'Jamie needs it. Your family needs it. What do *you* need, sweetheart? What is it you intend to withhold? What do you have left to hold on to except that hurt pride? Isn't it time you allowed me to fix it? Just remember this, that I may not know all there is to know about you, yet, I still know more than any other man exactly how that pride was damaged. And although it may be damaged, it's still in good working order. I will accept your offer, even on those terms. I will give them a place to live and make it habitable for them. I'll do whatever is necessary for their comfort. And for that, exactly what am I to expect?'

An end to this dreadful pretence, I wanted to cry, *for the pain of it is too terrible for me to bear much longer*. But how could I place my entire trust in such a man whose coldness had hurt me for so many years since that first meeting? Then, there was that one mad night. Then more bewildering indifference. And now this. What was I to believe? What could he expect from me except the same, on a longer time-scale? Passionate nights with intervals of icy coolness that would be as difficult for him to understand as it had been for me? Yes, at one time a certain pretence would have been necessary, for Linas's sake. But surely…oh, *surely* there could have been something to keep my heart from breaking. Had he thought that Jamie was *all* I wanted?

My hesitation was too much for him, and I felt his hands tighten over mine before sliding up to grasp my elbows, pulling me to my feet that were still trapped inside my muff. His grip moved up, his thumbs cruelly hooked beneath my arms, pulling me up to his mouth like a child with a puppet. My body swayed and bent.

His voice was hoarse with emotion, almost angry. 'Then I'll tell you what I expect, shall I? I expect everything you gave my brother, and more. You'll be in my bed each night and at my board by day. You'll be a friend to my friends and a mother to my children, my companion and helpmeet. In all things obedient. Now, is that what you can offer me, or have I missed something out, Miss Follet?'

Nothing material, I wanted to say. Only the mention of love, which apparently he did not expect. The bargain had only been waiting to be made, but I had not thought it would come like this, so prematurely. It was, after all, only a few short weeks since we'd begun to communicate. But my precious family were all I had, and I was responsible for them.

'Well?' he whispered. 'Second thoughts, is it?'

'No. That *is* what I'm offering. Just that.'

His eyes searched mine for doubts, but found none. 'Your family must mean much to you. Then we have a deal.'

I would have said yes, spit on my palm and shook hands on it as farmers do at market, signed something, exchanged some small token. But in the blink of an eye his mouth was upon mine, taking my breath away with a kiss as fierce as any I'd ever received, a kiss of victory and possession that I was helpless to soften in any way. His arms encircled my waist and shoulders, pushing my arm up to hold his head against me, cheek to cheek, and I heard his breathy whisper past my ear. 'Mine. *Mine.* You belong to *me*, Helene Follet. Me alone. I have you at last, woman.'

It was the talk of envy, jealousy, rivalry, not the words

of love or desire. It seemed to be repayment time. Collecting the winnings after an all-night game and a too-long wait. Though he had mentioned my needs, I could not expect him to dwell on them when his own were so great.

If my mind began to seek provisos, it was too late, but I had made no mention of the business, or my need to supplement what Linas had once provided. Presumably there would be no need for that in the future. So I did not mention it. One thing at a time, my common sense told me. Surprisingly, what my heart told me was very similar. *Comfort him*, it said. *He needs your comfort, for his pain is just as great as yours. It's up to you to find out why.*

Without a shred of understanding, I cradled his head inside the garland of my arms and rocked him gently like a mother, fondling his cheek and earlobe with my lips as if I knew where all this was coming from. We had both done our best to give, and to take what we believed was our due, and now the time had come to comfort each other for the price we had agreed. There was still so much explaining to be done, so much that I did not know about this business, long-held misconceptions about the relationship between two brothers. He had accepted my offer without demur, but I could sense the pain. Perhaps he felt an improper urgency so soon after his twin's demise. Or was there something else? Now was not the time to ask, for we were both tired, especially me.

In more normal circumstances, I would have gone early to bed and slept like a child, but this was not normal, nor could I imagine being held in his arms without wanting to belong to him in every sense, exhausted or not. It was not that I wished to reward him for coming to my rescue, for agreeing to help my family, or for offering me lifelong security. Nothing like that. He would have sensed the difference between a payment and a demand, I know. So while I aroused him with my lips, my hands delved beneath his tailcoat to find the hard muscle-bound valley of his back and to pull his shirt out of his breeches for a more intimate contact with his skin. Shamelessly demanding, I was, flaunting my honesty.

There was no pretence with him, either. No mock surprise or prudish rebuke of my brazenness, but a deep gasp of excitement from his throat as he bent to pick me up and swing me into his arms, dipping me at the door so that I could open it. Across the hall and up the stairs with no one to witness the abduction, only Debbie emerged from somewhere to open and then to close my bedroom door behind us without a word.

Then, since I had initiated the undressing, he allowed me to act as his valet, though with more haste and less reverence than he was used to, and punctuated by my kisses to every newly exposed area I could reach. How can one describe the soft tang of male skin, the scent of masculine intentions, or the air that breathes sexuality, anticipation and mastery? I had not managed to disguise my love from his father, and apparently I had not done so from him, either. Yet while I indulged myself in this way, exploring and fondling his body by the light of the fire, even down to his toes, I sensed no complacency or conceit in him that the affair had gone so soon in his favour, but rather an appreciation of the gentle ministrations after my earlier indignation.

My own garments were loose and easily undone, quickly slipped off my shoulders as I unbuckled, unbuttoned and untied him from complicated flaps and folds. I think I was bared before he was, kissed at intervals and caressed constantly until, at last, we could no longer delay the pleasure of the full-length contact our bodies demanded. Lifting me again, he carried me across to the bed where, with my arms still around his neck, he repeated the words he'd spoken earlier. 'Mine. *Mine.* No going back, sweetheart.'

I had carried my own version of that sentiment, though now it was already too late to put it into practice. In my dreams of retribution, I had thought to withhold myself, to blow hot and cold, to confuse him with my inconsistency. That was before the reality of our last night together, and now this—it would take more strength than I had to play the coquette with him.

In deference to my nightmarish day and extreme tiredness, his loving was exquisitely tender and undemanding, full of sweetness when his lips brushed across my eyelids, when he told me I was all a man could desire and how I was all *he* had ever desired enough to want to marry. Which, of course, I had difficulty believing, since he had not desired me enough to pursue me all those years ago, but had let his brother take up the hunt. I let it go, for his lips and hands lured me into other more immediate responses, and I was discovering a new kind of enjoyment in being dog-tired and being made love to by a sympathetic lover. He knew exactly how to comfort me better than I knew how to comfort him, how to bring me with patience to a star-bursting climax before taking his own pleasure as the stars fell earthwards. He knew to wipe me down and attend to the ease of my weary frame and, in his arms, I fell asleep almost immediately while thinking how different again this was from any previous experience. I ought not to have compared them, I know, for therein lay the root of unfairness. But I did.

It was still pitch dark when we woke, simultaneously stirring in each other's embrace, entwining, hungry for more sensation, our mouths seeking through a screen of my hair. Full length I lay upon him with my tresses making a tent over his face. His hands cupped my behind, pulling me into position, then rolling with me so that, in one quick flip, I was beneath him, possessed again, mindless with excitement and still only half-awake. There was no long languorous preparation this time, more like that first unreal night at Abbots Mere when no word was spoken, when we came together countless times, insatiable and desperate for consola-tion. It was like that now, as if making up for time lost, as if to remind ourselves and each other, even in half-sleep, that we had made a pact that could not be broken. He was powerful and purposeful and I matched him, urging him with my hands and lifting my hips to him, revelling in the knowledge that he would still be with me in the morning, and every morning to come.

Afterwards, comforted, I wondered whether that would be the right time to confirm his father's opinion that I was in love with him. But he had not spoken of love, only desire, and my pride was, as he had said, still in good working order. Time enough for talk of love, I decided. There would be as many difficult days ahead as there had been in the past, and some riddles to be solved about the exact nature of Lord Winterson's conquest. About my family's future, I was not half so sure.

Our breakfast together, taken well before Jamie was astir, was served by my footman as if Lord Winterson's presence there was now a foregone conclusion.

'I shall not be taking you with me,' he said, scraping up the last crumb of scrambled egg from his plate.

'Was that to your satisfaction?' I said. 'Not quite the way your Mrs Adamson does it.'

'The company more than makes up for it. Did you hear what I said?'

'I heard. But I don't see how you can do it without me. My mother is hardly going to deliver herself into the hands of complete strangers with all her goods and chattels. I wouldn't.'

'No, I dare say you would not. But she's had time to prepare herself, and I'm not exactly a complete stranger. You must have mentioned me from time to time, and your brothers will surely persuade her to trust me. Anyway, you said she was ailing.'

'So you think she'll quit like a lamb? It would not do to underestimate my mother's fighting spirit, my lord.'

'Like mother, like daughter, then.' Even passing his coffee cup to me for a refill was done gracefully, with a slide of his eyes over me as I poured.

'Please let me come,' I said. 'The shop will look after itself.'

His hand closed softly over mine. 'I know,' he said. 'You are a model of efficiency, but how will you prepare to receive guests if you're not here? They'll need places to put their things, places to sleep, bedding, food, whatever. You're needed here, sweetheart. Give Jamie some jobs to do.'

'Jamie? What can *he* do?'

'More than you think. Let him help. He enjoys it.'

I frowned, not best pleased to be told how to mother the child I'd reared more or less alone for three years.

Ignoring the stony response, he continued. 'I've sent to Abbots Mere for all the men and carts, and a boat to get them across the water. They'll bring all we need to do the job. And a carriage for the ladies. I shall pick up your phaeton, too.'

'And check that the supplies are still in it, if you please.'

'I'll bring them back. Now, just trust me, will you? I have to go. I expect it will take all day. You'd better clear out some of those storerooms at the back of the house. We shall need them.'

'You'll be dining here, too?'

'Probably not. My parents are still at Abbots Mere, so I'd better go back. Will you miss me?'

'Yes,' I said, before I could think about it.

His hand squeezed and released me, sliding down my fingers and changing the direction of my breath. He could have taken me on the floor. Anywhere. I argued no more, for he was quite right. I was needed here. Jamie needed me, after a day apart. Prue needed me, particularly.

The rain had stopped in favour of blue sky and fluffy

clouds pushed by a stiff breeze, bringing some colour back into the day. Our bargain had changed me too, though it was hard to say how except that I had reached another turning point, this time more permanent than any before it. My mother would think it was love at last, and she'd be delighted. And I dare say we'd be able, without too much effort, to convince her that she was right.

What had happened, however, was too important to be filed tidily away in a back drawer of my mind while I took on the day's duties, and there were times when I ought not to have been staring blankly out of the bedroom window, or trying to part Jamie's thick waves on the wrong side of his head.

'Mama!' he protested, clutching at the comb. 'What on *earth* are you doing with me?'

Mrs Goode, watching the process, tipped her head to indicate the problem, but her smile caught Jamie's eye and their indulgence was like a warm hug. After that, there appeared to be a mutual understanding that the whole messy business of too many guests was rather beyond me and that they ought, out of kindness, to send me off on some less mind-taxing mission. Nana Damzell, said Jamie, should have his room, and he would sleep with Goody. And since the sacrifice meant so much to him, neither of us denied him. After a talk with Mrs Carson and Mrs Neape, my housekeeper and cook, I left to visit Prue whom I'd not seen since Monday.

Prue was not a demonstrative lady, but on this occasion she wept in my arms as I smoothed her back and tried to find some comforting words to say, which turned out to be very unoriginal. 'Dear…dear Prue,' I said. 'I'm so sorry. So very sorry. Is there anything I can do? There must be something?'

'No, you've done more than enough, Helene. But thank you,' she said, drawing away. 'They were both very peaceful at the end, thanks to your help. They're at rest now, thank God.'

'Still together, Prue,' I said, feeling the sting of conscience that I had not sent for the doctor sooner, when I ought to have done. Would it have made any difference? That was something we would never know.

'Mother first, then Pop. Within the hour. After forty-four years.'

'When will you…they…?'

'Day after tomorrow. St Thomas's at Osbaldwick. They were born in that village, christened and married there too. Always went to St Thomas's.'

'I didn't know that. Did Mr Monkton visit them, Prue?'

'Nay,' she said with a huff of disapproval. 'Not him. I sent a message, but he never came to see them. Too busy, I reckon. It's only two miles beyond Walmgate, but young curates have more interesting things to do than visit their dying parishoners, these days. The undertakers are making all the arrangements for me.'

'Let me pay for it, Prue. Please. I shall be there with you, and the staff, and I shall close the shop on Friday.'

'Yes, I'd like that. They'll be very proud, will Ma and Pop.' She blew her nose and straightened her white lace cap. 'They were so weak, you know.'

'Yes, love. Quite a few others have been taken in the same way.'

'Aye. It's been a wicked winter so far.'

I went straight from Lop Lane to the shop to inform the staff, and to warn them that on Friday we would all be attending the funeral. I stayed for an hour to design some morning gowns for Lady Mirfield's seventeen-year-old overweight daughter, then returned home to find the place in the process of being rearranged, adjusted and turned upside down to find enough basic requirements for the invasion. What I had just heard about Medworth Monkton's indifference to Prue's request had both puzzled and shocked me, having always believed him to be the most diligent of curates. Could it have been Claude's birthday party that had prevented him? If not that, then what?

I had not been home above half an hour, spent stuffing pillows into cotton cases, when my footman came to say that Mr Medworth Monkton was downstairs in the drawing room, hoping for a few words with me. Which rather amazed me, considering that, in my mind, I had just been having a few well-chosen words with *him* about his parochial duties.

As always, his greeting was courteous and friendly towards me, despite my unorthodox links to his family. He had never been judgemental. In fact, if I were to criticise him at all, it would be on his ambivalence on matters which one might expect a man of God to have some kind of opinion. Sitting on the fence is all very well, and comfortable, but for those of us who welcome some direction from time to time, Medworth was probably not the one to ask. Not a highly practical man either, regardless of the medley of livestock he kept. Apart from being a good husband and a friendly scholarly curate, it was hard to know what else he was.

His bow was meticulous, his acceptance of a seat precisely timed to my being seated, his coat and breeches surprisingly free of animal hairs that show up so well on black. *His* hair, however, was as unruly as ever. Yet in the strong low winter light, I recognised a handsomeness akin to his brother's in the distinct jaw and nose that I had not been aware of before.

'Are you in town on business?' I said, thinking he might even now be on his way to Lop Lane. Better late than never.

'I came, Miss Follet, to ask about little Jamie and to apologise most sincerely for the accident. I was instructed,' he said, releasing a sheepish grin, 'to stay with the boys in the field. But one of my old friends insisted on distracting me with his chatter, and I'm afraid…well…I failed in my duty.'

It was kindly meant, and fair, to explain what happened for, since then, my opinion of his guardianship, temporary or not, was only lukewarm. 'Thank you,' I said. 'There's no harm done, Mr Monkton. Jamie is perfectly recovered. Your brother is going to teach him to swim.'

'Ah! How like Winterson to see the positive side. Excellent. He rarely lets a chance slip past him, does he?'

There was something in the tone of his question that seemed to have more behind it than polite rhetoric, followed by a smile that failed to lighten his eyes with the usual boyish mischief. Had he really come here to ask about Jamie, or was there something else?

'I don't know. I know much less about Lord Winterson than I did about his twin brother, you see. You know him better than I do.' I heard the artfulness of my reply. I was going to marry the man. 'But I do know that he makes an excellent guardian for my son.'

'Mmm, yes. Well, I suppose that will remain true as long as Jamie is too young to understand. I cannot help wondering, though, what will happen when Jamie reaches…er…the age of questioning.' Dropping his voice to a conspiratorial whisper, he observed me from beneath his brows, waiting for an appropriate reaction.

'Jamie has already reached the age of questioning, Mr Monkton, as you may recall when he told you of the remark made to him by Claude's little friend. That, you see, was the cause of the fracas at the mill-pond. Perhaps something ought to have been said at the time, don't you think?' My heartbeat had stepped up its pace in anticipation of a new phase in the conversation that had begun so amicably.

His eyes dropped away from mine as he nodded, and I could see that he had sucked in his bottom lip and let it out again, grimacing. 'Which is exactly the point I'm making, Miss Follet. That it's best to say something at the time, before it's too late.'

'Too late for what? About Jamie's parentage? I think that will all become clear in time, sir.'

'Er…well, not *that*, particularly. As you point out, that will be resolved eventually, I'm sure. It's the problem of my brother's lifestyle that concerns me most, and how it's going to affect a young impressionable boy like Jamie. Even though you claim to know so little about my brother, you must know what I'm referring to, Miss Follet. You yourself have been a part of it for some years now.'

Astonishment and indignation seethed in my breast, but I would not allow him to see. Instead, I smiled. 'Dear Mr Monkton,' I said, calmly, 'you must allow me to put your mind at rest, for I can see how misinformed you are about the kind of life I lead. I have *never* been part of Lord Winterson's...well... lifestyle, for want of a better expression. As for Jamie being affected by his guardian's behaviour, all I can say is that if Lord Winterson is only *half* as diligent, dutiful, loving, generous and caring to Jamie in the next three years as he has been in the last, I shall have nothing whatever to worry about. Nor will you.' Come to think of it, I had never spoken to anyone about Winterson in such terms, though there could never have been a better opportunity to say what I felt to one of his own family.

As if my praise of his brother gave him satisfaction, he nodded again, although the contortions of his mouth indicated that the matter would not be allowed to rest there. 'It does happen,' he said, 'that parenthood often brings out the best in even the most unusual circumstances, and it heartens me more than I can say to know that my brother has begun his duties so well. But I must refer you to my original concern, Miss Follet, about the kind of questions Jamie is sure to seek answers to in the future.'

'Do you have something specific in mind, sir?'

'Well, for one thing, about Winterson's love-child and its relationship to *him*. About who its mother is, and why—'

'Mr Monkton, please hold on a minute. You go too

fast for me. What exactly...*who* exactly are you talking about? Which mother?'

Sitting bolt upright, he pulled his chin deep into his collar like a runaway horse responding to the curb. His eyelids fluttered, but whether in mock or actual surprise I do not know. The whole conversation had an air of unreality about it, for I found it increasingly disturbing that a man usually so devoid of opinions should have come down so strongly against something that had not yet happened. Or had it?

His frown was childishly embarrassed, and one cheek went into a spasm as if it was all too painful for him. 'Oh, dear, what have I said?' he whispered. 'I thought you'd *know*. You seemed to be in each other's confidence.'

Confidence, I supposed, was his euphemism for pockets.

'Yes, what *have* you said, Mr Monkton? What is it you thought I'd know?'

'Er...about Lady Slatterly...and my brother.'

I don't know how I found the breath to say, 'What about them?'

'You saw that she was not quite herself at the ball, last weekend?'

'I had noticed it.'

'Did it not occur...? No, I see that it did not. My brother and she have always been very close, you know. It should hardly come as a surprise.'

'To know...?'

'That she's in,' he whispered, '*a delicate condition*.'

I must congratulate myself. I kept my voice level. 'It doesn't really surprise me at all, Mr Monkton, to know that Veronique is in the family way.' Yes, I felt justified, at that point, in using a little spicy vulgarity to bring the wretched man down to earth. 'In that, you are absolutely right. What *does* surprise me is that it hasn't happened sooner, after all the chances she's had.'

'I see,' he said, glancing wildly from side to side. My outspokenness had shaken him. 'But what about Winterson? That will surely not surprise you either, knowing something of his tendencies.'

I did not intend to give him the satisfaction of an answer to that. 'May I ask how you come to know this, sir? There are no visible signs of it yet. Is it not regarded as confidential at this early stage?'

He could not look at me, the father of three. Coyness had set in. 'The fashions, you know. They're very concealing, are they not?'

High waists, gathers and drapes, shawls and winter wraps. Yes, it was true. His own wife's bulge could be seen only from the side. Then I recalled Veronique's reaction as we joined them in the supper room, and there was I, thinking she was broody, like me. Breeding she was. Not broody. 'They are indeed, sir, but that doesn't answer my question. How do *you* come to know about Lady Slatterly's condition?'

'Old friends, Miss Follet. Veronique…er, Lady Slatterly has always found it easy to confide in me, both as curate and as Winterson's brother. She came to me some time ago for my advice.'

Advice? From Medworth? Now that *was* clutching at straws.

'In confidence, of course? How many others have you told, sir?'

He had the grace to look away, and I began to dislike him intensely. 'The point in my telling *you*, my dear Miss Follet, is that you and my brother have a legal share in Jamie's custody. A trust, as it were. And if that trust has been broken by one party, I feel it my bounden duty to inform the other of it, whether that breaks a confidence or not. I did hope that Winterson would have admitted his part in this affair by now, if only to discuss with you what steps he intends to take regarding his responsibilities. Marriage to Lady Slatterly would, of course, be the obvious solution, and this is why I am expressing some concern about the possible confusion in Jamie's mind concerning his exact relationships.'

'So you are certain about her condition. Are you equally certain who the father is, Mr Monkton?'

He adopted his pained expression again, as if I had challenged his veracity instead of Veronique's. 'I have her word on it,' he said, puffing out his chest a little, 'which I trust implicitly.'

'Then you are not as wise as you have always appeared to be, sir. You must surely be aware, in your role as confidante to the lady, that she's probably had more lovers than he? How can she possibly know who the father is? Has she kept notes?'

Wincing at my forthright turn of phrase, he was obviously rattled by my lack of conviction. 'She is absolutely certain of it, Miss Follet. I really do apologise for being the bearer of this distressing news, but I assumed, wrongly, I see, that my brother would have told you how things stand between him and Lady Slatterly. I came only to offer you the benefit of my advice and support, coming so soon after our mutual loss.'

'Your advice…ah…what would that be, in confidence, of course?'

His glance flickered uncomfortably in my direction as if I were a restless congregation. 'I find it is rarely successful to confront my brother with a problem head-on. He would deny it, naturally, as would most men in his position. As I said, he has an uncanny way of turning negatives into positives. No, perhaps the best way to handle the situation would be to distance yourself from him just a little more and then to allow him to broach the subject when he's decided what to do about it. Perhaps he already has, but I think it's much better for him to bear the bad tidings.'

'Of great joy.'

He did not, as Winterson had done, laugh and tell me not to go all biblical on him. Instead, he said, 'I beg your pardon?'

'You mean that, after all you've told me, I am now to pretend total ignorance of the matter? Then I'm supposed to appear shocked? On the other hand, is it really any of my business what your brother and Lady Slatterly get up to together? It would be if he were my husband, but he isn't, is he? And by the time Jamie is old enough to ask some searching questions about his half-relatives, he'll be old enough to be given some searching answers, I expect. He's quite intelligent. Regarding his own parentage, we have put in place a solution to that problem, such as it is. About other people's parentage, sir, I shall advise him to do as the rest of us try to do.'

'And that is?'

'Why, to mind our own business, of course, and

never... ever...to break a confidence unless it's a matter of life or death. And this isn't, is it?'

'It may be of great importance to young Jamie, Miss Follet.'

'Is that why you told him you had more important things to think about when one of your guests insulted him?'

That, apparently, was enough confrontation for the young curate of Osbaldwick who had already stayed longer than the regulation fifteen minutes. Standing up, he prepared to make his bow, though he could not resist a parting shot as he did so. 'I shall pray for you, Miss Follet. I came here as a friend out of the goodness of my heart to help you see your way out of an embarrassing situation. I suppose I must be relieved to find that you need no such help, but I shall always be available whenever you do.'

'That is very kind of you, Mr Monkton, and greatly appreciated. As you suspect, I am not in the least embarrassed by anything you've told me, though I imagine Lady Slatterly might be. Now, just remind me again, will you? Am I to tell your brother you called on me? Or not?'

His look of deep reproach convinced me that the interview had not gone according to plan, which had been to drive a wedge between me and his brother, as large a wedge as he could devise, and as plausible too. Everyone in the family, and plenty outside it, knew how Veronique Slatterly felt about Winterson, and who was I to blame her? But I knew also that, whether he was the father of her child or not, she would lose no time in laying her pregnancy at his door in the hope that, with enough pressure from all sides, he would do 'the honourable thing'.

But I had Winterson's categoric denial of any association, and whatever delinquencies he might be guilty of, dishonesty was not one of them. Quite the reverse. Too much honesty had kept us apart for years. I would not believe what Medworth was telling me. I would refuse to be upset by it. Nor would I challenge Winterson with this tale, as I knew full well Medworth wanted me to. Why else would he have come here to tell me? Why would he have come these two miles if he *expected* I'd already been told, when he couldn't be bothered to travel the same distance to administer God's grace to two of his dying parishoners? He was already halfway down the street before I remembered to ask him what had kept him from his duty to Prue's parents.

I would like to have felt as carefree as I seemed, but Medworth's visit had disturbed me deeply, both for its implications and the reasons why he should wish to cause a rift when he'd done no such thing during my association with Linas. There must have been other occasions when Winterson was thought to have fathered someone's child, yet nothing had ever been said to confirm it, or hold him to account. Furthermore, Linas's last few months had been spent in his brother's care at Abbots Mere, and I found it inconceivable that, during such a sad time of intensive nursing, Winterson would have been taking advantage of Veronique's generosity after so many years of refusals. The idea was ludicrous. No, I could not and *would* not believe it.

All the same, what if it was true?

Chapter Twelve

⌘

Those short dark February days, the cold, then the floods, seemed at the time more like a breeding ground for low spirits than the onset of spring when the first spears of snowdrops would normally have appeared, and birds building nests. In many respects I had much to be thankful for after a disastrous start, with my future set to become more secure than it had ever been, Jamie's problems alleviated and my family about to be relocated, albeit not a solution guaranteed to gladden them. In my do-gooding mode, it had hardly occurred to me that they might have other ideas when alternatives were so few, so I consoled myself with thoughts of their pleasure at the efforts I had made for them.

Jamie was ecstatic at the thought of having his own dear Nana Damzell, Greg and Finch to stay with us at last. His excited chatter and impractical suggestions made us smile; if it turned cold again, he said, his uncles could sleep with him and Goody in her large bed. But I did as Winterson suggested and allowed him to help, fearing that it would surely take me weeks to find anything as a result. And while the little fellow ran errands from kitchen to attic, I could not dismiss the absurdity of Medworth's errand and the plight of poor Veronique and what, if anything, I ought to say to Winterson about it.

As one problem was resolved, another had come to take its place, all set to strike at my most vulnerable parts. Knowing what I did of Winterson, how would I ever be sure? Was this what I would have to get used to, as the price of my uncontrollable love for him? The idea made me turn cold and sick, even while I smiled at Jamie's excitement. But just as disconcerting was Medworth's unusual officiousness and his alarming lapse of ethics that could hardly bode well for the future, especially when I had always regarded him as a firm ally. What a good thing I had never confided in him about my relationship with his brothers.

From a clear cold sky the light had begun to fade as we stood near the front windows to watch for signs of returning travellers. Behind us, last-minute adjustments were being made to the dinner table where places had been laid for eight people, candles and lamps lit, posies of ivy and hellebore arranged. Servants had been briefed, logs stacked in the hearth and jugs of ale brought up from the cellar, and wine too. My mother was fond of the sweet sauternes that Pierre obtained for her.

Jamie gave a yelp and wriggled like a worm off the window-seat, pulling the cushions with him. 'Uncaburl! Uncaburl!' His cries of welcome faded as he headed towards the hall. Through the gloom, I could make out

no accompanying carts or carriage, so assumed he must
have ridden on ahead to prepare us for their approach.
I held a hand to my shawl-covered bodice to still the
fluttering beneath, as the loud crack of the door-knocker
was cut short, then the high yelp echoed by the deeper
one followed by Jamie's chattery briefing. The limpet-
like cling of his embrace as Winterson tried to rid
himself of hat and gloves brought a laughing protest.
'Hold on, young man. I didn't come here to be smoth-
ered.' Trying to catch my eye round the little head, Winterson held him on one arm as he came to me,
unexpectedly bending for a kiss to both cheeks.

His skin was fresh and cold, and I could smell the
sweet scent of the moors upon it. 'Welcome, my lord,'
I said. 'We've been awaiting you.'

'So I see,' he whispered, greeting me with eyes that
held mine fractionally longer than etiquette required of a
man, soothing the fears that had dogged me since
Medworth's visit. 'Jamie,' he said, turning to the excited
child, 'be still. Your mama and I must talk before I go
home.'

I knew then, by the seriousness of his expression, that
my plans for my family's immediate future had fallen
through and that the reason for his lone visit was
because they were not on their way here, as we had
expected. Conflicting emotions passed through me as
we went from the hall into the well-prepared dining
room, and thankfulness that he was not about to leave
me alone to deal with Jamie's inevitable disappointment.

Perhaps sensing the unwelcome news, Mrs Goode
poured a glass of brandy and placed it beside his elbow

as he sat Jamie upon his knee and cuddled him, a Jamie who had suddenly become astonishingly composed.

'What is it?' I said. 'A change of plan? Things have worsened? Is it my mother?'

'According to your brothers,' Winterson said, 'your mother is in better health than she's been for some time. But you warned me about her fighting spirit. She's quite a lady, isn't she? And, no, things have not worsened.'

Anticipating, I felt the dead weight of failure. 'She wouldn't budge, then. Tch! So stubborn. I might have known it.'

'Wait. Don't jump to conclusions. I spent most of my time there talking with her and your brothers, and the rest of it in the boat looking round the buildings and the parts they've been farming.'

'And the devastation, too?'

'More at what they've achieved than what's been spoiled. Yes, there's still plenty of water coming over the foss, but less than before. The water levels have actually begun to drop. We got the boat across to the house, but I could see that they had no intention of moving, and, to be honest, Miss Follet, I believe they've made the right decision.'

'But didn't you tell them you'd decided to reclaim the land and demolish the buildings?'

'I didn't see the point. I took my bailiff and steward along with me to meet your brothers, and we could all see that it makes more sense to leave the Follethorpes there to farm it. We were very impressed by what we saw. They've done extremely well, considering the lack of help over the years and the unfavourable conditions they've lived in.'

'They had Pierre to help them. What happened?'

'He left after a…a difference of opinion.'

'Tell me the truth. He and my brothers always had a difference of opinion. What was so special about this one?'

Tenderly, he cradled Jamie's head against his chest, sliding his hand across the hair so like his own. Jamie's fist was already moving up towards his mouth, thumb first, his eyelids heavy with sleep. 'You,' said Winterson, very quietly. 'It was after Monsieur Follet had seen us together near the coffee house. Remember?'

How could I forget the look on Pierre's face? 'Yes,' I said.

'Well, he went back home and voiced some rather harsh comments.'

'Yes, I can imagine.'

'Your brothers were not aware. They'd never seen me until today. Now they can understand it, but when your cousin began to…'

'To throw insults about?'

'Yes, they told him he'd better leave. So he did. There and then. I don't know anything about their relationship, but neither of your brothers seems too concerned about his departure. Except for one thing.'

'You mean the loss of what he used to bring from Brid?'

'Worse. Prepare yourself for bad news. He took the savings with him.'

'Oh, no! All? Everything?' My sounds of despair widened Jamie's eyes for a second until his lids drooped again.

'Every penny. The lot.'

My sigh was deep and genuinely painful, for this I felt to be partly my fault. But whatever he thought of me, how *could* he have done that to my mother for whom he professed to care and to be grateful for those years of safety? 'Where has he gone? How are they managing? What does Mama have to say about his treachery?'

'I believe your mother is secretly relieved to have an end to the wrangling and bad feeling, Miss Follet. And I must say that young Finch makes an impressive head of the Follethorpe house. We saw very much eye to eye, your brothers and I. As to the loss of funds, well, none of them is too pleased about that because it was a considerable amount they'd put aside for renovations and living costs. They told me how you'd helped them financially at great personal cost to yourself. They're very proud of you, you know. That's why they refused to tolerate your cousin's criticisms.'

'Family loyalties. It works both ways,' I said.

'But they don't know where Monsieur Follet has gone. They've had other things to think about since he went. We rescued your phaeton, by the way, and delivered the supplies to your mother. She sends her thanks.'

'Thank you. But what happens now?' I said, trying to understand the implications of all this. 'Did you mean it when you said they should be left there to farm the land, just as they have been doing?'

'Not just as they have been doing. The place needs money spending on it, and a lot of extra hands to make it profitable.'

'But now they haven't *got* the money. *Or* the extra hands. *Have* they?'

'Shh!' he whispered, looking down at the sleeping bundle on his lap. Adjusting his position, he held Jamie closer to touch the cool forehead with his lips. For some moments, the conversation was suspended, then Mrs Goode caught my eye.

'Shall I take him up, ma'am?'

'No,' Winterson said, looking up at me with a smile. 'Wait a while. He's tired out. You allowed him to help you, then?'

'Practically non-stop. We're the exhausted ones.'

His smile broadened. 'Well, there's a lot to be done at Foss Beck. The men and I are going back there on Friday to take a longer look at what there is and what we may be able to do with it. By that time the water levels will have gone down further and we'll be able to see more. The house needs a lot of attention, and there'll be some of the other houses I can put tenants into, to help on the farm. If we start straight away, we could have it up and running by early summer.'

'I think,' I said, 'you should allow Mrs Goode to take Jamie up.' Without questioning, he passed the sleeping little body over to his nurse. 'I'll be up shortly,' I told her.

'Yes, ma'am. Goodnight, my lord.'

Winterson closed the door behind them and returned to his chair, anticipating me as I took a breath to begin my interrogation about these far-fetched plans of his. To silence me, he took my hands into his. 'Everything has changed, sweetheart,' he said, gently. 'I can see how you've slaved all day to prepare for them, but you had not allowed for their preferences, had you? You might have realised your mother would refuse to leave.'

'It's my father,' I said, gulping as the tears began to

prickle. 'She's said it before, but I really didn't think she'd be quite so obstinate. Besides, if you were to go ahead and demolish—'

'But I'm not, lass. I shall not demolish the place. They know that.'

'Did they tell you what happened, years ago, at Bridlington?'

'Of course. I didn't say that I already knew, naturally, but that business about being arrested for an offence your father committed all those years ago is utter nonsense. The law doesn't work that way. They've been badly misinformed.'

'What…misinformed…about…?'

'About having to stay hidden for fear of arrest. They're not in any danger. Never have been. If a wanted man dies, sweetheart, that's the end of the matter. Whoever told them otherwise is completely wrong. Or bluffing.'

'It was Pierre who insisted they must stay hidden.'

'Then it's just as well he's gone, even if he did take the money too.'

'Maybe he thought he was the one who'd earned it. And if he was not too familiar with English law, he might have assumed…'

'Rubbish!' he laughed softly, kissing my knuckles. 'French law is no different on that point. I intend to make some enquiries about your cousin.'

'Then there's something else you ought to know, Burl,' I said, feeling the warm imprint of his lips on my skin, such a simple tender gesture worth more to me than twenty springtimes.

A smile spread into his eyes and crinkled their

corners like fine tissue. 'You're calling me Burl,' he said. 'Say it again.'

'Burl. Sounds like pearl.'

'Sounds like angel voices to me. Go on.'

'Flirt. I was saying there's something…'

'Something I ought to know. He wanted to marry you. I know that.'

'No, about the shop. When the floods started. We had a visit.' I told him how the Customs and Excise Men had searched but found nothing, while his expression grew more and more concerned.

'Do you happen to know why they singled you out?'

'One of them mentioned my advertisement in the window. The one you saw. I thought that was what had aroused their suspicions, but I wondered just now if Pierre might have wanted to alert them after he'd seen us in town. But he wouldn't. He was never vindictive.'

'Vindictive enough to steal the family savings. I shall find out what I can. I know the Customs Controller. He'll tell me why you were investigated and who the men were.'

'You believe someone might have tipped them off?'

'Oh, not necessarily. Leave it to me.'

It was something he enjoyed saying, these days. Leave it to me. So I did. 'You said my family need stay in hiding no longer,' I said.

'There was never any need for it except that, without realising it, they had parked themselves on my land. Just as well they were quiet about that.'

'For which offence you will require compensation, in the Winterson tradition?'

'I thought we'd already settled that,' he said, letting go of my hands to take up the glass of brandy. 'Haven't we?'

'As you said, things have changed. You've decided not to force them out and not to find them alternative accommodation. But how are you expecting them to put the buildings and fields to rights without their funds?'

'Haven't I told you? I thought I had.'

'No, you haven't, my lord.'

'You *must* be exhausted,' he commented, drily. 'Is *this* contraband too?'

'No. It's one Linas used to drink. And I'm not so exhausted that I cannot remember what you said, or didn't say, a moment ago.'

'About?'

'Renovations. Restorations. Reclamations. All that.'

'Ah, I see. You wish to know exactly what you're getting on your side of the bargain, Miss Follet, now that they won't be here and homeless after all. Well, I didn't share the details of our bargain with your brothers, but…'

'I should hope not!'

'…but I did discuss with them, which *you* failed to do, what their preferences would be. In an ideal world, that is.'

'It was pouring with rain, and I had to shout across a lake.'

'Nevertheless, I find it more democratic to—'

'Oh, get on with it!'

'—not to take things too much for granted. So we sat down together over a bowl of *superb* vegetable broth and dumplings, to discuss their needs.'

'Their needs, or yours?'

'Theirs first, then mine. And if you insist on interrupting me, Miss Follet, I shall be here all night. Is that your intention?'

'Please, I won't interrupt. Just tell me.'

'Thank you. I was trying to.' Picking up the brandy, he sipped again and carefully replaced it, smiling, teasing. 'There was no mention of compensation, sweetheart,' he said. 'The property belongs to the Stillingfleete estate and it will be Stillingfleete money that will completely renovate and redecorate the house, install running water and proper cooking facilities, sanitation, everything they need. Your brothers have agreed to manage the extended farm for a monthly salary, and to work the fields that my men will plough and sow. The other fields will hold new stock, sheep and a few milk-cows, more horses and better machinery, some poultry yards and perhaps pens for rearing pheasants in. We may need an assistant gamekeeper, I think.

'We'll also have to decide which barns to repair and which fields to turn to arable and pasture. We can drain most of the arable land, and redirect the beck so that the farm can't be flooded again. After that, we'll rebuild some of the cottages for the farmhands. Eventually, we might even start to use the old church again, if I can find a curate willing to take it on. It's in a bit of a mess, isn't it?'

I listened to this as if it was all a dream, and I was waiting to wake at the first sound of discord. 'I can hardly believe it,' I whispered. 'What did Mama have to say?'

'Sharp as a bag of nails. She wanted to know why I was bothering with it, and did I intend first to marry you and accept Jamie as my own, which she had no doubt of, since we're as alike as two peas.'

'She said *that*? Tch! Oh, she's too outspoken for words, my lord.'

'Not a bit of it. She has the right to know. I told her she'd have to reconcile herself to being my mother-in-law.' He grinned like a mischievous schoolboy. 'Oh, then she wept a little.'

'Oh, dear. Poor Mama. She's been so very unwell.'

'She's not been so very unwell since Cousin Pierre left. For one thing, she stopped taking that concoction he was bringing her from York once a month, and immediately she began to improve. The boys tell me—' He stopped himself, directing his attention to the brandy.

'Tell you what? Do they suspect Pierre of something?'

'Probably not. It seems a strange coincidence, that's all.'

'Well, bargain or no bargain, I believe I'm in your debt, my lord. What you've agreed to do for them is—'

'For you, lass. I'm doing it for you.'

'Why?'

'Because I've got you, and my son. It's as simple as that.'

Something echoed inside me. *And I have the man I love, even though I'm not so certain of his heart or our future together.* 'I still have trouble believing it. It's everything they've dreamed of, and much more than I deserve. I really don't think the bargain is so very equal, is it?'

'That's one thing we shall agree to disagree on, so let's forget about it. I cannot have a wife whose family live like outlaws in derelict houses on my property, can I? That would never do.'

My heart staggered a little. 'No, of course not,' I said, lightly. 'That wouldn't do at all.' Too hastily for a skilful recovery, I changed the subject, telling him about Prue's recent bereavement and the Friday funeral.

He was all sympathy. 'Friday is when I'll be going over to Foss Beck again, so why not have a day at Abbots Mere tomorrow while your house is being put back together again? Jamie can stay overnight, then on Friday he and Mrs Goode can spend the morning with my parents and I'll have a coach bring them back here in the afternoon. Besides, I have something for him that I believe he'll like.'

I stared into his smiling eyes. 'Something with four legs and a tail?'

'Indeed. A lovely little Exmoor mare that I've had my eye on. She'll be perfect for him. One owner, grown too tall.'

'He'll be over the moon.'

'It'll help him get over the disappointment of not having his Nana Damzell to stay. Bring them tomorrow after breakfast, and be sure he has some stout breeches and boots. Now,' he said, getting to his feet, 'I must be off. I'm sorry about your spoilt preparations, but it's all for the best. Forgive me?' He held out his arms and I went into them with an enthusiasm that appeared to take him by surprise, since it was much less to do with either thanks or forgiveness than with my need to feel the security of his embrace. I needed that more than he would ever know, after what I'd heard that afternoon.

'Hold me,' I whispered.

He did better than that. His kisses were heady and brandy-flavoured, and I knew it would be easy to persuade him to stay. We reached the hall, both of us searching for the perfect reason why he could not possibly leave. He took up his hat and gloves from the hall table, catching sight of three calling-cards on the silver tray, one of which he recognised. 'Medworth?' he said. 'When did *he* visit you?'

'Today.'

'You didn't say.'

'I forgot. Just a social call while he was in town. He wished to apologise for not safeguarding Jamie too well on Tuesday.'

'Did he, indeed? I should damn well think so, too. Heaven only knows what kind of rector he'll make when Slatterly grants him his new living, if he cannot tend his flock better than that.'

'Rector? New living? What does Lord Slatterly have to do with it?'

'I'm surprised he didn't tell you. I thought he'd told everybody. The living at Osbaldwick is in Slatterly's gift, you see. It was he who made Medworth curate there, to help the old rector out. But the old chap has retired at last and now Medworth is to step into his shoes at Easter. Wear your riding habits tomorrow, you and Mrs Goode, and I'll find two horses for you. We'll ride across the estate with my parents, shall we?'

'Er…yes. Will my phaeton be repaired by then?'

'It was not broken, Miss Follet. Just stuck in a deep rut with a stone jamming it. The boys will have it all cleaned up by morning.'

'So I need not have…?'

While the footman had gone to stand impassively by the door with one hand on the knob, Winterson could do little but nod. His mouth, however, was struggling against an impulse to laugh. 'Goodnight,' he said. 'Sleep well, Miss Follet.'

My first call was to the kitchen to apologise to Mrs Neape for being the bearer of such unwelcome news. We had devised the menus with great care, choosing all my family's favourites, beef steak pudding with fricassée of turnips, roast saddle of venison with redcurrant jelly, cheesecakes, that kind of thing. She was philosophical. It could all be eaten cold, she said, seeing my bitter disappointment, and we would have enough to keep us going for a week.

Mrs Carson was equally sympathetic and quite unruffled by the extra work involved. She had seen it all before and by this time tomorrow, she said, everything would be back in its usual place.

Still dazed by the unexpected generosity showered upon me and my family by Lord Winterson, I went up to see Jamie, who had slept through his undressing and was in his own bed between lace-edged sheets meant for Nana Damzell, hugging the empty embroidered nightdress-case that smelled of lavender. Mrs Goode and I swapped smiles and tiptoed out. 'Come down to the kitchen with me,' I said. 'We'll dine with cook and Mrs Carson tonight.'

Afterwards, I gave in to the urge to begin putting things back where they belonged, and it was late when I went to bed in a silent house that I had expected to be warmed by my brothers' laughter and my mother's chatter to her companions. But now they had seen Winterson at last and had made the connection for themselves, leaving me with no explaining to do. He had eaten their vegetable broth and dumplings, and they would understand how easy it was for me to love him and, about the complications, they would not need to know. Nor did I ever expect them to ask.

Yet for all the resolution of problems, I could not help but feel the worrying undercurrents that nagged me, not like the broodiness of recent days but more like a fear that there was something I ought to know, brought on, no doubt, by Medworth's perplexing visit. Certainly something unusual had been agreed between Winterson and his sickly twin, something that even his father had no wish to pry into. But what could be Medworth's purpose, I wondered, in trying to rock his brother's boat? Had he anticipated our marriage? Did he have a problem with the inheritance? Was there an underlying jealousy that he'd managed, until now, to keep to himself? There was, after all, some difference in status between village curate—even rector—and titled landowner-farmer, heir to the estate. And although he and Cynthia managed to exude an aura of rather chaotic domestic bliss, could there be more than that behind the scenes, as I knew there was behind most marital façades? The thought of watching him in action for the first time on Friday failed to provide me with any hope, and it was a long time before I slept.

Even then, I dreamt of enormous lakes, and boats, and huge mill-wheels thrashing the water, and my little Jamie yelling to me, over and over, that he could swim, and ride, and fly. I called to him, but he didn't hear me.

His initial disappointment was soon overcome by the promise of a day at Abbots Mere and a stay overnight, though it did not escape his notice that Mrs Goode and I wore our riding habits for our journey in the shining phaeton. That, we said, was easy enough to explain, for the temperature had fallen to below freezing during the night, and the fields, once white with reflected clouds, were now white with ice and frost, blinding us with flashes from the mirrored sun. But when he saw that Nana Frances and Grandpa were also dressed for riding, he felt obliged to make the plaintive enquiry, 'Am I going to ride with Uncaburl again, Mama?'

Winterson held out a hand. 'Come with me, Jamie. There's someone out here who needs to take a look at you.'

'Look at *me*, Uncaburl?' he said, clasping the large hand. 'Who wants to look at me?'

'A lady called Penny. She's out here.'

We followed, eager to catch the first rapturous expression on Jamie's face at his introduction to the dark brown mare, which to my mind was too large for him. A twelve-hand Shetland would have been far more suitable for a child of three. Jamie had no such reservations. Speechless with joy, he and the polite little mare formed an immediate bond of friendship, for he was confident from the beginning, without fear, taking the reins as he'd seen Winterson do, responsive to every instruction, determined to do everything correctly. His little feet hardly cleared the saddle-flaps, but the smile of pride in being a horseman at last helped to lift the burdens from my heart as nothing else could do. Watching them set off, side by side, one as tall as a church and the other reaching no further than the stallion's saddle was a sight to pull at my heartstrings, though I think only Goody noticed the glisten of a tear upon my cheek. I thought then that if Jamie were the one to receive his father's love, instead of both of us, I would not complain or allow it to embitter me.

There was something else to give me food for thought that morning, not having ridden out with Winterson and his guests since last autumn when Linas's health began to deteriorate. Then, I had been left much to my own devices by our host, except when I was with Linas or another guest, Winterson never singling me out for a word as he had done on that isolated day in April 1802, forgotten by my lover. Nevertheless, someone must have taken the trouble to remind Linas after that, for on the day after our return home that year, a red rose appeared on my hall table which I placed before me at breakfast, lunch and dinner until it withered. The same thing happened on my birthday the following three years. Linas was always undemonstrative, and I dare say that was his way of saying what he could not say in words.

The difference on that sharp frosty morning is worth recording if only for the happiness it gave me to be one of the group instead of an outsider tolerated only for her relationship with a brother. That day, I was made to feel like one whose opinions were valued, drawn into conversation, laughed with and teased, occasionally. Jamie, of course, preferred to take his instructions directly from Winterson rather than me.

'Bear up, Miss Follet,' said Lord Stillingfleete in an aside that everyone could hear, 'mothers are not supposed to know a thing about horses. Frances suffered in exactly the same way, convinced that Burl's first pony was far too large for him. It didn't do him any harm, in the end.'

'I seem to recall,' said Winterson, straight-faced, 'that a certain three-year-old *end* was rather sore for a day or two. As you say, I recovered.'

'Burl Winterson,' his mother reprimanded, 'there are ladies present.'

'Yes, Mama,' he said. 'Keep your hands together, Jamie.'

'I've lost my stirrup, Uncaburl.'

Winterson drew on the leading-rein. 'All right. Sort it out. Ready?'

'Yes.'

'My lord,' I said, 'is it time for Jamie to take a rest now?'

'Yes, and tomorrow he can practise riding bareback in the paddock.'

Mrs Goode's sidelong glance at me showed that her thoughts ran parallel to mine, that we had entered men's territory and that, from now on, Jamie's infancy was on the wane.

With a view to discussing what Jamie could and could not do tomorrow, I lingered near the pony's empty loose-box after the others had gone into the house, certain that Winterson would want a private word with me concerning Jamie's shifting allegiance and my sharing of him. New experiences, and not comfortable for a possessive mother.

He entered the stable, stopped, looked, and saw me. I had not expected to feel such breathless girlishness as he came slowly towards me, bare-headed, stripping off his gloves. Laying them with his whip along the top edge of the box, he steered me backwards by one arm into the thick brass-topped doorpost. 'I suppose you must go home this afternoon?' he said, not waiting for an answer. 'Because if I have to spend another night without you, Miss Follet, I may be obliged to make violent love to you here. Would you mind that?'

'Lord Winterson, *please*! I waited here to speak with you in private.' I was not as shocked as I pretended, and he knew it, but nor did I take his request at all seriously. What is it about stables, I wonder?

'Sorry. It's the figure-hugging jacket that brings out my baser instincts.'

'Then I'd better go and change into something looser.'

'No. Stay as you are. You did well just now. It's not easy for you, is it, to watch him pass into someone else's hands? But don't worry about tomorrow. My father will be there, and my head groom, and Mrs Goode. They won't overtire him. They'll show him how to groom the mare. He'll be quite safe.'

'Yes. Thank you. I know he will. He's beside himself with happiness.'

'He's going to be good.'

'Like his father,' I whispered, unable to avoid the ambiguity.

But his reply was to take me in his arms as I'd wanted him to, instinctively knowing which twin I referred to. 'You were thinking, out there, of those other times. I know. I could see it. But there's no need to, sweetheart. It's all in the past. Let it go.'

'I would, gladly, if I knew what it was all about.'

'One day we'll talk about it. Give me time. It's hard for me too.'

'I can wait. But don't turn cold on me again, Burl. Previously, if I'd had the courage, I could have walked away from it all. This time, I shall not be able to do that, shall I?'

'There'll be no walking away, lass. There'll be no cause. No more of those wild parties and loose women. Only people we both like.'

The wild parties were the least of my problems. 'Were there many loose women?' I asked.

'Only a few. No one I allowed you to meet.'

'That sounds, my lord, as if you cared who I met, which I find hard to believe. Half the time you didn't even know I was here.'

'Wrong, Miss Follet. I knew *exactly* where you were *all* the time. Particularly I knew where you were on the eighteenth day of April in 1802 during the hours of—'

'Stop! We must go in, or they'll come looking for us.' I pushed myself away from him, but he pulled me back roughly by my shoulders and I felt the hard sting of his hands as his kiss demonstrated how his desire had not cooled. If he recognised the reasoning behind my queries, he had given me no hint of it, and though I was tempted to share my concerns with him about the Slatterly woman, those few snatched moments were too precious to spoil when I had so little evidence to go on, and even that was at third hand.

So I savoured the warm seeking thrill of his lips as well as the pain of his hands, then the dizzying shock of release that made my walk across the cobbled stable-yard more dangerous than usual.

Hot chocolate and shortbread awaited us by the crackling fire, but I had sacrificed my sense of taste for the more powerful sense of yearning, and I might as well have been eating sawdust while I smiled and chatted as if nothing out of the ordinary was happening to me. He knew, I'm sure.

He knew enough of my strangely elevated status to escort me all round the house into places I had never had reason to visit before, opening up all the rooms to my inspection to show me, I presumed, what I would soon be mistress of. The kitchens, the extensive pantries and larders where game and poultry hung in furry bundles beside hams and sides of venison. Fresh fish waited for attention, baskets of eggs, shallow bowls of cream, shelves of cheeses and butter, wooden churns, racks of vegetables and bunches of pot-herbs. The beautiful frosted kitchen garden too, with glass succession-houses I had never seen before, and the wide lacy arms of fruit trees pinned against the walls. His roses, he told me, bloomed throughout winter and into spring.

He took me through the long gallery built in the sixteenth century for King Henry VIII's overnight stay at Abbots Mere. I had attended routs and balls here with Linas very occasionally, but Winterson must have guessed that I had never been introduced to their brooding ancestors who lined the oak-panelled walls. It was an omission he put to rights as we walked, finding yet another way to make up for his brother's lack of attention, which I knew better than anyone was more to do with his illness than deliberate neglect.

Perhaps, I thought as we joined the others, Winterson had at last begun to realise that it was not so much Linas's thoughtlessness that had hurt me most but his own icy detachment. For my part, it was not so much being mistress of that beautiful house that would soothe my pride, but knowing that, for whatever reason, Burl Winterson wanted me.

Chapter Thirteen

With no Jamie or his nurse for company, the evening felt oddly vacant. Yet although the house on Blake Street was almost back to normal, there were still a few things left to be rearranged and put away, and by bedtime I felt sure of being able to sleep soundly. The fresh air had done its work; riding was something I hoped to do more of, for Winterson had some very fine horses and some wonderful gallops too.

But as I lay in my bed thinking things over, I realised that the pile of Linas's notebooks I had last seen on the side table in the parlour had not been replaced. Nor could I recall where I had put them. They would be sure to turn up unexpectedly, somewhere.

Friday was the morning of Prue's parents' funeral and I was up early to the shop to place a notice in the window, to pull the blinds halfway down and to tie a large black satin bow over the coloured tassels. The wearing of black had almost become a habit with me, these days, and I longed to wear colours other than greys and violet. But propriety was everything to Follet and Sanders, so I did my best to be worthy of Prue by adding a long black feather boa to my ensemble, a plume of ostrich on my bonnet and a fine edge of the same around my wrists. With black braid frogging down the sleeves and a narrow panel of it down the front of my pelisse, I felt that she would approve. Even at a time like this, Prue Sanders would be critical of what her staff were wearing.

For the second day, the rooftops shone with white frost, and the cobbles had been sprinkled with straw to make them less treacherous as Debbie and I walked down to Stonegate to pick up the phaeton. Having no reason to call at the front entrance, our approach through the ginnel into the rear stableyard was the most direct way to approach the phaeton and the groom who would accompany us. Winterson's coachman was there talking to the green-and-grey liveried young man, showing me, by the way their conversation lingered, that something had disturbed them.

'Good morning,' I said. 'Are we ready?'

'Indeed we are, ma'am,' they said, touching their grey beavers.

'Something wrong?'

A quick glance at each other told me there was. 'Er…well…not exactly wrong, ma'am,' said the senior coachman, getting his word in first. 'Mr Treddle's had a bit of a problem at the house just now. His lordship gave us all instructions, you see, not to allow anyone in while he's away, excepting yourself, ma'am. So it's a bit tricky when…well…' He touched his nose with a

knuckle, striving to be respectful in his bluff Yorkshire way.

'When someone demands an entry? Anyone I
know?'

'Lady Slatterly, ma'am. She was none too pleased
to find that his lordship's not here, you see. Didn't
believe Mr Treddle when he told her. Kicked up a bit
of a fuss, she did.'

'He's gone over to Foss Beck,' I said.

'Yes, ma'am, though we didn't tell her ladyship that.
She drove out of here like the devil himself was after
her. She'll ruin her horses if she drives 'em like that.'

I would like to have asked if she'd gone to Abbots
Mere where my Jamie was, but that would not have
been discreet. 'Yes,' I said, looking away down the
covered passage to the street beyond, imagining Veronique clattering through, desperate to see Winterson.
Well, there was nothing I could do about it, but my first
thoughts were for Jamie's safety rather than for
Veronique's peace of mind.

I cannot say I enjoyed the drive to Osbaldwick, being
forced to concentrate fully on the frozen mud ruts that
knocked the phaeton about in a most uncomfortable
fashion. I was obliged to walk the horses for most of
the way, to save their hooves. The countryside was
white, the dried grasses laced with cobwebs that shim-
mered in the sun, and soon we caught up with other carriages travelling towards the sound of tolling bells, then
groups of black-clad people walking from cottage to
church. It was obvious that Prue's parents had been
well loved, for there were several phaetons and car-

riages already lining the narrow street, and crowds passing through the lych-gate into St Thomas's Church.

Inside, I sat with our staff from the shop, and because I was placed to one side of a thick stone pillar, I doubt that Medworth Monkton knew I was there. But it gave me the chance to watch him closely, to see how he fluffed his lines and almost dropped his prayer book as he turned the pages with shaking hands. Something, I thought, was wrong with the man, usually so amiable and at ease. The traipse out to the burial site was, as always, a sombre affair that reminded me too closely of my late lover and his winter resting place, and had it not been for my promise to support Prue, I would have chosen to stand some distance away so as not to see. As it was, I stood with my arm around her shoulders as she had done for me, which appeared to do nothing to ease Medworth's trembling, and he hurried through the service of commital as if he too would rather have been elsewhere. Perhaps, I thought, this was too near his brother's burial for him to distance himself.

I looked for him after that, while Prue greeted her friends, but he had disappeared. This was very odd behaviour, for a curate ought to stay with the bereaved as a matter of courtesy, if not duty. So I slipped quietly back to the church ostensibly to congratulate him on his forthcoming advancement, though in fact to remind him where he was needed most. He had offered me the benefit of his advice; I would offer him some of mine.

The sound of voices from the vestry ought to have made me turn about and return to Prue, having only recently eavesdropped on a private conversation. I was not at all comfortable with the underhandedness of it, but while it was not in my nature to enjoy such a thing, my curiosity was at once alerted by Medworth's unusually sharp tone and by the answering one, in some distress, of Lady Veronique Slatterly. Yes, I was quite sure it was her because it was her name that Medworth snapped out, impatiently.

'You should not have come here, Veronique, on such a day. You *must* know I cannot see you. Go back home.'

There was a sound like a cough or a sob, and I froze, hating myself for staying, half-turning to go, but held back by my heart that told me I was in some way involved, willing or not. This was undoubtedly not a good time for her to seek counselling from her adviser, and his tone must have convinced her of his lack of sympathy, in case she had other ideas.

'You're avoiding me,' she whimpered from the vestry side of the curtain, a heavy purple thing with a fringe along the bottom meant to conceal the changing of vestments rather than conversations. 'Everybody is avoiding me. And you lied to me about Mrs Monkton.'

'Shh!'

She ignored his command. 'You told me you and Mrs Monkton were not intimate any more, but you were, weren't you? And you let me find out about her condition at the ball, of all places, when I couldn't…couldn't…' The sobbing voice faded and choked. 'So…so unkind of you. I don't suppose *she* knows about *my* condition, does she?'

'Hush, for pity's sake, Veronique. Of course she doesn't. Why would I tell her *that*? It has nothing to do with Cynthia. And I did *not* lie about not being… well…affectionate. It was true at the time.'

I heard again the sanctimonious tone he'd used to me, excusing, validating, squirming with righteousness. I wanted to burst through the curtain to take her side and demand a proper hearing, but perhaps I had no need, for he had made her angry too, and she was unwilling to be brushed aside simply because he had a funeral party to attend.

'Stop! Don't go!' she insisted. I saw the curtain billow. 'You'll *have* to tell her, Medworth. *This* is your doing too, you know.'

If I had not been told of her condition beforehand, I would not have guessed that she must be pointing to herself, the connection never having occurred to me after what he'd told me on Wednesday. Her accusation hit me like a thunderbolt. Not Winterson, but Medworth himself, taking advantage of those advisory sessions with his patron's unhappy daughter.

'Of *course* it isn't,' he rasped, half-whisper, half-yelp. 'And I have not been avoiding you. I have duties to perform that I've already neglected for your sake. And I told you before that it *must* be Winterson's. You know the reason, Veronique. He's free and I'm not, and with enough pressure from you and your father, and from me, and eventually from Miss Follet, he'll be obliged to accept it. Think of that. You'll be Lady Winterson. That's what you've always wanted, isn't it?'

'No!' she snapped. 'Not at *that* price, Medworth. He would not give in to that kind of pressure when he knows as well as I do that it cannot possibly be his.'

'Cannot? What nonsense is this? Of course it can.'

'No. I lied to you too.'

'What d'ye mean, lied? About what?'

'I've never been to bed with your brother. It's *your* child, not his.'

There was a pause, then the shocked, disbelieving reaction that I was fortunate not to have received from Linas when I'd told him about Jamie. That was something that had lain heavily on my conscience ever since, that I had been obliged to lie to everyone about the child's father for *his* sake, not for my own. It had been unforgivable, even while sparing me the gossip.

'I don't believe you,' Medworth said, coldly. 'You told me—'

'Of course I did. It was what you wanted me to say, wasn't it? That your brother and I had been lovers too. Well, now I'm telling you the truth—I have *never* been to bed with him, not ever. He would never be alone with me, and, yes, I *did* want him, have always wanted him more than anyone, but you didn't want to hear that, did you? You said you could offer me your comfort for his offhandedness, and now you don't want to know about it. But you can't foist it off on to your brother, Medworth. It won't work, and he knows it. It's his twin's woman *he's* always wanted, not me.' Her voice wavered and, at that point, I almost turned and left, for my guilty heart was not so well seasoned that I was immune to her anguish. She had felt his indifference too.

'You're lying again. I thought you and my brother would surely have…'

'I'm not lying. It's the truth. Why d'ye think I needed your comfort? Because you're irresistible? I've resisted better men than you, Medworth.'

'The father must be one of those you didn't resist, then. There have been plenty of them, I'm sure.'

'Not recently there haven't. You'll have to accept it because you're the only one responsible and there's no reason why I should pretend otherwise. *You* told me Mrs Monkton was ill and that you'd always wanted me. You said you loved me more than anyone. You didn't say she was ill with morning sickness, as I have been, did you?'

'Oh, God, this is terrible. It will be the end of me.'

'Have you told anyone about…about *my* condition?'

'No, of course not. I have to go, Veronique. I have people to see. I've done all I can for you. Really…no… let me go…*please*!'

The curtain billowed again as I watched, horrified, imagining the tussle that was being enacted in that confined space, her desperation, his determined cowardice, the terrible spinelessness that convinces men that black is white, that up is down, that no means yes if that is what will serve their purpose best. Guiltily, I shrunk back into the shadows, expecting one of them to emerge like a bullet within the next moment.

But it spoke volumes for Veronique's mettle when her shape appeared with arms outstretched, bulging across the curtain, preventing his escape. 'Oh, no,' she whispered, growling with menace, 'oh, no, Medworth Monkton. Don't you walk away this time and pretend innocence just because you think your word will be believed above mine. This time, there's your brother's word too, isn't there? Tell him about it, if you wish, and see what *he* tells you when he's stopped laughing. And tell my father too. *He* knows that Winterson isn't stupid enough to get *me* pregnant while he's hoping to catch Linas's woman, even if *you* are.'

'*You* tell your father,' he replied, cuttingly. 'You tell

him and see if he can't come up with half a dozen names who could easily have fathered your brat, Lady Slatterly. Why, you could have had a stableful by now with the kind of generosity *you* practise. How else could it have happened but by your own stupid carelessness?'

The bulge in the curtain disappeared, and a loud crack swayed it in the draught. Then, after a hiss of pain from within, the curtain was thrown aside with a rattle and Medworth stumbled through the gap with one hand pressed to the side of his head, bent very low.

Pressing myself back against the wall, I saw him pause and cling to one of the pews, take a look at his hand, then continue on round the corner to the small north door, the way he had apparently entered. Inside the vestry, the low sound of sobbing tore at my heart and filled my lungs with the painful beginnings of a wail. I could have gone in to her; I could have offered her whatever comfort a rival has to offer, but I had to choose between her and Prue. And I chose Prue because that was why I had gone there.

If I had been in the same dreadful position, I told myself, I would have preferred privacy after what had just happened, and that poor Veronique would probably want the same. And for all my odious guilt at having overheard what I had absolutely no right to know about, my regard for her privacy and my silence on the matter gave me some comfort all through the wake that followed the burial, the usual noisy gathering for refreshments, condolences and reminiscences.

Prue's appreciation was demonstrated in a motherly hug that, had she but known it, I was in need of almost as much as she, while the shock of what I'd discovered

resounded in my head like the clamour of church bells.
When Prue asked me where the curate had disappeared
to, I murmured something in his defence that he had
looked very unwell and had probably had to hurry
home, which was better than saying that he would not
wish to appear with a distinctly red hand-print on his
cheek.

Prue understood when I asked to leave the wake
before it had run its course, for now she was amongst
friends who would talk far into the evening. Naturally,
my mind dwelt on what I'd heard, on Medworth's
betrayal of his position, on Veronique's misery and on
my own decision to withhold offers of help for fear of
being thought intrusive. It was none of my business, my
conscience told me, without conviction. It was a lie, of
course. If it had not concerned me, I would not have
stayed to listen. Yet my guilt gave me little respite, and
my punishment was a pounding headache.

Back at Blake Street I sat beside a roaring fire with
my child and his nurse, a tray of tea, lemonade, and a
dish of buttery muffins hot from the kitchen, listening
to his back-to-front accounts of how he'd ridden
without a saddle, 'To strengthen my thighs,' he said,
glowing with three-year-old pride. 'And now they ache,
Mama, but Uncaburl's man says it's good for me.'

I hugged him to me, smelling the straw and stables
on him. 'Well done, little one,' I said. 'You shall have a
warm bath to soak the aches away. Did they show you
how to groom Penny and make her shine?'

'Yes, I stood on a box to reach her back an' she
stood still an' liked it, an I fed her carrots, and I ate all

my…' a mighty yawn interrupted the flow before the final '…greens for Nana Frances and Grandpa, Mama.'

To keep him awake until bedtime, I took him with me to the shop's deserted workrooms while I assessed all the available spaces in the property that Prue would have been able to use as living quarters if she'd not been obliged to live with her parents. There was no reason now why she could not live above the shop, rent free, if only we could clear some of the rooms and provide the basic amenities for her. It was an arrangement that might help to soften the blow of not having Pierre's bounty to sell.

After dinner that evening, as we sat by the fire in the drawing room, the sound of the door-knocker made us look up in the hope that it might be Lord Winterson, although I did not expect him. The footman tapped and entered. 'Lady Slatterly, ma'am,' he said.

My astonishment must have lingered on my face as she came forwards, for although she had indeed been at the forefront of my mind, I never expected her to show up here. 'What a pleasant surprise,' I said, responding to her curtsy. 'Please forgive the informality. Will you sit with us a while?'

I had seen her in all sorts of conditions over the years, ever since her first acid comments meant to wound me and, more recently, when she had been thankful to accept my goodwill. So my reading of her manner on this occasion was well informed, and clearly she was not a picture of happiness. There were red rims to her eyes, and she wore an air of uncertainty that was very different from the usual and, although she concealed her anguish with courage, it showed through in so many small ways. Forcing a smile, her eyes darted to Mrs Goode and Jamie.

'Mrs Goode,' I said, 'will you take Jamie up for his bath now, please?'

Once we were alone, Veronique's shoulders sagged with relief. As if unsure whether she was doing the right thing in approaching me this way, she took sleep-walking steps to the nearest chair and sat sideways on the edge of it. This was most unlike the Veronique I knew. And no wonder.

Fidgeting with her reticule, she blinked at me as if deciding how best to explain her visit. 'Helene,' she said at last, 'you were once kind enough to speak out for me.'

'At the ball. Yes, I remember. Men can be so insensitive, sometimes.'

'Yes. So I've come to ask…er…to ask you a favour. To ask your advice, actually…er…not for me, but for a friend of mine. She has a problem, you see, and I told her you might know how to…er…advise her what's best to do. She has no one else but me to turn to. Her other friends would not wish to be involved. It's all so…so difficult.'

My heart softened and ached for her. No one else to turn to but the one who had last said something kindly in her defence. Such unhappiness. What rejection she must be feeling. 'Of course I'll help your friend if I can,' I said. 'Is she about our age, or older?'

'Yes, she's our age. My age, actually. We've been close for years. She's done something foolish. Very… very…foolish.'

I saw that she struggled to hold back her tears, so

while she took a few moments to compose herself, I went to pour a glass of wine and place it beside her. 'Take a sip,' I said, 'then tell me how I can help your friend. I take it there may be a man involved?'

She sniffed, then nodded, but this time the fair ringlet did not bounce. The white fur collar reflected its pallor upon her mottled skin, and despite the brightly patterned pelisse-robe, she was far from the winter cheer it was meant to represent. At last, her wide-brimmed bonnet lifted. 'Yes, there is a man involved, but he doesn't want to know.'

'Know what, Veronique?'

'That she's going to be a mother. You're not shocked?'

'No, I'm not shocked. I am an unmarried mother too.'

'That's another reason why I thought you might know what to do.'

'If the man involved doesn't want to accept his responsibility, it makes life very difficult. Do her parents know about her problem?'

'No. She has only one parent.'

'I see. I had only one parent too.'

'Did you? That makes it even harder then, doesn't it?'

'Not really. Not if the parent is on her side, and loves her.'

Her eyebrows lifted at that. 'Doesn't it?' she said.

'No. There's only one opinion, one reaction, one shock. It often makes things simpler. Is there some reason why your friend may not wish to tell her parent? The point is, you see, that if she lives at home, her parent is going to discover it sooner or later, so perhaps it would be best if she said something herself before someone else does.'

'But it would hurt him so, wouldn't it?' she whispered.

'My dear, it would hurt him even more if he found out by accident. If it's from her father your friend is hoping for most help, then surely it's only fair to confide in him at the beginning so that they can discuss what to do about it. Is he the kind of man to fall into a rage, your friend's father?'

'No, he wouldn't do that. I'm sure of it.'

'He loves her very much, does he?'

'Indeed he does, but he'd want to know who's responsible, and she cannot tell him that.'

'She cannot…because…?'

'Because he's married, Helene. That's why he doesn't wish to accept the responsibility. I believe,' she added, as if she wasn't sure.

'Then I would not wish to persuade her otherwise,' I said, thinking quite the opposite. 'She's obviously a loyal young lady whose affection for the father runs very deep. Most of us would prefer him to be honest and admit that he has a part to play in the affair, and most parents would wish to know who'd sired their grandchild. But that decision must remain with your friend, after all.'

'I suppose it must,' she said, looking into the fire, 'and I'm sure she ought to take her father into her confidence. He'll be very upset, though.'

'Veronique, I think you'll find that fathers often understand how such things can happen. He may well be upset, and angry, and concerned for your friend, but if he loves her as you say he does, he won't wish to hurt her more than she is already. My advice would be for her to go and talk to him about it without delay, apologise for the pain she's caused and ask for his help. No hysterics. No blaming anyone. No threats or unkind words that she'll regret later. And no packing of bags, tell her.'

'Yes. I will. Thank you.'

'If you would like to talk about it some more, I shall be happy to listen, and to help, if I can. But go to your friend now and see what she thinks. Let me know, will you?'

'You've been very kind,' she whispered, pulling on her soft kid gloves. 'Men can be so unpredictable, can't they?' Placing a light hand on my arm, she brushed a kiss upon both my cheeks, which surprised me.

'Men are governed by different forces from us, but there are some exceptions out there. Does your friend have any exceptional men friends?'

Stretching out the fingers of one hand, she stroked the back of her glove as if imagining a wedding ring there. 'There is one... yes...who's been in love with me... *her*...for years. It's possible that he may help her out of her troubles. But it wouldn't be quite fair, would it?'

'Only if he's given the full story and is allowed to choose, not otherwise. He would have to know the facts and, even then, only if your friend truly believed she could be a loyal and faithful wife to him. Such things are not uncommon and often turn out to be very happy. I feel hardly in a position to act as adviser here, but it may be worth thinking about, especially since the child's father is not in a position to offer any help.'

'It would serve him right if I made his name known

to *everyone*,' she whispered, fiercely. 'He's getting away without a blemish.'

'Yes, probably. But he's not the only one who'd suffer, is he?'

She turned her hand over to stare at the palm, then closed her fist. 'He didn't let that thought bother him. I shall go and tell her what you've said, Helene. Thank you. It's at times like this when she misses her mama most.'

'When did your friend lose her mama, Veronique?'

'When I was fourteen, she left Papa for another man, but then she died only six months later in Scotland and we never saw her again. Papa was broken-hearted. He loved her too.' The distress still showed in her voice.

'Which is perhaps why,' I said, hearing the shift in her account from third to first person, 'you ought to confide in him, to let him know that he's needed. It sounds as if you may need each other's comfort.'

'Yes,' she said. 'I don't know why I didn't see it before.'

I surprised myself then by taking her into my embrace and holding the motherless miserable creature as if she were my sister while my secret knowledge burned holes in my conscience.

When she had gone, I found that my legs were shaking, whether from the effort of the last half-hour or from relief that Veronique had unwittingly verified all that Winterson had said about their relationship. I could not condone his apparent heartlessness any more than I could condone his earlier coldness to me, and I was sorry, in a way, that my own peace of mind had been bought at the price of her deep unhappiness. Yet it *had* been bought, and I was both glad and flattered that she had come to me, of all people, for honest objective advice. That was the least I could offer her, though I would like to have done more. On reflection, the only other thing I could do was to keep silent and respect her confidence, as her faithless lover had failed to do.

As for my enquiries about the possibility of a beau who might help her out, I had no qualms on that score, impersonal though it may seem. Wealthy fathers were often able to find bidders in the marriage stakes willing to take on an erring daughter, with enough inducement. The added benefit of knowing a man who had loved her for years cast a very positive light on the proceedings, and clearly Veronique was not against the idea in principle. In fact, I had never known her speak with such a lack of waspishness or self-pity.

With my head in my hands I stared into the fire, watching the flames lick around the logs and thinking how fortunate I had been compared to Veronique, whose life of wealth and luxury had not compensated one bit for the tragic loss of her mother at the age of fourteen. I was exactly that age when my father had gone from us in such frightening circumstances, yet although I'd had to venture out into the world owning next to nothing and expecting little, Fate had treated me with kindness, though until now I had failed to appreciate its methods. Is that what it had taken, I asked myself, to make me see how carefully Fate had taken me under her wing, providing me with a protector, then a child, and finally a promise of marriage to the man I loved? So, there had been deceptions, but not of the kind that Medworth used on Veronique and his loyal wife. There had been a loss of pride when I discovered how I had been used, as mistresses *are* used. But of what good was it to perpetuate my grumbles when I had my adored Jamie to bring me such joy? The rejection Veronique had suffered from both Winterson and his devious brother was of a more heartbreaking kind than I had suffered, including the thoughtlessness from his twin.

As my thoughts turned to Linas, I saw another day passing without having found the notebooks that might tell me, if nothing else, what his accounting was like and how much he had paid out for my upkeep. So when I had tucked Jamie up in bed, told him a story and said prayers, I left him in Goody's safekeeping and went down to begin the search again, eventually finding the books in a cupboard where the spare napkins and table covers had been put away.

Placing Veronique's untouched glass of wine at my elbow and the three leather-bound notebooks on my knees, I turned up the wick of the lamp and opened the first and smallest of them. As I suspected, it consisted of payments to the grocer, the chandler, the butcher and fishmonger, the carriage-maker and farrier, money paid to his tailor, bootmaker and hatter, the snuff-maker and, before my time with him, a record of payments to the jeweller for trinkets, a fob-watch, chain, and quizzing-glass. Running my finger down the more recent pages, I saw expenses for Jamie—bed linen, a cot, a small chair and a walking-frame from the carpenter—though all his clothes had been made by myself and Mrs Goode from fabrics obtained from the shop, costing Linas nothing. Even my own clothes, except for shoes, has cost Linas nothing. There were no surprises here.

The second notebook was no more than a catalogue of the volumes in his study on ethnography, geology and geography, on Greek and Roman sculptures and artifacts from Japan and India, on seashells and fossils, and rare plants from South America. Linas was never happier than when he was studying amongst his books.

The third one appeared to be a collection of his own essays on various topics, like one on Charles Townley's collection of antiques in his Park Lane house. That, I remembered, had been on our last visit together to London. Flipping through the pages, I saw another one headed 'Greek Vases in the Sir John Soane Collection', and another, 'On Earthquakes and Volcanoes'. I was just about to close it when I saw the familiar name of Helene, which I assumed would be Helen of Troy in that kind of company. It was his last entry, and I would have closed the book but for the word 'Burl' that sprang out of the pages as if it had been written in red ink instead of grey-black.

I was intrigued, feeling once more like the eavesdropper choosing to listen in to someone's private musings. This was getting to be a habit. I closed the book and sat with my hand on the cover, hearing the voices of conscience yet again, then Linas's voice telling me to go on.

Open it. Read it. It's meant for you.

I caressed the pages where his hand had rested, absorbing the touch of him from the faintly lined creamy paper. The voice faded and left me to my own devices and to the burning need to know why my name was there with Burl's. There was no heading to this last essay, only the date, October 10th, 1805, which was only days before he was taken to Abbots Mere to live out the last of his time. It was addressed to me, *Beloved Helene*.

Beloved? He had never called me that. 'Love' was his only tag for me, the usual Yorkshire form of address to anyone remotely friendly. 'C'mon, love,' he would call to me. Adjusting the book to catch the best light, I sat back in my chair and, to the sonorous ticking of the clock, began to read.

Chapter Fourteen

Beloved Helene. Dubiously, my gaze hung over the words.

The house is quiet now and I am unable to sleep until this story is told, for I shall leave here in the next day or two with little prospect of a return. You came to me this evening with our Jamie, as always, to perform those countless little services for me, too intimate to delegate to anyone except family. I never thought a three-year-old child could be so helpful or bring us such happiness, nor did I ever think I would have the love and devotion of a woman like you to take me to the end of my life. Beloved, I am truly blessed, and I wish I could say that I have no regrets, but, alas, that would be untrue. I have. And it is those regrets that must be explained while I still have time and strength, and although I would prefer to have explained them to you face to face, I fear that I would express myself so clumsily, thus undoing any advantage of spontaneity. No, I see you smile, spontaneity was never Linas's forte, was it? A planner, a deliberator, a scholar, perhaps, but hardly a creature of impulse.

You will know by now the regrets to which I refer, for although you never allowed that knowledge to colour your devotion to me, it placed upon you an unfair burden that was sometimes too hard for you to carry.

Oh, Linas, it *did* colour my devotion. If only you knew.

To tell you how and why may not earn your forgiveness, after all, but perhaps Burl will put in a good word for me now that he is claiming what was rightly his to begin with. How do I know that? Because I know my brother well; he would not delay for a day on something as important as this, and by now he will have begun his re-conquest of you.

You were seventeen when we met, beloved Helene— no, Linas, I was not seventeen until April—*a flower of a woman, a dazzling beauty who outshone every other female at the Assembly Rooms on that St Valentine's Day, and if I am not so articulate now, I was even less so then. Tongue-tied. Mute. I did not stand a chance with you. Together, Burl and I saw you enter, and I felt his reaction immediately. Yes, felt it. Don't ask me to define it. I cannot, except to say that his quietness took on a different quality that only a close relative would recognise. It was never his way, was it, to crowd in with the others?*

Nevertheless, it was not long before you stood up with him, nor was it long before everyone who saw you together knew that something momentous was happening before their eyes, and when Burl introduced us, I doubt if you heard a word he said. I remember it better than you think, dear Linas. *Still, you politely danced*

*with me without realising that I was as smitten as he.
How could you have known that my desire was like a
pain, all the more intense because whenever Burl
looked at a woman, she was as good as his?*

*You could not have known how it was between us,
Burl and me, close-coupled in mind and spirit, though
not in body. The very best of friends, yet rivals in love.
Whatever woman came my way, Burl's magnetism drew
her irrevocably towards him instead. Any woman I
managed to attract, one-tenth of Burl's tally, would
also see him, and whether he responded to her or not,
I might as well have been invisible for all the attention
I won. I grew used to it, yet I resented it even though I
knew it was never his intention, and, although I did
have flirtations, I was glad to move to Stonegate where
the chances of keeping a woman to myself for longer
were marginally better.*

*But that St Valentine's Ball, dearest Helene, was a
milestone for me, having just received from my doctor
a period of three years at the most in which to cram
every happy circumstance before it was too late. So live
life to the full, he advised me. I had never been strong,
as you know, but I think his prognosis surprised even
me. And now I had seen the woman of my dreams, the
one I wanted above all others, already beyond my
reach. What galled me most, I think, is that Burl's relationships with women had always been fleeting
affairs before the inevitable diversion of another more
alluring creature. Yes, it was the hunt that Burl enjoyed
most—the chase, the capture, the capitulation. And that
night, I saw the possibility of you being caught, flaunted
and then left while I watched again from the side, seeing*

*my chances and my life slip quietly away together. He
was in love with you, there is no doubt of that, but then
so was I. Impotently, disastrously, angrily in love.*

*But I knew something that, at the time, Burl did not
know, that you had no means, that your family were
unable to help you, that you had been supported by two
lovers for a short period, and that you worked for the
milliner and mantua-maker on Blake Street. How did I
know that? By overhearing the gossip that spread like
a forest fire through the ballroom while you and he were
dancing. You were vulnerable,* chère *Helene, and while
Burl would offer you the moon to hold for a few fabulous
weeks, or even months, I wanted to offer you the security
of my home and all the amenities that a mistress needs
who has nothing of her own. I had only three years left;
no long drawn-out sentence for you to endure and
better, I thought, than being yet one more of Burl's cast-
offs. I was what you needed, dearest love, and you were
what I needed. You were all ready to fall into my
brother's arms. I decided to take matters into my own
hands, truly the closest I have ever been to being spontaneous.*

*The next day I went to Abbots Mere, ostensibly to tell
Burl of my doctor's prediction for my short future. We
wept, trying to think of ways round the sentence, but
there were none. Our parents and Medworth should be
prepared, he said. It was only fair. He would see that I
had everything I wanted in my last years. Everything.
Nothing would be denied. What was it I wanted most?
Funds? To travel to Italy? Or Switzerland?*

*Wanting only you, I saw my chance. 'Miss Helene
Follet,' I said. 'She is my only desire.'*

Oh, Linas. Dear Linas. Is this how it happened, then?

I recall how Burl went to stand by the mantelpiece, resting his head on his arm across the shelf as if it was too heavy for him, and his silence almost made me change my mind. 'Why?' he said at last. 'Why her?'

'I need her,' I replied. 'Three more years are of no use to me unless I have her beside me, and I doubt I could even live them at all, seeing her with you, Burl. That's asking too much of me.'

It was asking too much of him too, I knew that, but I was convinced that although he too was in love with you then, it would not last and you would soon be broken-hearted, bewildered, and no better off materially than you were before. As love triangles go, this was the worst it could get, I thought. I was wrong, as you know.

For a while, the light seemed to go out of him, Helene. 'What do you want me to do?' he said.

'Leave her alone,' I told him. 'Leave her to me. She'll accept me, if only because I'm your brother and what I can offer her will be too good to refuse. She needs a patron, Burl. And anyway, I have only three years. If you feel the same way about her then as you do now, you'll be able to carry on from where you left off. She'll only be twenty. But I want an heir, Burl. Sounds daft, I know, but the thought of leaving without even a son to carry on my line is the saddest thing that could happen. I've never got a woman with child yet, but with her I could, I know it.'

'How can you be sure she'll accept you?' he said.

'I've told you. She needs a place of her own and long-term stability. If she becomes a mother to my child, she'll be glad of my protection.'

'At Stonegate? Let her have Blake Street, then. It's not far to walk.'

That much of the conversation I can remember clearly, but I was winning him over, Helene. Blake Street is his property, and he was already planning to give you the use of it as if it was mine. Looking back, I see that it must have given him some small pleasure to know that you would be living in his house, even if you didn't know it. He offered me the use of his servants, too. And to pay all the running costs. He was always generous.

He did, however, have some provisos of his own. About the offspring. If it happened, he said, that you were to produce a Monkton heir, then the child would need a guardian, the obvious person being himself. I must appoint him as such in my will. I agreed. It will bind you two together for many more years after I have gone, for one thing. Forgive me, Helene. I did it for the best. If I had known then what I know now, I would not have made such a fateful request of my brother, but how could I have foreseen that Burl's passion for you would burn so fiercely for so long? At the time of our agreement he tried to put me off, saying you were sure to be unreliable, a vision too good to be true. But my heart was already yours, my dear, and my three years already beginning to shine with contentment.

Ah, the unreliable part. I see now. But Burl's passion? Is that true?

He agreed to leave you alone, not to do anything to attract you or to win his regard, not to allow you one speck of hope or to add fuel to your desire for him. Oh, yes, I could see it, dear Helene. You tried to hide it, but yours are not the kind of emotions that can easily be hidden. And though you did your best to hide your anguish too, and your hurt, you kindly accepted my offer for reasons I shall never quite understand except that the arrangement would allow you to see the one who had misled you about his interest.

No, Linas, that was the hardest part of all, seeing him. I accepted your offer because, as you said, I needed you and you needed me, and the fact that the house on Blake Street was so convenient for my work with Prue Sanders.

Naturally, I had to tell you of my lifespan and to give you a choice; to do otherwise would have been barbaric. But you bore the news well, and maybe it was that which gave you a reason to put on a brave face and to give me all I could have wished for in devotion, nursing and loving. I always found it impossible to tell you, dearest beloved Helene, that your loving companionship was the heaven for which I had bargained with my brother. I should have written to you sooner about my adoration.

You may be wondering, beloved, when my regrets began. Not during those nights of tender lovemaking, to be sure, but on those days when we visited Abbots Mere and I could see how well Burl stuck to the letter of our agreement and, worse, its effect on you. There were times when I wanted to revoke it, to beg him to be a little kinder to you, but it was a risk I dared not take, being selfish, wanting you all for myself. I know now how very unhappy I made you even while you had my protection, yet my regrets on that score were to multiply.

Two years passed without a sign of my much-wanted

*heir, and my doctor and I were forced to the conclusion
that the infertility was linked to my illness, not to you.
You may also have wondered why I never asked you to
marry me in those early years, but to be honest I saw
no reason to. You will be well provided for when I am
no longer with you, dearest Helene, for I have always
known that Burl will claim you and our son, especially
as he was so far-sighted as to lay claim to my heir's
guardianship, even before he knew the exact circumstances. Moreover, widowhood brings its own complications of inheritance and relationship and, in short, I
felt that for you to remain as a spinster would make
things simpler for Burl and for you to come together
without blame or scandal. For both your sakes, I pray
that it has already happened.*

*But when I realised I was not likely to produce an
heir, I decided to share my concerns with Burl and, once
again, beg him to help me. I need not tell you how much
he fought against my suggestion, knowing how it would
immediately wreck the relationships we had put in
place, how distraught you would be by the second in-
explicable withdrawal of his affection, how bitter you
would have every right to be when you began to realise
the purpose of it, and how worried you would be about
the initial deception to myself, the one who had
provided for you. So I brought to bear all the ammunition to the argument, how I'd already used up two-
thirds of my predicted time and how, if you became
pregnant by him in the near future, I would have only
a few months in which to see my son. Could he deny me
that? I asked. Could he also deny himself, and you, one
night of bliss as a foretaste of what was to come? Would*

the damage outweigh the benefits, did he think? Were you likely to allow him access to your bed?

No, he said, you most certainly would not. You had pride, and who did I think I was talking about...a whore who shares her body with anyone she fancies? He could have one of those any day of the week, he said. He was astonished I could even ask. Yes, he was very angry.

I begged him, Helene. Yes, it was my doing, not his. I promised him I would not lay an ounce of blame on you or him, but take any offspring as my own, male or female, even though it would look like a miracle. I would love it as my own too. I told him I would not want the details, the how, or when, or where. I would leave it to him, and then to you to break the good news, having not the slightest doubt about the success. It was not, however, the kind of request I could expect to be answered there and then, and indeed he never did answer it in words, only in the deed. And even as I write, I am not in a position to guess how, or even if, he explained himself to you. Needless to say, the very thought of sharing you even briefly with my brother was like a knife wound in my soul.

Oh, dear Linas, I begin to wonder if you had a soul and, if so, where you hid it. How could anyone use a woman so, without a word to her?

But although my joy at Jamie's birth was boundless, dearest Helene, I saw how shame, humiliation and sadness showed through your lovely dark eyes, and how Burl's coolness towards you was unchanged, and there has not been a day since then when I have not tried hard to justify the impositions I placed on you both for my sake. Yes, to save my face, you lied to everyone for me about our Jamie's parentage. You swallowed your pride and hid your pain from everyone but Burl and me, yet I suffered not one word of reproach from either of you. I could give you no comfort, my Helene, because that would have been to admit my treachery, and ruin with distrust what were to have been my last few months. As it turned out, the wonders of fatherhood gave me an extended lease of life that I have always accepted as a precious gift from you, Burl and little Jamie. It has been more than I deserve. And now we have worked out the complicated plot and my story is at an end, at last.

Forgive me, dearest beloved. I have thought too much of my own desires and not enough of yours. When I am gone, you may find it in your heart to understand the kind of love I have for you that asks far more than love is allowed to ask. Or give. Burl has burned for you through all these years in a way I never believed was possible and, if I had not already done enough damage to last one lifetime, I would beg you to listen to him, and believe, if ever he tells you so. His suffering was for my sake, too.

God Bless you, dearest Helene, and our beloved son. Linas Monkton.

Yelping, gasping with grief, I put the book down, for it was trembling too much for me to read and my sobs shook my arms uncontrollably. Blinding hot tears crumpled my body into a heap, slamming the book shut between my knees and dropping it to the floor. His writing was so eloquent, yet he had never once hinted at his feelings in spoken words, never remembered special days, never voiced what his heart felt or what he knew death was about to take from him. But worse than that was the way he had abused his brother's love. I had accused Burl of using me; now I saw how he too had been manipulated, his emotions bribed into submission by Linas's demands. Knowing his brother's generosity, Linas had wrung him like a sponge to get what he wanted for his last three years and, although this had caused the birth of our darling Jamie, to do so in such a self-serving fashion at the expense of our happiness was unforgivable. He had asked for understanding, but my wretchedness could not find even the smallest crumb of it.

The clock struck nine and, as if obeying some kind of signal, I tried to slow my roaring into my handkerchief and clear my mind.

The tears began again. Stopped again.

The servants must not hear. They already had.

There was a tap on the door and Mrs Goode slipped into the room through a haze of my tears. Saying nothing, she came to hold me in her arms, bringing me back to earth with the smoothing and patting of her hands. 'It's the funeral isn't it?' she said. 'It's brought it all back to you. Shall I make you a cup of hot chocolate? I'll tell Debbie to go and warm your bed. You've had a busy day.' She bent to pick up the book and restore it to the pile, perhaps suspecting something in the handwritten pages.

'No, Goody. Bring me the woollen cloak. I'm going to Stonegate.'

She took me by the elbows. 'Can it not wait?' she whispered.

I shook my head, hoping she would not ask why.

'Shall I come with you?'

'No, you stay with Jamie. I just want…to…' Tears flowed again.

'Shh, it's all right, I know. But you ought not to go out alone.'

'It's not far. I won't be long.'

She brought my cloak and changed my shoes for me, frowning the perplexed footman into silence as I left the house. I clung to the railing beside the ice-covered steps, staggering like a drunk along the slippery pavement that twinkled with new frost under the lamps, passing the dark frontages of Blake Street, most of them shuttered for the night. Linas's house on Stonegate, now his brother's, was in darkness except for the brazier stuck into the metal holder beside the door.

Mr Treddle answered my knock, admirably concealing his surprise at my tear-stained face, extending a kindly hand to help me up the last step, drawing me like a father into the darkened hall as if he needed no explanation for my presence there. 'My dear lady,' he said. 'Come inside.' It was familiar, I know, but familiarity was what I had come for.

But if he had asked me why I had come, what I needed, what I would see, I could only have told him that I needed to be where Linas and I had been together, to try to make some sense out of those years, to chronicle the events and try to justify the pain he had inflicted on his over-generous brother. I pointed to the beautiful winding wrought-iron staircase. 'Up,' I whispered.

'Allow me to light your way, ma'am.' Picking up the hall lamp, he went very slowly ahead of me, waiting on the top landing for me to indicate the room I had once called my own. Passing through the doorway, now painted a fresh pale grey with gold beading, I saw that nothing inside had been changed, not even by a detail, same bed-curtains, same rather threadbare carpet, same towels and soap on the wash-stand, so dowdy compared to the rest of the house, newly decorated. 'Would you like me to draw the curtains, ma'am?' Mr Treddle said. 'And I can have a fire lit in no time, if you wish?'

'I only want to sit a while, Mr Treddle, thank you.'

'Very good, ma'am. I'm downstairs if you need anything.'

'I'll ring,' I said. The room smelled musty, damp and unloved.

Like a wraith he disappeared, and I sank down upon the velvet-cushioned window-seat that overlooked Stonegate's frosty cobbles, just as I had done countless times before to gather my thoughts together from the jumble of parts that intertwined like the figures in a dance. I had believed myself to be the one most wronged, the one most hurt by hopeless love, the one who had sacrificed most for Linas. Now I saw that it was not so. Burl had loved and wanted me and I had never known it, thinking that I was no more or less than a woman to be caught, and bedded, and then discarded once she had fulfilled her purpose. Now, all his coldness could be explained by Linas's dying wish that he should leave me well alone.

Mine. You belong to me, Helene Follet. Me alone. I have you at last.

Those words, fiercely spoken against my cheek, had haunted me for days, for they were words of possession, not love, though I had been right in my hunch that comfort was what he most needed then. It was what he'd needed for years, though he'd hidden it much better than me. How he must have suffered.

Sighing, I went to lie on my bed still, with my cloak wrapped round me, my mind unwinding the ravelled story that was too full of alternatives, assumptions and speculations to offer me any reason at all for forgiveness. The only mitigating factor I could dredge up from my charity was that Linas had been very ill, and desperate, and probably very afraid, and that in such an atmosphere, his resentment of Burl's success with women finally drove him to play God, before it was too late.

Downstairs, the muffled slam of a heavy door broke into my tangled reverie, hurting my head, but I thought no more of it until my bedroom door opened to let in another light and another figure, and then the cold icy scent of the night. Horses, leather, larches after rain.

'Burl!' I croaked. 'Oh Burl…dearest man…dearest beloved.'

Shadows lurched and skidded across the bed-curtains, and then I was being pulled up into his arms and held close with my wet face warmly nudged by his. Our lips met and breathed soft words into each other's mouths, words of wanting and the pain of loving too much.

'I didn't know, Burl. I didn't know until now,' I sobbed. 'I had no idea that's how it was for you. And I love you…love you…have always loved you…and you should not have allowed him to do this to us. It was so very cruel, my darling. Your pain, Burl, when…'

'Hush, my love. Sweetheart,' he whispered deep, low, velvety words that warmed me like fur, 'my only love, my darling Helene. You must not weep for me, lass. Come now, no more tears. It's done. Past. How long have you been here weeping?'

'Since I read it…oh, Burl. I'm so sorry.'

'For what, dear heart?'

'For my accusations. I've been so unfair and selfish. You did it for love of Linas, as you told me, but I thought it was some cold-hearted scheme you'd both devised to get Linas a son.'

'It was not cold-hearted on my part, my love. Anything but that. I had strong objections, but he made it too difficult for me to refuse him. I ought to have done, I know, but that day at Abbots Mere the chance arose and I took it. You were so unhappy, and I thought that just for one night I could show you how it could be. It was wrong, I admit it, but I had wanted you for so long and I felt that you wanted me too. Darling, it was never my desire to hurt you so much. Can you forgive me?'

'I didn't know you loved me, Burl. You kept it hidden.'

'I dared not let a word pass between us. That was part of the bargain. He pleaded with me to let him have first chance, thinking it would be for only three years, but then he took three more. How could any of us have known that would happen? It was almost unbearable. I didn't *want* his death, sweetheart, but I wanted you so desperately.'

'I think I might have left him, Burl, but for you. It was you who kept me here, that and the thought that I might lose Jamie. He was my comfort, my part of you that I never expected to have. If I'd known you loved me, I could have borne it all with patience, but he told you to leave me alone.'

'I couldn't let you suspect it. You would not have

been able to conceal your feelings. You've never been good at that, have you, sweetheart? But how did you discover all this? Has he left you a letter?'

'Yes, I found it this evening. Perhaps I ought to let you read it.'

'Poor Linas. So he explained his reasons?'

'Yes, and now that he's gone, Burl, I ought not to criticise him to you. He was your twin and my lover, and I suppose he *gave* us more than he demanded from us. At least he kept us together, didn't he? Like it or not.'

'I would have found a way, sweetheart, never fear. There's never been a woman, not one, that I would have waited six years for. Until you.' His arms tightened around me and, in his kiss, I felt all the longing and desolation of those six years, the ache of desire and the release of love that had been so long denied by us both. 'I knew I'd have to work hard to get you back,' he murmured, stroking the hair off my damp temples, 'but I didn't realise how useful your family would be, and the snow and ice, then the floods. And all that nonsense talk of rewards and prices, my darling, was only a device to trap you into accepting me. I had to do something to make your mind up. Think no more of it. For you, I would do whatever it takes, family or no family. So don't think too harshly of Linas if that's what he did too. They were his last years and his only chance to be the proud lover of Miss Helene Follet and, who knows, if I'd been in the same boat, I might have done the same.'

'You wouldn't, Burl. You're too big-hearted. You would never forget your sense of fairness. Linas seemed to forget everything.'

'We have six years of lost ground to make up. Shall I take you back home now, so we can make a start? And will you marry me now, Miss Follet, without any ifs and buts? No bargains? No delays?'

'I *will* marry you, Burl Winterson,' I said, feeling a strange sense of elation rush into my chest like the first stirrings of a young woman's heart. Breathless with happiness, I took hold of his head as I had done on that April night four years ago, letting my fingers roam in the semi-darkness to remind myself that this was not a dream. His skin had warmed, his lips kissed my finger-tips as they passed and I knew I was not dreaming. 'Yes, take me home. I have things to show you,' I said.

Under my fingers the lips smiled and whispered. 'You would not prefer to stay here, in your own room?'

'Not until it's been decorated,' I said. 'A pretty spring yellow, I think.'

Dear Mr Treddle ushered us out with a smile at my blotchy face. 'Goodnight, Miss Follet. Goodnight, my lord. The step is icy...take care...hold the railing, ma'am.'

That night, the short walk to my home was punctuated by several stops to remind ourselves and each other that, however many questions still awaited answers, the main one had at long last been resolved. Yes, it was true. Burl had loved me from the very beginning, and although I might have argued that for him to accept Linas's suggestion without consulting me was less than gentlemanly, I found it easier to forgive Burl than Linas. Though we had both suffered for it, we had also lived off that brief memory for four years, gaining an adorable child as a consolation that bound us together irrevocably. I could not blame him for that any longer. It was time to let the past take care of itself.

For me, the day had been packed with incident, most of which I was not at liberty to talk about. For Burl, who had been to Foss Beck again, the day had been a tiring one and he had plenty to tell me. Yet in the dim warm intimacy of my room at Blake Street, there were more important matters to keep us occupied than our respective families, for now our loving could take on a new dimension that would stretch ahead into years of trust and understanding. I had never thought that particular freedom would be mine so soon.

Setting all modesty aside in his honour, I first acted as his valet to make him comfortably naked in the chair beside the fire with a glass of wine, and myself standing some distance away where the lamplight could catch at only the palest surfaces. Although I was tired and emotionally drained, my slow and erotic removal of each item of clothing was suitably lethargic, like that of a sleepy woman who has other things on her mind. Each garter, each stocking was peeled off and discarded with a tantalising display of my body, just enough to delight him and, although he was relaxed and silent, I knew how focused was his attention and how delicious this was for him after a long day attending to my family's welfare.

Pretending to be alone, I took my time with each button, hook and tie, letting one side slip a little, then another, loosening my hair to reveal and conceal, swinging it aside, lifting it and letting it drop for me to make all those minute examinations of this limb, that hand, that foot, which we women make at such times as a matter of routine. Sliding my chemise down over one hip, inch by slow inch, I held it before me to conceal that part of me which I have never found particularly attractive, finally stepping out of the soft cotton fabric with the deep broderie-anglais hem while looking at him through the screen of my hair. I could go no further in my pretence.

Like a large cat, he stood up, dark against the firelight. 'Siren,' he whispered, 'you have captured my dream. How did you know, wicked black witch? Eh? Can you read my dreams now?' He came to me, taking the cotton shift out of my hand and tossing it on to the chair.

'Now I can,' I replied, softly. 'Now I can call you mine at last, after all these years. I can have you all, body and mind. And I am yours, my love.'

After bearing our child, and suckling him for nine months, my figure was no longer that of a seventeen-year-old. My hips and belly were rounded, my breasts full, still firm, but with all those years of virginal innocence gone for ever. Burl's heavy-lidded examination and the path of his hands over my body, however, was as leisured as my undressing had been, and I stood trembling like a girl with my knees turning to water at each touch, the tenderly teasing brush of his thumbs melting me, then his warm lips over my shoulders and neck.

No longer able to wait upon him, I linked my arms about his neck, knowing that he would lift me and take me those few short steps to the turned-down bed and lay me there with the blanket of his beautiful body to warm me, each of his kisses fusing into the next, emptying my mind. And because we were both physically weary, yet aware of the change in our relationship, our loving was sweetly languorous and indulgent, teasing time itself into eons of pleasure that washed over us like waves, taking us further and further into the deep waters of our passion. Our cries were softly calling, tuned to each other, wordless and evocative, arousing, yearning. With years of discovery ahead of us and no more misunderstandings, our loving was made all the sweeter and more poignant by words of love in all its forms, words we had saved in the secrecy of our hearts and never thought to use.

'Never leave me,' he whispered. 'Never…never leave me, Helene.'

'Beloved, I am yours. I have always been yours, even when you—'

'Don't say it. Darling woman, what can I do to make you forget?'

'That's easy, my lord. Brothers and sisters for Jamie, please.'

'I can arrange that, Lady Winterson. Leave it to me.'

'Now?'

'Of course now. Immediately. A little co-operation is all I ask.'

Needless to say, I co-operated fully. So well, in fact, that the deep sleep that followed our exhaustion took us through until dawn when Jamie and Debbie appeared to draw the curtains and place our tea-tray on the table. With no sign of surprise at seeing his Uncaburl in my bed, Jamie crawled across the prone and tousled body to burrow between us like a mole, grinning as if he was personally responsible.

Chapter Fifteen

$\sim\!\!\mathcal{O}\!\!\mathcal{O}\!\!\sim$

With our love for each other firmly established and our future as a family assured, everything else seemed to matter less than before, even though there were some serious issues still to be discussed. Linas's letter to me had certainly cleared my mind of misconceptions and left it wide open to receive his brother's love, but Burl himself had some doubts about the manner of Linas's explanation.

Some days later we sat by the fire in our house on Blake Street. Shaking his head, he closed the book and turned it over once or twice to study its leather binding. 'Tch!' he muttered. 'How like him to write it as an essay and then leave it to chance that you'd find it one day. It might have been *years* before you found it, Helene. What if I'd thrown the notebooks out, or put them into a bookshelf? Then you'd never have heard his side of the story, would you? Why couldn't he have told you, while there was still time?'

Snuggling deeper into his arms, I took the notebook

from him and returned it to its companions. 'Because he was unsure how I would take it,' I said. 'Because he could never have said it the way he could write it. Because he was not even sure he wanted me to know, after all. Let's not give it any more thought. It's of no consequence now. Tell me what you discovered about Pierre. You said you had something to tell me.'

'It was your brothers who solved the mystery, sweetheart. They were doing some clearing up ready for the renovations and they found some lists that Monsieur Follet had left behind in his hurry.'

'Lists of what?'

'Names. French prisoners of war kept in prison ships off the Essex coast, some of them crossed off or underlined. They showed it to me, and I recognised some of the names that have been circulated to all the Justices of the Peace in the county. They're men who've gone missing, presumed escaped. We've known for some time that there are French connections over here helping prisoners to get back home across the English Channel or the North Sea, but personally I never thought they'd come all this way up north. But it seems that some of them made their way up as far as York where your cousin has been meeting them.'

'In the coffee houses? Once a month, when he went to collect my mother's medication and bring the goods to the shop?'

'Very likely. The coffee houses are perfect meeting places.'

'Then the man who was with him when we saw him might have been one he was helping. He looked very rough and tired, didn't he?'

'Yes. He would have taken him to Bridlington to wait there for one of the smugglers' boats to ship him back to France. The men who come to collect these prisoners pay handsomely for human contraband, and Pierre has probably been doing it for several years, growing nicely wealthy from it.'

'Which is where the extra money comes from.'

'No more, dear heart. He pulled up the ladder and made a run for it. Things were getting too complicated for him. He'd waited for you, and then realised it was futile, and maybe he suspected I might know a thing or two about what was happening. Who knows? But Greg and Finch are not a bit sorry. They had no wish to call him brother.'

'So my mother has not been receiving her potions lately.'

'If I were you, I would not be too concerned about that,' he said, twisting a strand of my hair round his fingers. 'Your mother appears to be improving daily. Due, perhaps, to the absence of pain-killing drugs.'

'Burl…you cannot believe…*surely* not!'

'I'm keeping an open mind, sweetheart. I think we should allow the matter to drop, since it really serves no purpose to find out, does it? I don't think your mother suspects anything sinister.'

'So do you still think it was Pierre who told the Customs and Excise Men to look in our shop for French goods?'

'No. It was not him.' He answered with such finality that I knew his enquiries had revealed something.

'Do you want to tell me?' I said.

'Difficult. Maybe I should not.'

'Then it's someone I know. It would upset me. Is that it, my lord?'

He took a deep breath, and I thought how unlike him it was to hesitate. 'It upsets *me*,' he said, 'to think that I've had not one, but *two* brothers who see me so much as a rival that they are driven to prevent my happiness. On the other hand, Miss Follet, looking at you here in the crook of my arm with your hair all over the place and the neck of your bodice indecently open…'

'Which *you* opened, my lord!'

'…which I opened, I dare say I could forgive them both for wanting to knock me off my high horse, once in a while. However, I find it rather uncomfortable, to say the least…'

'Oh, *do* say the least, darling Burl. What *are* you saying, exactly? That Medworth…oh, no, you can't think that he…did he?'

'Yes, I'm afraid that's what I am saying. He dropped a rather indirect hint to two of the men who work for the Customs Controller, so I'm told, just as the floods began, a hint that they're trained to pick up with ears like bats. The truth is, my love, that although Medworth was quite content to see you as Linas's mistress, he's less than content to see you as my wife and mother of my son. Jealousy of my good fortune? Envy of my inheritance compared to his? Yes, love, he's not immune from the vices any more than the rest of us, though I'd not have believed he'd allow it to get as out of hand as he appears to have done.'

'He wanted to see me arrested? Oh, Burl, surely not.' My arms prickled, and the hair at the nape of my neck sent shivers down my spine.

'I really don't believe he'd thought too hard about what the exact consequences might be. I think he was more set on pulling us apart than what might happen to you. In a way, what he tried to do is potentially more serious than what Linas tried to do. Envy is a terrible thing.'

If ever the time was right for me to say what I knew about Medworth's other attempt to pull us apart, it was now. But I said nothing, for it was not my way to worsen a sibling relationship that had begun to falter. So I kept my peace, and I was glad that I did, for Burl himself told me the rest.

'He's moving house, by the way,' he said, 'so we shall be seeing less of him in the future. We had a meeting at Abbots Mere the other day, and my father has offered him a small living just on the other side of Harrogate, so he'll be near them. Mama is very pleased, of course.'

'Oh! That's rather sudden, isn't it? What of the rector's position at Osbaldwick? Has it…?'

'Fallen through. Lord Slatterly has found someone he believes will be more suitable. An older man. They'll be moving out next week.'

'I see. Is Medworth very disappointed?'

'He's philosophical about it. Cynthia won't want to leave, but curate's wives must move on. She'll take it in her stride. But I have some other news that will please you, Miss Follet. About Lord Slatterly's daughter.'

For one moment, I was not sure what I was meant to know and what to conceal. 'Veronique? Is she well?'

'Well and happy, according to her father. She's soon to be married.'

'Heavens above! That *is* good news. Anyone I know?'

'One of Viscount Wetherclough's sons. Been keen on her for years. He can't believe his luck, at last. I think I know how he feels.'

I hugged him. This was good news indeed. 'I must go and see her. We're on good terms now, you know.'

He looked down at me and smiled. 'Thanks to your kindness to her. You are, Miss Follet, the most wonderful woman, and I am the most fortunate of men. And if you hug me any closer, wench, your bodice will drop off altogether and I shall be shamelessly compromised. Is that the idea?'

'Mmm,' I said, as his hand moved the matter forwards.

'Wait, hussy,' he said, diverting the hand into his inside breast pocket. 'I have a halter to put round your neck while I have you half-naked here. Hold still.' Opening a flat red leather-covered box, he revealed a lining of white satin upon which lay a fine gold chain with a pendant hanging from it, the largest smokey-grey pearl I had ever seen. It was tear-drop shaped, with a diamond dripping from the base. 'Burl sounds like pearl,' he whispered. 'Keep saying it, sweetheart.'

'Burl,' I said. 'Thank you, dear heart. Thank you for waiting.'

'I would have waited for ever, my love, but I'm glad I didn't have to. Six years is more than enough to wait for a woman like you.'

It was on my birthday, April 18th, 1806, when the fifth red rose appeared on the hall table before breakfast, and it was then that I had to accept that the anonymous donor could not have been Linas, after all. Smiling, I placed it on my table between the toast and the milk-jug and waited for comments.

'Another rose, Mama?' said Jamie.

Burl looked across at me. 'Get them regularly, do you?'

'Mmm.' I nodded.

'Mama gets one every year on her birthday, Uncaburl. I think she should marry the handsome prince who gives 'em out. Shall you, Mama?'

'Yes, love. I think it's time I did. Will some time soon be good?'

Burl was staring, but then his expression changed, his eyes softening and desirous. 'Very soon, you mean?' he said, slowly.

'Yes, my lord. As soon as possible,' I said, nibbling at my lip.

His hand reached across the table to cover mine, caressing, protective and thoughtful. The tender expression deepened into a smile and I knew he understood that I was saying more than that, and I thought he looked like a young lad with his first girl. 'This time,' he whispered, 'I shall be able to do all those things I couldn't do before, shan't I? Shall we go over to Foss Beck and tell them? We can stay overnight at Fridaythorpe so as not to tire you.'

'To see Nana Damzell,' Jamie said. 'And when you marry Uncaburl, Mama, will he be my new papa then?'

We looked at each other without answering him, until he insisted. 'Will you, Uncaburl? If Mama gives the red rose to Papa, he won't mind then, will he? We'll tell him about it. Shall we?'

Tears prickled my eyes. 'That's what we'll do, little one. We'll call and see him on the way there, and you can give him the rose. He'll like that.'

So we did, making it the start of a tradition we kept up each year on my birthday, even when our retinue extended to our two nurses, the two younger boys and one girl, and a handsome young man of twelve who looked exactly like his papa.